A DANGEROUS DEAL

MELANIE
MILBURNE

KATE
HEWITT

CATHY
WILLIAMS

MILLS & BOON

IRRESISTIBLE ITALIANS: A DANGEROUS DEAL © 2023 by Harlequin Books S.A.

THE VENETIAN ONE-NIGHT BABY
© 2019 by Melanie Milburne
Australian Copyright 2019
New Zealand Copyright 2019

First Published 2019
Second Australian Paperback Edition 2023
ISBN 978 1 867 29835 9

THE BRIDE'S AWAKENING
© 2010 by Kate Hewitt
Australian Copyright 2010
New Zealand Copyright 2010

First Published 2010
Fourth Australian Paperback Edition 2023
ISBN 978 1 867 29835 9

THE TRUTH BEHIND HIS TOUCH
© 2012 by Cathy Williams
Australian Copyright 2012
New Zealand Copyright 2012

First Published 2012
Fourth Australian Paperback Edition 2023
ISBN 978 1 867 29835 9

This is a work of fiction. Names, characters, places, and incidents are either the product of the author's imagination or are used fictitiously, and any resemblance to actual persons, living or dead, business establishments, events, or locales is entirely coincidental.

Published by
Mills & Boon
An imprint of Harlequin Enterprises (Australia) Pty Limited (ABN 47 001 180 918), a subsidiary of HarperCollins Publishers Australia Pty Limited (ABN 36 009 913 517)
Level 19, 201 Elizabeth Street
SYDNEY NSW 2000
AUSTRALIA

MIX
Paper | Supporting responsible forestry
FSC® C001695
www.fsc.org

® and ™ (apart from those relating to FSC®) are trademarks of Harlequin Enterprises (Australia) Pty Limited or its corporate affiliates. Trademarks indicated with ® are registered in Australia, New Zealand and in other countries.
Contact admin_legal@Harlequin.ca for details.

Printed and bound in Australia by McPherson's Printing Group

CONTENTS

The Venetian
One-Night Baby

Melanie Milburne

Books by Melanie Milburne

Harlequin Modern

The Tycoon's Marriage Deal
A Virgin for a Vow
Blackmailed into the Marriage Bed
Tycoon's Forbidden Cinderella

Conveniently Wed!

Bound by a One-Night Vow

One Night With Consequences

A Ring for the Greek's Baby

The Ravensdale Scandals

Ravensdale's Defiant Captive
Awakening the Ravensdale Heiress
Engaged to Her Ravensdale Enemy
The Most Scandalous Ravensdale

The Scandal Before the Wedding

Claimed for the Billionaire's Convenience

Visit the Author Profile page
at millsandboon.com.au for more titles.

Melanie Milburne read her first Harlequin novel at the age of seventeen, in between studying for her final exams. After completing a master's degree in education, she decided to write a novel, and thus her career as a romance author was born. Melanie is an ambassador for the Australian Childhood Foundation and a keen dog lover and trainer. She enjoys long walks in the Tasmanian bush. In 2015 Melanie won the HOLT Medallion, a prestigious award honoring outstanding literary talent.

To Mallory (Mal) and Mike Tuffy. It was so lovely to meet you on the European river cruise a few years ago—it must be time for another one! It's wonderful to continue our friendship since. We always look forward to seeing you in Tasmania.
Xxx

CHAPTER ONE

SABRINA WAS HOPING she wouldn't run into Max Firbank again after The Kiss. He wasn't an easy man to avoid since he was her parents' favourite godson and was invited to just about every Midhurst family gathering. Birthdays, Christmas, New Year's Eve, parties and anniversaries he would spend on the fringes of the room, a twenty-first-century reincarnation of Jane Austen's taciturn Mr Darcy. He'd look down his aristocratic nose at everyone else having fun.

Sabrina made sure she had extra fun just to annoy him. She danced with everyone who asked her, chatting and working the room like she was the star student from Social Butterfly School. Max occasionally wouldn't show, and then she would spend the whole evening wondering why the energy in the room wasn't the same. But she refused to acknowledge it had anything to do with his absence.

This weekend she was in Venice to exhibit two of her designs at her first wedding expo. She felt safe from running into him—or she would have if the hotel receptionist could find her booking.

Sabrina leaned closer to the hotel reception counter. 'I can assure you the reservation was made weeks ago.'

'What name did you say it was booked under?' the young male receptionist asked.

'Midhurst, Sabrina Jane. My assistant booked it for me.'

'Do you have any documentation with you? The confirmation email?'

Had her new assistant Harriet forwarded it to her? Sabrina remembered printing out the wedding expo programme but had she printed out the accommodation details? She searched for it in her tote bag, sweat beading between her breasts, her stomach pitching with panic. She couldn't turn up flustered to her first wedding expo as an exhibitor. That's why she'd recently employed an assistant to help her with this sort of stuff. Booking flights and accommodation, sorting out her diary, making sure she didn't double book or miss appointments.

Sabrina put her lipgloss, paper diary, passport and phone on the counter, plus three pens, a small packet of tissues, some breath mints and her brand-new business cards. She left her tampons in the side pocket of her bag—there was only so much embarrassment she could handle at any one time. The only bits of paper she found were a shopping list and a receipt from her favourite shoe store.

She began to put all the items back in her bag, but her lipgloss fell off the counter, dropped to the floor, rolled across the lobby and was stopped by a large Italian-leather-clad foot.

Sabrina's gaze travelled up the long length of the expertly tailored charcoal-grey trousers and finally came to rest on Max Firbank's smoky grey-blue gaze.

'Sabrina.' His tone was less of a greeting and more of a grim *not you again*.

Sabrina gave him a tight, no-teeth-showing smile. 'Fancy seeing you here. I wouldn't have thought wedding expos were your thing.'

His eyes glanced at her mouth and something in her stomach dropped like a book tumbling off a shelf. *Kerplunk*. He blinked as if to clear his vision and bent down to pick up her lipgloss.

He handed it to her, his expression as unreadable as cryptic code. 'I'm seeing a client about a project. I always stay at this hotel when I come to Venice.'

Sabrina took the lipgloss and slipped it into her bag, trying to ignore the tingling in her fingers where his had touched hers. She could feel the heat storming into her cheeks in a hot crimson tide. What sort of weird coincidence was *this*? Of all the hotels in Venice why did he have to be at *this* one? And on *this* weekend? She narrowed her gaze to the size of buttonholes. 'Did my parents tell you I was going to be here this weekend?'

Nothing on his face changed except for a brief elevation of one of his dark eyebrows. 'No. Did mine tell you I was going to be in Venice?'

Sabrina raised her chin. 'Oh, didn't you know? I zone out when your parents tell me things about you. I mentally plug my ears and sing *la-de-da* in my head until they change the subject of how amazingly brilliant you are.'

There was a flicker of movement across his lips that could have been loosely described as a smile. 'I'll have to remember to do that next time your parents bang on about you to me.'

Sabrina flicked a wayward strand of hair out of her face. Why did she always have to look like she'd been through a wind tunnel whenever she saw him? She dared not look at his mouth but kept her eyes trained on his inscrutable gaze. Was he thinking about The Kiss? The clashing of mouths that had morphed into a passionate explosion that had made a mockery of every other kiss she'd ever received? Could he still recall the taste and texture of her mouth? Did he lie in bed at night and fantasise about kissing her again?

And not just kissing, but…

'*Signorina?*' The hotel receptionist jolted Sabrina out of her reverie. 'We have no booking under the name Midhurst. Could it have been another hotel you selected online?'

Sabrina suppressed a frustrated sigh. 'No. I asked my assistant to book me into this one. This is where the fashion show is being held. I have to stay here.'

'What's the problem?' Max asked in a calm, *leave it to me* tone.

Sabrina turned to face him. 'I've got a new assistant and somehow she must've got the booking wrong or it didn't process or something.' She bit her lip, trying to stem the panic punching against her heart. *Poomf. Poomf. Poomf.*

'I can put you on the cancellation list, but we're busy at this time of year so I can't guarantee anything,' the receptionist said.

Sabrina's hand crept up to her mouth and she started nibbling on her thumbnail. Too bad about her new manicure. A bit of nail chewing was all she had to soothe her rising dread. She wanted to be settled into her hotel, not left waiting on standby. What if no other hotel could take her? She needed to be close to the convention venue because she had two dresses in the fashion parade. This was her big break to get her designs on the international stage.

She. Could. Not. Fail.

'Miss Midhurst will be joining me,' Max said. 'Have the concierge bring her luggage to my room. Thank you.'

Sabrina's gaze flew to his. 'What?'

Max handed her a card key, his expression still as inscrutable as that of an MI5 spy. 'I checked in this morning. There are two beds in my suite. I only need one.'

She did *not* want to think about him and a bed in the same sentence. She'd spent the last three weeks thinking about him in a bed with her in a tangle of sweaty sex-sated limbs. Which was frankly kind of weird because she'd spent most of her life deliberately *not* thinking about him. Max was her parents' godson and almost from the moment when she'd been born six years later and become his parents' adored goddaughter, both sets of parents had decided how perfect they were for each other. It was the long-wished-for dream of both families that Max and Sabrina would fall in love, get married and have gorgeous babies together.

As if. In spite of both families' hopes, Sabrina had never got on with Max. She found him brooding and distant and arrogant. And he made it no secret he found her equally annoying...which kind of made her wonder why he'd kissed her...

But she was *not* going to think about The Kiss.

She glanced at the clock over Reception, another fist of panic pummelling her heart. She needed to shower and change and do her hair and makeup. She needed to get her head in order. It wouldn't do to turn up flustered and nervous. What sort of impression would she make?

Sabrina took the key from him but her fingers brushed his and a tingle travelled from her fingers to her armpit. 'Maybe I should try and see if I can get in somewhere else...'

'What time does your convention start?'

'There's a cocktail party at six-thirty.'

Max led the way to the bank of lifts. 'I'll take you up to settle you in before I meet my client for a drink.'

Sabrina entered the brass embossed lift with him and the doors whispered shut behind them. The mirrored interior reflected Max's features from every angle. His tall and lean and athletic build. The well-cut dark brown hair with a hint of a wave. The generously lashed eyes the colour of storm clouds. The faint hollow below the cheekbones that gave him a chiselled-from-marble look that was far more attractive than it had any right to be. The aristocratic cut of nostril and upper lip, the small cleft in his chin, the square jaw that hinted at arrogance and a tendency to insist on his own way.

'Is your client female?' The question was out before Sabrina could monitor her wayward tongue.

'Yes.' His brusque one-word answer was a verbal Keep Out sign.

Sabrina had always been a little intrigued by his love life. He had been jilted by his fiancée Lydia a few days before their wedding six years ago. He had never spoken of why his fiancée had called off the wedding but Sabrina had heard a whisper that it had been because Lydia had wanted children and he didn't. Max wasn't one to brandish his subsequent lovers about in public but she knew he had them from time to time. Now thirty-four, he was a virile man in his sexual prime. And she had tasted a hint of that potency when his mouth had come down on hers and sent her senses into a tailspin from which they had not yet recovered—if they ever would.

The lift stopped on Max's floor and he indicated for her to alight before him. She moved past him and breathed in the sharp citrus scent of his aftershave—lemon and lime and something else that was as mysterious and unknowable as his personality.

He led the way along the carpeted corridor and came to a suite that overlooked the Grand Canal. Sabrina stepped over the threshold and, pointedly ignoring the twin king-sized beds, went straight to the windows to check out the magnificent view. Even if her booking had been processed correctly, she would never have been able to afford a room such as this.

'Wow...' She breathed out a sigh of wonder. 'Venice never fails to take my breath away. The light. The colours. The history.' She turned to face him, doing her best to not glance at the beds that dominated the room. He still had his spy face on but she could sense an inner tension in the way he held himself. 'Erm... I'd appreciate it if you didn't tell anyone about this...'

The mocking arch of his eyebrow made her cheeks burn. 'This?'

At this rate, she'd have to ramp up the air-conditioning to counter the heat she was giving off from her burning cheeks. 'Me...sharing your room.'

'I wouldn't dream of it.'

'I mean, it could get really embarrassing if either of our parents thought we were—'

'We're not.' The blunt edge to his voice was a slap down to her ego.

There was a knock at the door.

Max opened the door and stepped aside as the hotel employee brought in Sabrina's luggage. Max gave the young man a tip and closed the door, locking his gaze on hers. 'Don't even think about it.'

Sabrina raised her eyebrows so high she thought they would fly off her face. 'You think I'm attracted to *you*? Dream on, buddy.'

The edge of his mouth lifted—the closest he got to a smile, or at least one he'd ever sent her way. 'I could have had you that night three weeks ago and you damn well know it.'

'*Had* me?' She glared at him. 'That kiss was...was a knee-jerk thing. It just...erm...happened. And you gave me stubble rash. I had to put on cover-up for a week.'

His eyes went to her mouth as if he was remembering the explosive passion they'd shared. He drew in an uneven breath and sent a hand through the thick pelt of his hair, a frown pulling at his forehead. 'I'm sorry. It wasn't my intention to hurt you.' His voice had a deep gravelly edge she'd never heard in it before.

Sabrina folded her arms. She wasn't ready to forgive him. She wasn't ready to forgive herself for responding to him. She wasn't ready to admit how much she'd enjoyed that kiss and how she had encouraged it by grabbing the front of his shirt and pulling his head down. Argh. Why had she done that? Neither was she ready to admit how much she wanted him to kiss her again. 'I can think of no one I would less like to "have me".'

Even repeating the coarse words he'd used turned her on. Damn him. She couldn't stop thinking about what it would be like to be *had by him*. Her sex life was practically non-existent. The only sex she'd had in the last few years had been with herself and even that hadn't been all that spectacular. She kept hoping she'd find the perfect partner to help her with her issues with physical intimacy but so far no such luck. She rarely dated anyone more than two or three times before she decided having sex with them was out of the question. Her first and only experience of sex at the age of eighteen—*had it really been ten years ago?*—had been an ego-smashing disappointment, one she was in no hurry to repeat.

'Good. Because we're not going there,' Max said.

Sabrina inched up her chin. 'You were the one who kissed me first that night. I might have returned the kiss but only because I got caught off guard.' It was big fat lie but no way was she going to admit it. Every non-verbal signal in her repertoire had been on duty that night all but begging him to kiss her. And when he finally had, she even recalled moaning at one point. Yes, moaning with pleasure as his lips and tongue had worked their magic. *Geez.* How was she going to live *that* down?

His eyes pulsed with something she couldn't quite identify. Suppressed anger or locked-down lust or both? 'You were spoiling for a fight all through that dinner party and during the trip when I gave you a lift home.'

'So? We always argue. It doesn't mean I want you to kiss me.'

His eyes held hers in a smouldering lock that made the backs of her knees fizz. 'Are we arguing now?' His tone had a silky edge that played havoc with her senses.

Sabrina took a step back, one of her hands coming up her neck where her heart was beating like a panicked pigeon stuck in a pipe. 'I need to get ready for the c-cocktail party...' Why, oh, why did she have to sound so breathless?

He gave a soft rumble of a laugh. 'Your virtue is safe, Sabrina.' He walked to the door of the suite and turned to look at her again. 'Don't wait up. I'll be late.'

Sabrina gave him a haughty look that would have done a Regency spinster proud. 'Going to *have* your client, are you?'

He left without another word, which, annoyingly, left her with the painful echo of hers.

Max closed the door of his suite and let out a breath. Why had he done the knight in shining armour thing? Why should he care if she couldn't get herself organised enough to book a damn hotel? She would have found somewhere to stay, surely. But no. He had to do the decent thing. Nothing about how he felt about Sabrina was decent—especially after that kiss. He'd lost count of how many women he'd kissed. He wasn't a man whore, but he enjoyed sex for the physical release it gave.

But he couldn't get *that* kiss out of his mind.

Max had always avoided Sabrina in the past. He hadn't wanted to encourage his and her parents from their sick little fantasy of them getting it on. He got it on with women he chose and he made sure his choices were simple and straightforward—sex without strings.

Sabrina was off limits because she was the poster girl for the happily-ever-after fairytale. She was looking for Mr Right to sweep her off her feet and park her behind a white picket fence with a double pram with a couple of chubby-cheeked progeny tucked inside.

Max had nothing against marriage, but he no longer wanted it for himself. Six years ago, his fiancée had called off their wedding, informing him she had fallen in love with someone else, with someone who wanted children—the children Max refused to give her. Prior to that, Lydia had been adamant she was fine with his decision not to have kids. He'd thought everything was ticking along well enough in their relationship. He'd been more annoyed than upset at Lydia calling off their relationship. It had irritated him that he hadn't seen it coming.

But it had taught him a valuable lesson. A lesson he was determined he would never have to learn again. He wasn't cut out for long-term relationships. He didn't have what it took to handle commitment and all its responsibilities.

He knew marriage worked for some people—his parents and Sabrina's had solid relationships that had been tried and tested and triumphed over tragedy, especially his parents. The loss of his baby brother Daniel at the age of four months had devastated them, of course.

Max had been seven years old and while his parents had done

all they could to shield him from the tragedy, he still carried his share of guilt. In spite of the coroner's verdict of Sudden Infant Death Syndrome, Max could never get it out of his mind that he had been the last person to see his baby brother alive. There wasn't a day that went by when he didn't think of his brother, of all the years Daniel had missed out on. The milestones he would never meet.

Max walked out of his hotel and followed the Grand Canal, almost oblivious to the crowds of tourists that flocked to Venice at this time of year. Whenever he thought of Daniel, a tiny worm of guilt burrowed its way into his mind. Was there something he could have done to save his brother? Why hadn't he noticed something? Why hadn't he checked him more thoroughly? The lingering guilt he felt about Daniel was something he was almost used to now. He was almost used to feeling the lurch of dread in his gut whenever he saw a small baby. Almost.

Max stepped out of the way of a laughing couple that were walking arm in arm, carrying the colourful Venetian masks they'd bought from one of the many vendors along the canal. Why hadn't he thought to book a room at another hotel for Sabrina? It wasn't as if he couldn't afford it. He'd made plenty of money as a world-acclaimed architect, and he knew things were a little tight with her financially as she was still building up her wedding-dress design business and stubbornly refusing any help from her doctor parents, who had made it no secret that they would have preferred her to study medicine like them and Sabrina's two older brothers.

Had he *wanted* her in his room? Had he instinctively seized at the chance to have her to himself so he could kiss her again? Maybe do more than kiss her?

Max pulled away from the thought like he was stepping back from a too-hot fire. But that's exactly what Sabrina was—hot. Too hot. She made him hot and bothered and horny as hell. The way she picked fights with him just to get under his skin never failed to get his blood pumping. Her cornflower-blue eyes would flash and sparkle, and her soft and supple mouth would fling cutting retorts his way, and it would make him feel alive in a way he hadn't in years.

Alive and energised.

But no. No. No. No. No.

He must *not* think about Sabrina like that. He had to keep his distance. He had to. She wasn't the sex without strings type. She wasn't a fling girl; she was a fairytale girl. And she was his parents' idea of his ideal match—his soul mate or something. Nothing against his parents, but they were wrong. Dead wrong. Sabrina was spontaneous and creative and disorganised. He was logical, responsible and organised to the point of pedantic. How could anyone think they were an ideal couple? It was crazy. He only had to spend a few minutes with her and she drove him nuts.

How was he going to get through a whole weekend with her?

CHAPTER TWO

SABRINA WAS A little late getting to the cocktail party, which was being held in a private room at the hotel. Only the designers and models and their agents and select members of the press were invited. She entered the party room with her stomach in a squirming nest of nibbling and nipping nerves. Everyone looked glamorous and sophisticated. She was wearing a velvet dress she'd made herself the same shade of blue as her eyes and had scooped her hair up into a bun and paid extra attention to her makeup—hence why she was late to the party.

A waiter came past with a tray of drinks and Sabrina took a glass of champagne and took a generous sip to settle her nerves. She wasn't good at networking…well, not unless she was showing off in front of Max. She always worried she might say the wrong thing or make a social faux pas that would make everyone snigger at her.

Large gatherings reminded her of the school formal the day after she'd slept with her boyfriend for the first time. The rumourmongers had been at work, fuelled by the soul-destroying text messages her boyfriend had sent to all his mates. Sabrina had heard each cruelly taunting comment, seen every mocking look cast in her direction from people she had thought were her friends.

She had stood behind a column in the venue to try and escape the shameful whispers and had heard her boyfriend tell a couple of his mates what a frigid lay she had been. The overwhelming sense of shame had been crippling. Crucifying.

Sabrina sipped some more champagne and fixed a smile on her face. She had to keep her head and not time-travel. She wasn't eighteen any more. She was twenty-eight and ran her own business, for pity's sake. She. Could. Do. This.

'You're Sabrina Midhurst, aren't you?' a female member of the press said, smiling. 'I recognised you from the expo programme photo. You did a friend's wedding dress. It was stunning.'

'Yes, that's me,' Sabrina said, smiling back. 'And I'm glad you liked your friend's dress.'

'I'd like to do a feature article on you.' The woman handed Sabrina a card with her name and contact details on it. 'I'm Naomi Nettleton, I'm a freelancer but I've done articles for some big-name fashion magazines. There's a lot of interest in your work. Would you be interested in giving me an interview? Maybe we could grab a few minutes after this?'

Sabrina could barely believe her ears. An interview in a glossy magazine? That sort of exposure was gold dust. Her Love Is in the Care boutique in London was small and she'd always dreamed of expanding. She and her best friend Holly Frost, who was a wedding florist, hoped to set up their shops side by side in Bloomsbury in order to boost each other's trade. At the moment, they were blocks away from each other but Sabrina knew it would be a brilliant business move if they could pull it off.

She wanted to prove to her doctor parents the creative path she'd chosen to follow wasn't just a whim but a viable business venture. She came from a long line of medicos. Her parents, her grandparents and both her brothers were all in the medical profession. But she had never wanted that for herself. She would much rather have a tape measure around her neck than a stethoscope.

She had been drawing wedding gowns since she was five years old. All through her childhood she had made dresses out of scraps of fabric. She had dressed every doll and teddy bear or soft toy she'd possessed in wedding finery. All through her teens she had collected scrapbooks with hundreds of sketches and cuttings from magazines. She'd had to withstand considerable family pressure in order to pursue her dream and success was her way of proving she had made the right choice.

Sabrina arranged to meet the journalist in the bar downstairs after the party. She continued to circulate, speaking with the models who had been chosen to wear her designs and also with the fashion parade manager who had personally invited her to the event after her daughter had bought one of Sabrina's designs.

She took another glass of champagne off a passing waiter.

Who said word of mouth didn't still work?

Max came back to the hotel after the dinner with his client had gone on much later than he'd originally planned. He hadn't intended having more than a drink with Loretta Barossi but had ended up lingering over a meal with her because he hadn't wanted to come back to his room before Sabrina was safely tucked up and, hopefully, asleep in bed. Unfortunately, he'd somehow given the thirty-six-year-old recently divorced woman the impression he'd been enjoying her company far more than he had, and then had to find a way to politely reject her broadly hinted invitation to spend the night with her. But that was another line he never crossed—mixing business with pleasure.

He was walking past the bar situated off the lobby when he saw Sabrina sitting on one of the plush sofas talking to a woman and a man who was holding a camera in his lap. As if she sensed his presence, Sabrina turned her glossy honey-brown head and saw him looking at her. She raised her hand and gave him a surreptitious fingertip wave and the woman with her glanced to see to whom she was waving. The woman leaned forward to say something to Sabrina, and even from this distance Max could see the rush of a blush flooding Sabrina's creamy cheeks.

He figured the less people who saw him with Sabrina the better, but somehow he found himself walking towards her before he could stop himself. What had the other woman said to make Sabrina colour up like that?

Sabrina's eyes widened when he approached their little party and she reached for her glass of champagne and promptly knocked it over. 'Oops. Sorry. I—'

'You're Max Firbank, the award-winning architect,' the young woman said, rising to offer her hand. 'I've seen an article about your work in one of the magazines I worked for a couple of years ago. When Sabrina said she was sharing a room with a friend, I didn't realise she was referring to you.' Her eyebrows suggestively rose over the word *friend*.

Sabrina had stopped trying to mop up her drink with a paper napkin and stood, clutching the wet and screwed-up napkin in her hand. 'Oh, he's not *that* sort of friend,' she said with a choked little laugh. 'I had a problem with my booking and Max offered me his bed, I mean *a* bed. He has two. Two big ones— they look bigger than king-sized, you could fit a dozen people in each. It's a huge room, so much space we hardly know the other is there, isn't that right, Max?' She turned her head to look at him and he almost had to call for a fire extinguisher because her cheeks were so fiery red.

Max wasn't sure why he slipped his arm around her slim waist and drew her to his body. Maybe it was because she was kind of cute when she got flustered and he liked being able to get under her skin for a change, the way she got under his. Besides, he didn't know any other woman he could make blush more than her. And, yes, he got a kick out of touching her, especially after That Kiss, which she enjoyed as much as he had, even though she was intent on denying it. 'You don't have to be shy about our relationship, baby.' He flashed one of his rare smiles. 'We're both consenting adults.'

'Aw, don't you make a gorgeous couple?' the woman said. 'Tim, get a photo of them,' she said to the man holding the camera. 'I'll include it in the article about Sabrina's designs. That is, if you don't have any objection?'

Hell, yeah. He had one big objection. He didn't mind teasing a blush or two out of Sabrina but if his family got a whiff of him sharing a room with her in Venice they would be measuring him for a morning suit and booking the church. Max held up his hand like a stop sign. 'Sorry. I don't make a habit of broadcasting my private life in the press.'

The woman sighed and handed him a business card. 'Here are my details if you change your mind.'

'I won't.' He gave both the journalist and the photographer a polite nod and added, 'It was nice meeting you. If you'll excuse us? It's been a big day for Sabrina. She needs her beauty sleep.'

Sabrina followed Max to the lift but there were other people waiting to use it as well so she wasn't able to vent her spleen. What was he thinking? She'd been trying to play down her relationship with Max to the journalist, but he'd given Naomi Nettleton the impression they were an item. She stood beside him in the lift as it stopped and started as it delivered guests to their floors.

Max stood calmly beside her with his expression in its customary inscrutable lines, although she sensed there was a mocking smile lurking behind the screen of his gaze. She moved closer to him to allow another guest into the lift on level ten and placed her high heel on Max's foot and pressed down with all her weight. He made a grunting sound that sounded far sexier than she'd expected and he placed the iron band of his arm around her middle and drew her back against him so her back was flush against his pelvis.

Her mind swam with images of them locked together in a tangle of sweaty limbs, his body driving into hers. Even now she could feel the swell of his body, the rush of blood that told her he was as aroused as she was. Her breathing quickened, her legs weakened, her heart rate rocketed. The steely strength of his arm lying across her stomach was burning a brand into her flesh. Her inner core tensed, the electric heat of awakened desire coursing through her in pulses and flickers.

The mirrors surrounding them reflected their intimate clinch from a thousand angles but Sabrina wasn't prepared to make a scene in front of the other guests, one of whom she had seen at the cocktail party. After all, she had a professional image to uphold and slapping Max's face—if indeed she was the sort of person to inflict violence on another person—was not the best way to maintain it.

But, oh, how she longed to slap both his cheeks until they were as red as hers. Then she would elbow him in the ribs and stomp on his toes. Then she would rip the clothes from his body, score her fingernails down his chest and down his back until he begged for mercy. But wait…why was she thinking of ripping his clothes off his body? No. No. No. She must not think about Max without clothes. She must not think about him naked.

She. Must. Not.

Max unlocked the door and she brushed past him and almost before he had time to close it she let fly. 'What the hell were you playing at down there? You gave the impression we were sleeping together. What's *wrong* with you? You know how much I hate you. Why did you—?'

'You don't hate me.' His voice was so calm it made hers sound all the more irrational and childish.

'If I didn't before, I do now.' Sabrina poked him in the chest. 'What was all that about in the lift?'

He captured her by the waist and brought her closer, hip to hip, his eyes more blue than grey and glinting with something that made her belly turn over. 'You know exactly what it was about. And just like that kiss, you enjoyed every second of it. Deny it if you dare.'

Sabrina intended to push away from him but somehow her

hands grabbed the front of his jacket instead. He smelt like sun-warmed lemons and her senses were as intoxicated as if she had breathed in a potent aroma. An aroma that made her forget how much she hated him and instead made her want him with every throbbing traitorous cell of her body. Or maybe she was tipsy from all the champagne she'd had downstairs at the party and in the bar. It was making her drop her inhibitions. Sabotaging her already flagging self-control. Her head was spinning a little but didn't it always when he looked at her like that?

His mouth was tilted in a cynical slant, the dark stubble around his nose and mouth more obvious now than earlier that evening. It gave him a rakish air that was strangely attractive. Dangerously, deliciously attractive. She was acutely aware of every point of contact with his body: her hips, her breasts and her belly where his belt buckle was pressing.

And not just his belt buckle, but the proud surge of his male flesh—a heady reminder of the lust that simmered and boiled and blistered between them.

The floor began to shift beneath her feet and Sabrina's hands tightened on his jacket. The room was moving, pitching like a boat tossed about on a turbulent ocean. Her head felt woolly, her thoughts trying to push through the fog like a hand fumbling for a light switch in the dark. But then a sudden wave of nausea assailed her and she swayed and would have toppled backwards if Max hadn't countered it with a firm hand at her back.

'Are you okay?' His voice had a note of concern but it came from a long way off as if he was speaking to her through a long vacuum.

She was vaguely aware of his other hand coming to grasp her by the shoulder to stabilise her, but then her vision blurred and her stomach contents threatened mutiny. She made a choking sound and pushed Max back and stumbled towards the bathroom.

To her mortifying shame, Max witnessed the whole of the undignified episode. But she was beyond caring. And besides, it had been quite comforting to have her hair held back from her face and to have the soft press of a cool facecloth on the back of her neck.

Sabrina sat back on her heels when the worst of it was over. Her head was pounding and her stomach felt as it if had been scraped with a sharp-edged spoon and then rinsed out with hydrochloric acid.

He handed her a fresh facecloth, his expression wry. 'Clearly I need some work on my seduction routine.'

Sabrina managed a fleeting smile. 'Funny ha-ha.' She dragged herself up from the floor with considerable help from him, his hands warm and steady and impossibly strong. 'Argh. I should never drink on an empty stomach.'

'Wasn't there any food at the cocktail party?'

'I got there late.' She turned to inspect her reflection in the bathroom mirror and then wished she hadn't. Could she look any worse? She could almost guarantee none of the super-sophisticated women he dated ever disgraced themselves by heaving over the toilet bowl. She turned back around. 'Sorry you had to witness that.'

'You need to drink some water. Lots of it, otherwise you're going to have one hell of a hangover in the morning.' His frown and stern tone reminded her of a parent lecturing a binge-drinking teenager.

'I don't normally drink much but I was nervous.'

His frown deepened and he reached for a glass on the bathroom counter and filled it from the tap and then handed it to her. 'Is this a big deal for you? This wedding expo?'

Sabrina took the glass from him and took a couple of sips to see how her stomach coped. 'It's the first time I've been invited to exhibit some of my designs. It's huge for me. It can take new designers years to get noticed but luckily the fashion show floor manager's daughter bought one of my dresses and she liked it so much she invited me along. And then Naomi, the journalist in the bar, asked for an interview for a feature article.

It's a big opportunity for me to get my name out there, especially in Europe.' She drained the glass of water and handed it back to him.

He dutifully refilled it and handed it back, his frown still carving a trench between his brows. 'What did you tell her about us?'

'Nothing. I didn't even mention your name. I just said I was sharing a room with a friend.'

'Are you sure you didn't mention me?'

Sabrina frowned. 'Why would I link my name with yours? Do you think I want anyone back home to know we're sharing a room? Give me a break. I'm not *that* stupid. If I let that become common knowledge our parents will have wedding invitations in the post before you can blink.' She took a breath and continued, 'Anyway, you were the one who made it look like we were having a dirty weekend. You called me "baby", for God's sake.'

'Drink your water,' he said as if she hadn't spoken. 'You need to get some rest if you want to look your best for tomorrow.'

Sabrina scowled at him over the top of her glass. 'Do you have to remind me I look a frightful mess?'

He released a slow breath. 'I'll see you in the morning. Goodnight.'

When Sabrina came out of the bathroom after a shower there was no sign of him in the suite. She wondered if he'd left to give her some privacy or whether he had other plans. Why should she care if he hooked up with someone for a night of unbridled passion? She pulled down the covers on one of the beds and slipped between the cool and silky sheets and closed her eyes...

Max went for a long walk through the streets and alleys of Venice to clear his head. He could still feel the imprint of Sabrina's body pressing against him in the lift. He'd been hard within seconds. His fault for holding her like that, but the temptation had caught him off guard. Had it been his imagination or had she leaned back into him?

He wanted her.

He hated admitting it. Loathed admitting it but there it was. He was in lust with her. He couldn't remember when he'd started noticing her in that way. It had crept up on him over the last few months. The way his body responded when she looked at him in a certain way. The way his blood surged when she stood up to him and flashed her blue eyes at him in defiance. The way she moved her dancer-slim body making him fantasise about how she would look naked.

He had to get over it. Ignore it or something. Having a fling with Sabrina would hurt too many people. Hadn't he hurt his parents enough? If he started a fling with her everyone would get their hopes up that it would become permanent.

He didn't do permanent.

He would get his self-control back in line and get through the weekend without touching her. He opened and closed his hands, trying to rid himself of the feeling of her soft skin. Trying to remove the sensation of her touch. What was wrong with him? Why couldn't he just ignore her the way he had for most of his adult life? He'd always kept his distance. Always. He avoided speaking with her. He had watched from the sidelines as she'd spoken to everyone at the various gatherings they'd both attended.

There was no way a relationship between them would work. Not even a short-term one. She had fairytale written all over her. She came from a family of doctors and yet she had resisted following the tradition and become a wedding-dress designer instead. Didn't that prove how obsessed with the fairytale she was?

His mistake had been kissing her three weeks ago. He didn't understand how he had gone from arguing with her over something to finding her pulling his head down and then his mouth coming down on hers and… He let out a shuddering breath. Why was he *still* thinking about that damn kiss? The heat of their mouths connecting had tilted the world on its axis, or at least it had felt like it at the time. He could have sworn the floor had shifted beneath his feet. If he closed his eyes he could still taste her sweetness, could still feel the soft pliable texture of her lips moving against his, could still feel the sexy dart of her tongue.

The worst of it was he had lost control. Desire had swept through him and he still didn't know how he'd stopped himself from taking her then and there. And *that* scared the hell of out him.

It would not—*could* not—happen again.

When Max entered the suite in the early hours of the morning, Sabrina was sound asleep, curled up like a kitten, her brown hair spilling over the pillow. One of her hands was tucked under the cheek; the other was lying on the top of the covers. She was wearing a cream satin nightie for he could see the delicate lace trim across her décolletage peeking out from where the sheet was lying across her chest.

The desire to slip into that bed and pull her into his arms was so strong he had to clench his hands into fists. He clearly had to do something about his sex life if he was ogling the one woman he wanted to avoid. When was the last time he'd been with someone? A month? Two…or was it three? He'd been busy working on multiple projects, which hadn't left much time for a social life. Not that he had a much of a social life. He preferred his own company so he could get on with his work.

Work. That's what he needed to concentrate on. He moved past the bed to go to the desk where he had set up his laptop the day before. He opened one of the accounts he was working on and started tinkering.

There was a rustle from the bed behind him and Sabrina's drowsy voice said, 'Do you have to do that now?'

Max turned around to look at her in the muted light coming off his laptop screen. Her hair was a cloud of tangles and one of her cheeks had a linen crease and one spaghetti-thin strap of her nightie had slipped off her shoulder, revealing the upper curve of her left breast. She looked sleepy, sexy and sensual and lust hit him like a sucker punch. 'Sorry. Did I wake you?'

She pushed back some of her hair with her hand. 'Don't you *ever* sleep?'

I would if there wasn't a gorgeously sexy woman lying in the bed next to mine.

Max kept his features neutral but his body was thrumming, hardening, aching. 'How's your head? Have the construction workers started yet?'

Her mouth flickered with a sheepish smile. 'Not yet. The water helped.'

He pushed a hand through his hair and suppressed a yawn. 'Can I get you anything?'

'You don't have to wait on me, Max.' She peeled back the bed covers and swung her slim legs over the edge of the bed. She padded over to the bar fridge and opened it, the light spilling from inside a golden shaft against her long shapely legs.

'Hair of the dog?' Max injected a cautionary note in his tone.

She closed the fridge and held up a chocolate bar. 'Nope. Chocolate is the best hangover cure.'

He shrugged and turned back to his laptop. 'Whatever works, I guess.'

The sound of her unwrapping the chocolate bar was loud in the silence. Then he heard her approaching from behind, the soft *pfft, pfft, pfft* of her footsteps on the carpet reminding him of a stealthy cat. He smelt the fragrance of her perfume dance around his nostrils, the sweet peas and lilacs with an understory of honeysuckle—or was it jasmine?

'Is that one of your designs?' She was standing so close behind him every hair on the back of his neck lifted. Tensed. Tickled. Tightened.

'Yeah.'

She leaned over his shoulder, some of her hair brushing his face, and he had to call on every bit of self-control he possessed not to touch her. Her breath smelt of chocolate and temptation. In the soft light her skin had a luminous glow, the creamy perfection of her skin making him ache to run his finger down the slope of her cheek. He let out the breath he hadn't realised he'd been holding and clicked the computer mouse. 'Here. I'll give you a virtual tour.' He showed her the presentation he'd been working on for a client, trying to ignore the closeness of her body.

'Wow…' She smiled and glanced at him, her head still bent close to his. 'It's amazing.'

Max couldn't tear his eyes away from the curve of her mouth. Its plump ripeness, the top lip just as full as the lower one and the neat definition of the philtrum ridge below her nose. He met her gaze and something in the atmosphere changed. The silence so intense he was sure he could hear his blood pounding. He could certainly feel it—it was swelling his groin to a painful tightness. He put his hand down on hers where it was resting on the desk, holding it beneath the gentle but firm pressure of his. He felt her flinch as if his touch electrified her and her eyes widened into shimmering pools of cornflower blue.

The tip of her tongue swept over her lips, her breath coming out in a jagged stream. 'Max…' Her voice was whisper soft, tentative and uncertain.

He lifted her hand from the desk and toyed with her fingers, watching every micro-expression on her face. Her skin was velvet soft and he was getting off thinking about her hands stroking his body. Stroking *him*. Was she thinking about it? About the heat they generated? About the lust that swirled and simmered and sizzled between them? She kept glancing at his mouth, her throat rising and falling over a series of delicate swallows. Her breathing was uneven. He was still seated and she was standing, but because of the height ratio, he was just about at eye level with her breasts.

But the less he thought about her breasts the better.

Max released her hand and rose from the desk chair in an

abrupt movement. 'Go back to bed, Sabrina.' He knew he sounded as stern as a schoolmaster but he had to get the damn genie back in the lamp. The genie of lust. The wicked genie that had been torturing him since he'd foolishly kissed Sabrina three weeks ago.

'I was sound asleep in bed before you started tapping away at your computer.' Sabrina's tone was tinged with resentment.

Max let out a long slow breath. 'I don't want to argue with you. Now go to—'

'Why don't you want to argue with me?' Her eyes flashed blue sparks. 'Because you might be tempted to kiss me again?'

He kept his expression under lockdown. 'We're not doing this, Sabrina.'

'Not doing what?' Her mouth was curved in a mocking manner. 'You were going to kiss me again, weren't you? Go on. Admit it.'

Max gave his own version of a smile and shook his head as if he was dealing with a misguided child. 'No. I was not going to kiss you.'

She straightened her shoulders and folded her arms. 'Liar.'

Max held her gaze, his body throbbing with need. No one could get him as worked up as her. No one. Their verbal banter was a type of foreplay. When had it started to become like that? For years, their arguments had just been arguments—the clash of two strong-willed personalities. But over the last few months something had changed. Was that why he'd gone to the dinner party of a mutual friend because he'd known she'd be there? Was that why he'd offered to drive her home because her car was being serviced? There had been other people at the dinner who could have taken her but, no, he'd insisted.

He couldn't even recall what they'd been arguing about on the way home or who had started it. But he remembered all too well how it had ended and he had to do everything in his power to make sure it never happened again. 'Why would I kiss you again? You don't want another dose of stubble rash, do you?'

Her combative expression floundered for a moment and her teeth snagged her lower lip. 'Okay…so I might have been lying about that…'

Max kept his gaze trained on hers. 'You're not asking me to kiss you, are you?'

The sparkling light of defiance was back in her eyes. 'Of course not.' She gave a spluttering laugh as if the idea was ludicrous. 'I would rather kiss a cane toad.'

'Good.' He slammed his lips shut on the word. 'Better keep it that way.'

CHAPTER THREE

SABRINA STALKED BACK to her bed, climbed in and pulled the covers up to her chin. Of course she'd wanted Max to kiss her. And she was positive he'd wanted to kiss her too. It secretly thrilled her that he found her so attractive. Why wouldn't it thrill her? She had all the usual female needs and she hadn't made love with a man since she was eighteen.

Not that what had happened back then could be called, by any stretch of the imagination, making love. It had been selfish one-sided sex. She had been little more than a vessel for her boyfriend to use to satisfy his base needs. She'd naively thought their relationship had been more than that. Much more. She had thought herself in love. She hadn't wanted her first time to be with someone who didn't care about her. She had been so sure Brad loved her. He'd even told her he loved her. But as soon as the deed was done he was gone. He'd dumped her and called her horrible names to his friends that still made her cringe and curl up in shame.

Sabrina heard Max preparing for bed. He went into the bathroom and brushed his teeth, coming out a few minutes later dressed in one of the hotel bathrobes. Was he naked under that robe? Her mind raced with images of his tanned and toned flesh, her body tingling at the thought of lying pinned beneath him in the throes of sizzling hot sex.

She couldn't imagine Max ever leaving a lover unsatisfied. He only had to look at her and she was halfway to an orgasm. It was embarrassing how much she wanted him. It was like lust had hijacked her body, turning her into a wanton woman who could think of nothing but earthly pleasures. Even now her body felt restless, every nerve taut with the need for touch. *His* touch. Was it possible to hate someone and want them at the same time? Or was there something wrong with her? Why was she so fiercely attracted to someone she could barely conduct a civil conversation with without it turning into a blistering argument?

But why *did* they always argue?

And why did she find it so…so stimulating?

It was a little lowering to realise how much she enjoyed their verbal spats. She looked forward to them. She got secretly excited when she knew he was going to be at a function she would be attending, even though she pretended otherwise to her family. No wonder she found joint family functions deadly boring if he didn't show up. Did she have some sort of disorder? Did she crave negative interaction with him because it was the only way she could get him to notice her?

Sabrina closed her eyes when Max walked past her bed, every pore of her body aware of him. She heard the sheets being pulled back and the sound of him slipping between them. She heard the click of the bedside lamp being switched off and then he let out a sigh that sounded bone-weary.

'I hope you don't snore.' The comment was out before she could stop herself.

He gave a sound that might have been a muttered curse but she couldn't quite tell. 'No one's complained so far.'

A silence ticked, ticked, ticked like an invisible clock.

'I probably should warn you I've been known to sleepwalk,' Sabrina said.

'I knew that. Your mother told me.'

She turned over so she was facing his bed. There was enough soft light coming in through the gap in the curtains for her to see him. He was lying on his back with his eyes closed, the sheets pulled to the level of his waist, the gloriously naked musculature of his chest making her mouth water. He looked like a sexy advertisement for luxury bed linen. His tanned skin a stark contrast to the white sheets. 'When did she tell you?'

'Years ago.'

Sabrina propped herself up on one elbow. 'How many years ago?'

He turned his head in her direction and opened one eye. 'I don't remember. What does it matter?'

She plucked at the sheet covering her breasts. What else had her mother told him about her? 'I don't like the thought of her discussing my private details with you.'

He closed his eye and turned his head back to lie flat on the pillow. 'Bit late for that, sweetheart.' His tone was so dry it could have soaked up an oil spill. 'Your parents have been citing your considerable assets to me ever since you hit puberty.'

Sabrina could feel her cheeks heating. She knew exactly how pushy her parents had been. But so too had his parents. Both families had engineered situations where she and Max would be forced together, especially since his fiancée Lydia had broken up with him just before their wedding six years ago. She even wondered if the family pressure had actually scared poor Lydia off. What woman wanted to marry a man whose parents staunchly believed she wasn't the right one for him? His parents had hardly been subtle about their hopes. It had been mildly embarrassing at first, but over the years it had become annoying. So annoying that Sabrina had stubbornly refused to acknowledge any of Max's good qualities.

And he had many now that she thought about it. He was steady in a crisis. He thought before he spoke. He was hard working and responsible and organised. He was a supremely talented architect and had won numerous awards for his designs. But she had never heard him boast about his achievements. She had only heard about them via his parents.

Sabrina lay back down with a sigh. 'Yeah, well, hate to tell you but your parents have been doing the same about you.' She kicked out the rumples in her bed linen with her feet and added, 'Anyone would think you were a saint.'

'I'm hardly that.'

There was another silence.

'Thanks for letting me share your room,' she said. 'I don't know what I would have done if you hadn't offered. I heard from other people at the cocktail party that just about every-where else is full.'

'It's fine. Glad to help.'

She propped herself back on her elbow to look at him. 'Max?'

He made a sound that sounded like a *God, give me strength* groan. 'Mmm?'

'Why did you and Lydia break up?' Sabrina wasn't sure why she'd asked the question other than she had always wondered what had caused his fiancée to cancel their wedding at short notice. She'd heard the gossip over the children issue but she wanted to hear the truth from him.

The movement of his body against the bed linen sounded angry. And the air seemed to tighten in the room as if the walls and ceiling and the furniture had collectively taken a breath.

'Go to sleep, Sabrina.' His tone had an intractable *don't push it* edge.

Sabrina wanted to push it. She wanted to push him into re-vealing more about himself. There was so much she didn't know about him. There were things he never spoke about—like the death of his baby brother. But then neither did his parents speak about Daniel. The tragic loss of an infant was always devastat-ing and even though Max had been only seven years old at the time, he too would have felt the loss, especially with his parents so distraught with grief. Sometimes she saw glimpses of his parents' grief even now. A certain look would be exchanged between Gillian and Bryce Firbank and their gazes would shadow as if they were remembering their baby boy. 'Someone told me it was because she wanted kids and you didn't. Is that true?'

He didn't answer for such a long moment she thought he must have fallen asleep. But then she heard the sound of the sheets rustling and his voice broke through the silence. 'That and other reasons.'

'Such as?'

He released a frustrated-sounding sigh. 'She fell in love with someone else.'

'Did you love her?'

'I was going to marry her, wasn't I?' His tone had an edge of impatience that made her wonder if he had been truly in love with his ex-fiancée. He had never seemed to her to be the falling-in-love type. He was too self-contained. Too private with his emotions. Sabrina remembered meeting Lydia a couple of times and feeling a little surprised she and Max were a couple about to be married. The chemistry between them had been on the mild instead of the wild side.

'Lydia's divorced now, isn't she?' Sabrina continued after a long moment. 'I wonder if she ever thinks she made the wrong decision.'

He didn't answer but she could tell from his breathing he wasn't asleep.

Sabrina closed her eyes, willing herself to relax, but sleep was frustratingly elusive. Her body was too strung out, too aware of Max lying so close by. She listened to the sound of him breathing and the slight rustle of the sheets when he changed position. After a while his breathing slowed and the rustling stopped and she realised he was finally asleep.

She settled back down against the pillows with a sigh...

Max could hear a baby crying...the sound making his skin prickle with cold dread. Where was the baby? What was wrong with it? Why was it crying? Why wasn't anyone going to it? Should he try and settle it? Then he saw the cot, his baby brother's cot…it was empty… Then he saw the tiny white coffin with the teddy bear perched on top. *No. No. No.*

'Max. Max.' Sabrina's voice broke through the nightmare. 'You're having a bad dream. Wake up, Max. Wake up.'

Max opened his eyes and realised with a shock he was holding her upper arms in a deathly grip. She was practically straddling him, her hair tousled from being in bed or from him manhandling her. He released her and let out a juddering breath, shame and guilt coursing through him like a rush of ice water. 'I'm sorry. Did I hurt you?' He winced when he saw the full set of his fingerprints on her arms.

She rubbed her hands up and down her arms, her cheeks flushed. 'I'm okay. But you scared the hell out of me.'

Max pushed back the sheets and swung his legs over the edge of the bed, his back facing her. He rested his hands on his thighs, trying to get his heart rate back to normal. Trying not to look at those marks on her arms. Trying not to reach for her.

Desperately trying not to reach for her.

'Max?' Her voice was as soft as the hand she laid on his shoulder.

'Go back to sleep.'

She was so close to him he could feel her breath on the back of his neck. He could feel her hair tickling his shoulder and he knew if he so much as turned his head to look at her he would be lost. It had been years since he'd had a nightmare. They weren't as frequent as in the early days but they still occasionally occurred. Catching him off guard, reminding him he would never be free from the pain of knowing he had failed his baby brother.

'Do you want to talk about your nightmare?' Sabrina said. 'It might help you to—'

'No.'

Sabrina's soft hand was moving up and down between his shoulder blades in soothing strokes. His skin lifted in a shiver, his blood surging to his groin. Her hand came up and began to massage the tight muscles of his neck and he suppressed a groan of pleasure. Why couldn't he be immune to her touch? Why couldn't he ignore the way she was leaning against him, one of her satin-covered breasts brushing against his left shoulder blade? He could smell her flowery fragrance; it teased and tantalised his senses. He felt drugged. Stoned by her closeness.

He drew in a breath and placed his hands on either side of his thighs, his fingers digging into the mattress. He would *not* touch her.

He. Would. Not.

Sabrina could feel the tension in his body. The muscles in his back and shoulders were set like concrete, even the muscles in his arms were bunched and the tendons of his hands white and prominent where he was gripping the mattress. His thrashing about his bed had woken her from a fitful sleep. She had been shocked at the sound of his anguish, his cries hadn't been all that loud but they had been raw and desperate and somehow that made them seem all the more tragic. What had he been dreaming about? And why wouldn't he talk about it? Or it had it just been one of those horrible dreams everyone had from time to time?

Sabrina moved her hand from massaging his neck to trail it through the thickness of his hair. 'You should try and get some sleep.'

'You're not helping.' His voice was hard bitten like he was spitting out each word.

She kept playing with his hair, somehow realising he was like a wounded dog, snipping and snarling at anyone who got too close. She was close. So close one of her breasts was pressing against the rock-hard plane of his shoulder blade. The contact, even through the satin of her nightie, made her breast tingle and her nipple tighten. 'Do you have nightmares often?'

'Sabrina, please...' He turned and looked at her, his eyes haunted.

She touched his jaw with the palm of her hand, gliding it down the rough stubble until she got to the cleft in his chin. She traced it with her finger and then did the same to the tight line of his mouth, exploring it in intimate detail, recalling how it felt clamped to hers. 'Do you ever think about that night? The night we kissed?' Her voice was barely more than a whisper.

He opened and closed his mouth, the lips pressing together as if he didn't trust himself to use them against hers. 'Kissing you was a mistake. I won't be repeating it.'

Sabrina frowned. 'It didn't feel like a mistake to me... It felt...amazing. The best kiss I've ever had, in fact.'

Something passed through his gaze—a flicker of heat, of longing, of self-control wavering. Then he raised a hand and gently cupped her cheek, his eyes dipping to her mouth, a shudder going through him like an aftershock. 'We shouldn't be doing this.' His voice was so gruff it sounded like he'd been gargling gravel.

'Why shouldn't we?' Sabrina leaned closer, drawn to him as if pulled by an invisible force.

He swallowed and slid his hand to the sensitive skin of her nape, his fingers tangling into her hair, sending her scalp into a tingling torrent of pleasure. 'Because it can't go anywhere.'

'Who said I wanted it to go anywhere?' Sabrina asked. 'I'm just asking you to kiss me, not marry me. You kiss other women, don't you?'

His breath came out and sent a tickling waft of air across the surface of her lips. 'The thing is... I'm not sure I can *just* kiss you.'

She stared at him in pleasant surprise. So pleasant her ego got out of the foetal position and did a victory dance. 'What are you saying?' She couldn't seem to speak louder than a whispery husk.

His eyes had a dark pulsing intensity that made her inner core contract. 'I want you. But I—'

'Can we skip the but?' Sabrina said. 'Let's go back to the *I want you* bit. Thing is, I want you too. So, what are we going to do about it?'

His gaze drifted to her mouth and then back to her eyes, his eyes hardening as if he had called on some inner strength to keep his self-control in check. 'We're going to ignore it, that's what.' His tone had the same determined edge as his gaze.

Sabrina moistened her lips, watching as his gaze followed the movement of her tongue. 'What if I don't want to ignore it? What if I want you to kiss me? What if I want you to make love to me just this once? No one needs to know about it. It's just between us. It will get it out of our system once and for all and then we can go back to normal.'

She could hardly believe she had been so upfront. She had never been so brazen, so bold about her needs. But she could no longer ignore the pulsing ache of her body. The need that clawed and clenched. The need that only *he* triggered. Was that why she hadn't made love with anyone for all these years? No one made her feel this level of desire. No one even came close to stirring her flesh into a heated rush of longing.

'Sabrina…please…' His voice had a scraped-raw quality as if his throat had been scoured with a bristled brush.

'Please what? Don't tell it like it is?' Sabrina placed her hand on his chest where his heart was thud, thud, thudding so similar to her own. 'You want me. You said so. I felt it when you kissed me three weeks ago. And I know you want me now.'

Max took her by the hands, his fingers almost overlapping around her wrists. At first, she thought he was going to put her from him, but then his fingers tightened and he drew her closer. 'This is madness…' His smoky grey-blue gaze became hooded as it focussed on her mouth as if drawn to it by a magnetic force too powerful for his willpower.

'What is mad about two consenting adults having a one-night

stand?' There she went again—such brazen words spilling out of her mouth, as if she'd swallowed the bad girl's guide to hook-up sex. Who was this person she had suddenly become since entering his hotel room? It wasn't anyone Sabrina recognised. But she wasn't going to stop now. She couldn't. If she didn't have sex with Max, someone she knew and trusted to take care of her, who else would she get to do the deed? No one, that's who.

Ten years had already passed and her confidence around men had gone backwards, not forwards. It was do or die—of sexual frustration. She wanted Max to cure her of her of her hang-ups... not that she was going to tell him about her lack of a love life. No flipping way. He'd get all knight-in-shining-armour about it and refuse to make love to her.

Max brushed the pad of his thumb over her bottom lip, pressing and then releasing until her senses were singing like the Philharmonic choir. 'A one-night stand? Is that really what you want?'

Sabrina fisted her hands into the thickness of his dark brown hair, the colour so similar to her own. She fixed her gaze on his troubled one. 'Make love to me, Max. Please?' *Gah.* Was she begging now? Was that how desperate she had become?

Yep. That desperate.

Max tipped up her chin, his eyes locking on hers. 'One night? No repeats? No happy ever after, right?'

Sabrina licked her lips—a mixture of nerves and feverish excitement. 'I want no one and I mean no one to find out about this. It will be our little secret. Agreed?'

One of his dark brows lifted above his sceptical gaze. But then his gaze flicked back to her mouth and he gave a shuddery sigh, as if the final restraint on his self-control had popped its bolts. 'Madness,' he said, so low she almost couldn't hear it. 'This is madness.' And then his mouth came down and set fire to hers.

CHAPTER FOUR

Six weeks later...

'SO, ARE YOU still keeping mum about what happened between you and Max in Venice?' Holly asked when she came into Sabrina's studio for a wedding-dress fitting.

Sabrina made a zipping-the-lips motion. 'Yep. I promised.'

Holly's eyes were twinkling so much they rivalled the sparkly bridal tiaras in the display cabinet. 'You can't fool me. I know you slept with him. What I don't understand is why you haven't continued sleeping with him. Was he that bad a lover?'

Sabrina pressed her lips together to stop herself from spilling all. So many times over the last six weeks she'd longed to tell Holly about that amazing night. About Max's amazing lovemaking. How he had made her feel. Her body hadn't felt the same since. She couldn't even think of him without having a fluttery sensation in her stomach. She had relived every touch of his hands and lips and tongue. She had repeatedly, obsessively dreamed about his possession, the way his body had moved within hers with such intense passion and purpose.

She picked up the bolt of French lace her friend had chosen and unrolled it over the cutting table. 'I'm not going to kiss and tell. It's...demeaning.'

'You kiss and told when he kissed you after he drove you home that night a few weeks back. Why not now?'

'Because I made a promise.'

'What?' Holly's smiling expression was exchanged for a frown. 'You don't trust me to keep it a secret? I'm your best friend. I wouldn't tell a soul.'

Sabrina glanced across the table at her friend. 'What about Zack? You guys share everything, right?'

Holly gnawed at her lip. 'Yeah, well, that's what people in love do.'

She tried to ignore the little dart of jealousy she felt at Holly's happiness. Her friend was preparing for her wedding to Zack Knight in a matter of weeks and what did Sabrina have on her love radar? Nothing. *Nada.* Zilch.

A mild wave of nausea assailed her. Was it possible to be lovesick without actually being in love? Okay. She was in love. In love with Max's lovemaking. Deeply in love. She couldn't stop thinking about him and the things he had done to her. The things they had done together. The things she had done to him. She placed a hand on her squeamish tummy and swallowed. She had to get a grip. She couldn't be bitter and sick to her stomach about her best friend's joy at marrying the man she loved. So what if Holly was having the most amazing sex with Zack while all Sabrina had was memories of one night with Max?

Holly leaned across the worktable. 'Hey, are you okay? You've gone as white as that French lace.'

Sabrina grimaced as her stomach contents swished and swirled and soured. 'I'm just feeling a little…off.'

Holly did a double blink. 'Off? As in nauseous?'

She opened her mouth to answer but had to clamp her hand over it because a surge of sickness rose up from her stomach. 'Excuse me…' Her hand muffled her choked apology and she bolted to the bathroom, not even stopping to close the door.

Holly came in behind her and handed her some paper towels

from the dispenser on the wall. 'Is that a dodgy curry or too much champagne?'

Sabrina looked up from the toilet bowl. 'Ack. Don't mention food.'

Holly bent down beside her and placed a hand on Sabrina's shoulder. 'How long have you been feeling unwell?'

'Just today...' Sabrina swallowed against another tide of excessive saliva. 'I must have a stomach bug...or something...'

'Would the "or something" have anything to do with your weekend in Venice with Max, which you, obstinately and totally out of character, refuse to discuss?'

Sabrina's scalp prickled like army ants on a military parade. Max had used a condom. He'd used three over the course of the night. She was taking the lowest dose of the Pill to regulate her cycle because the others she'd tried had messed with her mood. 'I can't possibly be pregnant...'

Holly helped her to her feet. 'Are you saying you didn't sleep with him?'

Sabrina pulled her hair back from her face and sighed. 'Okay, so I did sleep with him. But you have to promise you won't tell anyone. Not even Zack.'

'Honey, I can trust Zack to keep it quiet.' Holly stroked Sabrina's arm. 'Did Max use a condom?'

Sabrina nodded. 'Three.'

Holly's eyes bulged. 'At a time?'

'No, we made love three times.' She closed the toilet seat and pressed the flush button. 'We made a promise not to talk about it. To anyone. Ever.'

'But why?'

Sabrina turned to wash her hands and face at the basin. 'We both agreed it was the best thing considering how our families go on and on about us getting together. We had a one-night stand to get it out of our system. End of story. Neither of us wants be involved with the other.'

'Or so *you* say.' Holly's tone was so sceptical she could have moonlighted as a detective.

Sabrina made a business of drying her face and hands. 'It's true. We would be hopeless as a couple. We fight all the time.'

Holly leaned against the door jamb, arms folded. 'Clearly not all the time if you had sex three times. Unless it was combative sex?'

Sabrina glanced at her friend in the reflection of the mirror. 'No...it wasn't combative sex. It was...amazing sex.' She had to stop speaking as the tiny frisson of remembered delight trickled over her flesh.

'Have you seen Max since that weekend?'

'No. We agreed to keep our distance as if nothing happened.' Sabrina sighed. 'He even checked out early from the hotel after our night together. He wasn't there when I woke up. He sent me a text from the airport to say he'd covered the bill for the suite and that's the last time I heard from him.' It had hurt to find the suite empty the next morning. Hurt badly. So much for her following the Fling Handbook guidelines. She'd foolishly expected a good morning kiss or two...or more.

'If you're not suffering from a stomach bug, then you'll have to see him sooner or later,' Holly said.

Sabrina put her hand on her abdomen, her heart beginning to pound with an echo of dread. She couldn't possibly be pregnant... *Could she?* What on earth would she say to Max? Max, who had already made it known he didn't want children. How could she announce *he* was the father of her child?

But wait, women had pregnancy scares all the time. Her cycle was crazy in any case. She had always planned to have kids, but not yet. She was still building up her business. Still trying to prove to her family her career choice was as viable, rewarding and fulfilling as theirs.

She'd had it all planned: get her business well established, hopefully one day fall in love with a man who would treat her the way she had always longed to be treated. Not that she had actively gone looking for the love of her life. She had been too worried about a repeat of her embarrassing falling-in-love episode during her teens. But getting married and having babies was what she wanted. One day. How could she have got it so messed up by falling pregnant? Now? While being on the Pill and using condoms? She was still living in a poky little bed-sit, for God's sake.

Sabrina moved past Holly to get out of the bathroom. 'I can't tell him until I know for sure. I need to get a test kit. I have to do it today because there's a Midhurst and Firbank family gathering tomorrow night and I can't do a no-show. It's Max's mother's birthday. She'd be hurt if I didn't go.'

'You could say you've got a stomach bug.'

Sabrina gave her a side-eye. 'My parents and brothers will be there and once they hear I've got a stomach bug, one or all of them will be on my doorstep with their doctor's bag.' She clutched two handfuls of her hair with her hands. 'Argh. Why am I such a disaster? This wasn't meant to happen. Not *no-o-o-w.*' To her shame, her last word came as a childish wail.

'Oh, sweetie, you're not a disaster. Falling pregnant to a guy you love is not a catastrophe. Not in this day and age in any case.'

Sabrina dropped her hands from her head and glared at her friend. 'Who said I was in love with Max? Why do you keep going on about it?'

Holly placed her hands on her hips in an *I know you better than you do yourself* pose. 'Hello? You haven't slept with any-one for ten years, and then you spend a night in bed with a man you've known since you were in nappies? You wouldn't have slept with him if you didn't feel something for him.'

Sabrina rolled her lips together and turned away to smooth the fabric out on the worktable. 'Okay, so maybe I don't hate him as much as I used to, but I'm not in love with him. I wouldn't be so...so...stupid.' *Would she?* She had promised herself she would never find herself in that situation again. Fancying herself in love with someone who might reject her in the end like her teenage boyfriend had. Falling in love with Max would be asking for the sort of trouble she could do without. More trouble, that was, because finding herself pregnant to him was surely trouble enough.

Holly touched Sabrina on the arm. 'Do you want me to stay with you while you do the test?'

Sabrina gulped back a sob. 'Oh…would you?'

Holly smiled. 'That's what best friends are for—through thick and thin, and sick and sin, right?'

If it hadn't been his mother's birthday Max would have found some excuse to not show up. Not that he didn't want to see Sabrina. He did, which was The Problem. Wanting to see her, wanting to touch her, wanting to kiss her, wanting, wanting, wanting to make love to her again. He had told himself one night and one night only and here he was six weeks later still replaying every minute of that stolen night of seriously hot sex. Sex so amazing he could still feel aftershocks when he so much as pictured her lying in his arms. Sex so planet-dislodging he hadn't bothered hooking up with anyone else and wondered in his darkest moments if he ever would.

He couldn't imagine touching another woman after making love with Sabrina. How could he kiss another mouth as sweet and responsive as hers? How could he slide his hands down a body so lush and ripe and feminine if it didn't belong to Sabrina?

Max arrived at his parents' gracious home in Hampton Court, and after greeting his mother and father took up his usual place at the back of the crowded room to do his people-watching thing. He searched the sea of faces to see if Sabrina was among them, more than a little shocked at how disappointed he was not to find her. But then a thought shot like a stray dart into his brain. What if she brought someone with her? Another man? A new date? A man she was now sleeping with and doing all the sexy red-hot things she had done with him?

Max took a tumbler of spirits off the tray of a passing waiter and downed it in one swallow. He had to get a hold of himself. He was thirty-four years old, not some hormone-driven teenager suffering his first crush. So what if Sabrina slept with someone else? What business was it of his? They'd made an agreement of one night to get the lust bug out of the way.

No repeats.

No replays.

No sequel.

No happy-ever-after.

Max turned to put his empty glass down on a table next to him and saw Sabrina greeting his mother on the other side of the room. The way his parents adored her was understandable given they hadn't had any children after the loss of Daniel. Sabrina, as their only godchild, had been lavished with love and attention. Max knew their affection for her had helped them to heal as much as was possible after the tragic loss of an infant. Not that his parents hadn't adored him too. They had been fabulous parents trying to do their best after such sad circumstances, which, in an ill-advised but no less understandable way, had fed their little fantasy of him and Sabrina one day getting together and playing happy families.

But it was a step too far.

Way, way too far.

Sabrina finally stepped out of his mother's bone-crushing hug and met his gaze. Her eyes widened and then flicked away, her cheeks going an intense shade of pink. She turned and hurriedly made her way through the knot of guests and disappeared through the door that led out to the gallery-wide corridor.

Max followed her, weaving his way through the crowd just in time to see Sabrina scuttling into the library further down the corridor, like a terrified mouse trying to escape a notoriously cruel cat. In spite of the background noise of the party, the sound of the key turning in the lock was like a rifle shot. Or a slap on the face.

Okay, so he had left her in Venice without saying goodbye in person but surely that didn't warrant *this* type of reaction?

Max knocked on the library door. 'Sabrina? Let me in.'

He could hear the sound of her breathing on the other side of the door—hectic and panicked as if she really was trying to avoid someone menacing. But after a moment the key turned in the lock and the door creaked open.

'Are you alone?' Sabrina's voice sounded as creaky as the door, her eyes wide and bluer than he had ever seen them. And, he realised with a jolt, reddened as if she'd been recently crying. A lot.

'Yes, but what's going on?' He stepped into the room before she could stop him and closed the door behind him.

Sabrina took a few steps back and hugged her arms around her middle, her eyes skittering away from his. 'I have something to tell you…'

Here we go. Max had been here so many times before. The *I want more than a one-night stand* speech. But this time he was okay with it. More than okay. He could think of nothing he wanted more than to have a longer fling with her. Longer than one night, that was. A week or two, a month or three. Long enough to scratch the itch but not long enough for her to get silly ideas about it being for ever. 'It's okay, Sabrina. You don't have to look so scared. I've been thinking along the same lines.'

Her smooth brow crinkled into a frown. 'The same…lines?'

Max gave a soft laugh, his blood already pumping at the thought of taking her in his arms. Maybe even here in the quiet of the library while the guests were partying in the ballroom. What could be sexier than a clandestine affair? 'We'd have to keep it a secret, of course. But a month or two would be fun.' He took a step towards her but she backed away as if he was carrying the Black Plague.

'No.' She held up her hands like stop signs, her expression couldn't have looked more horrified than if he'd drawn a gun.

No? Max hadn't heard that word from a woman for a long

time. Weird, but hearing it from Sabrina was unusually disappointing. 'Okay. That's fine. We'll stick to the original agreement.'

She gave an audible swallow and her arms went back around her middle. 'Max...' She slowly lifted her gaze back to his, hers still wide as Christmas baubles. 'I don't know how to tell you this...'

His gut suddenly seized and he tried to control his breathing. So she'd found someone else. No wonder his offer of a temporary fling had been turned down. She was sleeping with someone else. Someone else was kissing that beautiful mouth, someone else was holding her gorgeous body in their arms.

'It's okay, Sabrina.' How had he got his voice to sound so level? So damn normal when his insides were churning with jealousy? Yes, jealousy—that thing he never felt. Ever. Not for anyone. The big green-eyed monster was having a pity party in his gut and there was nothing he could do about it.

One of Sabrina's hands crept to press against her stomach. She licked her lips and opened her mouth to speak but couldn't seem to get her voice to work.

Max called on every bit of willpower he possessed to stop himself from reaching for her and showing her why a temporary fling with him was much a better idea than her getting involved permanently with someone else. A hard sell to a fairytale girl, but still. His hands stayed resolutely by his sides, but his fingers were clenching and unclenching like his jaw. 'Who is it?' There. He'd asked the question his pride had forbidden him to ask.

Sabrina's brow creased into another puzzled frown. 'I... You think there's someone...*else*?'

Max shrugged as if it meant nothing to him what she did and whom she did it with. But on the inside he was slamming his fist into the wall in frustration. Bam. Bam. Bam. The imaginary punches were in time with the thud, thud, thud of his heart. 'That's what this is about, isn't it?'

'Have *you* found someone else?' Her voice was faint and hesitant as if it was struggling to get past a stricture in her throat.

'Not yet.'

She closed her eyes in a tight squint as if his answer had pained her. She opened her eyes again and took a deep breath. 'In a way, this is about someone else...' She laced her fingers together in front of her stomach, then released them and did it again like a nervous tic. 'Someone neither of us has met...yet...'

Max wanted to wring his own hands. He wanted to turn back time and go back to Venice and do things differently. He had to get control of himself. He couldn't allow his jealousy over a man who may or may not exist to mess with his head. He took a calming breath, released it slowly. They would both eventually find someone else. He would have to get used to seeing her with a husband one day. A man who would give her the family she wanted. The commitment and the love she wanted. And Max would move from woman to woman just as he had been doing for the last six years. 'So, you're saying you're not actually seeing someone else right at this moment?'

'No.' Her face screwed up in distaste. 'How could you think I would want to after what we shared?'

'It was just sex, Sabrina.' He kept his tone neutral even though his male ego was doing fist pumps. Damn good sex. Amazing sex. Awesome sex he wanted to repeat. Then a victory chant sounded in his head. *There isn't anyone else. There isn't anyone else.* The big green monster slunk away and relief flooded Max's system.

'Yeah, well, if only it had been just sex...' Something about her tone and her posture made the hairs of the back of his neck stand up. Her hand kept creeping over the flat plane of her belly, her throat rising and falling over a swallow that sounded more like a gulp.

Max was finding it hard to make sense of what she was saying. And why was she looking so flustered? 'I'm not sure where this conversation is heading, but how about you say what you want to say, okay? I promise I won't interrupt. Just spit it out, for God's sake.'

Her eyes came back to his and she straightened her spine as if girding herself for a firing squad. 'Max... I'm pregnant.'

CHAPTER FIVE

MAX STEPPED BACK as if she had stabbed him. His gut even clenched as if a dagger had gone through to his backbone. *Pregnant?* The word was like a poison spreading through his blood, leaving a trail of catastrophic destruction in its wake. His heart stopped and started in a sickening boom-skip-boom-skip-boom-skip rhythm, his lungs almost collapsing as he fought to take a breath. His skin went hot, then cold, and his scalp prickled and tightened as if every hair was shrinking away in dread.

'You're...pregnant?' His voice cracked like an egg thrown on concrete, his mind splintering into a thousand panicked thoughts. A baby. They had made a baby. Somehow, in spite of all the protection he had used, they had made a baby. 'Are you sure?'

She pressed her lips together and nodded, her chin wobbling. 'I've done a test. Actually, I've done five. They were all positive.'

Max scraped a hand through his hair so roughly he nearly scalped himself. 'Oh, God...' He turned away, a part of him vainly hoping that when he turned back he wouldn't find himself in the library of his parents' mansion with Sabrina telling him he was to be a father. It was like a bad dream. A nightmare.

His. Personal. Nightmare.

'Thanks for not asking if it's yours.' Sabrina's soft voice broke through his tortured reverie.

He swung back to face her; suddenly conscious of how appallingly he was taking her announcement. But nothing could have prepared him for this moment. He had never in his wildest imaginings ever thought he would be standing in front of a woman—any woman—bearing this bombshell news. Pregnant. A baby. *His* baby. 'I'm sorry, but it's such a shock.' Understatement. His heart was pounding so hard he wouldn't have been out of place on a critical care cardiac ward. Sweat was pouring down between his shoulder blades. Something was scrabbling and scratching like there was a frantic animal trapped in his guts.

He stepped towards her and held out his hands but she stepped back again. His hands fell back by his sides. 'So… what have you decided to do?'

Her small neat chin came up and her cornflower-blue eyes hardened with determination. 'I'm not having a termination. Please don't ask me to.'

Max flinched. 'Do you really think I'm the sort of man to do something like that? I'm firmly of the opinion that it's solely a woman's choice whether she continues with a pregnancy or not.'

Relief washed over her pinched features but there was still a cloud of worry in her gaze. 'I'm not against someone else making that difficult choice but I can't bring myself to do it. Not under these circumstances. I don't expect you to be involved if that's not what you want. I know this is a terrible shock and not something you want, but I thought you should know about the pregnancy first, before it becomes obvious, I mean.' Her hand went protectively to her belly again. 'I won't even tell people it's yours if you'd rather not have them know.'

Max was ashamed that for a nanosecond he considered that as an option. But how could he call himself a man and ignore his own flesh and blood? It wasn't the child's fault so why should it be robbed of a relationship with its father? He had grown up with a loving and involved father and couldn't imagine how different his life might have been without the solid and dependable support of his dad.

No. He would do the right thing by Sabrina and the baby. He would try his hardest not to fail them like he had failed his baby brother and his parents. He stepped forward and captured her hands before she could escape. 'I want my child to have my name. We'll marry as soon as I can arrange it.'

Sabrina pulled out of his hold as if his hands had burned her. 'You don't have to be so old-fashioned about it, Max. I'm not asking you to marry me.'

'I'm not asking you. I'm telling you what's going to happen.' As proposals went, Max knew it wasn't flash. But he'd proposed in a past life and he had sworn he would never do it again. But this was different. This was about duty and responsibility, not foolish, fleeting, fickle feelings. 'We will marry next month.'

'Next month?' Her eyes went round in shock. 'Are you crazy? This is the twenty-first century. Couples don't have to marry because they happened to get pregnant. No one is holding a gun to your head.'

'Do you really think I would walk away from the responsibility to my own flesh and blood? We will marry and that's final.'

Sabrina's eyes flashed blue sparks of defiance and her hands clenched into fists. 'You could do with some work on your proposal, buddy. No way am I marrying you. You don't love me.'

'So? You don't love me either,' Max said. 'This is not about us. This is about the baby we've made. You need someone to support you and that someone is me. I won't take no for an answer.'

Her chin came up so high she could have given a herd of mules a master class in stubbornness. 'Then we're at an impasse because no way am I marrying a man who didn't even have the decency to say goodbye in person the night we…had sex.'

Max blew out a breath and shoved a hand back through his hair again. 'Okay, so my exit might have lacked a little finesse, but I didn't want you to get any crazy ideas about our one night turning into something else.'

'Oh, yeah? Well, because of the quality of your stupid condoms, our one-night has turned into something else—a damn baby!' She buried her face in her hands and promptly burst into tears.

Max winced and stepped towards her, gathering her close against his body. This time she didn't resist, and he wrapped his arms around her as the sobs racked her slim frame. He stroked the back of her silky head, his mind whirling with emotions he had no idea how to handle. Regret, shame and blistering anger at himself. He had done this to her. He had got her pregnant. Had the condoms failed? He was always so careful. He always wore one. No exceptions. Had he left it on too long? At one point he had fallen asleep with her wrapped in his arms, his body still encased in the warm wet velvet of hers.

Was that when it had happened? He should never have given in to the temptation of touching her. He had acted on primal instinct, ruled by his hormones instead of his head. 'I'm sorry. So sorry. But I thought you said you were on the Pill?'

She eased away from his chest to look up at him through tear-washed eyes. 'I'm on a low dose one but I was so caught up with nerves about the expo, I had an upset tummy the day before I left for Venice. Plus, I was sick after having that champagne at the cocktail party.' She tried to suppress a hiccup but didn't quite manage it.

Max brushed the hair back from her face. 'Look, no one is to blame for this other than me. I shouldn't have touched you. I shouldn't have kissed you that first time and I definitely shouldn't have booked you into my room and—'

'Do you really regret what happened between us that night?' Her expression reminded him of a wounded puppy—big eyes, long face, fragile hope.

He cradled her face in his hands. 'That's the whole trouble. I don't regret it. Not a minute of it. I've thought of that night thousands of times since then.' He brushed his thumbs over her cheeks while still cupping her face. 'We'll make this work, Sabrina. We might not love each other in the traditional way, but we can make do.'

She tugged his hands away from her face and stepped a metre away to stand in front of the floor-to-ceiling bookshelves. 'Make do? Is that all you want out of life? To...' she waved her hand in a sweeping gesture '...*make do*? What about love? Isn't that an essential ingredient of a good marriage?'

'I'm not offering you that sort of marriage.'

Her eyes flashed and she planted her hands on her hips. 'Well, guess what? I'm not accepting *that* sort of proposal.'

'Would you prefer me to lie to you?' Max tried to keep his voice steady but he could feel ridges of anger lining his throat. 'To get down on bended knee and say a whole lot of flowery words we both know I don't mean?'

'Did you say them to Lydia?'

'Let's keep Lydia out of this.' This time the anger nearly choked him. He hated thinking about his proposal six years ago to his ex-fiancée. He hated thinking about his failure to see the relationship for what it had been—a mistake from start to finish. It had occurred to him only recently that he had asked Lydia to marry him so his parents would back off about Sabrina. Not the best reason, by anyone's measure.

'You still have feelings for her, don't you? That's why you can't commit to anyone else.'

Max rolled his eyes and gave a short bark of a laugh. 'Oh, please spare me the pop psychoanalysis. No, I do not still love Lydia. In fact, I never loved her.'

Sabrina blinked rapidly. 'Then why did you ask her to marry you?'

He walked over to the leather-topped mahogany desk and picked up the paperweight he had given his father when he was ten. He passed it from hand to hand, wondering how to answer. 'Good question,' he said, putting the paperweight down and turning to look at her. 'When we first dated, she seemed fine with my decision not to have kids. We had stuff in common, books, movies, that sort of thing.' He gave a quick open-close movement of his lips. 'But clearly it wasn't enough for her.'

'It might not have been about the kid thing. It might have been because she knew you didn't love her. I never thought your chemistry with her was all that good.'

Max moved closer to her, drawn by a force he couldn't resist. 'Unlike ours, you mean?' He traced a line from below her ear to her chin with his finger, watching as her pupils darkened and her breath hitched. Her spring flowers perfume danced around his nostrils, her warm womanly body making his blood thrum and hum and drum with lust. *Don't touch her.* His conscience pinged with a reminder but he ignored it.

Her hands came up to rest against his chest, the tip of her tongue sweeping over her rosebud lips. But then her eyes hardened and she pushed back from him and put some distance between them. 'I know what you're trying to do but it won't work. I will not be seduced into marrying you.'

'For God's sake, Sabrina,' Max said. 'This is not about seducing you into changing your mind. You're having my baby. I would never leave you to fend for yourself. That's not the sort of man I am.'

'Look, I know you mean well, but I can't marry you. I'm only just pregnant. I can't bear the thought of everyone talking about me, judging me for falling pregnant after a one-night stand, especially to you when I've done nothing but criticise you for years. Anyway, what if I were to have a miscarriage or something before the twelve-week mark? Then you'd hate me for sure for trapping you in a marriage neither of us wanted in the first place.'

The mention of miscarriage gave him pause. He had seen his mother go through several of them before and after the death of Daniel. It had been torture to watch her suffer not just physically but emotionally. The endless tears, the longing looks at passing prams or pregnant women. He had been young, but not too young to notice the despair on his mother's face. 'Okay. So we will wait until the twelve-week mark. But I'm only compromising because it makes sense to keep this news to ourselves until then.'

Sabrina bit her lower lip and it made him want to kiss away the indentation her teeth made when she released it. 'I've kind of told Holly. She was with me when I did the test.'

'Can you trust her to keep it to herself?'

'She'll probably tell Zack, but she assures me he won't blab either.'

Max stepped closer again and took her hands, stroking the backs of them with his thumbs. 'How are you feeling? I'm sorry I didn't ask earlier. Not just about how you're feeling about being pregnant but are you sick? Is there anything you need?'

Fresh tears pooled in her eyes and she swallowed a couple of times. 'I'm a bit sick and my breasts are a little tender.'

'Is it too early to have a scan?'

'I'm not sure, I haven't been to see the doctor yet.'

'I'll go with you to all of your appointments, that is, if you want me there?' Who knew he could be such a model father-to-be? But, then, he figured he'd had a great role model in his own dad. Even so, he wanted to be involved for the child's sake.

'Do you want to be there or would you only be doing it out of duty?'

'I want to be there to see our baby for the first time.' Max was a little surprised to realise how much he meant it. But he needed to see the baby to believe this pregnancy had really happened. He still felt as if he'd stepped into a parallel universe. Could his and Sabrina's DNAs really be getting it on inside her womb? A baby. A little person who would look like one or the other, or a combination of both of them. A child who would grow up and look to him for protection and nurturing. Did he trust himself to do a good job? How could he when he had let his baby brother down so badly?

The door suddenly opened behind them and Max glanced over his shoulder to see his mother standing there. 'Oh, there you two are.' Her warm brown eyes sparkled with fairy godmother delight.

Sabrina sprang away from Max but she bumped into the mahogany desk behind her and yelped. 'Ouch!'

Max reached for Sabrina, steadying her by bringing her close to his side. 'Are you okay?'

She rubbed her left hip, her cheeks a vivid shade of pink. 'Yes…'

'Did I startle you?' Max's mother asked. 'Sorry, darling, but I was wondering where you'd gone. You seemed a little upset earlier.'

'I'm not upset,' Sabrina said, biting her lip.

His mother raised her eyebrows and then glanced at Max. 'I hope you two aren't fighting again? No wonder the poor girl gets upset with you glaring at her all the time. I don't want my party spoilt by your boorish behaviour. Why can't you just kiss and make up for a change?'

Max could have laughed at the irony of the situation if his sense of humour hadn't already been on life support. He'd done way more than kiss Sabrina and now there were consequences he would be dealing with for the rest of his life. But there was no way he could tell his mother what had gone on between them. No way he could say anything until she was through the first trimester of her pregnancy. It would get everybody's hopes up and the pressure would be unbearable—even more unbearable than it already was.

'It's fine, Aunty Gillian. Max is being perfectly civil to me,' Sabrina said, carefully avoiding his gaze.

Max's mother shifted her lips from side to side. 'Mmm, I'm not sure it's safe to leave you two alone for more than five minutes. Who knows what might happen?'

Who knew, indeed?

* * *

As soon as the door closed behind Gillian Firbank, Sabrina swung her gaze to Max. 'Do you think she suspects anything?'

'I don't think so. But we have to keep our relationship quiet until you get through the first trimester. Then we can tell everyone we're marrying.'

She stared at him, still not sure how to handle this change in him. So much for the one night and one night only stance he'd taken before. Now he was insisting on marrying her and wouldn't take no for an answer.

She blew out a breath, whirled away and crossed her arms over her middle. 'You're being ridiculous, Max. We can't do this. We can't get married just because I'm pregnant. We'd end up hating each other even more than we do now.'

'When have I ever said I hated you?' Max's jaw looked like it was set in stone. A muscle moved in and out next to his flattened mouth as if he was mentally counting to ten. And his smoky blue eyes smouldered, making something fizz at the back of her knees like sherbet.

'You don't have to say it. It's in your actions. You can barely speak to me without criticising something about me.'

He came to her and before she could move away he took her by the upper arms in a gentle but firm hold. Deep down, Sabrina knew she'd had plenty of time to escape those warm strong fingers, but right then her body was craving his touch. Six long weeks had passed since their stolen night of passion and now she was alone with him, her senses were firing, her needs clamouring, her resolve to resist him faltering. 'I don't hate you, Sabrina.'

But you don't love me either.

She didn't say the words out loud but the silence seemed to ring with their echo. 'We'd better get back to the party otherwise people will start talking.'

His hands tightened. 'Not yet.' His voice was low and deep

and husky, his eyes flicking to her mouth as if drawn by a force he couldn't counteract.

Sabrina breathed in the clean male scent of him, the hint of musk, the base note of bergamot and a top note of lemon. She leaned towards him, pushed by the need to feel him close against her, to feel his body respond to hers. He stirred against her, the tempting hardness of his body reminding hers of everything that had passed between them six weeks ago. 'Max... I can't think straight when you touch me.'

'Then don't think.'

She stepped out of his hold with a willpower she hadn't known she possessed. 'I need a couple of weeks to get my head around this...situation. It's been such a shock and I don't want to rush into anything I might later regret.'

She didn't want to think about all the madly-in-love brides who came to her for their wedding dresses. She didn't want to think about Max's offer, which had come out of a sense of duty instead of love. But she didn't want to think about bringing up a baby on her own either. She walked to the library door, knowing that if she stayed a minute longer she would end up in his arms.

'Where are you going?' Max asked.

She glanced over her shoulder. 'The party, remember?'

He dragged a hand over his face and scowled. 'I hate parties.'

CHAPTER SIX

BY THE TIME Max dragged himself out of the library to re-join the party there was no sign of Sabrina. He moved through the house, pretending an interest in the other guests he was no-where near feeling, surreptitiously sweeping his gaze through the crowd to catch a glimpse of her. He didn't want to make it too obvious he was looking for her, but he didn't want her to leave his parents' house until he was sure she was okay.

He was having enough trouble dealing with the shock news of her pregnancy, so he could only imagine how it was impact-ing on her. Even though he knew she had always wanted chil-dren, she wanted them at the right time with the right guy. He wasn't that guy. But it was too late to turn back the clock. He was the father of her child and there was no way he was going to abandon her, even if he had to drag her kicking, screaming and swearing to the altar.

Max wandered out into the garden where large scented can-dles were burning in stands next to the formal garden beds. There was no silky honey-brown head in the crowd gathered outside. The sting of disappointment soured his mood even fur-ther. The only way to survive one of his parents' parties was to spar with Sabrina. He hadn't realised until then how much he looked forward to it. Was he weird or what? Looking forward to their unfriendly fire was not healthy. It was sick.

And so too was wanting to make love to a woman you got pregnant six weeks ago. But he couldn't deny the longing that was pounding through him. He'd wanted to kiss her so badly back in the library. Kiss her and hold her and remind her of the chemistry they shared. Hadn't it always been there? The tension that vibrated between them whenever their gazes locked. How the slightest touch of her hand sent a rocket charge through his flesh. That first kiss all those weeks ago had set in motion a ferocious longing that refused to be suppressed.

But it *had* to be suppressed. It *must* be suppressed. He was no expert on pregnancy, having avoided the topic for most of his adult life, but wasn't sex between the parents dangerous to the baby under some circumstances? Particularly if the pregnancy was a high-risk one? How could he live with himself if he harmed the baby before it even got a chance to be born? Besides, he didn't want their families to get too excited about him and Sabrina seeing each other. He could only imagine his mother's disappointment if she thought she was going to be a grandmother only to have it snatched away from her if Sabrina's pregnancy failed.

No. He would do the noble thing. He would resist the temptation and get her safely through to the twelve-week mark. Even if it damn near killed him.

Max's mother came towards him with half a glass of champagne in her hand. 'Are you looking for Sabrina?'

'No.' *Shoot.* He'd delivered his flat denial far too quickly.

'Well, if you are, then you're wasting your time. She went home half an hour ago. Said she wasn't feeling well. I hope it wasn't your fault?' The accusatory note in his mother's voice grated along his already frayed nerves.

Yep, it was definitely his fault.

Big time.

* * *

Sabrina managed to make it back to her tiny flat without being sick. The nausea kept coming and going in waves and she'd been worried it might grip her in the middle of the party celebrations. She had decided it was safer to make her excuses and leave. Besides, it might have looked suspicious if her mother or Max's noticed she wasn't drinking the champagne. After all, the party girl with a glass of bubbles in her hand and a dazzling smile on her face whilst working the room was her signature style.

But it seemed Sabrina had left one party to come home to another. The loud music coming from the upstairs flat was making the walls shake. How would she ever get to sleep with that atrocious racket going on? She only hoped the party wouldn't go on past midnight. Last time the neighbours had held a party the police had been called because a scuffle had broken out on the street as some of the guests had been leaving.

It wasn't the nicest neighbourhood to live in—certainly nowhere as genteel as the suburbs where her parents and two older brothers lived and where she had spent her childhood. But until she felt more financially stable she didn't feel she had a choice. Rents in London were continually on the rise, and with the sharing economy going from strength to strength, it meant there was a reduced number of properties available for mid- to long-term rent.

She peeled off her clothes and slipped her nightgown over her head. She went to the bathroom and took off her makeup but then wished she hadn't. Was it possible to look that pale whilst still having a functioning pulse?

Sabrina went back to her bedroom and climbed into bed and pulled the covers over her head, but the sound of heavy footsteps clattering up and down the stairs would have made a herd of elephants sound like fairies' feet. Then, to add insult to injury, someone began to pound on her front door.

'Argh.' She threw off the covers and grabbed her wrap to cover her satin nightgown and padded out to check who was there through the peephole. No way was she going to open the door if it was a drunken stranger. But a familiar tall figure stood there with a brooding expression. 'Max?'

'Let me in.' His voice contained the thread of steel she had come to always associate with him.

She unlocked the door and he was inside her flat almost before she could step out of the way. 'What are you doing here?'

He glanced around the front room of her flat like a construction official inspecting a condemned building. 'I'm not letting you stay here. There isn't even an intercom on this place. It's not safe.'

Pride stiffened her spine and she folded her arms across her middle. 'I don't plan to stay here for ever but it's all I can afford. Anyway, you didn't seem to think it was too unsafe when you kissed me that time you brought me home.'

'My mind was on other things that night.' There was the sound of a bottle breaking in the stairwell and he winced. 'Right. That settles it. Get dressed and pack a bag. You're coming with me.'

Sabrina unfolded her arms and placed them on her hips. 'You can't just barge into my home and tell me what to do.'

'Watch me, sweetheart.' He moved past her and went to her bedroom, opening drawers and cupboards and throwing a collection of clothes on the bed.

Sabrina followed him into her bedroom. 'Hey, what the hell do you think you're doing?'

'If you won't pack, then I'll do it for you.' He opened another cupboard and found her overnight bag and, placing it on the bed, began stuffing her clothes into it.

Sabrina grabbed at the sweater he'd picked up and pulled on it like a dog playing tug-of-war. 'Give it back.' *Tug. Tug. Tug.* 'You're stretching it out of shape.'

He whipped it out of her hands and tossed it in the bag on the bed. 'I'll buy you a new one.' He slammed the lid of the bag down and zipped it up with a savage movement. 'I'm not letting you stay another minute in this hovel.'

'Hovel?' Sabrina snorted. 'Did you hear that clanging noise? Oh, yes, that must be the noise of all those silver spoons hanging out of your mouth.'

His grey-blue eyes were as dark as storm clouds with lightning flashes of anger. 'Why do you live like this when you could live with your parents until you get on your feet?'

'Hello? I'm twenty-eight years old,' Sabrina said. 'I haven't lived with my parents for a decade. And nor would I want to. They'd bombard me constantly with all of your amazingly wonderful assets until I went stark certifiably crazy.'

There was the sound of someone shouting and swearing in the stairwell and Max's jaw turned to marble. 'I can't let you stay here, Sabrina. Surely you can understand that?'

She sent him a glare. 'I understand you want to take control.'

'This is not about control. This is about your safety.' He scraped a hand through his hair. 'And the baby's safety too.'

Sabrina was becoming too tired to argue. The noise from upstairs was getting worse and there would be no hope of sleeping even if by some remote chance she convinced Max to leave her be. Besides, she secretly hated living here. The landlord was a creep and kept threatening to put up the rent.

Sabrina was too proud, too determined to prove to her parents she didn't need their help. But it wasn't just herself she had to think about now. She had to take care of the baby. She'd read how important it was for mothers-to-be to keep stress levels down and get plenty of rest for the sake of the developing foetus. Was Max thinking along the same lines? 'Why did you come here tonight?' she asked.

'I was worried about you. You left the party early and I worried you might be sick or faint whilst driving home. I'm sorry. I should have offered to drive you but I was still reeling from your news and—'

'It's okay.' She tossed her hair back over one shoulder. 'As you see, I managed to get home in one piece.'

He stepped closer and took her hands in his. His touch made every nerve in her skin fizz, his concerned gaze striking a lethal blow to her stubborn pride. 'Let me look after you, Sabrina. Come home with me.'

Her insides quivered, her inner core recalling his intimate presence. The memories of that night seemed to be swirling in the air they shared. Her body was so aware of his proximity she could feel every fibre of her satin nightgown against her flesh. Was he remembering every moment of that night? Was his body undergoing the same little pulses and flickers of remembered pleasure? 'Live with you, you mean?'

'We'll have separate rooms.'

She frowned. 'You don't want to...?'

'I don't think it's a good idea.' He released her hands and stepped back. 'Not until you get through the first trimester. Then we'll reassess.' His tone was so matter-of-fact he could have been reading a financial report.

Sabrina couldn't quell her acute sense of disappointment. He didn't want her any more? Or maybe he did but he was denying himself because he'd set conditions on their relationship. 'But how will we keep our...erm...relationship or whatever we're now calling it a secret from our families if we're living under the same roof?'

'In some ways, it'll make it easier. We won't be seen out and about together in public. And I travel a lot for work so we won't be on top of each other.'

Doubts flitted through her mind like frenzied moths. Sharing a house with him was potentially dangerous. Her body was aflame with lust as soon as he came near, living with him would only make it a thousand times worse. She ached to feel his arms around her, his kiss on her mouth, his body buried within hers. What if she made a fool of herself? Wanting him so badly she begged him to make love to her?

What if she fell in love with him?

He wasn't offering her love, only his protection. Food and shelter and a roof over her head. And a stable but loveless marriage if the pregnancy continued. But wasn't that a pathway to heartbreak? How could she short-change herself by marrying someone who wasn't truly in love with her?

Max came closer again and took her hands. 'This is the best way forward. It will ensure your safety and my peace of mind.'

She looked down at their joined hands, his skin so tanned compared to the creamy whiteness of hers. It reminded her of the miracle occurring inside her body, the cells dividing, DNA being exchanged, traits and features from them both being switched on or off to make a whole new little person. A little person she was already starting to love. 'I don't know...'

His hands gave hers a small squeeze. 'Let's give it a try for the next few weeks, okay?'

Sabrina let out a sigh and gave him a wry glance. 'You know, you're kind of scaring me at how convincing you can be when you put your mind to it.'

He released her hands and stepped back with an unreadable expression. 'I'll wait for you out here while you get changed out of your nightgown. Any toiletries you need from the bathroom before we get going?'

She sighed and turned back for the bedroom. 'I'll get them once I've got changed.'

Max waited for Sabrina while she gathered her makeup and skincare products from the bathroom. He would have paced the floor but there wasn't the space for it. He would have taken out a window with his elbow each time he turned. It was true that he hadn't noticed how appalling her flat was when he'd brought her home that night all those weeks ago. The flat wasn't so bad inside—she had done her best to tart things up with brightly coloured scatter cushions and throw rugs over the cheap sofa, cute little knick-knacks positioned here and there and prints of artwork on the walls. There was even a bunch of fresh flowers, presumably supplied by her best friend Holly, who was a florist.

But it was what was on the outside of Sabrina's front door that worried him. Apart from the stale cooking smells, there were no security cameras, no intercom to screen the people coming in and out of the building. How could he sleep at night if he left her here with who knew what type of people milling past? Criminals? Drug dealers? Violent thugs?

No. It was safer for her at his house. Well, safe in one sense, dangerous in another. He had made a promise to himself that he would keep his hands off her. He knew he was locking the stable door even though the horse was well on its way to the maternity ward, but he had to be sensible about this. Sleeping with her before the three-month mark would make it even harder to end their relationship if the pregnancy failed.

Something tightened in his gut at the thought of her losing that baby. *His* baby. He had never imagined himself as a father. For most of his life he had blocked it out of his mind. He wasn't the type of man who was comfortable around kids. He actively avoided babies. One of his friends from university had asked him to be godfather to his firstborn son. Max had almost had a panic attack at the church when his friend's wife had handed him the baby to hold.

But now *he* was going to be a father.

Sabrina came out after a few minutes dressed in skinny jeans and a dove-grey boyfriend sweater that draped sensually over her bra-less breasts. On her feet she was wearing ballet slippers, and on her face an expression that was one part resignation and one part defiance. He tore his gaze away from the tempting globes of her breasts, remembering how soft they had felt in his hands, how tightly her nipples had peaked when he'd sucked on them. In a few months her body would be ripe with his child.

A child *he* had planted in her womb.

He had never considered pregnancy to be sexy but somehow with Sabrina it was. Damn it, everything about her was sexy.

Wasn't that why he'd crossed the line and made love to her last month in Venice?

But now he had drawn a new line and there was no way he was stepping over it.

No. Freaking. Way.

Sabrina hadn't realised she had slept during the drive from her flat to Max's house in Notting Hill. She woke up when the car stopped and straightened from her slumped position in the passenger seat. She hadn't been to this new house of his before—but not for want of trying by his and her parents. She had walked past it once or twice but was always so keen to avoid him that she had stopped coming to the Portobello Road markets for fear of running into him.

The house was one in a long row of grand four-storey white terrace houses. Each one had a black wrought-iron balustrade on the second-floor balcony and the same glossy black decorative fencing at street level.

When Max led the way inside, she got a sense of what Lizzie Bennet in *Pride and Prejudice* had felt when seeing Pemberley, Mr Darcy's estate, for the first time. *This could be your home if you marry him.*

She turned in a circle in the black and white tiled foyer, marvelling at the décor that was stylish and elegant without being over the top. The walls and ceiling were a bone white but the chandelier overhead was a black one with sparkling crystal pendants that tinkled with the movement of air. There was a staircase leading to the upper floors, carpeted with a classic Persian runner with brass rods running along the back of each step to hold it in place. Works of art hung at various points, which she could only presume were originals. He didn't strike her as the sort of man to be content with a couple of cheap knock-offs to adorn his walls, like she had done at her flat.

'I'll show you to your room,' Max said. 'Or would you like something to eat and drink first?'

Sabrina tried to smother a yawn. 'No, I think I'll go straight to bed. I'm exhausted.'

He carried her small bag and led the way up the stairs, glancing back at her every few steps to make sure she was managing okay. It would have been touching if it hadn't been for how awkward the situation between them was. She was very much aware of how she had rocked his neat and ordered life with her bombshell news. She was still trying to come to terms with it herself. How was she going to run her business and look after a baby? What was she going to say to her parents and brothers?

Oh, by the way, I got myself knocked up by my mortal enemy Max Firbank.

'I'll show you around tomorrow, but the main bathroom is on the ground floor, along with the kitchen and living areas,' Max said. 'On this floor there's my study, second door on the left, and the guest bedrooms, each with its own bathroom. My room is on the third floor. There's a gym on the top floor.'

Sabrina stopped on the second-floor landing to catch her breath. 'Who needs a gym with all these stairs?'

He frowned and touched her on the arm. 'Are you okay?'

'Max, I'm fine. Please stop fussing.'

He drew in a breath and released it in a whoosh, his hand falling away from her forearm. 'Tomorrow I'll have the rest of your things brought over from your flat.'

'How am I going to explain why I'm not at home if my parents or brothers drop by? Where will I say I'm staying?'

'Tell them you're staying with a friend.'

Sabrina arched her eyebrows. 'Is that what you are now? My...friend?'

He glanced at her mouth before meeting her gaze with his inscrutable one. 'If we're going to be bringing up a child together then we'd damn well better not be enemies.'

She had a feeling he was fighting hard not to touch her. One of his hands was clenching and unclenching and his chiselled jaw was set in a taut line. 'This is your worst nightmare, isn't it? Having me here, pregnant with a baby you didn't want.'

'Let's not talk any more tonight. We're both tired and—'

'I'm not so tired that I can't see how much you're hating this. Hating *me*.' She banged her fist against her chest for emphasis. 'I didn't do it deliberately, you know.'

'I never said you did.'

Sabrina was struggling to contain her overwrought emotions. Her life was spiralling out of her control and there was nothing she could do about it. She swallowed a sob but another one followed it. She turned away and squeezed her eyes shut to stop the sting of tears.

Max put the bag down and placed his hands on her shoulders, gently turning her to face him, his expression etched with concern. 'Hey...' His finger lifted her face so her eyes met his. 'Listen to me, Sabrina. I do not hate you. Neither do I blame you for what's happened. I take full responsibility. And because of that, I want to take care of you in whatever way you need.'

But I need you. The words stayed silent on her tongue. She would not beg him to make love to her again. She wanted him to own his desire for her. To own it instead of denying it. She blinked the moisture away from her eyes. 'I'm worried about how I'll cope with my work and a baby. What if I lose my business? I've worked so hard to get it to this stage.'

His hands tightened on her shoulders. 'You will not lose your business. You can appoint a manager or outsource some work. The golden rule in running a business is only to do the stuff that only you can do.'

'I've been trying to do that by hiring a part-time assistant but she messed up my booking for Venice,' Sabrina said.

'It takes time to build up your confidence in your staff but if you train them to do things the way you want them done, and check in occasionally to see if they're on track, then things will eventually run the way you want them to.' He removed his hands from her shoulders and picked up her bag again. 'Now, young lady, it's time for you to get some shut-eye.'

He led her to one of the guest bedrooms further down the corridor. It was beautifully decorated in cream and white with touches of gold. The queen-sized bed was made up with snowy white bedlinen, the collection of standard and European pillows looking as soft as clouds. The cream carpet threatened to swallow her feet up to the ankle and she slipped off her shoes and sighed as her toes curled against the exquisite comfort of luxury fibres.

Max put Sabrina's bag on a knee-high chest near the built-in wardrobes. 'I'll leave you to settle in. The bathroom is through there. I'll see you in the morning.' His tone was so clipped he could have trimmed a hedge. He walked the door to leave and she wondered if he was thinking about the last time they had been alone together in a room with a bed. Did he regret their lovemaking so much that he couldn't bear the thought of repeating it? It felt uncomfortably like her boyfriend walking away, rejecting her. Hurting her.

'Max?'

He turned back to face her. 'Yes?'

Sabrina had to interlace her fingers in front of her body to keep from reaching out to him. She couldn't beg him to stay with her. Wouldn't beg him. The risk of him rejecting her would be too painful. 'Nothing…' A weak smile flickered across her lips. 'Goodnight.'

''Night.' And then he left and closed the door with a firm click.

CHAPTER SEVEN

MAX WENT DOWNSTAIRS before he was tempted to join Sabrina in that damn bed. What was wrong with him? Hadn't he done enough damage? He wanted slip in between those sheets with her, even if just to hold her against his body. He hadn't forgotten how it felt to have her satin-soft skin against his. He hadn't forgotten how it felt to glide his hands over her gorgeous breasts or how it felt to bury himself deep into her velvet warmth.

But he must *not* think about her like that. He had to keep his distance otherwise things could get even more complicated than they already were. Relationships got complicated when feelings were involved and he was already fighting more feelings than he wanted to admit. Everything was different about his relationship with Sabrina. Everything. And if that wasn't enough of a warning for him to back off in the feelings department, he didn't know what was.

He couldn't remember the last time he'd had a sleepover with a lover. It hadn't been in this house as he'd only moved in a few months ago once the renovations had been completed. He hadn't even shared his previous house with Lydia in spite of her broad hints to move in with him.

Max sat at his desk in his study and sighed. For the next six weeks he would have to make sure he kept his relationship with

Sabrina completely platonic. Since when had he found it sexy to make love to a pregnant woman? But now he couldn't stop thinking about the changes her body was undergoing.

Changes *he* had caused.

His gaze went to the framed photograph of his family on his desk. It had been taken just days before Daniel had died. His mother and father were sitting either side of him and he was holding his brother across his lap. Everyone was smiling, even Daniel.

Max wondered if he would ever be able to look at that photograph without regret and guilt gnawing at his insides. Regret and guilt and anger at himself for not doing more to help his little brother. It had taken many years for his parents to smile again, especially his mother.

Would the birth of his parents' first grandchild heal some of the pain of the past?

When Sabrina woke the next morning, it took her a moment to realise where she was. The room was bathed in golden sunlight, and she stretched like a lazy cat against the marshmallow-soft pillows. It was a Sunday so there was no rush to get out of bed…although staying in bed would be a whole lot more tempting if Max was lying here beside her. She'd heard him come up the stairs to his room on the floor above hers in the early hours of the morning. Didn't the man need more than three or four hours of sleep?

There was a tap at the door and she sat up in the bed. 'Come in.'

Max opened the door, deftly balancing a tray on one hand as he came in. 'Good morning. I thought you might like some tea and toast.'

'Oh, lovely, I haven't had breakfast in bed in ages.'

He came over to the bed and placed the tray, which had fold-down legs, across her lap. This close she could smell his freshly shampooed hair and the citrus fragrance of his aftershave. He straightened and gave his version of a smile. 'How are you feeling?'

'So far, so good,' Sabrina said. 'Sometimes the nausea hits when I first stand up.'

'Good reason to stay where you are, then.'

She picked up the steaming cup of tea and took a sip. 'Mmm…perfect. How did you know I take it black?'

His expression was wry. 'I think it's safe to say your parents have told me just about everything there is to know about you over the years.'

Not quite everything.

Sabrina had never told her parents about her first sexual experience. The only person she'd told was Holly. It was too embarrassing, too painful to recall the shame she'd felt to hear such horrible rumours spread about her after giving herself to her boyfriend. 'Seriously, they told you how I take my tea?'

He gave a half smile. 'Only joking. No, I've been observing you myself.'

She put her tea back on the tray and picked up a slice of toast and peeped at him from half-lowered lashes. 'I've noticed.'

'Oh?'

'Yep. You got really annoyed when I danced with one of the guys at that party at my parents' house a few months back.' She nibbled on the toast and watched his expression go from that mercurial smile to a brooding frown. She pointed the toast at him. 'There. That's exactly how you looked that night.'

He rearranged his features back into a smile but it didn't involve his eyes. 'You imagined it. I was probably frowning about something else entirely.'

Sabrina examined her slice of toast as if it were the most interesting thing in the world. 'Thing is… I've never been all that comfortable with the dating scene.'

'But you're always going on dates.' Max's frown was one of confusion. 'You've nearly always got someone with you when you go to family gatherings.'

So, he'd noticed that too, had he? Interesting. Sabrina shrugged. 'So? I didn't want everyone to think I was a freak.' She hadn't intended to tell him about her past. It hadn't seemed necessary the night they'd made love. Max's magical touch had dissolved all of her fears of physical intimacy. Well, most of them. But it wasn't physical intimacy that was her problem now. Emotional intimacy was the issue. What if she developed feelings for him that weren't reciprocated? Real feelings. Lasting feelings. *Love* feelings.

'When was the last time you had sex with a guy?' His voice had a raw quality to it.

She looked at the toast in her hand rather than meet his gaze. 'Other than with you? Ten years.'

'Ten years?' The words all but exploded from his mouth.

Sabrina could feel her colour rising. 'I'm sure that seems like a long time to someone like you, who has sex every ten minutes, but I had a bad experience and it put me off.'

He took the toast out of her hand and held her hand in both of his. 'Sabrina...' His thumbs began a gentle stroking of her wrist, his eyes meshing with hers. 'The bad experience you mentioned...' His throat rose and fell as if he was trying to swallow a boulder. 'Were you—?'

'No, it was completely consensual,' Sabrina said. 'I was eighteen and fancied myself in love and felt ready to have sex for the first time. I never wanted my first time to be outside the context of a loving relationship. But my so-called boyfriend had another agenda. He just wanted to crow to his friends about getting it on with me. I overheard him telling his friends I was hopeless in bed. The gossip and rumours did the rounds of my friendship group. It was humiliating and I wanted to die from shame. Up until you, I hadn't been brave enough to sleep with anyone else.' She chanced a glance at him from beneath her lowered lashes. 'Go on, say it. Tell me I'm a frigid freak.'

His frown carved a deep V into his forehead, his hands so soft around hers it was as if he were cradling a baby bird. 'No...'

His voice had that raw edge again. 'You're no such thing. That guy was a jerk to do that to you. You're gorgeous, sensual and so responsive I can barely keep my hands off you.'

His words were like a healing balm to her wounded self-esteem. So what if he didn't love her? He desired her and that would have to be enough for now. His gentle touch made her body ache to have him even closer, skin on skin. She leaned in and pressed a soft-as-air kiss to his mouth, just a brush of her lips against his. 'Thank you...'

His mouth flickered as if her light kiss had set off an electric current in his lips. He drew her closer, one of his hands going to the back of her head, the other to glide along the curve of her cheek, his mouth coming down to within a breath of hers. But then he suddenly pulled back to frown at her again. 'But that night we made love... My God, I probably hurt you. Did I?'

Sabrina wound her arms around his neck, sending her fingers into the thickness of his hair. 'Of course you didn't. You were amazingly gentle.'

'But you were practically a virgin.' His expression was etched with tension. 'I should have taken more time. I shouldn't have made love to you more than once. Were you sore? Did I do anything you didn't like?'

She shook her head. 'No, Max. I enjoyed every second of our lovemaking. I just wish...' She bit her lip and lowered her gaze.

'Wish what?'

'Nothing. I'm being silly.'

Max inched up her chin with the end of his finger. 'Tell me.'

Sabrina took a breath. 'I've only had sex four times in my life, one time I don't want to even think about any more. The other three times were so amazing that I sometimes wonder if I imagined how amazing they were.'

'What are you saying?'

'I'm asking you to make love to me again.'

His eyes searched hers. 'Is that really what you want?'

She looked into his smouldering eyes. 'I want you. You want me too...don't you?'

His hand slid under the curtain of her hair. 'It scares me how much I want you. But I don't want to complicate things between us.'

'How will it complicate things if we sleep together? It's not as if I'm going to get pregnant.' Her attempt at humour fell flat if his reaction was anything to go by.

He closed his eyes in a slow blink, then he removed her hand from him and stood up. 'I'm sorry, Sabrina, but I can't. It wouldn't be fair to you.' He scraped a hand through his still-damp-from-a-shower hair. 'You're not thinking straight. It's probably baby brain or something.'

'Baby brain?' Sabrina choked out a humourless laugh. 'Is that what you think? Really? Don't you remember how amazing that night in Venice was?'

'Sabrina.' His stern schoolmaster tone was another blow to her flagging self-esteem.

She pushed the tea tray off her legs and set it on the other side of the bed. 'Or maybe sex is always that amazing for you. Maybe you can't even distinguish that night from the numerous other hook-ups you've had since.' She threw him a glance. 'How many have there been, Max?' Tears smarted in her eyes but she couldn't seem to stop herself from throwing the questions at him, questions she didn't really want answered. 'Is that why you've refused to sleep me with since that night? How many have you had since then? One or two a week? More?'

He drew in a long breath and then released it. 'None.'

'None?'

He came and sat beside her legs on the bed and took her hand again, his fingers warm and strong around hers. 'None.'

Sabrina used the back of her free hand to swipe at her tears. 'Are you just saying that to make me feel better?'

'It's the truth. There hasn't been anyone because...' He

looked down at her hand in the cage of his, a frown pulling at his forehead.

'Because?'

His gaze met hers and a wry smile flickered across his mouth. 'I'm not sure.'

Sabrina moistened her dry lips. 'Was it…amazing for you too? That night in Venice, I mean?'

He gave her hand a squeeze. 'How can you doubt it? You were there. You saw what you did to me.'

She lowered her gaze and looked at their joined hands, thinking of their joined bodies and the sounds of their cries of pleasure that night. His deep groans and whole-body shudders. 'It's not like I have much experience to draw on…'

He brought up her chin with the end of his finger. 'It was amazing for me, sweetheart. You were everything a man could ask for in a lover.' His frown came back, deeper than before. 'I just wish I'd known you were so inexperienced. Are you sure I didn't hurt you?'

Sabrina placed her other hand on top of his. 'Max, listen to me. You didn't hurt me.'

He brought her hand up to his mouth, pressing his lips against the back of her knuckles, his gaze locked on hers. 'When I saw you at my mother's party last night I was considering offering you more than a one-night fling.' He lowered her hand to rest it against his chest. 'I would've been breaking all of my rules about relationships in doing so, but I couldn't get you out of my mind. Or stop thinking about how good we were together.'

'Then why won't you make love to me again?'

His irises were a deep smoky grey, his pupils wide and ink black, and they flicked to her mouth and back to her gaze. 'You're making this so difficult for me.' His voice was gravel rough and he leaned closer until his lips were just above hers. 'So very difficult…' And then his mouth came down and set hers aflame.

It was a soft kiss at first, slow and languorous, his lips rediscovering the contours of her mouth. But it soon changed when his tongue stroked across her bottom lip. She opened to him and his tongue met hers, his groan of satisfaction as breathless as her own. His hands came up to cradle her face, his fingers splaying across her cheeks, his mouth working its mesmerising magic on hers. The movement of his tongue against hers set off fireworks in her blood. Her pulse raced, her heart thumped, her need for him rising in a hot tide of longing that left no part of her body unaffected. Her breasts tingled at the close contact as he drew her closer, the satin of her nightgown sliding sensually over her flesh.

He lifted his mouth to blaze a hot trail of kisses along her neck to the scaffold of her left clavicle. 'God, I want you so damn much...' His voice came out as a growl, the warmth in his lips as hot as fire. He was making her burn for him. She could feel it smouldering between her legs, the slow burn of lust that he had awakened in her.

'I want you too.' She breathed the words against his lips, her tongue stroking his lower lip, tasting him, teasing him.

He sealed her mouth with his, massaging her lips in a tantalising motion that made her pulse and ache with feverish desire. His tongue danced with hers, an erotic choreography that made her senses sing. One of his hands slipped the shoestring strap of her nightgown down her shoulder, uncovering her right breast. He brought his mouth down to its rosy peak, his caress so gentle it made her shiver with delight. His teeth lightly grazed her nipple, his tongue rolling over and around it until she gave a gasp of pleasure. He lowered the other strap off her left shoulder, the satin nightgown slithering down to her waist, revealing her body to his feasting gaze.

'You are so damn beautiful.'

Sabrina began to lift his T-shirt, desperate to touch his warm male skin. 'I want to touch you.'

He pulled back to haul his T-shirt over his head, tossing it to the floor. He stood and came over to remove the tea tray from the bed and set it on top of a chest of drawers. He came back to her. 'Are you sure about this?'

'Never surer.' Sabrina wriggled out of her nightgown, a part of her a little shocked at her lack of shyness. But hadn't he already seen all there was to see? She loved the way he looked at her with eyes blazing with lust. It was the most ego-boosting thing to see him struggle to keep control. No one had ever made her feel as beautiful as he did. No one had ever made her feel proud to be a woman, proud of her curves, proud of her sounds as desire shuddered through her.

Max swallowed and stared at her for a long moment, seemingly still struggling with the tug-of-war between his body and his brain. Sabrina drank in the sight of him naked, his taut and tanned torso cut and carved with well-defined muscles that would have made Michelangelo drool and sharpen his chisel. She had never thought of a man as being beautiful before—it was a term usually applied to women. But in Max's case it was entirely appropriate. There was a classical beauty about the structure of his face and body, the aristocratic lines and planes and contours reminding her of heroes—both fictional and historical—from times past.

Max gathered her close, his touch as gentle as if he were handling priceless porcelain. It made her skin lift and shiver in a shower of goose-bumps. 'Are you cold?' He frowned and glided his hand over her thigh.

Sabrina smiled and brushed her hand down the wall of his chest, suddenly feeling shy about touching him. But she ached to touch him. To caress him. 'I'm not cold. I'm just enjoying being touched. You have such incredible hands.'

He brought his mouth back to hers in a lingering kiss that made her need of him throb deep in her core. Every movement of his lips, every touch of his tongue, every contact point of his body with hers made her desire build to the point of pain. There was a storm gathering in her feminine flesh, a tight turbulence that spread from her core to each of her limbs like all her nerves were on fire. There was a deep throbbing ache between her legs and every time his tongue flicked against hers, it triggered another pulse of lust that made it throb all the more. She moved against him restively, wanting more but not sure how to ask for it.

Perhaps he sensed her shyness, for he took one of her hands and brought it down between their bodies. 'You can touch me.' His voice was so deep and husky it made her skin tingle to think she was having such an effect on him.

Sabrina stroked him with her fingers, enjoying the satin-wrapped steel of his male flesh. He drew in a sharp breath as if her touch thrilled him as much as his thrilled her. 'Am I doing it right?'

'Everything you're doing is perfect.' His breathing increased its pace, his eyes dark and glittering with need.

She moved her hand up and down his shaft, enjoying the feel of him without the barrier of a condom. Skin on skin. The smoothness and strength of him making everything that was female in her do cartwheels of delight.

After a moment, he removed her hand and pressed her down so he was balanced above her on his elbows. 'I don't want to rush you.'

'Rush me?' Sabrina gave a soft laugh. 'I'm practically dying here I want you so much.'

His slow smile made her heart trip and kick. 'Slow is better. It makes it more enjoyable for both of us.'

She reached down to stroke him again. 'Isn't it killing you to hold on so long?'

His jaw worked as if he was reining in his response to her touch. 'I want this to be good for you. Better than good.'

Sabrina's heart was asking for more room inside her chest. He was the dream lover, the lover she had fantasised about for most of her adult life. A lover who put her needs ahead of his own. A lover who respected her and made sure she enjoyed every second of their lovemaking.

But she wanted more. More of him. All of him. He moved over her, gathering her close, nudging her entrance with his erection, taking his time to move, waiting for her to get used to him before going further.

It was so different from her first time as a teenager. So very different it made her chest tighten with emotion. If only *he* had been her first lover. Her body responded to him like fuel to fire. It erupted into sensations, fiery, pulsating sensations that rippled through her entire body. She welcomed him into her with a breathless gasp of pleasure, her inner muscles wrapping tightly around him, moving with him as he began to slowly thrust. Her need built and built within her, his rhythmic movements triggering electrifying sensations that made every cell of her body vibrate. Tension gathered again in her core, a teasing tantalising tension that was more powerful than before. It was taking over her body, taking over her mind, pulling her into one point of exquisite feeling...

But she couldn't quite complete the journey. Her body was poised on a vertiginous precipice, needing, *aching* to fall but unable to fly.

Max brought his hand down to her tender flesh, caressing, providing that blessed friction she needed to finally break free. And fly she did, in waves and ripples and pulses that left no part of her body unaffected. It was like being tossed into a whirlpool, her senses scattering as shockwave after shockwave rocketed through her. Sabrina heard someone gasping and crying in a breathless voice and realised with a jolt that those primal and earthy sounds had come from her.

Max waited until her storm had eased before he increased his pace, bringing himself to his own release with a series of shuddering movements that made her wonder if he had been as affected by their lovemaking as she. Or was this normal for him? Was sex simply sex for him and nothing else? The physical satiation of primal needs that could be met with any willing female? Or had he been as moved as she had been by the flow and ebb of sensations that were still lingering in her body like waves gently washing against a shore?

He began to play with her hair, running his fingers through the tousled strands, the slight pull on her scalp sending a frisson down her spine. How could one person's touch be so powerful? Evoke such incredible sensations in her body?

After a long moment, he raised his head to look down at her, his hand now cradling the back of her head. His expression was confusing to read, it was as if he had pulled down an emotional screen on his face but it hadn't gone all the way down, leaving a gap where a narrow beam of light shone through. The contours of his mouth that hinted at a smile, the smoky grey-blue of his eyes, the pleated brow that wasn't quite a frown made her wonder if he—like her—was privately a little shocked at how good they were together. 'You were wonderful.' His voice had that gravel and honey thing going on. 'Truly wonderful.'

Sabrina let out a shuddery sigh—just thinking about the sensations he had caused made her shiver in delight. 'Is it like that for you all the time?'

He didn't answer for a moment and she wished she hadn't gone fishing for compliments. Stupid. Stupid. Stupid. Of course it wasn't different for him. Of course it wasn't special. Of course it wasn't unique.

She wasn't special.

She wasn't unique.

Max's hand cupped the side of her face, his gaze more blue than grey—a dark, intense blue that made her think of a midnight sky. 'It's not often as good as that. Rarely, in fact.'

Sabrina's heart lifted like it was attached to helium balloons. 'But it sometimes is?' Why couldn't she just let it drop? But she had to know. She longed to know if he felt even a portion of what she'd felt. Her body would never be the same. How could it? It had experienced a maelstrom of sensations that even now were lingering in her flesh in tiny tingles and fizzes.

A small frown appeared on his brow and his eyes moved

between each of hers in a back and forth motion as if he were searching for something he didn't really want to find. 'Sabrina…' He released a short sigh. 'Let's not make this any more complicated than it already is.'

Sabrina knew she was wading into the deep end but couldn't seem to stop herself. 'What's complicated about asking you if the sex we just had was run-of-the-mill for you?'

He held her gaze for a beat and then pushed himself away. He got off the bed and rubbed a hand over the back of his neck, tilting his head from side to side as if to ease a knot of tension.

He let out another sigh and turned back to face her, a twisted smile ghosting his mouth. 'Okay, you win. It was great sex. Awesome. The best I've had in years, which was why I was going to offer you a longer fling yesterday at my mother's party.'

Sabrina searched his expression, wondering whether to believe him or not. How silly was she to push for a confession from him only to doubt it when he gave it to her? 'Do you mean it?' Her voice was as soft as a whispered secret, uncertain and desperately seeking reassurance.

Max came back to sit on the bed beside her. He took one of her hands and brought it up to his mouth, kissing each of her fingertips in turn, his eyes holding hers. 'You're a beautiful and sexy woman. I can't remember a time when I've enjoyed sex more.' He gave another rueful twist of his mouth. 'Maybe I've been dating the wrong type of woman.'

Sabrina lowered her gaze and chewed one side of her mouth. 'Better than not dating at all, I suppose…' She didn't want to think about him dating other women. Now that they'd made love again, it made her sick to think of him kissing and caressing someone else. Thank God he hadn't been with anyone since their night in Venice, but how would she feel if he had? But if she didn't marry him, he would be at liberty to sleep with whomever he wished.

It was her call.

Max tipped up her chin with his finger, meshing his gaze

with hers. 'What happened to you when you were eighteen would be enough to put most people off dating for a decade. But you have no need to feel insecure. You're one hell of a sexy partner, sweetheart. That night we first kissed? I wanted you so badly it was all I could do to tear myself away.'

'Really?'

His smile made something in her chest ping. He leaned down to press a soft kiss to her mouth. 'Couldn't you tell?'

Sabrina smiled against his mouth. 'It was kind of an enthusiastic kiss now that I think about it.'

He kissed her again, a longer kiss this time, the movement of his lips stirring her senses into overdrive. He lifted his mouth just above hers, his eyes sexily hooded. 'Is that enthusiastic enough for you?'

She traced the line of his mouth with her finger, her body tingling with excitement at the way his hard body was pressing against her. 'Getting there.'

He captured her finger with his teeth, holding it in a soft bite, his eyes pulsating with lust. 'I want you.'

Sabrina shivered in anticipation and looped her arms around his neck. 'I want you too.'

He brought his mouth back down to hers, kissing her long and deep, his tongue gliding into her mouth with a slow thrust that made her body tremble. His hands cradled her face, his upper body pressing down on her breasts, the skin-on-skin contact thrilling her senses all over again. She could feel the swollen ridge of his erection against her lower body, and her inner core responding with tight contractions and clenches. The sweet tension was building, all her pleasure points in heightened awareness of his touch. One of his hands went to her breast in a slow caress that made her skin tighten and tingle. His thumb rolled over her nipple, back and forth until it was a hard pebble of pleasure. The sensations travelled from her breasts to her belly and below as if transmitted by a sensual network of nerves, each one triggered and tantalised by his spine-tingling touch. He went lower to caress her intimately, his clever fingers wreaking havoc on her senses, driving up her need until she was breathless with it.

But he coaxed her only so far, leaving her hanging in that torturous zone that made her wild with longing. Wild and wanton and racked with primitive urges she'd had no idea she possessed. She felt like she would *die* if he didn't let her come. The need was like a pressure cooker inside her flesh. Building. Building. Building.

He gently pressed her down with his weight, his body entering hers with a smooth deep thrust that made her gasp and groan in delight. Her body welcomed him, worshipped him, wrapped around him in tight coils of need that sent pulses of pleasure ricocheting through her flesh.

He set a slow rhythm at first, but then he gradually increased his pace and she went with him, holding him, stroking his back and shoulders, her body so finely tuned to his that she was aware of every breath he took, every sound he made, every movement of his body within hers.

He rolled her so she was lying on top of him, his hands gripping her hips, encouraging her to move with him in an erotic rhythm that intensified her pleasure. She should have felt exposed and vulnerable but she didn't, instead she felt sexy and desirable. His eyes gleamed with delight as she rode him, naked flesh to naked flesh, hers soft and yielding, his hard and commanding.

Sabrina could feel the tight tingle in the core of her being; the slow build was now a rush of heady sensation threatening to consume her like a swamping wave. It was terrifying and yet tantalising as her body swept her up into a tumult of powerful pulses of pleasure, blissful, frightening pleasure that stole her breath and blanked out her thoughts. She heard herself cry out, a high wail that sounded almost primitive, but she was beyond caring. Her body was riding out a cataclysmic storm that made every pore of her skin tingle and tighten as the waves of orgasm washed over her.

Max continued to move within her, his hands holding her by the hips now, his face screwed up in intense pleasure as he pumped his way to paradise. It was as thrilling as the orgasm she'd just had to watch him shudder through his. The way his hands tightened on her almost to the point of pain, the clench of the toned muscles of his abdomen, the momentary pause before he allowed himself to fly. The raw sexiness of his response made her feel proud of her femininity in a way she had never before.

He arched his head back on the pillow and let out a ragged-sounding sigh as his whole body relaxed. He ran a light hand up and down her right arm, his touch like an electrical current on her sensitised-by-sex skin.

His eyes meshed with hers, holding them in a lock that communicated on another level—a level she could feel deep in her flesh. Their bodies were still connected, neither of them had moved. She hadn't been able to. Hadn't wanted to.

He gave a crooked smile and gathered her close so she was sprawled across his chest. She laid her head against the thud of his heart, and sighed as his hand went to the back of her head in a slow-moving caress that made every hair on her scalp shiver at the roots.

Words didn't seem necessary, although Sabrina had plenty she wanted to say. But she kept her mouth closed. He might hold her like a romantic lover but this was not a love match. She had to keep her head. She had to keep her heart out of this. She closed her eyes and nestled against him, breathing in the musky scent of their coupling. For so long Max had been her enemy. The man she actively avoided or if she couldn't avoid him, she fought with him. But how would she be able to conceal her body's involuntary response to him? How would she stop herself from betraying how he made her feel?

Max wasn't her ideal husband. How could he be when he'd always made it clear he didn't want children? He'd been prepared to marry his ex-fiancée but only on the proviso that the marriage would be childless. He didn't want the things Sabrina wanted, the things she'd wanted since she was a little girl. But now circumstances had forced them together because he refused to walk away from her and their child.

Max moved so he was lying beside her and leaning on one elbow. His free hand moved from her face in a slow caress down between her breasts to rest against the flat plane of her belly. There was a faintly disturbing gravitas about his expression that made her wonder if he was already regretting making love to her. Regretting the child they had made.

Sabrina searched his tense features, noted the shadows behind his eyes. 'Does your decision never to have children have something to do with what happened to your brother Daniel?' She knew she was crossing a line by bringing up the subject of his baby brother. Some of the tiny muscles on his face flinched as if she'd slapped him with the pain of the past.

His hand fell away from her belly and he rolled away and got off the bed, his back turned towards her. 'I was the last person to see him alive.' The words were delivered in a hollow tone that echoed with sadness. 'You didn't know that, did you?' His glance over his shoulder was almost accusing.

Sabrina pressed her lips together and shook her head. 'No... no, I didn't...'

He turned back around and drew in a savage-sounding breath, releasing it in a gust. 'No. Because my parents wanted to protect me from blame.' Guilt was etched on his features and shadowing his gaze in smoky clouds.

She frowned in confusion. Why was he blaming himself for his baby brother's death? 'But Daniel died of SIDS, didn't he?'

'Yes, but I can't help blaming myself.' His throat rose and fell. 'I was seven years old. Surely that's old enough to know if something was wrong with my baby brother? But I must have missed it. I thought he was asleep. If only I had acted earlier, called Mum to check on him or something.'

Sabrina thought of Max as a young child, confused and dis-traught by the death of his baby brother. Even adults blamed themselves, particularly mothers, when a baby tragically died of Sudden Infant Death Syndrome, so how much more would Max shoulder the blame from his immature and somewhat ig-norant perspective as a young child?

'But, Max, you were so young. You shouldn't be blaming yourself for Daniel's death. It was a tragic thing but no way was it your fault. Your parents don't blame you, surely?' She had heard nothing of this from his parents or her own, who were such close friends of Gillian and Bryce Firbank.

'No, of course they don't,' Max said in the same grim tone. 'They were in shock and grieving terribly at the time but they were always careful to make sure I was shielded from any sense of responsibility for Daniel's death. But I couldn't stop blaming myself. Still can't, to be perfectly honest.' He gave a twisted movement of his mouth that was as sad to see as the shadows in his eyes.

'Oh, Max…' Sabrina got off the bed and went to him, put her arms around him and hugged him close. After a moment, she leaned back to look up into his eyes. 'I don't know what to say… I can't bear the thought of you blaming yourself all this time. Have you talked to your parents about it?'

He shook his head, his shoulders going down on a sigh. 'We hardly ever mention Daniel's name now. It upsets Mum too much.'

'Understandable, I guess.'

Max's arms fell away from around her body and he stepped back, his expression difficult to read. 'My mother had several miscarriages before and after Daniel died. That's why there was such a gap between Daniel and me. She desperately wanted another child after he died, but each time another pregnancy ended, I saw another piece of her fade away.' Something flick-ered in his gaze. 'I've always felt guilty about my decision not to have children. My parents would love grandchildren. But

I realised I can't tell them about this baby of ours until we're through the danger period. It would destroy them to have their hopes raised and then dashed.'

'Your poor mum. I'm not sure I knew about the miscarriages,' Sabrina said. 'Mum's never mentioned it. Neither has your mum.'

'She doesn't talk about it. Hasn't for decades. She's always so upbeat and positive but I know she must still think about it.' He sighed again. 'And that's another thing I blame myself for. My parents' marriage has been tested way too much because of my failure to protect my brother.'

'But your parents are happy together, aren't they? I mean, they always look like they are. Your dad adores your mum and she adores him.'

His mouth gave a twisted movement, his eyes shadowed. 'But how much happier would they have been if I hadn't let them down?'

Sabrina placed her hand on his arm. 'Max, you haven't let them down. It's not your fault. They're amazingly proud of you. They love you.'

He covered her hand with his and attempted a smile. 'You're a sweet girl, Sabrina. But I have a habit of letting people down in the end. That's why I keep my relationships simple. But nothing about us is simple now, is it? We've made a baby.'

Sabrina hadn't realised until now how deeply sensitive Max was. He was aware of the pain his mother had suffered and was doing all he could to protect Sabrina during the early days of her pregnancy. But marrying him was a big step. Sleeping with him six weeks ago had changed her life in more ways than she had thought possible. 'Max…this offer of yours to marry me…'

His hands came up to cradle her face, his eyes moving back and forth from her gaze to her mouth. His breathing had altered, so too had hers. Their breaths mingled in the small space between their mouths, weaving an intoxicating spell on her senses. 'Maybe I need to work a little harder to convince you, hmm?'

His mouth came down and covered hers, his lips moving in soft massaging movements that made every bone in her body feel like it had been dissolved. She swayed against him, dizzy with need, her body on fire with every spine-tingling stroke and glide of his tongue. The dance of their mouths was like sophisticated choreography, no one else could have kissed her with such exquisite expertise. No one else could have made her mouth feel so alive, so vibrantly, feverishly alive. Her heart picked up its pace, sending blood in a fiery rush to all the erogenous zones of her body, making her acutely aware of pleasure spots that ached to be touched, longed to be caressed. Longed to be filled with his intimate invasion.

Max lifted his mouth off hers, his eyes still gleaming with arousal. 'That one night was never going to be enough. We both know that.'

'Then why didn't you contact me afterwards?'

His mouth shifted in a rueful manner. 'We agreed to stay clear of each other but there wasn't a day that went past that I didn't regret agreeing to that rule.'

Sabrina hadn't been too enamoured with that rule either. Every day of those six weeks she'd ached to see him. Ached to touch him. Ached to give herself to him. But that was how she'd got in to this mess in the first place. Max and she had made a child together from their one night of passion.

Passion but not love.

Max didn't love her and was only offering to marry her because of their child. Her dreams of a romantic happily ever after with a man who adored her were fast disappearing.

'Do you regret this?' Sabrina couldn't hold back the question. 'Taking our relationship to this level?'

His frown deepened and his hand stilled on her hair. 'No.' He released a jagged sigh and added, 'But I don't want you to get hurt. I'm offering you marriage. Not quite the sort you're after but it's all I can offer.'

Sabrina aimed her gaze at his Adam's apple. 'I know what you're offering, Max... I'm just not sure I can accept it...'

He brought her chin up with his finger and did that back and forth thing again with his eyes, searching hers for any trace of ambiguity. 'We're good together, Sabrina. You know that. We can make a go of this. We've both come from stable backgrounds so we know it'll be the best thing for our child to have both its parents together.'

She felt torn because there was nothing she wanted more than to give her baby a stable upbringing like the ones she and Max had experienced. Didn't every mother want that for her baby? But would marrying a man who didn't love her be enough in the long run? He might come to love their child, but would he ever come to love her as well? And why was she even asking such a question? She wasn't in love with Max. *Was she?* She had to keep her feelings out of it. If she fell for him it would make her even more vulnerable than she already was.

But she couldn't ignore the chemistry between them when her body was still tingling from head to foot from his lovemaking. Neither could she ignore the dread that if she refused to marry him, he would be free to go back to his playboy life. Sure, he would be an involved father but not permanently on site like hers had been. Sabrina released a sigh and rested her hand against his thudding heart.

'Okay, I will marry you, but we can't tell anyone until after the twelve-week mark. We'll have to keep our relationship secret from our families until then, because no way am I going to be subject to pressure and well-meaning but unsolicited advice from our families.'

The frown relaxed slightly on his forehead but it seemed to lurk in the grey shadows of his eyes. He brushed back her hair from her face and pressed a soft kiss to her lips. 'They won't hear about it from me.'

CHAPTER EIGHT

Two weeks passed and Sabrina's noisy and cramped flat became a distant memory. All of her things had now been moved and were either in storage or at Max's house. She was touched by his attention to detail, the way he made sure everything was perfectly set up for her. Nothing seemed too much trouble for him, but she couldn't help wondering if he was finding the rapid change in his neat and ordered life a little confronting.

But for her, living with him showed her how seriously she had misjudged him in the past. It made it harder and harder to remember exactly why she had hated him so much. Or had that been a defence mechanism on her part? Somehow her heart had recognised that he was the one man who could make her fall for him and fall hard.

Each time Holly came in for a fitting, Sabrina had to quell her own feelings of disappointment that her wedding wasn't going to be as she had dreamed and planned for most of her life.

But Holly wasn't Sabrina's best friend for nothing and it didn't take her long to pick up on Sabrina's mood at her fitting that afternoon. 'You don't seem yourself today, Sabrina. Is something wrong?'

Sabrina placed another pin in the skirt of Holly's gown to mark where she needed to take it in. 'Other than my husband-to-be is only marrying me out of duty because I'm pregnant with his baby?'

'Oh, honey,' Holly sighed. 'Do you really think Max doesn't care about you? Personally, I think he's been in love with you for months.'

Sabrina sat back on her heels and looked up at her friend. 'What makes you think that?'

Holly lifted one shoulder. 'It's just a vibe I got when I saw him at that party a few months ago. He was acting all dog-in-the-manger when you were dancing with that other guy.'

'So? He was probably just annoyed with me for drawing attention to myself.' Sabrina picked up another pin. 'Turn a little to the left. That's it.' She inserted the pin at Holly's waistline. 'Have you been dieting? This is the third time I've had to take this dress in.'

Holly laughed. 'Wedding nerves. Or excitement more like.'

There was a silence broken only by the rustle of fabric as Sabrina fiddled with the alterations on the dress.

'Have you and Max set a date for the wedding?' Holly asked.

Sabrina scrambled to her feet and stabbed the pins back in her pincushion. 'Not yet...' she sighed. 'I can't see him wanting a big one. He's never been one for large gatherings. He missed out on the Firbank party animal gene.'

Holly's look was as probing as a spotlight. 'Have you decided what you feel about him?'

Sabrina made a business of tidying up her dressmaking tools. She had been deliberately avoiding thinking about her feelings for Max. They were confusing and bewildering, to say the least. He was the last person she had thought she would fall in love with, but how could she not lose her heart to such a wonderful man? He was everything she wanted in a life partner. He was stable and strong and dependable. He had good family values, he was hard working and supportive.

Yes, he was nervous about becoming a father, which was understandable given what had happened to his baby brother. But she wished he would open up more to her about his concerns. To let her in to his innermost doubts and fears. She had hated him for so long, loathed and resented him, and yet these days she only had to think of him and her heart would flutter and a warm feeling spread through her body. 'It's complicated...' She glanced at her friend. 'I used to think I hated him but now I wonder if I ever did. Was it like that for you with Zack?'

Holly's toffee-brown eyes melted at the sound of her fiancé's name. 'It was exactly like that. I hated him when I first met him but as soon as he kissed me...' she gave a dreamy smile '... I think that's when I fell completely and hopelessly in love.'

Sabrina knew from earlier conversations with Holly that handsome playboy Zack Knight had fallen in love with Holly the moment he'd met her. With Zack's reputation as a celebrity divorce lawyer and Holly a twice-jilted wedding florist, their romance had been the talk of London. And while Sabrina was thrilled Holly and Zack were so in love and looking forward to their wedding in a few weeks' time, it made her situation all the more heart-wrenching. She longed for Max to love her the way she had come to love him. Her feelings for him—now that she'd acknowledged them—were intense and irreversible.

But would she be happy knowing, deep down, he was only marrying her out of a sense of duty?

Max was still privately congratulating himself on keeping his relationship with Sabrina a secret from his family. There was something deeply intimate about keeping their involvement quiet. The bubble of secrecy made every moment with her intensely special, as if they were the only two people left on the planet. He had never felt that close to anyone else before and it was both terrifying and tempting. Tempting to think it could grow and develop into something he had told himself never to aspire to because he didn't deserve it.

Worried he would somehow jinx it, destroy it.

It was still too early for Sabrina to be showing her pregnancy, but just knowing his baby was nestled inside her womb made him feel things he had never expected to feel. Not just fear, although that was there big-time, but flickers of excitement, anticipation, wonder. He caught himself wondering what their child would look like, who it would take after, what traits or quirks of personality it would inherit. He had even stopped avoiding people with prams and now took covert glances at the babies inside.

And he had gone to London's most famous toyshop and bought two handmade teddy bears—one with a blue ribbon and one wearing a pink tutu, because, for some reason, he couldn't get the idea of a tiny little girl just like Sabrina out of his mind. He was keeping the bears for when he and Sabrina came home from their first ultrasound appointment.

The day of the appointment, Max cleared his diary for the whole day because he was in no fit state to work even though it would only take up half an hour or so. He was barely able to speak on the way to the radiography centre as he was so lost in his tangled thoughts. His stomach pitched and pinched, his heart raced and his pulse rioted. What if there was something wrong with the baby?

He hadn't realised until now how much he cared about that little bunch of cells. The feelings ambushed him, making him wonder if other fathers felt like this. Men were mostly at arm's length from a pregnancy, distant from what was going on in their partner's body as it nurtured and sustained new life. But he felt an overwhelming sense of love for the child that was growing in Sabrina's womb. What was ahead for their child? What sort of person would they become? How could he as its father make sure it had everything it needed for a long and fulfilling and healthy life?

Max sat beside Sabrina in the waiting room, took her hand and rested it on his thigh. 'Nervous?'

She gave a wobbly smile. 'A little. Are you? You've been awfully quiet.'

He squeezed her hand. 'Sorry. I'm still getting my head around everything.'

A flicker of worry passed through her blue gaze and she looked down at their joined hands. 'I'm sorry about all of this... I can't help feeling it's my fault we're in this situation.'

'Sabrina.' He tipped up her chin and locked his eyes with hers. 'It's not your fault. If it's anyone's fault it's mine.'

Max was relieved Sabrina had finally agreed to marry him. He wanted nothing more than to provide a stable and loving home for their child. And it would be a loving relationship, though perhaps not in the most romantic sense. He genuinely cared about Sabrina, she had been a part of his life for so long, and yet it had only been recently that he had found out the more complex layers to her personality.

He had been deeply touched when she'd revealed to him what had happened to her as a teenager. He wished she had told him that night in Venice but she hadn't and he had to accept it. Would he have still made love to her? He couldn't answer that question. The need between them was so strong and seemed to be getting stronger.

Sabrina's name was called and they were led into the examination room. Max continued to hold her hand as the sonographer moved the probe over Sabrina's still flat abdomen. How could a baby—his baby—be growing inside her? It didn't seem real until he saw the image of the foetus come up on the screen. He could barely register what the sonographer was saying. All he could think was that was his child floating around in the amniotic sac that would feed and nurture it until it was born in seven months' time.

His chest suddenly felt tight with emotion, his heart thumping with a combination of dread and wonder. What sort of father would he be? How could he trust that he would always do the right thing by his child? He had never thought this day would occur and yet here he was sitting with his wife-to-be and staring at a 3D image of their baby.

His wife-to-be. Sabrina, his fiancée. The mother of his child.

Sabrina's hand grasped his tighter. 'Isn't it incredible?' Her eyes shone with the same wonder he was feeling. 'That's our baby.'

Max squeezed her hand and smiled. 'It sure is.'

'You have a few more weeks to decide if you want to know the sex,' the sonographer said. 'It's usually pretty clear from about eighteen to twenty weeks.'

'Do you want to know the sex of the baby?' Sabrina asked Max after the scan was completed.

'Do you?'

'I asked you first.'

'I'm not a great one for surprises, as you probably know,' Max said. 'But I'll go with what you decide. It's your call.'

Her teeth did that lip-chewing thing that never failed to make him want to kiss away the teeth marks on her pillow-soft lips. 'I kind of want to know but I kind of don't. Does that make sense?'

He smiled and brought her hand up to his lips, kissing her bent knuckles. 'It makes perfect sense. At least you've got a bit of time to make up your mind.'

She nodded and gave a fleeting smile. 'It's a little scary now that I've seen the baby... I mean, it makes it so...so real, doesn't it?'

Max kept her hand in his. 'You don't have to be afraid, sweetie. I'll be with you every step of the way.'

She looked at the printed photo of their baby that the sonographer had given them. 'I wonder who it will take after? You or me? Or maybe a bit of both of us.'

'As long as it's healthy, that's all that matters,' Max said. And even then things could happen. Bad things. Tragic things. His gut churned at the thought and his heart started tripping and hammering again. Boom. Trip. Boom. Trip. Boom. Trip. Boom.

Sabrina must have sensed his disquiet and placed her other hand over their joined ones. 'You'll be a wonderful father, Max. I know you will.'

He tried to smile but it didn't quite work. 'Come on. Let's get you home so you can rest.'

Sabrina wasn't tired when they got home but she was concerned about Max. He had seemed preoccupied at the appointment and he'd kept looking at the photo of the baby since then with a frown pulling at his brow. Was he thinking of all the things that could go wrong even after a healthy baby was born? There were no words to settle his fears because no one could guarantee that nothing would happen to their baby. Even after gestation and infancy, there was still the treacherous landscape of childhood and adolescence. But worrying about it wouldn't change what fate had decided—or so she kept telling herself.

Max came into the bedroom where she was resting a short time later, carrying two shopping bags. He sat on the edge of the bed and passed them to her. 'For the baby, whatever sex it is.'

Sabrina opened the first bag to find a handmade teddy bear wearing a blue ribbon. 'So you think it's a boy?'

He gave a one-shoulder shrug. 'I'm hedging my bets. Open the other bag.'

She opened the bag and pulled out another teddy bear but this one was wearing a pink tutu. It touched her that Max had already gone shopping for their baby. It made her wonder if his growing feelings for the baby would somehow, one day, include her. 'They're so cute, Max. That was so thoughtful of you.'

He picked up the blue-ribboned teddy bear and balanced it on his knee, his finger absently flicking the ribbon around its neck. 'Both Daniel and I had one of these. Our grandparents gave them to us.' Something drifted over his features like a shadow across the sky. 'Daniel's was buried with him; it sat on the top of his coffin during the service. I'm not sure if Mum kept mine or not. I think she found it hard to look at it once Daniel had died.'

Her heart ached at what Max must have felt at his baby brother's funeral. And she felt deeply moved that he had shared with her a little more about his childhood and the sadness he still carried. Sabrina took the bear out of Max's hands and set it beside the pink-tutu-dressed one by her side. She took his hand in hers and stroked the strong tendons running over the back of his hand. 'I have a feeling this baby is going to bring a lot of joy to both our families, but especially to yours. You'll be a fabulous dad. I just know it.'

He gave a ghost of a smile and lifted her hand up to his mouth, pressing a soft kiss to the backs of her knuckles. 'I wish I had your confidence.' He lowered her hand to his lap and circled one of her knuckles with his thumb, a frown settling between his eyebrows. 'I'll do my best to protect you and the baby. But what if I fail?'

Sabrina grasped his hand, squeezing it. 'You won't fail. Don't even think like that, Max. Everyone feels a bit daunted by the prospect of parenthood. It's normal.'

He gave another fleeting smile but a shadow remained in his gaze. 'That reminds me...' He let go of her hand and pulled a small velvet box out of his trouser pocket. 'I have something else for you.' He handed the box to her. 'Open it. If you don't like it we can change it for something else.'

Sabrina took the box and prised open the lid. Inside was an exquisite diamond ring that glinted as the light caught all its facets. Being in the business she was in, she saw lots of engagement rings but none had been as gorgeous as this one. 'Oh, Max, it's beautiful...' She glanced up at him. 'But it looks frightfully expensive.'

'And why wouldn't I buy you an expensive ring?'

Because you don't love me.

She didn't have to say it out loud. It was loud enough in her conscience to deafen her. She looked back at the ring and carefully took it out of its velvet home.

Max suddenly took the ring from her and lifted her hand and slipped it over her ring finger. 'There. What about that? A perfect fit.'

'How did you guess my size? Or is that another thing my parents have told you over the years?'

He gave a twisted smile. 'They might well have. But, no, this time I guessed.'

Sabrina looked down at the ring winking on her finger. She tried not to think about how different this moment might have been if they were like any other normal couple. A couple who had met and fallen in love the old-fashioned way. 'It's a gorgeous ring, Max. Truly gorgeous.'

A frown appeared on his forehead. 'Would you have preferred to choose one yourself?'

'No. This one's perfect.' She glanced at him again. 'But I'll have to only wear it in secret for another month because if either of our parents see this giant sparkler on my hand—'

'Maybe we should tell them.'

Sabrina frowned. 'But I thought we agreed to keep it quiet until the twelve-week mark?'

He took her hand and toyed with the ring on her finger, his inscrutable gaze meshing with hers. 'I know but we've had the first ultrasound and everything looks healthy so—'

She tugged her hand out of his and held it close to her body. 'No, Max. I think we should wait. It's only another month and then we can tell everyone about the baby and…and set a date for the wedding.' Every time she thought about the wedding she had a panic attack. How was she going to get a dress made in time? What if she ballooned and looked nothing like the picture she had in her mind of the bride she had always wanted to be?

But it wasn't just about looking the part…what if Max *never* came to love her? People who genuinely loved you never deserted you. It was love that sheltered and sustained a relationship, not an overblown sense of duty.

Max captured her hand again and stroked it in warm, soothing motions. 'I don't want you to think I'm hiding you from my parents out of shame or embarrassment, like we're having some tawdry little affair. I'm proud to be your partner.'

Sabrina squeezed his hand. 'Oh, Max, that's so sweet of you. But I'm kind of enjoying our little secret. I'm surprised we've managed to keep it quiet this long. But I'm sure that's only because my mum and dad are away on holiday at the moment. I told Mum when she phoned me that I was moving out of my flat to stay with a friend. Unusually for her, she didn't ask which one, but it won't be long before she does.'

'But would it be such a problem to tell her you're staying with me? I don't want to come between you and your parents, especially your mother. And especially now you're pregnant.'

Sabrina rolled her eyes. 'You know what my parents are like, always telling me what I should do. I know they mean well, but as soon as they know I'm pregnant they'll whip out their medical bags and whisk me off to have every test under the sun. I just want to have time to get used to it myself. I'm enjoying the secrecy and the privacy for now.'

Max turned her hand over and traced a lazy circle in her palm. 'I'm enjoying it too.'

'You are?'

His eyes glinted. 'So much so, I think we should go away for the weekend.'

A bubble of excitement formed in her chest. 'Where to?'

'It's a secret.'

Sabrina gave him a coy look. 'You kind of like your secrets, don't you?'

He gave a quick grin that transformed his face. 'More than I realised. Can you take the time off work? I know you usually work on a Saturday but—'

'It's fine. My assistant Harriet is getting better all the time so she can take over while I'm away. I figured she's going to have to do more and more for me the further along I get with the pregnancy.'

Max stroked his hand over the back of her head. 'How long will you work? I can support you if you'd like to take more time off and—'

'I love my job, Max. Pregnancy isn't a disease. I'm perfectly healthy and—'

'I just worry about you doing too much. Running a business more or less singlehandedly is not an easy task. You need to out-source so you're not overburdened with unnecessary work. We have a wedding to plan and a baby on the way and that needs to take priority, surely?'

How could he suggest she take time out from the business she loved as if it was nothing more than a fill-in job? Sabrina swung her legs over the edge of the bed and stood. 'Will you stop lecturing me about what I should do? You're starting to sound like my parents.'

'Yeah, well, maybe your parents are onto something.' Max's tone tightened.

She glared at him, stung by his betrayal in siding with her parents. 'What's that supposed to mean?'

He released a rough-sounding breath. 'Look, I don't want to argue with you. I'm just saying you need to do things a little differently. You're a talented designer, no question about that, but you can't possibly make every single dress yourself.'

'I don't make every one myself. I have a small team of seam-stresses but I do all the hand-sewing myself because that's my signature touch.'

'Would it help if I set up a workroom for you here?' Max asked. 'You could work from home and get your assistant to run the shop so you can rest when you need to.'

It was a tempting offer. She had often thought of working from home without the distraction of phones and walk-ins who were 'just browsing'. Some of her hand sewing was compli-cated and painstaking work and she needed to concentrate. And truth be told, she had been feeling a little overwhelmed with it all even before she'd found out she was pregnant. 'You wouldn't mind?'

'Why would I mind?'

'I don't know… I just thought weddings weren't your thing.'

He came back to take her hands in his. 'There is only one wedding I'm interested in right now and that's ours. And the sooner it happens the better.'

Sabrina chewed the side of her mouth. 'But I need time to make myself a dress.'

'Don't you have one in stock you could use?'

She rolled her eyes and pulled her hands away. 'Duh. I've been planning my wedding since I was four years old. No. I cannot wear a dress from stock. I want to make it myself.'

He frowned. 'How long will it take to make one?'

'I usually have a six-month lead time for most of my clients. I'm only doing Holly's in a shorter time frame because she's my best friend.'

'*Six months?*' His tone was so shocked she might have well as said it would take a century.

'I might be able to rustle something up a little earlier but I want my dress to be something I can be proud of when I look back on our wedding day.' Not to mention her relationship with Max. But would she look back on that with pride or despair?

'You're stalling.' The note of schoolmaster censure was back in his tone. 'I don't want to wait for months on end to get married. We've made the decision so let's get on with it.'

'I am not stalling,' Sabrina said. 'Weddings are not dinner parties where you invite a few guests, cook some food and open some wine. It takes months of planning and—'

'So we'll hire a wedding planner.'

'Max, you're not listening to me,' Sabrina said. 'I want to plan my own wedding. I want to make my own dress. I don't want it to be a rushed shotgun affair.'

His jaw worked for a moment. 'I'd like to be married before the baby is born. I want it to have my name.'

'The baby will have your name regardless.' Sabrina sighed and came over to him, touching him on the forearm. 'Maybe we can compromise a bit. I can't say I want to walk up the aisle

with a big baby bump on show. That's not quite what I envisaged for myself when I was growing up.'

His hands came to rest on the tops of her shoulders, his eyes
searching hers. 'Would you be happy with a small and simple
wedding, just family and a few close friends?'

She would have to be happy with it because she was starting
to realise there wasn't time for her to plan anything else. How
far from her childhood dreams had she come? 'Is that what you
would like? Something small and intimate?'

One of his hands went to the nape of her neck, the other to
cradle the side of her face. 'I'm sorry I can't give you exactly
what you want but we can make do.'

Make do. There was that annoying phrase again. But Sabrina
was increasingly aware of her habit of idealising stuff and ending up disappointed when nothing met her standards. Maybe
it was better this way. To lower her expectations and be pleasantly surprised when it worked out better than she thought. She
pasted on a smile. 'Then that's what we'll do. Make do.'

CHAPTER NINE

BY THE TIME the weekend came, Sabrina had almost convinced herself her relationship with Max was just like that of any other young couple in love and preparing for their marriage and a baby. Almost. He whisked her out of London on Friday afternoon, with their weekend bags loaded in the boot of his car, and drove a couple of hours into the countryside to a gorgeous Georgian mansion a few kilometres from a quiet village.

The mansion had been recently renovated for the garden was still showing signs of having had tradesmen's workboots and ladders and other construction paraphernalia all over it. But even in the muted late evening summer light she could see the neglected garden's potential. Roses bloomed in messy abundance, clematis and fragrant honeysuckle climbed rampantly over a stone wall, and along the pathway leading to the front door she could see sweet alyssum filling every crack and crevice in a carpet of white and purple.

'What a gorgeous place,' Sabrina said, glancing at him as helped her out of the car. 'Is it yours?'

'Yes. Do you like it?'

'I love it.' She breathed in the clove-like scent of night stocks and sighed with pleasure. 'Wow. It's just like out of a fairytale.

I'm almost expecting fairies or goblins to come dancing out of that back section of the wild garden.'

Max took her hand. 'Come on. I'll show you around.' He led her to the front door, taking care she didn't trip over the cracked pathway. 'I bought it a while back. I've been coming down when I can to do some of the work myself.'

She gave him a sideways glance. 'Well, I know from personal experience how good you are with your hands.'

He grinned back and squeezed her hand. 'Cheeky minx. Careful, the sandstone step here is a bit uneven. I was going to replace it but I quite like the fact it's been worn down over the years.'

It was becoming more and more apparent to Sabrina that Max was a traditionalist at heart. He was always careful in his designs to respect a building's history and incorporate it cleverly into any new development on the same site, just as he had done with his house in Notting Hill. And wasn't his determination to marry her because of the baby another indication of his commitment to his strong values?

Max unlocked the door and led her inside the house, switching on lights as he went. The interior had been tastefully decorated in mostly neutral colours, which brought in more light. The furniture was a mixture of old and new and she wondered if he'd chosen it himself or got an interior decorator to do it for him. He would certainly know plenty in the course of running his architectural firm. Most of whom would be female.

Sabrina swung her gaze back to his. 'You have excellent taste. Or did you get someone to do the decorating for you?'

He kicked at the crooked fringe on the rug on the floor with his foot to straighten it out. 'There's a woman I use now and again. She's good at listening to what I want and getting on with it.'

The big green-eyed monster was back and poking at Sabrina's self-esteem. 'Is that all you use her for?'

Max frowned. 'Pardon?'

Sabrina wished she hadn't spoken. She turned away and ran her hand over a beautiful walnut side table. 'Nothing...'

He came up behind her and placed his hands on her shoulders and turned her to face him. 'Sabrina. Listen to me.' His voice was gentle but firm. 'You and I are in a committed relationship. You don't have to worry that I'll be looking at any other woman. Ever. Understood?'

She chewed at her lower lip. 'I'm sorry but I can't help feeling a little insecure. It's not like we're in love or anything. How can you be so certain you won't fall in love with someone else?'

His hands tightened on her shoulders. 'Stop torturing yourself with unlikely scenarios. I realise this is a tricky time for you. You have crazy hormonal stuff happening and a lot has happened in a short period of time. But believe me when I say I'll remain faithful to our marriage vows. You have my word on that, sweetheart.'

Sabrina looked into his grey-blue eyes and wished there was a magic spell she could cast that would make him fall in love with her. It would be so much easier to relax and enjoy every facet of their relationship if she thought it was founded on the things that were most important to her.

He was offering commitment without love. Other men offered love and then reneged on the commitment. Could she continue to hope and pray Max would find the courage to relax the guard around his heart and love her as she longed to be loved? She stretched her mouth into a smile. 'Thank you.'

He inched up her chin and planted a kiss on her lips. 'Come on. I'll show you upstairs.'

Sabrina followed him up the staircase to the landing, where eight bedrooms each with their own bathroom were situated. The master bedroom was huge with a gorgeous window seat that overlooked the rambling garden and the landscape beyond. Sabrina knelt on the chintz-covered cushioned seat and looked at the wonderful view of rolling fields and the dark green fringe of forest and wondered if she had ever seen such a beautiful setting. 'Gosh, it's so private. Are there any neighbours?'

'Not close by,' Max said. 'That's why I bought it. It's nice to get away from the hustle and bustle every now and again.'

Sabrina rose from the window seat. 'Do you plan to live here one day? It's a big house for one person. I mean, you weren't planning on settling down and all.'

He reached past her to open the window to let in some fresh air. 'It's more of a weekender. I find it relaxing to be surrounded by nature instead of noise. It clears my head so I can work on my designs.'

Sabrina bit her lip and fiddled with the brass knob the curtains were held back by. 'As big as this place is, you might not get much head space when there's a wailing baby in the house...'

He took her hands in his, his thumbs stroking the backs of her hands. 'Are you nervous about being a mum?'

'A little...yeah, actually a lot.' She sighed. 'I know women have been having babies for ever but it's my first baby and I can't help feeling a little worried I won't be good enough.'

He cut back an incredulous laugh and squeezed her hands. 'Not good enough? You'll be the best mum in the world. You're a natural nurturer.'

'But don't you worry about how this baby is going to change both our lives? I mean, a bit over a month ago we were both single and hating each other. Now we're having a baby and getting married.'

'I have never hated you.' His tone had a strong chord of gravitas.

But what did he feel for her? 'You certainly gave me that impression. Not that I can talk, of course.'

His expression was cast in rueful lines. 'Yes, well, with our parents watching us like hawks for any sign of a melting of the ice between us, I guess we both did or said things we regret now.'

Sabrina moved closer as his hands went to her hips. It never ceased to amaze her how neatly they fitted together like two pieces of a puzzle. 'You're being far too gracious, Max. I seem to remember being an absolute cow to you on a number of occasions.'

He dropped a kiss to the tip of her nose and smiled. 'You're forgiven.'

She smiled back, struck again by how much a smile transformed his features. She lifted her hand to his face and traced the contours of his mouth. 'You have such a nice smile. I don't think I ever saw you smile at me before a few weeks ago.'

'Maybe you're teaching me to lighten up a bit.'

'By accidentally falling pregnant? Yeah, like that's the way to do it.'

He brushed her hair back from her forehead. 'What's done is done. We're moving forward now and it won't help either of us to focus on the negatives about how we got together.' He stepped back with a brief flash of a smile. 'I'm going to bring in our things while you settle in. I've brought some supper for us.'

Sabrina sat on the end of the bed once he'd gone, her thoughts in a messy tangle. Was she being too negative about their situation? She was a lot better off than many young women who suddenly found themselves pregnant after a one-night stand. Max was determined to stand by her and support her. He was bending over backwards and turning himself inside out to be the best partner he could be.

She was grateful he was standing by her, but it didn't stop her hoping his concern for her and the baby would grow and develop into lasting love.

When Sabrina came downstairs, Max had unpacked the car and loaded the fridge with the food he had brought. She was touched by how much effort he had put into making their weekend away so stress-free for her. She hadn't had to do anything but pack her overnight bag.

He came back into the sitting room with a glass of fresh

orange juice and some nibbles on a plate. 'Here you go. I've just got to warm up the dinner.'

Sabrina took the juice and smiled. 'Who knew you were so domesticated?'

'Who indeed?'

He sat down beside her and slung his arm along the back of the sofa near her shoulders. His fingers played with the loose strands of her hair, making her scalp tingle and her skin lift in a frisson of delight. 'Not too tired?' he asked.

She leaned forward to put her juice on the coffee table in front of the sofa, then sat back to look at him. 'Not too tired for what?'

His eyes did that sexy glinting thing. 'No way am I making love to you until you've had something to eat, young lady.'

Sabrina shifted so she was straddling his lap, her arms going around his neck. 'But what if all I want right now is you?'

He ran his hands down the length of her arms, his touch lighting fires along her flesh. 'Those pregnancy hormones really are going crazy, hey?'

She had a feeling it had nothing to do with her hormones. It had everything to do with him. How he made her feel. 'Could be.' She brought her mouth down to his, meeting his lips in a kiss that sent a river of flame straight to her core. She could feel the pulsing ache of her body pressed so close to the burgeoning heat of his. The surge of his male flesh reminding her of the erotic intimacy to come.

He drew in a harsh breath as if the leash on his self-control had snapped. One of his hands going to the back of her head to keep her mouth crushed to his. His tongue thrust between her lips, meeting hers in a hot sexy tangle that sent another shiver racing down her spine.

Sabrina set to work on undoing the buttons on his shirt, peeling it away from his body so she could touch his warm hard flesh. He slid his hands under her top, the glide of his slightly calloused hands on her naked skin making her ache for his possession. He deftly unclipped her bra and brought his hands around the front of her body to cradle her breasts. His thumbs stroked back and forth over her nipples, turning them into achingly hard peaks that sent fiery shivers to her core.

'God, you're so damn sexy I can hardly control myself.' His voice was deep and sounded like it had been dragged over a rough surface.

'Don't control yourself, then.' Sabrina licked his lower lip, relishing in the way he shuddered at her touch. 'You can do what you want to me if you'll let me do what I want to you, okay?'

He didn't answer but drew in a ragged breath and brought his mouth back to hers in a long drugging kiss that involved tongues and teeth and lips and mutual desire so ferocious it threatened to engulf them both.

Sabrina wrenched at his belt fastening, finally getting it undone and tugging it through the lugs of his trousers. She tossed it to the floor over her shoulder and it landed in a snake-like slither on the carpeted floor. She wriggled down off his lap, quickly removing the rest of her clothes, a frisson passing over her flesh when she saw his eyes feasting on her. It amazed her how quickly his body responded to hers and how quickly hers responded to his. Even now she could feel the tight pulses and flickers of need deep in the core of her womanhood, the tender flesh swelling in high arousal, the blood pumping through her veins at breakneck speed.

'Take your trousers off.' Sabrina was a little shocked at how forthright she was being. Shocked but thrilled to be discovering her sensual power. For so many years she had doubted herself, felt ashamed and insecure. But with Max she felt powerfully sexy and feminine. There was no room for shame, only room for the celebration of her sensual awakening.

He stood and stepped out of his trousers, his expression a mixture of rampaging desire and caution at what she might do to him. She pushed him back down on the sofa, bending down on her knees in front of his seated form. 'Now I get to play naughty girl with you.'

Max sucked in another breath and put his hands on her shoulders. 'You don't have to do that—'

'I want to.'

'Oh, God...' He groaned as her hands encased him, moving up and down in massaging strokes the way he had taught her. But she wanted more. She wanted to taste him the way he had tasted her.

Sabrina gave him one long stroke with her tongue from base to tip, delighting in the whole-body shudder he gave. It gave her the impetus to keep going, to torture him with her tongue the way he had done to her. She stroked him again with her tongue, back and forth like she was enjoying her favourite ice cream, casting him wicked temptress glances from beneath half-mast lashes. His breathing rate increased, his body grew more and more tense, every muscle and sinew struggling to keep control. Sabrina opened her mouth over him, drawing him in, sucking and stroking until he was groaning in blissful agony.

Max pulled himself away before he came, breathing hard, his eyes glazed with lust. 'Not all the way, sweetheart.'

'Why won't you let me?'

He got to his feet and picked her up in his arms. 'Because I have other plans for you.'

She linked her arms around his neck and shivered in anticipation. 'Ooh, that sounds exciting.'

He gave her a glinting smile and walked up the stairs, carrying her as if she weighed no more than one of the cushions off the sofa. When they got to the master bedroom, he laid her on the bed and came down beside her, his thighs in an erotic tangle with hers. He cupped one of her breasts in his hands, bringing his mouth down to take her tight nipple into his mouth. He swirled his tongue around its pointed tip, then gently drew on her with a light sucking motion that sent arrows of heat to her core. He moved to her other breast, pleasuring her with the gentle scrape of his teeth and the flick and stroke of his tongue.

Sabrina moved restlessly beneath him. 'Please. I want you

so much…' Her body was throbbing with the need to feel him inside her. The hollow ache between her legs was unbearable, every nerve primed and poised for the erotic friction it craved.

'I want you too, so damn much, I'm nearly crazy with it.' He moved down her body, holding her hips with his hands as he kissed her abdomen from her belly button down to the top of her mound. She drew in a sharp breath as his mouth came to the heart of her desire. He separated her with the stroke of his tongue, moving along her sensitive flesh in a series of cat-like licks that made every hair on her head shiver at the roots.

It was too much and it wasn't quite enough. Her nerves were tight as an over-tuned cello string, vibrating with the need for release. And then she was suddenly there, falling apart under the ministrations of his lips and tongue, shattering into a million pieces as the tumult of sensations swept through her. She cried, she laughed, she bucked and moaned and clutched at his hair, but still he kept at her until the very last aftershock left her body. She flung her head back against the bed, her breathing still hectic. 'Oh, my God…that was incredible.'

Max placed a hand on her belly, a triumphant smile curving his mouth. 'But wait. There's more.' He moved back over her, careful not to crush her with his weight, and entered her with a smooth, thick thrust, making her gasp all over again.

He set a slow rhythm at first, but then he increased the pace at her urging. She wanted him as undone as she had been. She moved her hands up and down the bunched muscles of his arms, then placed them on his taut buttocks, kneading and stroking the toned flesh as his body moved intimately within hers.

'You feel so damn good.' His voice was part moan, part groan as his mouth came back to hers.

Sabrina kissed him back, using her lips and tongue and even her teeth at one point. The intensity of his passion for her was thrilling. The movement of his body, the touch and taste of him delighting her senses into an intoxicating stupor. She arched her spine, desperate to get closer, to trigger the orgasm she could feel building in her body.

He slipped a hand underneath her left hip, lifting her pelvis and shifting slightly to change the contact of their hard-pressed bodies. And just like that she was off again in a heart-stopping release that sent shockwaves through every inch of her flesh. It was like fireworks exploding, fizzing and flickering with blinding light and bursts of colour like a shaken kaleidoscope.

Sabrina was conscious of the exact moment he let go. She felt every shudder, every quake, felt the spill of his essence and held him in the aftermath, listening to the sound of his breathing slowly return to normal. There was something almost sacred about the silence that fell between them. The quiet relaxation of their bodies, the synchronisation of their breathing, the mingling of their sensual fragrances and intimate body secretions was so far removed from her first experience of sex it made her love for Max deepen even further.

Max leaned on one elbow and placed his other hand on her thigh. 'Was that exciting enough for you?'

Sabrina smiled a twisted smile and touched his stubbly jaw in a light caress. 'You know it was.'

He captured her hand and kissed her fingertips, holding her gaze with his. 'I've never been with a more responsive partner. Every time we make love you surprise me.'

She aimed her gaze at his Adam's apple, feeling suddenly emotional. 'I know I've said it before, but I wish you'd been my first lover. I can't believe I let that jerk mess with my head so much and for so long.'

He cradled her close, his hand gently brushed back her hair from her forehead. 'Sweetie, if I were ever to find myself alone with that creep I would delight in giving him a lesson on how to respect women. What he did to you was disgusting and unforgiveable.'

Sabrina couldn't help feeling touched by the flare of righteous anger in his eyes. It was wonderful to have someone stand up for her, someone who respected and cared about her welfare. Even if he didn't love her the way she wanted to be loved, surely it was enough that he would move heaven and earth to take care of her and their baby? 'You're such a good man, Max.'

He pressed a soft kiss to her lips and then lifted himself off the bed. 'Stay here and rest. I'll bring supper up in few minutes.'

Sabrina propped herself up on the elbows. 'Are you sure you don't want some help?'

He pointed a finger at her but there was a smile in his eyes. 'Stay. That's an order.'

She gave him a mock-defiant look. 'You know how obstreperous I get when you issue you with me orders. Are you sure you want to take that risk?'

His eyes ran over her naked form in a lustful rove that made her want him all over again. 'Are you spoiling for a fight, young lady?' His voice was a low deep growl that did strange things to the hairs on the back of her neck.

Sabrina got off the bed and sashayed across to him with a sultry smile. She sent her hand from the top of his sternum to the proud bulge of his erection. 'I was thinking more along the lines of making love, not war. Are you on?'

He shuddered at her touch and pulled her closer. 'I'm on.' And his mouth came down on hers.

CHAPTER TEN

AN HOUR OR so later, Max sat across from Sabrina in the cosy kitchen of the cottage and watched as she devoured the supper of soup and fresh bread and fruit he'd brought with him. He wondered if he would ever get tired of looking at her. Her hair was all tousled where his hands had been in it, her lips were swollen from his kisses and her cheeks had a beautiful creamy glow.

She looked up to see him looking at her and her cheeks went a faint shade of pink. She licked her lips and then, finding a crumb or two, reached for her napkin and dabbed at her mouth. 'What?'

Max smiled and pushed his untouched bread roll towards her. 'I like watching you eat. You remind me of a bird.'

'Yeah? What type? A vulture?' She picked up the bread roll and tore it into pieces. 'Seriously, I can't believe my appetite just now. I'm starving.'

'Must be the hormones.'

She gave him a sheepish look. 'Or the exercise.'

His body was still tingling from said exercise. And that was another thing he wondered if he'd ever tire of—making love with her. 'I should have fed you earlier. It's almost midnight.'

'I love midnight feasts.' She popped another piece of bread in her mouth, chewed and swallowed, and then frowned when she saw his water glass. 'Hey, didn't you bring any wine with you? I'm the one who isn't drinking while I'm pregnant, not you.'

'That hardly seems fair,' Max said. 'I'm not a big drinker in any case.'

'Oh, Max, that's so thoughtful of you. But I don't mind if you have a glass of wine or two.'

'It's not a problem.' He passed her the selection of fruit. 'Here, have one of these peaches.'

After a while, she finished her peach and sat back with a contented sigh. 'That was delicious.'

He got up to clear the table. 'Time for bed?'

She smothered a yawn. 'Not before I help you clear this away.' She pushed back her chair and reached for the plates.

'I'll sort it out. You go up and get comfortable.'

She was halfway to the door when she turned around to look at him with a small frown wrinkling her forehead. 'Max?'

'What's up, sweetie?'

'Have you brought anyone else down here? Another woman, I mean?'

'No. I've only just finished the renovations.' He picked up the plates and cutlery and added, 'I wasn't going to share it with anyone, to be perfectly honest. Even my parents don't know about it.'

'Why haven't you told them?'

'There are some things I like to keep private.'

She chewed at her lip. 'I've been thinking... It must have been hard for Lydia, knowing your parents didn't think she was right for you.'

Funny, but Max could barely recall what his ex-fiancée looked like now. 'Yes, it probably was hard for her.' He frowned and continued. 'I sometimes wonder if I only got engaged to her to stop them banging on about you.'

Something flickered through her gaze. 'Not the best reason to get engaged.'

'No.'

'Have you seen her since?'

'No. What would be the point? We've both moved on.'

She gave him a thoughtful look. 'But have you?'

'Have I what?'

'Moved on.'

Max turned and loaded the dishwasher. 'You can rest easy, Sabrina. I have no lingering feelings for Lydia. You're my priority now.'

'But in a way, it's the same, isn't it?'

He closed the dishwasher with a snap. 'What's the same?'

'The way you felt about her is similar to how you feel about me. You weren't in love with her and you're not in love with me.'

Max didn't like where this conversation was heading. He wasn't incapable of love. He just chose not to love in *that* way. It wasn't called 'falling in love' for nothing. You lost all control when you loved someone to that degree. He was worried that if he fell in love he would eventually let the person down. Hadn't he always done so? His parents? His baby brother? Even Lydia had been short-changed and had gone off looking for someone who could love her the way she wanted.

'Sabrina.' He let out a long sigh. 'Let's not have this discussion this late at night. You're tired and—'

'What are you afraid of?'

He gave a short laugh to lighten the atmosphere. 'I'm not afraid of anything. Now, be a good girl and go upstairs and I'll be up in a second.'

She looked like she was going to argue, but then she let out a sigh and turned and headed upstairs.

Max leaned his hands on the kitchen counter and wondered if this was always going to be a stumbling block in their relationship. But he assured himself that Sabrina wasn't in love with him so what was the problem? If she had been, wouldn't she have said so? No, they were two people forced together because of circumstance and they were both committed to making the best of the situation. They had put their enmity aside, they liked each other, desired each other and respected each other. If that wasn't a positive thing, what was? Their relationship had a lot more going for it than others he'd seen. And it was certainly better than any relationship he'd had in the past.

Way better.

Sabrina spent the rest of the weekend with her mouth firmly closed on the subject of Max's feelings for her. She didn't want to spoil the relaxing time together because she could see how hard he was trying to do everything right by her. Her feelings weren't the top priority right now. They had a baby on the way and she had to somehow reassure Max he would be a wonderful father. She knew it still troubled him and she ached to ease that painful burden for him.

She consoled herself that in time he might relax the guard around his heart, open himself to loving her once he fell in love with their baby. Didn't most new parents say the experience of bringing a child into the world was a defining moment? A time when overwhelming love flooded their beings? It was her hope, her dream and unceasing prayer that Max would feel that groundbreaking love for their child and include her in it.

A few days later, Max left for a brief trip to Denmark, where he had a project on the go. Sabrina could sense his reluctance to leave her but she assured him she would be fine as she had work aplenty of her own to see to. Most days her nausea was only mild and if she was sensible about getting enough rest she was able to cope with the demands of her job.

Living at his house had far more benefits than she had first realised, not least the warm protective shelter of Max's arms when she went to sleep each night and when she woke each morning. Staying at his house was like living in a luxury hotel but much less impersonal. There were reminders of him everywhere—books, architectural journals he was reading, one with a feature article on him—and even the house itself with its stylish renovation that perfectly married the old with the new.

There was that word again—*marriage*.

But she couldn't bring herself to regret her acceptance of his proposal. She had to concentrate on what was best for the baby and put her own issues aside. Max cared about her otherwise he wouldn't have made such a fuss over her, looking after her, insisting on her living with him and doing a hundred other things for her that no one had ever done for her before.

The evening he was due to come back, Sabrina found a photo of him with his family in the study, taken before his baby brother had died. She had seen the photo at his parents' house in the past but somehow she hadn't really looked at it in any detail before. She traced her finger over Max's bright and happy smile as a seven-year-old boy and wondered if the birth of their baby would heal some of the pain of the past. There was no doubt in her mind that he would make an excellent father.

The sound of the doorbell ringing almost made her drop the photo frame. Max was due home any minute, but surely if it was him he would use his key rather than the doorbell? She placed the photo back on Max's desk and went out to check the security monitor in the foyer to see who was at the door. Her heart nearly jumped out of her chest when she saw it was her mother standing there with Max's mother Gillian. She had thought her mother would be away for another week in France…or had she got the dates wrong?

Sabrina stepped backwards away from the monitor, hoping Gillian Firbank and her mother hadn't heard her footsteps on the black and white tiles of the foyer, but in her haste she stumbled and bumped against the hall table. She watched in horror as the priceless vase that was sitting there wobbled and then crashed to the floor, shattering into pieces.

'Max?' Gillian said, rapping firmly at the door. 'Is that you? Are you okay?'

Sabrina stood surrounded by the detritus of the vase, her heart hammering faster than that of a rabbit on the run. Should she open the door? But how could she explain why she was at

Max's house? They were supposed to be keeping their relationship a secret. But if their mothers found her in situ at Max's home...

'Perhaps it's a burglar,' Sabrina's mother said. 'We'd better call the police.'

Sabrina had no choice but to open the door before her mother summoned half of London's constabulary to Max's house. 'Hi,' she said. 'I'm...erm...housesitting for Max.'

Gillian's and Sabrina's mother's eyes widened and then they exchanged a twinkly-eyed glance.

'Housesitting? For... Max?' Her mother's voice rose in a mixture of disbelief and hope.

'Yes. Just while he's in Denmark. He's coming back tonight. In fact, I thought he would be home before this. Perhaps his flight's been delayed.'

Gillian's mouth was tilted in a knowing smile. 'I knew something was going on with you two at my party.'

'Nothing's going on,' Sabrina lied, not very well by the look on the two women's faces.

'I wanted to show your mother Max's new renovations,' Gillian said. 'We were in the area and saw the lights on and thought we'd pop in. But if Max isn't home we'll come back another time.'

'You told me the other day you were staying at a friend's house.' Her mother's expression was one part accusatory, one part delighted.

'Yes, well, that's sort of true,' Sabrina said.

'So you two are friends now?' Her mother's eyes danced like they were auditioning for a part in *La Cage aux Folles*.

'Mum, it's not what you think—'

'Actually, it is what you think,' Max said as he came up the path to the front door carrying his travel bag with his laptop case slung over his shoulder. 'Sabrina and I are getting married.'

'Married?' The mothers spoke in unison, their faces so aglow with unmitigated joy they could have lit up the whole of London.

Max put his arm around Sabrina's waist and drew her close to his side. 'Yes. We haven't set a date yet but we'll get around to it soon.'

Sabrina glanced at him with a question in her eyes but he simply smiled and bent down to kiss her. 'Miss me, darling?' he said.

'You have no idea how much.' Sabrina bit her lip. 'I'm sorry about your vase...'

'What vase?'

She pointed to the shattered pieces of porcelain strewn over the foyer behind them. 'I bumped it when I was checking the security monitor. Please tell me it wasn't valuable.'

'Not as valuable as you,' he said, and kissed her again.

'Oh, look at you two gorgeous things.' Gillian grabbed Sabrina's mother's arm to lead her inside Max's house. 'We need to celebrate. Let's open some champagne.'

Sabrina gave him a *what do we do now?* look, but his expression remained calm. 'They had to find out sooner or later,' he said, sotto voce, and led her inside behind the older women.

Before she knew it, Max had efficiently cleaned up the pieces of the vase and Sabrina found herself sitting beside him on one of the sofas in the main sitting room. Her mother and Gillian were sitting opposite with glasses of champagne raised in a toast.

'Why aren't you drinking yours, Sabrina?' her mother asked after everyone else had sipped theirs. Max had only taken a token sip, however.

Sabrina cradled her glass in her hands, her cheeks feeling so hot she could have stripped the paint off the walls. 'Erm...'

'Oh, my God!' Gillian shot to her feet as if a spring in the sofa had jabbed her. 'You're pregnant?'

Max looked like he was the one suffering morning sickness. Sabrina's mother Ellen looked like she didn't know whether to laugh or cry.

Sabrina decided there was no point denying it. Besides, she

wanted her mother to be one of the first to know and not find out some other way. 'Yes, I am pregnant but only eight weeks. We're not telling everyone until the twelve-week mark.'

There were hugs and kisses and hearty congratulations all round and finally, after promising they would only tell their husbands and Sabrina's brothers about the pregnancy, the mothers left.

Max closed the door on their exit with a sigh. 'I'm sorry. I forgot I told my mother to drop in sometime to see the completed renovations.'

Sabrina frowned. 'But why did you have to tell them we're getting married? Why not just say we're having a fling or something? You know how I feel about this. Now they'll be in full on wedding fever mode, telling everyone our business and—'

'I was thinking about it while I was away,' Max said. 'Trying to keep our involvement a secret is going to cause you more stress than you need right now. I figured it was safer to get this out in the open. I didn't realise my mother would twig about the pregnancy, though.'

Sabrina sank back into the sofa and hugged one of the scatter cushions, eyeing her untouched glass of champagne as if it had personally insulted her. 'If I hadn't broken that damn vase, trying to avoid them, we might still have kept our secret safe. Argh. I hate how out of control my life is right now.'

He hunkered down next to her and grazed his knuckles across her cheek, his eyes warm and tender. 'It was going to come out sooner or later. And there's no reason to think your pregnancy isn't going to continue.'

'Would you prefer it if I lost the baby?'

He flinched. 'No. How can you ask that?'

She shrugged one shoulder and tossed the cushion to one side. 'I've done a pretty good job of stuffing up your neatly controlled life.'

He straightened and then came to sit beside her on the sofa, his hand slipping under the curtain of her hair to the nape of her neck, his expression wry. 'Maybe it needed shaking up a bit.'

Sabrina could feel every inch of her body responding to his touch. She placed her arms around his waist, loving the strength and warmth of his body so close to hers. She rested her head against his chest and sighed. 'At least our families are happy for us.'

He lifted her face off his chest and meshed his gaze with hers. 'It's a good start.'

'But what if we make each other miserable? I mean, further down the track?'

He brushed an imaginary hair away from her face. 'We're both mature adults. We can handle the odd difference of opinion, surely? Besides, I quite like arguing with you.'

A smile tugged at her mouth, a hot tide of longing pooling in her core. 'Do you fancy a fight now?'

His eyes glinted. 'Bring it on.' And he scooped her up in his arms and carried her to the bedroom.

CHAPTER ELEVEN

A FEW DAYS LATER, Sabrina had left the shop early, leaving Harriet in charge so she could get home to make a special dinner. They had been eating out mostly but she wanted to have a night at home for once. She suspected he took her out for dinner so often so she wouldn't have to cook but she enjoyed cooking and wanted to do something for him for a change.

Max's once-a-week housekeeper had been through the house and left it spotless. Holly had given Sabrina some fresh flowers and she placed them in the new vase she'd bought to replace the one she'd broken.

He came in just as she was stirring the Provençale chicken casserole on the cooktop and she put the spoon down and smiled. How could a man look so traffic-stopping gorgeous after a long day at work? 'How was your day?'

'Long.' He came over and planted a kiss on the top of her head. 'Mmm…something smells nice.'

Sabrina held up the spoon for him to have a taste. 'It's one of your favourites. Your mum told me.'

He tasted the casserole and raised his brows in approval. 'Delicious. But why are you cooking? Shouldn't you be resting as much as possible?'

'I like cooking.'

'I know, but you don't have to wait on me. I could have picked up a takeaway to save you the bother.'

Sabrina popped the lid back on the pot. 'I'm not waiting on you. I just wanted to do something for you for a change. You've been so good about everything and I—'

'Hey.' He placed his hands on her shoulders and turned her so she was facing him. 'I like doing things for you. I want to make this relationship work.'

She bit down on her lip. 'I know. For the baby's sake, right?'

His hands gave her shoulders a gentle squeeze. 'Not just for the baby. For you. I care about you, Sabrina. Surely you know that?'

She gave an on-off smile. Would caring be enough for her? 'I know but—'

He placed a finger over her lips. 'No buts. I care about you and will do everything in my power to make you happy.' He lowered his hand and brought his mouth to hers instead, kissing her leisurely, beguilingly until she melted into his arms.

Sabrina wound her arms around his neck, pressing herself closer to the tempting hard heat of his body. Her inner core already tingling with sensation, his mouth triggering a tumultuous storm in her flesh. His tongue met hers and she made a sound of approval, her senses dazzled by the taste of him, the familiar and yet exotic taste that she craved like a potent drug. His hands cradled her face as he deepened the kiss, his lips and tongue wreaking sensual havoc, ramping up her desire like fuel tossed on a naked flame. It whooshed and whirled and rocketed through her body, making her aware of every point of contact of his body on hers.

With a groan Max lifted his mouth from hers. 'How long can dinner wait?'

Sabrina pulled his head back down. 'Long enough for you to make love to me.'

He kissed her again, deeply and passionately. Then he took

her hand and led her upstairs, stopping to kiss her along the way. 'I've been thinking about doing this all day.'

'Me too,' Sabrina said, planting a series of kisses on his lips. 'I'm wild for you.'

He smiled against her mouth. 'Then what's my excuse? I've been wild for you for months.'

He led her to the master bedroom, peeling away her clothes and his with a deftness of movement that made her breathless with excitement. The touch of his warm strong hands on her naked skin made her gasp and whimper, his hands cupping her breasts, his lips and tongue caressing them, teasing her nipples into tight peaks of pleasure. The same tightly budded pleasure that was growing in her core, the most sensitive part of her hungry, aching for the sexy friction of his body.

Max worked his way down her body, gently pushing her back against the mattress so she was lying on her back and open to him. It was shockingly intimate and yet she didn't have time to feel shy. Her orgasm was upon her as soon as his tongue flicked against the heart of her and she came apart in a frenzied rush that travelled through her entire body like an earthquake.

He waited until she came down from the stratosphere to move over her, entering her with a deep but gentle thrust, a husky groan forced from his lips as her body wrapped around him. Sabrina held him to her, riding another storm of sensation, delighting in the rocking motion of his body as he increased his pace. Delighting in the strength and potency of him, delighting in the knowledge that she could do this to him—make him breathless and shuddering with ecstasy.

Max collapsed over her, his breathing hard and uneven against the side of her neck. 'You've rendered me speechless.'

Sabrina stroked her hands over his lower back. 'Same.'

He propped himself up on his elbows, his eyes still dark and glittering with spent passion. 'I mean it, sweetie. I don't think I've ever enjoyed sex as much as I have with you.'

She couldn't imagine making love with anyone but him. The

thought appalled her. Sickened her. She snuggled closer, her arms around his middle, wondering if it were possible to feel closer to him than she did right now.

After a long pause he stroked a strand of hair away from her face, his eyes dark with renewed desire. 'How do you think dinner is holding up?'

She rubbed her lower body against his pelvis and smiled her best sexy siren smile. 'It'll keep.' And she lifted her mouth to the descent of his.

Max had a run of projects that urgently needed his attention. He'd been neglecting his work in order to take care of Sabrina, making sure she had everything she needed in the early weeks of her pregnancy. But his work could no longer be postponed. He had big clients who expected the service they paid good money for. He hated leaving Sabrina but he had a business to run and people relying on him.

Travelling out of town meant he would have to stay overnight and that's what he hated the most. Not waking up next to her. Not having her sexy body curled up in his arms, the sweet smell of her teasing his nostrils until he was almost drunk on it. He informed her of his business trip over breakfast and she looked up from buttering her toast with disappointed eyes. So disappointed it drove a stake through his chest.

Her smile looked forced. 'Oh… Thanks for telling me.'

He scraped a hand through his hair. Clearly he had some work to do on his communication skills. And his timing. 'I'm sorry. I should have told you days ago. I thought I could manage it at a distance but the client is getting restless.'

She got up from the table and took her uneaten toast to the rubbish bin and tossed it in. 'I know you have a business to run. So do I.'

'Why aren't you eating? Do you feel sick?'

She turned from the bin with a combative look her on face. 'I'm fine, Max. Stop fussing.'

He came over to her and took her stiff little hands in his. 'Do you think I really want to leave you? I hate staying in hotels. I would much rather wake up with you beside me.'

Her tight expression softened. 'How long will you be away?'

'Two nights,' Max said, stroking the backs of her hands. 'I'd ask you to come with me but I know you're busy with Holly's dress. Which reminds me, we need to set a wedding date. My mother has been on my back just about every day to—'

'Yeah, mine too.' Her mouth twisted. 'But I don't want to get married close to Holly's wedding day. But neither do I want to be showing too much baby bump on ours. I don't know what to do. Ever since I was a little girl, I've dreamed of my wedding day. Not once in those dreams did I picture myself waddling up the aisle pregnant. I'm stressing about it all the time. Whenever I think about it I just about have a panic attack.'

He cupped her cheek in his hand. 'Oh, sweetie, try not to stress too much. We'll talk some more when I get back, okay?'

She sighed. 'Okay...'

Max kissed her on the forehead, breathing in her summer flowers scent. 'I'll call you tonight.' He touched her downturned mouth with his fingertip. 'Why don't you ask Holly to stay with you while I'm away? I'm sure she wouldn't mind.'

'She spends every spare minute with Zack.' A spark of annoyance lit her gaze. 'Besides, I don't need flipping babysitting.'

'I can't help worrying about you.'

She slipped out of his hold and picked up her tote bag where it was hanging off the back of a chair. 'You worry too much. I'll be fine. I have plenty to keep me occupied.'

Max placed his hands on her shoulders, turning her to face him. 'You'll have to be patient with me, Sabrina. I'm not the world's best communicator. I'm used to going away for work at a moment's notice. But obviously that's going to have to change once we become parents.'

She let out a soft sigh. 'I'm sorry for being so snippy. I'm just feeling a little overwhelmed.'

He brought up her chin with his finger, meshing his gaze with her cornflower-blue one. 'It's perfectly understandable. We'll get through this, sweetheart. I know we will.'

She gave another fleeting smile but there was a shadow of uncertainty behind her eyes. 'I have to run. I have a dress fitting first thing.'

He pressed a kiss to her lips. 'I'll miss you.'

'I'll miss you too.'

Sabrina was ten minutes late to her fitting with her client, which was embarrassing as it had never happened before. But she couldn't seem to get herself into gear. Ever since she'd found out Max was going away, she'd felt agitated and out of sorts. It wasn't that she wanted to live in his pocket. She had her own commitments and responsibilities, but she had come to look forward to their evenings together each day. She loved discussing the events of the day with him over dinner, or curling up on the sofa watching television. She had even got him hooked on one of her favourite TV series. She loved the companionship of their relationship. It reminded her of her parents' relationship, which, in spite of the passage of years, seemed to get stronger.

And then there was the amazing sex.

Not just amazing sex, but magical lovemaking. Every time they made love, she felt closer to him. Not just physically, but emotionally. It was like their bodies were doing the talking that neither of them had the courage to express out loud. She longed to tell him she loved him, but worried that if she did so he would push her away. She couldn't go through another humiliation of rejection. Not after what had happened when she was eighteen. But even so, she had to be careful not to read too much into Max's attentive behaviour towards her. He cared for her and he cared about their baby.

That was what she had to be grateful for.

Holly came in for her final fitting later that afternoon just on closing time. 'Hiya.' She swept in, carrying a bunch of flowers, but then noticing Sabrina's expression frowned. 'Hey, what's up?'

Sabrina tried to smile. 'Nothing.'

Holly put the flowers down. 'Yeah, right. Come on, fess up.'

Sabrina was glad Harriet had left for the day. She closed the shop front door and turned the 'Closed' sign to face the street. 'Come out the back and I'll do your fitting while we chat.'

'Forget about the fitting—we can do that another day,' Holly said, once they were out the back. 'The wedding isn't for another few weeks. What's wrong?'

Sabrina put her hand on her belly. Was it her imagination or had she just felt a cramp? 'I'm just feeling a bit all over the place.'

'Are you feeling unwell?'

'Sort of...' She winced as another cramp gripped her abdomen.

Holly's eyes widened. 'Maybe you should sit down. Here...' She pulled out a chair. 'Do you feel faint?'

Sabrina ignored the chair and headed straight to the bathroom. 'I need to pee.'

She closed the bathroom door, taking a breath to calm herself. Tummy troubles were part and parcel of the first weeks of pregnancy. Nausea, vomiting, constipation—they were a result of the shifting hormones. But when she checked her underwear, her heart juddered to a halt. The unmistakable spots of blood signalled something was wrong. She tried to stifle a gasp of despair as a giant wave of emotion swamped her.

Was she about to lose the baby?

Holly knocked on the bathroom door. 'Sabrina? Are you okay?'

Sabrina came out a short time later. 'I think I need to go to hospital.'

Max was in a meeting with his client when he felt his phone vibrating in his pocket. Normally he would have ignored it—

clients didn't always appreciate their time with him being in-terrupted. Especially this client, by far the most difficult and pedantic he had ever had on his books. But when he excused himself and pulled out his phone, he didn't recognise the num-ber. He slipped the phone back into his pocket, figuring who-ever it was could call back or leave a message. But he only had just sat back down with his client when his phone pinged with a text message. He pulled the phone out again and read the text.

Max, it's Holly. Can you call me ASAP?

Max's chest gave a painful spasm, his heart leaping and lodg-ing in his throat until he could scarcely draw breath. There could only be one reason Sabrina's friend was calling him. Something must be wrong. Terribly wrong. He pushed back his chair and mumbled another apology to his client and strode out of the room. He dialled the number on the screen and pinched the bridge of his nose to contain his emotions. 'Come on, come on, come on. Pick up.'

'Max?'

'What's happened?' Max was gripping the phone so tightly he was sure it would splinter into a hundred pieces. 'Is Sabrina okay?'

'She's fine. She's had a slight show of blood but nothing since so that's good—'

Guilt rained down on him like hailstones. He should never have left her. This was *his* fault. She'd been out of sorts this morning and he'd made it a whole lot worse by springing his trip on her without warning. What sort of job was he doing of looking after her when the first time he turned his back she ended up in hospital? Was there something wrong with him? Was there a curse on all his relationships, especially the most important one of all? His guts churned at the thought of her losing the baby. Of *him* losing her. Dread froze his scalp and churned his guts and turned his legs to water.

'Are you sure she's okay? Can I speak to her?'

'She's still with the doctor but I'll get her to call you when she's finished. She didn't want to worry you but I thought you should know.'

Damn right he should know. But he still shouldn't have left her. He had let her down and now he had to live with his old friend, guilt. 'Thanks for calling. I'll be back as soon as I can.'

'You're free to go home now, Sabrina,' the doctor said, stripping off her gloves. 'The cervix looks fine and the scan shows the placenta is intact. A break-through bleed at this stage, especially one as small as yours, is not unusual. Some women have spotting right through the pregnancy. Just make sure you rest for a day or two and if you have any concerns let us know.'

Sabrina tried to take comfort in what the doctor had said but her emotions were still all over the place. 'I'm not going to lose the baby?'

'I can't guarantee that. But, as I said, things look fine.' The doctor glanced at the engagement ring on Sabrina's hand and smiled. 'Get your fiancé to take extra-special care of you for the next few days.'

Her fiancé...

Sabrina wished Max were waiting outside instead of Holly. Her friend was fabulous and had swung into action as if she had been handling fretting pregnant women all her life. But the person Sabrina most wanted by her side was Max. She felt so alone facing the panic of a possible miscarriage. What if she had lost the baby? What if she *still* lost it? The doctor was right, there were no guarantees. Nature was unpredictable.

Holly swished the curtain aside on the cubicle. 'The doctor said you're fine to go home. Max is on his way.'

'You called him? How did you get his number?'

Holly patted Sabrina's tote bag, which was hanging from Holly's shoulder. 'I found his number on your phone. I didn't feel comfortable calling him on your phone so I called him on mine. I know you didn't want to worry him but if something had happened, imagine how he'd feel?'

Sabrina got off the bed, testing her legs to see if they were as shaky as they had been earlier when panic had flooded her system. 'He would probably feel relieved.'

'What? Do you really think so?'

'I know so.' Sabrina cast her friend a weary glance. 'The only reason we're together is because of the baby.'

Holly frowned. 'But he cares about you. I could hear it in his voice. He was so worried about you and—'

'Worrying about someone doesn't mean you love them,' Sabrina said. 'It means you feel responsible for them.'

'You're splitting hairs. That poor man almost had a heart attack when I told him you were in hospital.'

'I wish I had what you have with Zack,' Sabrina said. 'I wish Max loved me the way Zack loves you. But wishing doesn't make it happen.'

'Oh, honey, I'm sure you're mistaken about Max. You're feeling emotional just now and this has been a huge scare. You might feel better once he's back home with you.'

But what if she didn't?

Max risked speeding tickets and any number of traffic violations on the way back to London. He'd called Sabrina several times but she must have turned her phone off. He called Holly and she told him Sabrina was back at his house, resting.

'Can you stay with her until I get back?' Max glanced at the dashboard clock. 'I'm about an hour away.'

'Sure.'

'Thanks. You're a gem.' He clicked off the call and tried to get his breathing under control. But every time he thought of what could have happened to Sabrina he felt sick to his guts. Miscarriages were dangerous if help wasn't at hand. It might be the twenty-first century but women could still haemorrhage to death. He couldn't get the picture of a coffin out of his mind.

Two coffins. One for Sabrina and another for the baby. How could he have let this happen? How could he have put his work before his responsibilities towards her and their child?

It felt like an entire millennium later by the time Max opened his front door. Holly had obviously been waiting for him as she had her bag over her shoulder and her jacket over her arm.

'She's upstairs,' Holly said.

'Thanks for staying with her.'

'No problem.' She slipped out and Max was halfway up the stairs before the door closed.

Sabrina was standing in front of the windows with her back to him, her arms across her middle. She turned when she heard his footfalls but he couldn't read her expression.

Max wanted to rush over to her and enfold her in his arms but instead it was like concrete had filled his blood and deadened his limbs. He opened and closed his mouth, trying to find his voice, but even that had deserted him. His throat was raw and tight, blocked with emotions he couldn't express.

'You're back.' Her voice was as cold as the cruel icy hand gripping his throat.

'I came as fast as I could. Are you all right?'

She was holding herself almost as stiffly as he was but he couldn't take a step towards her. His legs felt bolted to the floor, his guts still twisting and turning at what might have been.

'I'm fine.'

'And the baby?' He swallowed convulsively. 'It's still—?'

'I'm still pregnant.'

Relief swept through him but still he kept his distance. He didn't trust his legs to work. He didn't trust his spiralling emotions. They were messing with his head, blocking his ability to do and say the things he should be saying. Things he wasn't even able to express to himself, let alone to her. 'Why aren't you in bed? You need to rest.'

A shuttered look came over her eyes. 'Max, we need to talk.'

He went to swallow again but his throat was too dry. Something was squeezing his chest until he could barely breathe. 'You scared the hell out of me. When I got that call from Holly...' His chest tightened another notch. 'I thought... I thought...' In his mind he could see that tiny white coffin again and another bigger one next to it. Flowers everywhere. People crying. He could feel the hammering of his heartbeat in time with the pulse of his guilt.

Your fault. Your fault. Your fault.

'Max, I can't marry you.'

He went to reach for her but she stepped back, her expression rigid with determination. 'You're upset, sweetie. You've had a big shock and you'll feel better once you've—'

'You're not listening to me.' Her voice with its note of gravity made a chill run down his neck.

'Okay.' He took a breath and got himself into some sort of order. 'I'm listening.'

She rolled her lips together until they almost disappeared. 'I can't marry you, Max. What happened today confirmed it for me.'

'For God's sake, do you think I would have left town if I thought you were going to have a miscarriage? What sort of man do you think I am?'

Her expression remained calm. Frighteningly calm. 'It's not about the miscarriage scare. You could have been right beside me at the hospital and I would still have come to the same decision eventually. You were wrong to force your proposal on me when you can't give your whole self to the relationship.'

'Forced?' Max choked back a humourless laugh. 'You're having my baby so why wouldn't I want you to marry me?'

'But if I had lost the baby, what then?' Her gaze was as penetrating as an industrial drill. 'Would you still want to marry me?'

Max rubbed a hand down his face. He had a headache that was threatening to split his skull in half. Why did she have to do this now? He wasn't over the shock of the last few hours.

Adrenaline was still coursing through him in juddering pulses. 'Let's not talk about this now, Sabrina.'

'When will we talk about it? The day of the damn wedding? Is that what you'd prefer me to do? To jilt you like Lydia did?' Her words came at him like bullets. *Bang. Bang. Bang.*

Max released a long, slow breath, fighting to keep his frustration in check. He couldn't talk about this now, not with his head so scrambled, thoughts and fears and memories causing a toxic poison that made it impossible for him to think straight. Impossible for him to access the emotions that went into automatic lockdown just as they had done all those years ago when he'd seen his mother carrying the tiny limp body of his baby brother. It felt like he was a dead man standing. A robot. A lifeless, emotionless robot.

'I put marriage on the table because of the baby. It would be pointless to go ahead with it if you were no longer pregnant.'

Nothing showed on her face but he saw her take a swallow. 'I guess I should be grateful you were honest with me.'

'Sabrina, I'm not the sort of man to say a whole bunch of words I can't back up with actions.'

Tears shone in her eyes. 'You act like you love me. But I can't trust that it's true. I need to hear you say it, but you won't, will you?'

'Are you saying you love me?'

Her bottom lip quivered. 'Of course I love you. But I can't allow myself to be in a one-sided relationship. Not again. Not after what happened when I was eighteen.'

Anger whipped through him like a tornado. 'Please do me the favour of not associating anything I do or say with how that creep treated you. You know I care about you. I only want the best for you and the baby.'

'But that's my point. If there wasn't a baby there wouldn't be an us.' She turned to the walk-in wardrobe.

'Hey, what are you doing?'

'I'm packing a bag.'

Max caught her by the arm. 'No, you're damn well not.'

She shook off his hold, her eyes going hard as if a steel curtain had come down behind her gaze. 'I can't stay with you, Max. Consider our engagement over. I'm not marrying you.'

'You're being ridiculous.' Panic was battering inside his chest like a loose shutter in a windstorm. 'I won't let you walk away.'

She peeled off his fingers one by one. 'You're a good man, Max. A really lovely man. But you have serious issues with love. You hold everyone at a distance. You're scared of losing control of your emotions so you lock them away.'

'Spare me the psychology session.' Max couldn't keep the sarcasm in check. 'I've tried to do everything I can to support you. I've bent over backwards to—'

'I know you have but it's not enough. You don't love me the way I want to be loved. And that's why I can't be with you.'

Max considered saying the words to keep her with him. How hard could it be? Three little words that other people said so casually. But he hadn't told anyone he loved them since he'd told his baby brother, and look how that turned out. He felt chilled to the marrow even thinking about saying those words again. He had let her down and there was nothing he could do to change it. He wasn't good enough for her. He had never been good enough and he'd been a fool to think he ever could be. 'Will you at least stay here for a bit longer till I find you somewhere to live?'

A sad smile pulled at her mouth. 'No, Max, I don't think that would be wise. I'll stay with my parents for bit until I find somewhere suitable.'

Later, Max could barely recall how he'd felt as Sabrina packed an overnight bag and handed him back the engagement ring. He hadn't even said, *No, you keep it.* He'd been incapable of speech. He drove her to her parents' house in a silence so thick he could almost taste it. His emotions were still in an emergency lockdown that made him act like an automaton, stripping every expression off his face, sending his voice into a monotone.

It was only days later, when he got back home to his empty house after work, where the lingering fragrance of her perfume haunted him, that he wondered if he should have done more to convince her to stay. But what? Say words she knew he didn't mean? He would be no better than that lowlife scum who'd hurt her so badly all those years ago.

But why did his house seem so empty without her there? He had got used to the sound of her pottering about. Damn it, he'd even got used to the mindless drivel she watched on television. He would have happily watched a test pattern if he could just sit with his arm around her. He could get through watching just about anything if he could hear the sound of her laughter and her sighs, and patiently hand her his handkerchief when she got teary over the sad bits of a movie.

But he would have to get used to not having her around.

Sabrina dragged herself through the next few days, worn down by sadness that her life wasn't turning out like that of the dewy-faced brides that filed through her shop. It was like having salt rubbed into an open and festering wound to see everyone else experiencing the joy and happiness of preparing for a wedding when her dreams were shattered. Why was her life destined to fall short of her expectations? Was there something wrong with her? Was she too idealistic? Too uncompromising?

But how could she compromise on the issue of love?

Moving back in with her parents might not have been the wisest move, Sabrina decided. She was engulfed by their disappointment as well as her own. It seemed everyone thought Max was the perfect partner for her except Max himself. But she couldn't regret her decision to end their engagement. She couldn't remain in a one-sided relationship. The one who loved the most was always the one who got hurt in the end. She wanted an equal partnership with love flowing like a current between them. Like it flowed between both sets of parents, long and lasting and able to withstand calamity.

No. This was the new normal for her. Alone.

And the sooner she got used to it the better.

A few miserable days later, Max went into his study and sat at his desk. He found himself sitting there every night, unable to face that empty bed upstairs. He sighed and dragged a hand over his face. His skull was permanently tight with a headache and his eyes felt gritty.

His eyes went to the photograph of his family before Daniel had died. There was nothing he could do to bring his brother back. Nothing he could do to repair the heartache he had caused his parents by not being more vigilant. His phone rang and he took it out of his pocket and swore when he saw it was his mother. The gossip network was back at work after a few days' reprieve. No doubt Sabrina's mother Ellen had called his mum to tell her the wedding was off. He was surprised Ellen hadn't done so the moment it had happened but maybe Sabrina had wanted things kept quiet for a bit. He answered the phone. 'Mum, now's not a good time.'

'Oh, Max. Ellen told me Sabrina called off the engagement.'

'Yep. She did.'

'And you let her?'

'She's an adult, Mum. I can't force her to be with me.' Even though he'd damn well given it a good shot.

'Oh, darling, I'm so upset for you and for her,' his mum said. 'I can't help thinking your father, Ellen, Jim and I have been putting too much pressure on you both. We just wanted you to be happy. You're perfect for each other.'

'I'm not perfect for anyone. That's the problem.' He let out a jagged sigh. 'I can't seem to help letting down the people I care about. You, Dad and Daniel, for instance. I do it without even trying. It's like I'm hard-wired to ruin everyone's lives.'

'Max, you haven't ruined anyone's lives,' his mother said after a small silence. 'I know you find it hard to allow people close to you. You weren't like that as a young child, but since we lost Daniel you've stopped being so open with your feelings. It was like a part of you died with him. I blame myself for not being there for you but I was so overwhelmed by my own grief I didn't see what was happening to you until it was too late. But you weren't to blame for what happened, you know that, don't you?'

Max leaned forward to rest one elbow on the desk and leaned his forehead against his hand. 'I should have known something was wrong. You asked me to check on him and he seemed fine.'

'That's because he *was* fine when you checked on him. Max, the coroner said it was SIDS. Daniel might have died in the next ten minutes and there was nothing you could have done to change that.' She sighed and he heard the catch in her voice. 'Darling, do you think I haven't blamed myself? Not a day goes past that I don't think of him. But it would be an even bigger tragedy if I thought you weren't living a fulfilling life because you didn't think you deserved to love and be loved in return.'

'Look, I know you mean well, Mum, but I can't give Sabrina what she wants. What she deserves. I'm not capable of it.'

'Are you sure about that, Max? Totally sure?'

Max ended the call and sat back in his chair with a thump. It was slowly dawning on him that he had made the biggest blunder of his life. His feelings for Sabrina had always been confusing to him. For years he'd held her at arm's length with wisecracking banter, but hadn't that been because he was too frightened to own up to what was going on in his heart? She had always got under his skin. She had always rattled the cage he had constructed around his heart.

And up until he'd kissed her he'd done a damn fine job of keeping her out. But that one kiss had changed everything. That kiss had led to that night in Venice and many nights since of the most earth-shattering sex of his life. But it wasn't just about amazing sex. There was way more to their relationship than that.

He *felt* different with her.

He felt alive. Awakened.

Hopeful.

His sexual response to her was a physical manifestation of what was going on in his heart. He was inexorably drawn to her warm and generous nature. Every time he touched her, he felt a connection that was unlike any he'd experienced before. Layer by layer, piece by piece, every barricade he'd erected had been sloughed away by her smile, her touch. Her love. How could he let her walk away without telling her the truth? The truth that had been locked away until now. The truth he had shied away from out of fear and cowardice.

He loved her.

He loved her with every fibre of his being. His love for her was the only thing that could protect her. Love was what had kept his family together against impossible odds. Love was what would protect their baby, just as he had been protected. His and her parents were right—he and Sabrina were perfect for each other. And if he didn't exactly feel perfect enough, he would work damn hard on it so he did.

Because he loved her enough to change. To own the feelings he had been too fearful to name. Feelings that he needed to express to her because they were bubbling up inside him like a dam about to break.

Sabrina's parents fussed over her so much each night when she came home from work that she found it claustrophobic. They were doing it with good intentions but she just wanted to be alone to contemplate her future without Max. Thankfully, that night her parents had an important medical function to attend, which left Sabrina to have a pity party all by herself.

The doorbell rang just as she was deciding whether she could be bothered eating the nutritious meal her mother had left for her. She glanced at the security monitor in the kitchen and her heart nearly stopped when she saw Max standing there. But before she allowed herself to get too excited, she took a deep calming breath. He was probably just checking up on her. Making sure she'd settled in okay.

She opened the door with her expression cool and composed. 'Max.' Even so, her voice caught on his name.

'I need to talk to you.' His voice was deep and hoarse, as if he had swallowed the bristly welcome mat.

'Come in.' Sabrina stepped away from the door to allow him to follow but she didn't get far into the foyer before he reached for her, taking her by the hands.

'Sabrina, my darling, I can't believe it has taken me this long to realise what I feel about you.' His hands tightened on hers as if he was worried she would pull away. 'You've been in my life for so long that I was blind or maybe too damn stubborn to see you're exactly what our parents have said all this time. You're perfect for me. Perfect because you've taught me how to feel again. How to love. I love you.'

Sabrina stepped a little closer or maybe he tugged her to him, she wasn't sure. All she knew was hearing him say those words made something in her chest explode with joy like fireworks. She could feel fizzes and tingles running right through her as she saw the look of devotion on his face. 'Oh, Max, do you mean it? You're not just saying it to get me back?'

He wrapped one arm around her like a tight band, the other hand cupped one side of her face, his eyes shining like wet paint. 'I mean it with every breath and bone and blood cell in my body. I love you so much. I've been fighting it because on some level I knew you were the only one who could make me feel love again and I was so worried about letting you down. And then I went and did it in the worst way possible. I can't believe I stood there like a damn robot instead of reaching for you and telling you I loved you that night you came home from hospital. Please marry me, my darling. Marry me and let's raise our baby together.'

She threw her arms around his neck and rose up on tiptoe so she could kiss him. 'Of course I'll marry you. I love you. I think I might have always loved you.'

Max squeezed her so tightly she thought her ribs would crack. He released her slightly to look at her. 'Oh, baby girl, I can't believe I nearly lost you. I've been such a fool, letting you leave like that. How devastated you must have felt when you told me you loved me and I just stood there frozen like a statue.'

Sabrina gazed into his tender eyes. 'You're forgiven, as long as you forgive me for being such a cow to you for all those years.'

He cradled her face with his hands and brushed his thumbs across her cheeks. 'There's nothing to forgive. I enjoyed every one of those insults because they've brought us here. You are the most adorable person in the world. I wish I could be a better man than I am for you, but I give you my word I'll do my best.'

Sabrina blinked back tears of happiness. 'You are the best, Max. The best man for me. The only man I want. You're perfect just the way you are.'

He gave her a lingering kiss, rocking her from side to side in his arms. After a while, he lifted his head to look at her, his eyes moist with his own tears of joy. 'Hang on, I forgot something.' He reached into his trouser pocket and took out her engagement ring and slipped it on her finger. 'There. Back where it belongs.'

Sabrina smiled and looped her arms around his neck again. 'We are both back where we belong. Together. Ready to raise our little baby.'

He hugged her close again, smiling down at her. 'I'm more than ready. I can't wait to be a father. You've taught me that loving someone is the best way of protecting them and I can safely say you and our baby are not going to be short of my love.' He kissed her again and added, 'My forever love.'

EPILOGUE

A FEW WEEKS LATER, Max stood at the end of the aisle at the same church in which he and his baby brother had been christened, and looked out at the sea of smiling faces, his friends and family. He saw Zack sitting with Sabrina's family with a grin from ear to ear, having just got back from his honeymoon. Holly was the maid of honour so Zack would have to do without his new bride by his side while the ceremony was conducted.

Max drew in a breath to settle his nerves of excitement. The church was awash with flowers thanks to Holly. He couldn't believe how hard everyone had worked to get this wedding under way in the short time frame. But wasn't that what friends and family were for? They pulled together and the power of all that love overcame seemingly impossible odds.

The organ began playing 'The Bridal March' and Holly, as Sabrina's only bridesmaid, and the cute little flower girl, the three-year-old daughter of one of Max's friends from University, began their procession.

And then it was time for his bride to appear. Max's heart leapt into his throat and he blinked back a sudden rush of tears. Sabrina was stunning in a beautiful organza gown that floated around her, not quite disguising the tiny bump of their baby. She looked like a fairytale princess and her smile lit up the church and sent a warm spreading glow to his chest.

She was wearing something borrowed and something blue, but when she came to stand in front of him he saw the pink diamond earrings he had bought her after they had found out at the eighteen-week ultrasound they were expecting a baby girl. They had decided to keep it a secret between themselves and it thrilled him to share this private message with her on this most important of days. One day they would tell their little daughter of the magic of how she brought her parents together in a bond of mutual and lasting love.

Sabrina came to stand beside him, her eyes twinkling as bright as the diamonds she was wearing, and the rush of love he felt for her almost knocked him off his feet. He took her hands and smiled. 'You look beautiful.' His voice broke but he didn't care. He wasn't ashamed of feeling emotional. He was proud to stand and own his love for her in front of all these people. In front of the world.

Her eyes shone. 'Oh, Max, I can't believe my dream came true. We're here about to be married.'

He smiled back. 'Our dream wedding.' He gave her hands a little squeeze. 'My dream girl.'

* * * * *

The Bride's Awakening

Kate Hewitt

KATE HEWITT discovered her first Harlequin romance on a trip to England when she was thirteen, and she's continued to read them ever since. She wrote her first story at the age of five, simply because her older brother had written one and she thought she could do it, too. That story was one sentence long—fortunately, they've become a bit more detailed as she's grown older.

She studied drama in college, and shortly after graduation moved to New York City to pursue a career in theater. This was derailed by something far better—meeting the man of her dreams, who happened also to be her older brother's childhood friend. Ten days after their wedding they moved to England, where Kate worked a variety of different jobs—drama teacher, editorial assistant, youth worker, secretary and, finally, mother.

When her oldest daughter was one year old, she sold her first short story to a British magazine. Since then she has sold many stories and serials, but writing romance remains her first love—of course!

Besides writing, she enjoys reading, traveling and learning to knit—it's an ongoing process, and she's made a lot of scarves. After living in England for six years, she now resides in Connecticut with her husband, her three young children and the possibility of one day getting a dog.

Kate loves to hear from readers. You can contact her through her website, www.kate-hewitt.com.

CHAPTER ONE

VITTORIO RALFINO, the Count of Cazlevara, stood on the threshold of San Stefano Castle and searched the milling guests for the woman he intended to be his wife. He wasn't certain what she looked like for, beyond a single small photo, he hadn't seen her in sixteen years. Or if he had seen her, she hadn't made much of an impression. Now he planned to marry her.

Anamaria Viale wasn't readily apparent amidst the tuxedo and evening gown-clad crowd circulating through the candlelit foyer. All he remembered from when he'd seen her at her mother's funeral was a sad, sallow face and too much dark hair. She'd been thirteen years old. The photo in the magazine gave little more information; she had good teeth. Still, her looks—or lack of them—did not interest Vittorio. Anamaria Viale possessed the qualities he was looking for in a wife: loyalty, health and a shared love of this land and its grapes. Her family's vineyard would be an asset to his own; together they would rule an empire and create a dynasty. Nothing else mattered.

Impatiently, he strode into the castle's medieval hall. Shadows danced along the stone walls and he felt the curious stares of neighbours, acquaintances and a few friends. He heard the murmur of speculative whispers travel around the ancient hall in a ripple of suppressed sound and knew he was their subject.

He hadn't been back in Veneto for more than a day or two at a time in the last fifteen years. He'd kept away from the place and its memories and regrets. Like a hurt little boy, he'd run away from his past and pain, but he was a man now and he was home for good—to find a wife.

'Cazlevara!' Someone clapped him on the back, thrusting a glass of wine into his hand. His fingers closed around the fragile stem as a matter of instinct and he inhaled the spicy, fruity scent of a bold red. 'You must try this. It's Busato's new red—he's blended his grapes, *Vinifera* and *Molinara*. What do you think?'

Vittorio took a practised sip, swilling the rich liquid in his mouth for a moment before swallowing. 'Good enough,' he pronounced, not wanting to get into a detailed discussion about the merits of mixed grapes, or whether Busato, one of the region's smaller winemakers, was going to give Castle Cazlevara, his own winery—the region's largest and most select—any competition. He wanted to find Anamaria.

'I heard the rumours. You're home then? You're going to make some wine?'

Vittorio glanced at the man who had been speaking to him: Paolo Prefavera, a colleague of his father's. His round cheeks were already rosy with drink and he smiled with the genial bonhomie of an old family friend, although his eyes were shrewd.

'I've always been making wine, Paolo. Castle Cazlevara produces nine hundred thousand bottles a year.'

'While you've been touring the world—'

'It's called marketing.' Vittorio realized he was speaking through his teeth. He smiled. 'But yes, I'm home for good.' Home, so he could rein his grasping brother Bernardo back in, before he squandered the rest of the winery's profits. Home, so he could keep his treacherous mother from taking what was his—and his heir's. At this thought, his forced smile turned genuine, even though his eyes remained hard. 'Have you seen Anamaria Viale?' Paolo's eyebrows rose and Vittorio stifled a curse. He was too impatient; he knew that. When he made a decision, he wanted it carried out immediately, instantly. He'd decided to marry Anamaria Viale nearly a week ago; it felt like an eternity. He wanted it done; he wanted her vineyard joined to his, he wanted *her* joined to him, in his bed, by his side, being a wife.

Paolo smiled slyly and Vittorio forced himself to smile back. Now there would be whispers, rumours. Gossip. 'I have a question to ask her,' he explained with a shrug, as if it were no matter.

'She was over by the fireplace, last time I saw her.' Paolo gave a small chuckle, more of a guffaw. 'How could you miss her?'

Vittorio didn't understand what Paolo meant until he neared the huge stone fireplace. An alarmingly large stuffed boar's head was mounted above the hearth and a few men were gathered underneath, sipping wine and chatting quietly. At least he thought they were all men. Narrowing his eyes, he realized the tall, strong figure in the centre of the group was actually a woman. Anamaria.

His mouth tightened as he took in his intended wife, dressed in an expensive-looking but essentially shapeless trouser suit. Her long dark hair was held back in a clip and looked as thick and coarse as a horse's tail. She held a glass of wine as most of the castle's guests did; the evening was, after all, a wine-tasting for the province's premier winemakers and guests. She had, Vittorio saw, strong, even features; pretty was not necessarily a word he would use to describe them. There was something too earthy and bold about her, he decided. He preferred the women he took to his bed to be more delicate, fragile even. *Slim.*

Not, he amended, that Anamaria Viale was overweight. Not at all. Big-boned was the word he might have chosen, although his mother would have sneered and called her *grassa*. Fat.

Vittorio's mouth thinned at the thought of his mother. He could hardly wait to see the look on the old bitch's face when he told her he was getting married. Bernardo, her precious favourite, fool that he was, would never inherit. Her plans—the plans she'd cherished since the moment his father's will had been read—would come to nothing.

Vittorio smiled at the thought, little more than a bitter twisting of his mouth, and dismissed his bride's looks as a matter of no importance. He didn't want a beautiful woman; beautiful women, like his mother and his last mistress, were never satisfied, always finding fault. He'd left his mistress in Rio pouting for more time, money, even love. He'd told her he would never set eyes on her again.

Anamaria, he was sure, would take what she was given and be grateful, which was exactly what he wanted. A wife—a humble, grateful wife—the most important accessory a man could ever possess.

Surveying her tall, strong form, Vittorio was quite sure a woman like her was unused to male attention; he anticipated her stammering, blushing pleasure when the Count of Cazlevara singled her out.

He stepped forward, straightening his shoulders, and adopted an easy-going, self-assured smile whose devastating effect he knew well.

'Anamaria.' His voice came out in a low, suggestive hum.

She turned, stiffening in surprise when she saw him. Her eyes widened and a smile dawned on her face, a fragile, tremulous gesture of joy, brightening her whole countenance for the barest of moments. Vittorio smiled back; he almost laughed aloud. This was going to be so easy.

Then she drew herself up—her height making Vittorio appreciate Paulo's comment once more—and raked him with one infuriatingly dismissive glance, that amazed smile turning cool and even—could it be?—contemptuous. He was still registering the change in her expression and mood—his smug satisfaction giving way to an uneasy alarm—when she spoke.

'Hello, Lord Cazlevara.' Her voice was low, husky. Almost, Vittorio thought with a flicker of distaste, like a man's. Although, he noted, there was nothing particularly unpleasing about her features: straight brows and nose, dark grey eyes, the good teeth he'd noticed before. She was not, at least, ugly; rather, she was exceedingly plain. He let his smile deepen to show the dimple in his cheek, determined to win this plain spinster over. A woman like Anamaria would surely appreciate any charm thrown her way.

'Let me be the first to say how lovely you look tonight.'

She raised her eyebrows, the flicker of that cool smile curling her mouth and glinting in her eyes. They had, he saw, gold flecks that made them seem to shimmer. 'You will indeed be the first to say so.'

It took Vittorio a moment to register the mockery; he couldn't believe she was actually making fun of him—as well as of herself. Feeling slightly wrong-footed—and unused to it—Vittorio reached for her hand, intending to raise it to his lips even as he cursed the way he'd phrased his flattery. For flattery it was indeed, and she knew it. She was not stupid, which he supposed was a good thing. She let his lips brush her skin, something darkening her eyes—those gold flecks becoming molten— before she quite deliberately pulled her hand away.

The crowd around them had fallen back, yet Vittorio was conscious of avid stares, intent ears and, even more so, his own mounting annoyance. This first meeting was not going the way he'd anticipated—with him firmly in control.

'To what do I owe such a pleasure?' Anamaria asked. 'I don't believe we've seen each other in well over a decade.' Her voice caught a little, surprising him. He wondered what she was thinking of, or perhaps remembering.

'I'm simply glad to be back home,' Vittorio replied, keeping his voice pitched low and smooth, 'among beautiful women.'

She snorted. She actually snorted. Vittorio revised his opinion; the woman was not like a man, but a horse. 'You have learned honeyed words on your trips abroad,' she said shortly. 'They are far too sweet.' And, with a faintly mocking smile, she turned and walked away from him as if he were of no importance at all. *She* left *him*.

Vittorio stood there in soundless shock, his fury rising. He'd been summarily dismissed, and he, along with the little knot of spectators around him, was conscious of it. He felt the stares, saw a few smug smiles, and knew he'd been put properly in his place, as if he were a naughty schoolboy being disciplined by a mocking schoolmarm. It was a feeling he remembered from childhood, and he did not like it.

Standing there, Vittorio could not escape the glaringly—and embarrassingly—obvious conclusion: as far as opening gambits went, his had been an utter failure.

He'd been planning to ask her to marry him, if not tonight, then certainly in the next few days. When he decided a thing—even to marry—he wanted it done. Completed. Over. He had no time or patience for finer emotions, and frankly he'd considered the wooing of such a woman to be an easy exercise, a mere dispensing of charm, a few carefully chosen compliments.

After reading the article about her—and seeing her photo—he'd assumed she would be grateful for whatever attention she received. She was unmarried and nearing thirty; his proposal would be, he'd thought, a gift. Maybe even a miracle.

Perhaps he had been arrogant, or at least hasty. The wooing and winning of Anamaria Viale would take a little more thought.

Vittorio smiled. He liked challenges. Admittedly, time was of the essence; he was thirty-seven and he needed a wife. An heir. Yet surely he had a week—or two—to entice Anamaria into marriage? He wasn't interested in making the woman fall in love with him, far from it. He simply wanted her to accept what was a very basic business proposition. She was the candidate he'd chosen, the most suitable one he could find, and he wasn't interested in any others. Anamaria Viale would be his.

Still, Vittorio realized, he'd acted like a fool. He was annoyed with himself for thinking a woman—any woman—could be charmed so thoughtlessly. It was a tactical error, and one he would not make again. The next time he met Anamaria Viale, she would smile at him because she couldn't help herself; she would hang on his every word. The next time he met her, it would be on his terms.

Anamaria made sure she didn't look back as she walked away from the Count of Cazlevara. Arrogant ass. Why on earth had he approached her? Although they were virtually neighbours, she hadn't seen him in at least a decade. He hadn't had more than two words for her in the handful of times she *had* seen him, and yet now he'd expressly sought her out at tonight's tasting, had looked for her and given her those ridiculous compliments.

Beautiful women. She was not one of them, and she knew it. She never would be. She'd been told enough. She was too tall, too big-boned, too mannish. Her voice was too loud, her hands and feet too big; everything about her was awkward and unappealing to men like Vittorio, who had models and starlets and bored socialites on his arm. She'd seen the photos in the tabloids, although she pretended not to know. Not even to look. She did, on occasion anyway, because she was curious. And not just curious, but jealous, if she were honest with herself, which Anamaria always tried to be. She was jealous of those tiny, silly slips of women—women she'd gone to school with, women who had no use for her—who could wear the skimpy and sultry clothes she never could, who revelled in their own femininity while she plodded along, clumsy and cloddish. And Vittorio knew it. In the split second before she'd spoken, she'd seen the look in his eyes. Disdain, verging on disgust.

She knew that look; she'd seen it in Roberto's eyes when she'd tried to make him love her. Desire her. He hadn't. She'd seen it in other men's eyes as well; she was not what men thought of—or liked to think of—when they considered a woman. A pretty woman, a desirable one.

She'd become used to it, armoured herself with trouser suits and a practical, no-nonsense attitude, the best weapons a woman like her could have. Yet tonight, from Vittorio—stupidly— that look of disdain had hurt. She'd been so glad to see him, for that split second. Stupidly glad. She'd actually thought he'd remembered—

Why on earth had he approached her with that asinine flattery? Had he been attempting some sort of misguided chivalry, or worse, had he been mocking her? And why had he sought her out so directly in the first place?

He was the Count of Cazlevara—he could have any woman he wanted—and yet he'd entered the party and made straight for her. She only knew that because she'd seen him enter the castle, and felt her heart skip and then completely turn over. Even from afar, he was magnificent; well over six feet, he walked with a lithe grace, his suit of navy silk worn with careless elegance. His eyes—as black as polished onyx—had narrowed and his assessing gaze had swept the hall as if he were looking for someone.

That was all she'd seen before she'd been pulled into another conversation, and now Anamaria wondered if he'd actually been looking for *her*.

Stupid. Fanciful. Wishful thinking, even. Vittorio could have anyone he wanted. Why on earth would he bother with her for a moment?

And yet, for some reason, he *had*.

Anamaria's cheeks burned and she took a hasty sip of wine, barely tasting the superb vintage—she was, ironically, drinking one of Cazlevara's own. It seemed, she acknowledged bleakly, far more likely that he'd been mocking her. Amusing himself with a little easy flattery of a woman who would surely only lap it up gratefully. She knew the type. She'd dealt before with men who treated her with condescending affection, and acted surprised when they were rebuffed. Yet Vittorio hadn't been surprised by her rebuff—he'd been furious.

Anamaria's lips curved into a smile. *Good.*

She knew very little about Vittorio. She knew the facts, of course. He was the richest man in Veneto, as well as a Count. His winery—the region's best—had been run by the Cazlevaras for hundreds of years. In comparison, her own family's three hundred year heritage seemed paltry.

His father had died when he was a teenager; she, along with several thousand others, had been at the memorial service at San Marco in Venice. The funeral had been a quiet family affair at the Cazlevara estate. As soon as he reached his majority, he'd gone travelling—drumming up more business for the winery—and hardly ever came home. He'd been more or less absent—gone—for nearly fifteen years. Anamaria could only imagine that a man like Vittorio needed more entertainment than the rolling hills and ancient vineyards Veneto could provide.

She pictured him now, remembering how he'd looked at her from those gleaming onyx eyes. He was a beautiful man, but in a hard way. Those high, sharp cheekbones seemed almost cruel—at least they did when his eyes were narrowed in such an assessing manner, his mouth pursed in telling disdain before he'd offered her such a false smile.

Yet, even as she considered how she'd seen him only a few moments ago, another memory rose up and swamped her senses. The only real memory she had of Vittorio Cazlevara. The memory that had made her smile when she'd seen him again—smile with hope and even, pathetically, with joy.

It had been at her mother's funeral. November, cold and wet. She'd been thirteen and hadn't grown into her body yet, all awkward angles, her limbs seeming to fly out of their own accord. She'd stood by the graveside, her hand smeared with the clump of muddy dirt she'd been asked to throw on her mother's casket. It had landed with a horrible thunk and she'd let out an inadvertent cry, the sound of a wounded animal.

As the mourners had filed out, Vittorio—he must have been around twenty years old then—had paused near her. It was only later that she'd wondered why he'd come at all; their families were acquaintances, nothing more. She hadn't registered the tall, dark presence for a moment; she'd been too shrouded in her own pall of grief. Then she'd looked up and those eyes—those beautiful eyes, dark with compassion—had met hers. He'd touched her cheek with his thumb, where a tear still sparkled.

'It's all right to be sad, *rondinella*,'—swallow—he'd said, softly enough so only she could hear. 'It's all right to cry.' She'd stared at him dumbly, his thumb still warm against her chilled cheek. He smiled, so sadly. 'But you know where your mother is now, don't you?' She shook her head, not wanting to hear some paltry platitude about how Emily Viale was happy now, watching her daughter from some celestial cloud. He took his thumb, damp with her tears, and touched it to his breastbone. 'In here. *Tua cuore.*' Your heart. And with another sad, fleeting smile, he had moved away.

She'd known then that he'd lost his father a few years before. Even so, she hadn't realized another person could understand her so perfectly. How someone—a stranger—had been able to say exactly the right thing. How later, when she wept scalding tears into her pillow, wept until she felt she'd be sick from it and her mind and body and heart all felt wrung, wasted, she'd remember his words.

It's all right to cry.

He'd helped her to grieve. And when the pain had, if not stopped, then at least lessened, she'd wanted to tell him that. She'd wanted to say thank you, and she supposed she'd wanted to see if he still understood her. Understood her more, even, than before. And she'd wanted to discover if she, perhaps, understood him too. A ridiculous notion, when that passing comment was the only conversation they'd ever really shared.

Over the years, she'd almost—almost—forgotten about Vittorio's words at her mother's graveside. Yet in that second when she'd seen him again, every frail, childish hope had leapt to life within her and she'd thought—she'd actually *believed*—that he remembered. That it had meant something.

Her pathetic foolishness, even if only for a second, annoyed her. She wasn't romantic or a dreamer; any dreams of romance—love, even—she'd once entertained as a child had died out years ago, doused by the hard reality of boarding school, when she'd been a picked-on pigeon among swans. Ana's mouth twisted cynically. Perhaps not a pigeon, but a swallow, a plain and unprepossessing bird, after all.

They'd flickered briefly back to life in her university days, enough so that she had been willing to take a risk with Roberto.

That had been a mistake.

And, just now, the moment Vittorio Ralfino's mouth had tightened in disdain and then uttered words Anamaria knew to be false…the last faint, frail hope she hadn't even known she'd still possessed had flickered out completely. Mockery or lies. She didn't know which. It hardly mattered.

Anamaria took another sip of wine and turned to smile at another winemaker—Busato, a man in his sixties with hair like cotton wool and a smile as kind as that of *Babbo Natale*. As one of the few female winemakers in the room, she appreciated his kindness, as well as his respect. And, she told herself firmly, she would dismiss Vittorio Cazlevara completely from her mind, as he had undoubtedly dismissed her from his. A few words exchanged nearly seventeen years ago hardly mattered now. She wouldn't be surprised if Vittorio didn't remember them; it certainly shouldn't *hurt*. He'd merely been offering her a few pleasantries, scraps tossed from his opulent table, no doubt, and she vowed not to give them a second thought.

A light gleamed in one of the downstairs windows of Villa Rosso as she headed up the curving drive. Her father was waiting for her, as he always did when she went to these events; just a few years ago he would have gone with her, but now he chose to leave such things entirely to her. He claimed she needed her independence, but Anamaria suspected the socialising tired him. He was, by nature, a quiet and studious man.

'Ana?' His voice carried from the study as she entered the villa and slipped off her coat.

'Yes, Papà?'

'Tell me about the tasting. Was everyone there?'

'Everyone important,' she called back, entering the study with a smile, 'except you.'

'Bah, flattery.' Her father sat in a deep leather armchair by the fireplace; a fire crackled in the hearth to ward off the night's chill. A book lay forgotten in his lap and he took off his reading spectacles to look at her, his thin, lined face creasing into a smile. 'You needn't say such things to me.'

'I know,' she replied, sitting across from him and slipping off her shoes, 'and so I should, since I was the subject of a flatterer myself tonight.'

'Oh?' He shut his book and laid it on the side table, next to his spectacles. 'What do you mean?'

She hadn't meant to mention Vittorio. She'd been trying to forget him, after all. Yet somehow he'd slipped right into their conversation before it had even started, and it couldn't even surprise her because, really, hadn't he been in her mind all evening?

'The Count of Cazlevara has returned,' she explained lightly. 'He made an appearance tonight. Did you know he was back?'

'Yes,' Enrico said after a moment and, to Ana's surprise, he sounded both thoughtful and guarded. 'I did.'

'Really?' She raised her eyebrows, tucking her feet under her as she settled deeper into the armchair of worn, butter-soft leather. 'You never told me.' She couldn't quite keep the faint note of reproach from her voice.

Her father hesitated and Ana had the distinct feeling he was hiding something from her. She wondered how she even knew it to be a possibility, when their relationship—especially in the years after her mother had died—had been so close, so open. It hadn't always been that way, God knew, but she'd worked at it and so had he, and yet now...? Was he actually hiding something from her?

She gave a little laugh. 'Well, Papà?'

He shrugged. 'It didn't seem important.'

Ana nodded, accepting, because of course it shouldn't be important. She barely knew Vittorio. That one moment by her mother's graveside shouldn't even count. 'Well, it's late,' she finally said, smiling. 'I'm tired, so I think I shall go to bed.'

Ana scooped up her shoes, letting them dangle from her fingers as she walked slowly from the library through the darkened foyer and up the marble stairs that led to the second floor of the villa. She walked past darkened room after darkened room; the villa had eight bedrooms and only two were ever used. They rarely had guests.

Vittorio's few words had unsettled her, she realized as she entered her room and began to undress for bed. They shouldn't have—what a meaningless conversation it had been! Barely two sentences, yet they reverberated through her mind, her body, their echoes whispering provocatively to her.

She hadn't expected to have such a reaction to the man when she'd barely spared him a thought these last years. Yet the moment he'd entered the castle, she'd been aware of him. Achingly, alarmingly, *agonizingly* aware, her body suddenly springing to life, as if it had been numb or asleep, or even dead.

She slipped on her pyjamas and let her hair out of its restraining clip.

Outside her window, the moon bathed the meadows in silver and she could just make out the shadowy silhouettes in the vineyard that gave Villa Rosso both its name and fortune—*rosso* for the colour of the wine those grapes produced, a rich velvety red that graced many a fine table in Italy and, more recently, abroad.

Ana sat in her window seat, her legs drawn up to her chest, her chin resting on her knees. The wind from the open window stirred her hair and cooled her cheeks—she hadn't realized they'd been heated. Had she been blushing?

And what for? If she had any sort of social life at all, that tiny exchange with Vittorio would have meant less than nothing. Yet the hard fact was that she didn't, and it had. She was twenty-nine years old, staring at her thirtieth birthday in just a few months, without even the breath of hope of a social life beyond the winemaking events and tastings she went to, mostly populated by men twice her age. Not exactly husband material.

And was she even looking for a husband? Ana asked herself sharply. She'd given up that kind of dream years ago, when it had been pathetically, painfully obvious that men were not interested in her. She'd chosen to fill her life with business, friends and family—her father, at least—rather than pursue romance—love—that had, over the years, always seemed to pass her by. She'd *let* it go by, knowing those things were not for her. She'd accepted it…until tonight.

Still, she wished now that Vittorio hadn't come back, wished his absurd flattery—false as it so obviously was—hadn't stirred up her soul, reminded her of secret longings she'd forgotten or repressed. She'd been ignored so long—as a woman—that she'd become invisible, even to herself. She simply didn't think of herself that way any more.

She leaned her head back against the cool stone, closing her eyes as the wind tangled her hair and rattled in the trees outside.

She wanted, she realized with a sharp pang, Vittorio Cazlevara to look at her not with disdain or disgust, but with desire. She wanted him to say the things he'd said to her tonight—and more—and mean them.

She wanted to feel like a woman. For once.

CHAPTER TWO

'SIGNORINA VIALE, you have a visitor.'

'I do?' Ana looked up from the vine she'd been inspecting. It was the beginning of the growing season and the vines were covered in tiny unripened fruit, the grapes like perfect, hard little pearls.

'Yes.' Edoardo, one of the office assistants, looked uncomfortable—not to mention incongruous—in his immaculate suit and leather loafers. He must have been annoyed at having to tramp out to the vineyard to find her, but Ana always seemed to forget to bring her mobile. 'It is Signor Ralfino... I mean the Count of Cazlevara.'

'Vittorio...?' Ana bit her lip as she saw Edoardo's surprised look. The name had slipped out before she could stop herself, yet she was hardly on intimate terms with the Count. Why was he here? It had been only three days since she'd last seen him at the wine-tasting event and now he'd come to Villa Rosso, to her home, to find her? She felt a strange prickling along her spine, a sense of ominous yet instinctive foreboding, the way she did before a storm. Even when the sun beat down from a cloudless sky, she could tell when rain was coming. She knew when to cover the grapes from frost. It was one of the things that made her a natural—and talented—winemaker. Yet she had no idea if her instincts were right when it came to men. She'd hardly had enough experience to find out. 'Is he in the office?' she asked, a bit abruptly, and Edoardo nodded.

The sun was hot on her bare head and Ana was suddenly conscious of her attire: dusty trousers and a shirt that stuck to her back. It was what she normally wore on her regular inspection of the Viale vineyards, yet she hardly expected to receive visitors in such clothing…and certainly not Vittorio.

Why was he here?

'Thank you, Edoardo. I'll be with him shortly.' Disconcerted by the sudden heavy thudding of her own heart, Ana turned back to the vines, stared blindly at the clusters of tiny grapes. She waited until she heard him leave, and the rustle of vines as he passed, and then she drew in a long shuddering breath. She unstuck her shirt from her back and brushed a few sweaty strands of hair from her forehead. She was a mess. This was not how she wanted the Count of Cazlevara to see her.

Unfortunately, she had no choice. She could hardly walk the half-kilometre back to the villa to change if Vittorio was already waiting in the winery office.

She'd undoubtedly kept him waiting long enough. Vittorio Cazlevara did not, Ana acknowledged, seem like a patient man. Taking another deep breath, she tried her best to straighten her clothes—how had her shirt become so untucked and with a long streak of dirt on one sleeve?—and, throwing back her shoulders, she headed towards the office.

The long, low building with its creamy stone and terracotta tiles was as much a home to Ana as the villa was. It was a place where she felt confident and in control, queen of her domain, and that knowledge gave her strength as she entered. Here, it didn't matter what she looked like or how she dressed. Here, she was Vittorio's equal.

Vittorio stood by the sofa that was meant for visitors, a coffee table scattered with glossy magazines in front of it. His hands shoved deep in his pockets, he prowled the small space with a restless energy that radiated from his powerful body. He looked like a caged panther, full of contained power, dark and vaguely threatening.

Yet why should she be threatened by him? He was just a man…but what a man. He wore an exquisite suit made of Italian silk, perfectly tailored and hugging his powerful frame—his tall frame, for he had at least four inches on her own five foot eleven. His hair was inky-dark and cut close, emphasizing those hooded onyx eyes, the slashes of his severe brows. He looked up and those knowing eyes fixed on her, making Ana realize she'd been gawping like a schoolgirl. She straightened, managing a small, cool smile.

'Count Cazlevara. An unexpected pleasure.'

'Vittorio, please.' His gaze swept her in an instant, his mouth tightening in what Ana recognized as that now familiar disdain. He didn't even realize how he gave himself away, she thought with a strange little pang of sorrow. Was he going to try some more asinine flattery on her? She braced herself, knowing, no matter what, it would hurt. 'I'm sorry if I've interrupted you,' Vittorio said, and Ana gestured to her dishevelled clothes, even managing a wry smile as if her attire was not humiliating, despite him being dressed with such exquisite care.

'I'm afraid I was not expecting visitors. I was out in the vineyard, as you can see.'

'How are your grapes?'

'Growing.' She turned away from him, surreptitiously tucking in her blouse, which seemed determined on coming untucked at every opportunity. 'The weather has been good, thank God. May I offer you refreshment?'

He paused, and she glanced back at him. His head was cocked, and he was studying her with a thoughtful thoroughness she decided she didn't like. 'Yes, thank you. It is a warm day.'

Did his eyes linger on her heated face, her sticky shirt? Ana willed herself not to flush even more. If even the Count of Cazlevara was going to arrive unannounced, he would have to take her as she was. 'Indeed. Why don't we adjourn to the tasting room? It is more comfortable in there.' Vittorio gave a terse little jerk of his head, and Ana led the way to the room at the back of the winery that was meant for public gatherings.

The room was light and airy, with a vaulted ceiling and large windows that let in the late morning sunshine. A few tables, made from retired oak barrels, were scattered around with high stools. Ana sat down on one of the leather sofas positioned in one corner, meant for a more intimate conversation. She sat down, smoothing her dusty trousers and offering Vittorio another smile, bright and impersonal. Safe. 'How may I help you, Vittorio?' She stumbled only slightly over his Christian name; she wasn't accustomed to using it, even if she had been thinking it to herself.

He didn't reply, instead giving her an answering smile that showed the white flash of his straight, even teeth and said, 'You've done well for yourself these last years, Anamaria. The Viale label has grown in stature—not to mention price.'

'Please call me Ana. And thank you. I've worked hard.'

'Indeed.' He steepled his fingers under his chin, surveying her with that knowing little smile that she now found irritated her. 'And you've stayed at Villa Rosso all these years?'

She gave a little shrug, trying not to be defensive. 'It is my home.'

'You haven't wanted to travel? Go to university? See a bit of the world?'

'I'm happy where I am, Vittorio,' Ana replied, her voice sharpening just a little bit. 'And I did go to university. I took a degree in viticulture at the University of Padua.'

'Of course.' He nodded. 'I forgot.' Ana almost asked him how he would have known such a thing in the first place, but she decided to hold her tongue. 'Your father must be very glad of your dedication and loyalty to Viale Wines—and to him, of course. You've lived with him all these years?'

'Yes.' Ana tilted her head, wondering where these seemingly

innocuous comments were coming from. Why did the Count of Cazlevara care what she had been doing these last ten or fifteen years? What interest could he possibly have in Viale Wines? 'I cannot imagine doing anything else,' Ana said simply, for it was the truth. Viale Wines had become her life, her blood. Besides her father and her home, she had little else. Vittorio smiled, seeming pleased by her answer, and an assistant bustled in with a pitcher of iced lemon water and two frosted glasses.

'Thank you,' Ana murmured and, after the assistant had left, she poured two glasses and handed one to Vittorio. 'So,' she said when they'd both sipped silently for a moment, 'you're back at last from your travels abroad. To stay this time?'

'It would seem so. I have, I realize, been gone too long.' His mouth tightened, his eyes looking hard, and for a moment Ana was discomfited, wondering just what had brought him back to Veneto.

'Are you glad to be back?' she asked and his eyes, still hard with some unnamed emotion, met hers.

'Yes.'

Ana nodded. 'Still, it must have been nice to see so many places.' Could she sound more inane? She resisted the urge to wipe her damp palms on her trousers. She wanted to demand to know why he was here, what he wanted from her. This was the second time he'd sought her out, and she could not fathom why he was doing so. Why he would *want* to.

'It was.' He set his glass down on the coffee table with a quiet clink. 'And it was, of course, business.'

'Yes.'

Vittorio still gazed at her in that assessing manner, saying nothing. His silence unnerved her, made her edgy and a little desperate. She wasn't used to feeling so at odds; she'd become accustomed to being in control of her own life, especially here at the winery, her own little kingdom.

'Sometimes business and pleasure mix, however,' he finally said, his words seeming heavy with meaning, and Ana gave a little nod and smile although she hardly knew what he was saying, or why.

'Indeed.' Her nerves now taut and starting to fray, she forced another little laugh and said, 'I must confess, Vittorio, I don't know why you're here. It is good to have you back in Veneto, of course, but if I am to be frank, we've had very little to do with one another.' There. It was said. If she'd been rude, Ana didn't care; his presence, so confident—arrogant—and supremely male, unsettled her. It made her heart jump and her palms sweat and, worst of all, it made some sweet, nameless longing rise up in her like a hungry tide. She swallowed and kept her gaze firmly on him.

He leaned forward to take his glass once more, and the scent of his cologne—something faintly musky—wafted over her. Inadvertently, instinctively, she pressed back against the sofa cushions. He lifted his gaze to meet hers once more, yet she could tell nothing from those onyx eyes. They were as blank as polished marble. 'Actually, Ana, I came to ask you to dinner.'

The words seemed to fall into the stillness of the room, and of her heart. Did he mean a date? she wondered incredulously, even as a sense of sudden fierce pleasure rushed through her. A *date*. When was the last time she'd been on one of those, and with a man like Vittorio Ralfino? She felt her cheeks heat—how easily she gave herself away—and to cover her confusion, she reached for her glass and took a sip.

'I see I've surprised you.'

'Yes.' She pressed the glass against her hot cheek, lifting her gaze to smile wryly at him. 'We have not seen each other in years and, in any case—' She stopped, biting her lip, pulling it between her teeth and nipping it hard enough to draw a drop of blood. She tasted it on her tongue, hard and metallic. Vittorio smiled, his eyes on her mouth, and Ana knew he'd witnessed that traitorous little display of her own uncertainty.

'In any case?' he prompted gently.

She gave a helpless little shrug. 'I'm not exactly the kind of woman—' She stopped again, wishing she had not revealed so much. She didn't know how *not* to; she was terrible at lying, or even dissembling. She could only speak her heart, always had. It had never been dangerous before.

And it had been so long—forever—since a man had asked her out. Since she'd even *hoped* a man might ask her out.

'The kind of woman I take out to dinner?' Vittorio filled in. 'But how would you know what kind of woman I take out to dinner?'

'I don't,' Ana said quickly, too quickly. 'But I know—' She stopped again. There was no way of saving herself or her pride, it seemed. 'I am surprised, that's all,' she finally said, and pressed her lips tightly together to keep from revealing anything more.

Vittorio didn't answer, and Ana couldn't tell a thing from his expression. Surprisingly, she found she was not blushing now; instead, she felt cold and lifeless. This—this feeling of terrible numbness—was why she'd stopped looking for a man, for love. It hurt too much.

She put her glass back down on the table. Memories rushed in to fill the blank spaces in her mind and heart. The cruel laughter of the girls at boarding school, the interminable school dances where she'd clutched a glass of lukewarm punch and tried to make herself invisible. It hadn't been hard to do; no one had wanted to see her anyway.

Stupid schoolgirl memories, yet how they still hurt. How another man's attention—and his disdain—brought it all back.

'I see,' he said finally and, on opening her eyes, Ana felt he saw too much. The last thing she wanted was his pity. 'Actually,' Vittorio continued, watching her carefully, 'I want to discuss a business proposition with you.' He waited, still watching, and Ana's eyes widened in horror. Now the blush came, firing her body from the roots of her hair to the tips of her toes. She'd made *such* a fool of herself, assuming he was asking her out. And of course he hadn't corrected her, she realized with a vicious little stab of fury. He'd probably enjoyed seeing her squirm, relished her awful confession. *I'm not exactly the kind of woman...* He knew just what she'd meant, and his expression told her he agreed with her. As many had before.

'A business proposition,' she finally repeated, the silence having gone on, awkwardly, for at least a minute. 'Of course.'

'It might not be the kind of business proposition you're expecting,' Vittorio warned with a little smile and Ana tried for an answering laugh, though inwardly she was still writhing with humiliation and remembered pain.

'Now you have me intrigued.'

'Good. Shall we say Friday evening?'

Ana jerked her head in acceptance. 'Very well.' It didn't seem important to pretend she needed to check some schedule, that she might be busy. That she might, in fact, have a *date*. Vittorio would see right through her. He already had.

'I'll pick you up at Villa Rosso.'

'I can meet you—'

'I am a gentleman, Ana,' Vittorio chided her wryly. 'I shall enjoy escorting you somewhere special.'

And where exactly was somewhere special? Ana wondered. And, more alarmingly, what should she wear? Her wardrobe of businesslike trouser suits hardly seemed appropriate for a dinner date...except it wasn't a date, had never been meant to be a date, she reminded herself fiercely. It was simply a business proposition. A trouser suit would have to do. Still, Ana was reluctant to don one. She didn't want to look like a man; she wanted to feel like a woman. She didn't dare ask herself why. For over ten years—since her university days—she'd dressed and acted not purposely like a man, more like a sexless woman. A woman who wasn't interested in fashion, or beauty, or even desire. Certainly not love. It had been safer that way; no expectations or hopes to have dashed, no one—especially herself—to disappoint. There was no earthly reason to change now. There was every reason to keep as she'd been, and stay safe.

* * *

On Friday night she stood in front of the full-length mirror in her bedroom, gazing rather ruefully at her reflection. She wore a pair of fitted black trousers with a rather unfortunately boxy jacket; it had looked better on the rack. Her one concession to femininity was the cream silk beaded tank top she wore underneath, and that was completely hidden by the jacket. She piled her hair up on top of her head, wincing a little bit at the strands that insisted on escaping to frame her face and curl with surprising docility along her neck. She couldn't decide if the loose tendrils gave her a look of elegance or dishevelment. She didn't attempt any make-up, as she'd never mastered the art of doing her face without looking like a child who had played in her mother's make-up box.

'There.' She nodded at her reflection, determined to accept what she saw. Wearing a sexy cocktail dress or elegant gown would have been ridiculous, she told herself. She never wore such things—she didn't own such things—and, considering Vittorio's business proposition, there was no reason to start now.

Her father was, as usual, in the study when Ana came downstairs. Most evenings he was content to hole up in the villa with a book or a game of solitaire.

Enrico looked up from his book, raising his eyebrows at her outfit. 'Going out, my dear?'

Ana nodded, suppressing a little pang of guilt. She hadn't told her father about this dinner with Vittorio; she told herself she'd simply forgotten, but she knew that wasn't true. She hadn't wanted him to know, and start reading more into this dinner than there was or ever could be.

'Yes,' she said now, dropping a kiss on the top of his thinning hair. 'Dinner.'

'A date?' Enrico asked, sounding pleased. Ana shook her head and stepped away to look out of the window. Twilight was stealing softly upon the world, cloaking the landscaped gardens in violet.

'No. Just business.'

'Always business,' her father said a bit grumpily, and Ana smiled.

'You know I love it.' And she did love it; the wine, the grapes were in her blood. Her father loved to tell the story about when he had taken her to the vineyards when she was only two years old. He'd hoisted her up to the vines and she'd plucked a perfectly ripe grape, deeply purple and bursting with flavour, and popped it into her mouth. Then, instead of saying how tasty it was, she'd pronounced in a quite grown-up voice, *'Sono pronti.'* They're ready.

'I worry you work too much.'

Ana said nothing, for she knew she had no argument. She did work too much; she had nothing else. In the last few years her father had stepped back from the winery business, as he'd never really wanted to be more than a gentleman vintner, tending the family grapes. Ana wanted more. She dreamed of the day when Viale wines were in every fine restaurant in Europe, and even America. When they were held in reserve for special customers, the bottles dusty and precious. When they rivalled Cazlevara Wines.

Just then she saw headlights pierce the growing darkness, and a navy Porsche swept up the drive. Ana watched from the window, her heart starting to thud with hard, heavy beats as Vittorio stepped from the car. In the lengthening shadows she couldn't see what he wore, yet she could tell he looked magnificent. She felt it in her own shivery response.

The doorbell rang.

'Someone is coming for you?' Enrico asked, his book forgotten in his lap.

'Yes—' Ana started from the study.

'Whoever it is,' Enrico called after her, 'invite him in.'

By the time she reached the door she was breathless and flushed, simply from nerves. Vittorio stood there, hands thrust deep into his pockets, looking as magnificent as Ana knew he would in an immaculately tailored suit of navy silk. His shirt was crisp and white and a tie of aquamarine silk was knotted at the brown column of his throat.

Ana swallowed, her mouth dry, her head empty of thoughts. She could not think of a single thing to say.

'Hello, Ana.' He smiled, a quick flash of white teeth. 'Are you ready?'

Ana nodded, conscious of both how Vittorio had not complimented her—or even commented on—her appearance, and that her father was sitting in the next room, waiting for her to usher in her guest. She swallowed. 'Yes, but would you like to come in for a moment? My father…' She trailed off, hating how hesitant she sounded. 'My father would like to say hello,' she said firmly, and then turned to lead Vittorio to the study without looking back to see if he followed.

Once in the study Ana stepped aside as her father looked up and smiled. He didn't, she realized with a jolt, look very surprised. 'Good evening, Vittorio.'

'Good evening, sir.'

Enrico smiled, pleased by the sign of respect. 'You are going out for dinner?'

'In a manner of speaking. I thought we could eat at Castle Cazlevara.'

Ana looked at him in surprise. Dinner in his own castle? She'd been to the castle once, for a Christmas party when she was a child. She remembered a huge Christmas tree, twenty feet high, in the castle's soaring entrance hall, and eating too many sweets.

Uneasily, Ana realized Vittorio and her father had been talking, and she hadn't heard a word. Now Vittorio turned to her, smiling solicitously. 'We should go.'

'Yes, all right.'

One hand rested lightly on the small of her back—the simple touch seemed to burn—as Vittorio said goodbye to Enrico and then led her out to the softly falling darkness and his waiting car.

* * *

Vittorio opened the passenger door for Ana before sliding in the driver's side. She was nervous, he saw, and her clothes were utterly atrocious. He'd been about to compliment her when she'd first opened the door and had just stopped himself from uttering what they both knew would be more unwanted false flattery.

He drummed his fingers against the steering wheel as Ana fastened her seat belt. He felt impatient, as he so often did, and also, strangely, a little uncertain. He didn't like either feeling. He didn't know how best to approach Ana, how to court her, if such a thing could even be done. He doubted he could act convincingly enough. As intelligent and decent a human being as she obviously was, she was not a woman to take to bed. Yet if this marriage was to work—if he were to have an heir—then he would be taking her to bed, and more than once.

Vittorio dwelt rather moodily on that scenario before pushing it aside. He could have chosen another woman, of course; there were plenty of pretty—gorgeous, even—socialites in Italy who would relish becoming the Contessa of Cazlevara. Women he would gladly take to bed but, ironically perhaps, he did not wish to marry them.

Their vineyards did not border his own; they were not dedicated to winemaking, to the region. They were not particularly loyal. They were not, any of them, wife material.

Ana was. When he'd contemplated taking a wife, Ana Viale had ticked every box quite neatly. Experienced in winemaking, running her own vineyard, a dutiful daughter, healthy and relatively young.

And, of course, loyalty. He'd read of her loyalty to her family, and her family's vineyard, in that magazine article. Loyalty was a necessity, an absolute; he would not be betrayed again, not by those closest to him.

No, Anamaria Viale was the wife he wanted. The only wife he wanted.

His hands tightened on the steering wheel as he thought of

the other reason—really, the main reason—he wished to marry at all. He needed an heir. God willing, Ana would provide him with one, and would keep his brother—treacherous Bernardo—from ever becoming Count, as his mother had so recently told him she wanted.

The conversation, as it always was with Constantia, the current Countess, had been laced with bitterness on both sides. She'd rung asking for money; had there ever been anything else she wanted from him?

'I don't know why you hoard all your money, Vittorio,' she'd said a bit sulkily. 'Who are you keeping it for?'

He'd been distracted by the business emails on his computer screen, her words penetrating only after a moment. 'What do you mean?'

She'd sighed, the sound impatient and a bit contemptuous; it was a sound he remembered well from childhood, for it had punctuated nearly every conversation he'd had with his mother. 'Only that you are getting on in years, my son,' she had said, and he had heard the mocking note in her voice. 'You're thirty-seven. You are not likely to marry, are you?'

'I don't know,' he'd replied, and she'd laughed softly, the sound making the hair on the nape of his neck prickle.

'But if you don't marry, Vittorio, you can't produce an heir. And then you know what happens, don't you?' She sighed again, the sound different this time, almost sad. 'Bernardo becomes Count.'

He'd frozen then, his hand curled around the receiver, his eyes dark with memory and pain. That was what his mother had always wanted, what his brother had wanted. He'd known it for years, ever since they'd first tried to steal his inheritance from him, his father barely in the grave.

He didn't forget.

And how could he have forgotten the importance of marriage, of children? He'd been so intent on improving Cazlevara Wines, of forgetting the unhappiness he knew waited for him back home. He'd never considered the future, his future. His heirs.

Now he did. He'd considered carefully, chosen his bride as he would a fine wine. Now he just needed to decide when to decant it.

Vittorio drummed his fingers against the steering wheel again and saw Ana slide him a wary glance. How to approach his chosen bride? She sat tensely, one hand clenched around the door handle as if she would escape the speeding car. The suit she wore looked like something pulled out of a convent's charity box and it did nothing for her tall, generous figure. Not that there was something to be done for her figure, but Vittorio imagined that some decent clothes and make-up could go some way to improving his intended bride's appearance.

His mouth twisted. What would Ana think if she knew he planned to marry her—and as soon as possible? Of course, any woman should be thrilled to become part of the Cazlevara dynasty, yet he felt instinctively that Ana Viale might balk. He knew from the other night at San Stefano Castle that she would not be fooled by his attempts to flatter or romance her, and why should she? God knew, the women he usually had on his arm or in his bed did not look or dress or even talk like Ana Viale. Yet he didn't want to marry them. He wanted to marry Ana. It was a matter of expediency, of business.

And that, Vittorio decided, was how he would present the marriage to her. She appreciated plain speaking, and so he would speak as plainly as possible. The thought appealed to him. He wouldn't have to waste time pretending to be attracted to her. Most women would enjoy a little flattery, but he knew now that it would only annoy Ana, perhaps even hurt her.

A tiny twinge of something close to guilt pierced his conscience. Would Ana want some kind of *real* marriage? Was she waiting for love?

With him it was impossible, and she needed to know that from the start. Surely a woman like her was not still holding out for love? She seemed too practical for that, not to mention too plain. Besides, she could always say no.

Except Vittorio would make sure she didn't.

Ana pressed back against the leather seat as the darkened countryside, rolling hills and clusters of oak trees, sped by. She sneaked another glance at Vittorio's rather forbidding profile. He hadn't spoken since they'd got in the car, and he didn't look as if he was up for a chat. His jaw was tight, his eyes narrowed, his hands clenched around the steering wheel. What was he thinking? Ana didn't want to ask. She turned towards the window, tried to still the nerves writhing in her middle. They drove for at least twenty minutes without speaking, and then Ana saw the lights of Castle Cazlevara on a hill in the distance, mere pinpricks in the unrelenting darkness. Vittorio turned into the mile-long private drive that wound its way up the hill to his home.

Ana had seen photos of the castle on postcards, and of course she'd been there the one time. Yet, even so, the sight of the huge medieval castle perched on jutting stone awed and even intimidated her. Its craggy turrets rose towards the darkened sky and an ancient-looking drawbridge was now lowered over the drained moat. At one point the castle had been an imposing fortress, perched high on its hill, surrounded by a deep moat. Now it was simply Vittorio's home.

'So your own home is the "somewhere special"?' she asked lightly, and was rewarded with the flicker of a smile.

'I must admit I find Castle Cazlevara rather special.'

Gazing up at the castle's soaring walls and towers, Ana could only agree. Special, and a bit scary.

Vittorio drove across the drawbridge and parked the car in the castle's inner courtyard, now paved over with slate, providing a perfect backdrop for the Porsche. The building had been updated from the time it had served as a fortress against barbarian invaders—and, if Ana remembered her history, the Pope's own army—although it still retained much of its charm.

Though charm was hardly the word, Ana thought as Vittorio came around to open her door before she could even touch the handle. It was darkly impressive, forbiddingly beautiful. Like its owner. Gas-lit torches flickered on either side of the entrance doors as Vittorio led her up the stone stairs.

The huge entryway was filled with dancing shadows, a thick Turkish carpet laid over the ancient stones. Polished mahogany doors led to several large reception rooms, now lost in shadow, but Vittorio forewent these in favour of a small passageway in the back of the main hall. Ana followed him, conscious of the castle all around them, huge, dark and silent.

'Have you ever wanted to build something else?' she asked to Vittorio's back. The narrow corridor was cold and dark. 'A palazzo somewhere, something modern?'

Vittorio stiffened slightly, yet noticeable still to Ana. She was so aware of him: his powerful shoulders and long back, the muscles rippling under the smooth silk of his suit, even the faint musk of him. Aware of his moods, changing like quicksilver, even though he did not look at her or speak. It was strange, being so aware. So *alive*. She wasn't used to it.

'The Counts of Cazlevara have always lived here,' he said simply. 'And their families. Although my mother lives near Milan for much of the year, in a palazzo like you mentioned.' There was a sharp note to his voice, a hint of something dark and even cruel, something Ana couldn't understand. He turned, his eyes gleaming from the light of the sconces positioned intermittently along the stone walls. 'Could you not imagine living in such a place as this?'

In a flash of insight—or perhaps just imagination—Ana *could* see herself living there. She pictured herself in the gracious drawing rooms, presiding over a Christmas party like the one she'd gone to as a child. Overseeing a feast in the ancient dining hall, as if she were the Contessa herself, inviting the citizens of Veneto into her gracious home. Such images caused longing to leap within her. Surprised by its intensity, she pushed the images away; they were absurd, impossible, and surely not what Vittorio meant.

'There is certainly a great deal of history here,' she said, once again to his back.

'Yes. Many centuries. Yet your own family has been in Veneto a long time.'

'Three hundred years,' Ana conceded wryly. 'No more than a day compared to yours.'

'A bit more than a day,' Vittorio said, laughter in his voice. He stopped in front of a polished wooden door which he opened so Ana could enter. 'And now. Dinner.'

Ana took in the cosy room with a mixture of alarm and anticipation. Heavy velvet curtains were drawn at the windows, blocking out the night. A fire crackled in the hearth and sent dancing shadows around the candlelit room. A table for two had been laid in front of the fire, with a rich linen tablecloth and napkins, the finest porcelain and crystal. On a small table to the side, a bottle of red had already been opened to breathe. It was an intimate scene, a romantic scene, a room ready not for business, but seduction.

Ana swallowed. She walked to the table, one hand on the back of a chair. When had she last had a meal like this, shared a meal like this? Never. The idea of what was to come filled her with a dizzying sense of excitement that she told herself she had no right to feel. She shouldn't even want to feel it. Yet still it came, bubbling up inside of her, treacherous and hopeful. This felt like a date. A real date. She cleared her throat. 'This all looks lovely, Vittorio. Somewhere special indeed.'

Vittorio smiled and closed the door behind him. They were completely alone; Ana wondered whether there was anyone else in the castle at all. 'Do you live here alone since you've returned?' she asked.

Vittorio shrugged. 'My brother Bernardo and my mother Constantia are in Milan. They come and go as they please.'

His tone was strange, cold, and yet also almost indifferent. It made Ana wonder if he considered his brother and mother—the only family he had left—as nothing more than interlopers in his own existence. Surely not. Ever since her own mother had died, she'd clung to her father, to the knowledge that he was her closest and only relative, that all they had was each other. Surely Vittorio felt the same?

He pulled back her chair and Ana sat, suppressing a shiver of awareness as he took the heavy linen napkin and spread it across her lap, his thumbs actually brushing her inner thighs. Ana jerked in response to the touch, a flush heating her cheeks, warming her insides. She had never been touched so intimately, and the thought was shaming. He'd just been putting a napkin in her lap.

She supposed it was her lack of experience with men that made her so skittish and uncertain around Vittorio, hyper-aware of everything he did, every sense stirring to life just by being near him. That had to be it; nothing else made sense. This aching awareness of him was just due to her own inexperience. She didn't go on dates and she didn't flirt. She did not know what it felt like to be desired.

And you're not desired now.

This dinner—this room—with all of its seeming expectations was going to her head. It was setting her up, Ana realized, for a huge and humiliating fall. She'd fallen before, she reminded herself, her would-be boyfriend at university had had to spell out the plain truth.

I'm just not attracted to you.

Neither was Vittorio. He wasn't even pretending otherwise. She mustn't forget that, no matter what the trappings now, Vittorio was not interested in her as a woman. This was simply how he did business. It had to be.

And so it would be how she did business as well.

'Wine?' Vittorio asked and held up the bottle. With a little dart of surprised pleasure, Ana realized it was one of Viale's labels. The best, she acknowledged as she nodded and Vittorio poured.

He sat down across from her and raised his glass. Ana raised her own in response. 'To business propositions.'

'Intriguing ones, even,' Ana murmured, and they both drank.

'Delicious,' Vittorio pronounced, and Ana smiled.

'It's a new blend—'

'Yes, I read about it.'

She nearly spluttered in surprise. 'You did?'

'Yes, in the in-flight magazine on my trip home.' Vittorio placed his glass on the table. 'There was a little article about you. Have you seen it?' Ana nodded jerkily. The interview had been short, but she'd been glad—and proud—of the publicity. 'You've done well for yourself, Ana, and for Viale Wines.'

'Thank you.' His words meant more to her than they ought, she knew, but she couldn't keep the fierce pleasure at his praise from firing through her. Ana had worked long and hard to be accepted in the winemaking community, to make Viale Wines the name it was.

A few minutes later a young woman, diminutive and dark-haired, came in with two plates. She set them down, Vittorio murmured his thanks and then she left as quietly as she had come.

Ana glanced down at the paper-thin slices of prosciutto and melon. 'This looks delicious.'

'I'm glad you think so.'

They ate in silence and Ana's nerves grew more and more taut, fraying, ready to break. She wanted to demand answers of Vittorio; she wanted to know just what this business proposition was. She wasn't good at this, had never been good at this; she couldn't banter or flirt, and at the moment even idle chatter seemed beyond her.

It was too much, she thought with a pang. Being here with a devastatingly handsome man—with Vittorio—eating delicious food, drinking wonderful wine, watching the firelight play with shadows on his face—all of it was too much. It made her remember all the things she'd once wanted that she'd long ago accepted she'd never have. A husband. Children. A home of her own. She'd made peace with that, with the lack in her life, because there was so much she had, so much she loved and enjoyed. She'd *thought* she'd made peace with it, but now she felt restless and uncertain and a little bit afraid. She *wanted* again.

She had no idea why Vittorio—Vittorio, of all people, who was so unbearably out of her league—made her feel this way. Made her remember and long for those things. Made her, even now, wonder if his hair felt as crisp as it looked, or if it would be soft in her hands. If she touched his cheek would she feel the flick of stubble against her fingers? Would his lips be soft? Would he taste like her own wine?

Ana nearly choked on a piece of melon, and Vittorio looked up enquiringly. 'Are you all right?' he asked, all solicitude, and she nodded almost frantically.

'Yes—yes, fine.' She could hardly believe the direction her thoughts had taken, or the effect they were having on her body. Her limbs felt heavy and warm, a deep, pleasurable tingling starting low in her belly and then suddenly, mischievously flaring upwards, making her whole being clench with sudden, unexpected spasms of desire.

She'd never thought to feel this way, had thought—hoped, even—she'd buried such desperate longings. For surely they were desperate. This was *Vittorio*. Vittorio Ralfino, the Count of Cazlevara, and he'd never once looked at her as a woman. He never would.

They ate in near silence, and when they were finished the woman came back to clear the plates and replace them with dishes of homemade ravioli filled with fresh, succulent lobster.

'Have you missed home?' Ana asked in an effort to break the strained silence. Or perhaps it wasn't strained and she only felt it was because her nerves were so fraught, her body still weak with this new desire, desperate for more. Or less. She was torn between the safety of its receding and the need for it to increase. To actually touch. Feel. *Know.*

Vittorio seemed utterly unaware of her dilemma; he sat sprawled in his chair, cradling his glass of wine between his palms.

'Yes,' he replied, taking a sip. 'I shouldn't have stayed away so long.'

Ana was surprised by the regret in his voice. 'Why did you?'

He shrugged. 'It seemed the right thing to do at the time. Or, at least, the easy thing to do.' Vittorio took a bite of ravioli. 'Eat up. These ravioli are made right here at the castle, and the lobster were caught fresh only this morning.'

'Impressive,' Ana murmured, and indeed it was delicious, although she barely enjoyed a mouthful for she felt the tension and the need building inside her, tightening her chest and making it hard even to breathe. She wanted to ask him what she was doing here; she wanted to reach across the table and touch him. The need to touch was fast overriding the need to know. Action would replace words and if she had just one more glass of wine she was afraid she would do just what she was thinking—fantasising—about and actually touch him.

She wondered how Vittorio would react. Would he be stunned? Flattered? Repulsed? It was too dangerous to even imagine a scenario, much less to want it—crave it…

She could stand it no more. She set down her fork and gave Vittorio as direct a look as she could. 'As lovely as this meal is, Vittorio, I feel I have to ask. I must know.' She took a breath and let it out slowly, laying her hand flat on the table so she didn't betray herself and reach out to touch him. 'Just what is this business proposition you are thinking of?'

Vittorio didn't answer for a long moment. He glanced at the wine in his glass, ruby-red, glinting in the candlelight. He smiled almost lazily—making her insides flare with need once more—and then set his glass down on the table.

'Well,' he said with a wry little smile, 'if you must know, it is simply this. I want you to marry me.'

CHAPTER THREE

THE WORDS SEEMED to ring in the empty air, filling the room, even though the only sound was the crackle of the fire as the logs settled into the grate, scattering a bit of ash across the carpet.

Ana stared, her mind spinning, her mouth dry. Once again, she couldn't think of a single thing to say. She wondered if she'd heard him correctly. Surely she'd imagined the words. Had she wanted him to say such a thing? Was she so ridiculous, pathetic, that she'd *dreamed* it?

Or had he been joking? Common sense returned. Of course he was joking. She let her lips curve into a little smile, although she knew the silence had gone on too long. She reached for her wine. 'Really, Vittorio,' she said, shaking her head a little bit as if she actually shared the joke, 'I want to know why.'

He leaned forward, all lazy languor gone, replaced with a sudden intentness. 'I'm serious, Ana. I want to marry you.'

She shook her head again, unable to believe it. Afraid to believe it. He must be joking, even if it was a terrible joke. A cruel one.

She'd known cruel jokes before. Girls hiding her clothes after gym, so she had to walk through the locker rooms in a scrap of a towel while they giggled and whispered behind their hands.

The boy who had asked her to dance when she was fifteen—she'd accepted, incredulously, and he'd laughed and run away. She'd seen the money exchange grubby adolescent hands, and realized he'd only asked her as a bet. And of course the one man she'd let into her life, had wanted to give her body to, only to be told he didn't think of her that way. Roberto had acted affronted, as if she'd misunderstood all the time they'd spent together, the dinners and the late nights studying. Perhaps she had misunderstood; perhaps she was misunderstanding now.

Yet, looking at Vittorio's calm face, his eyes focused intently on hers, Ana slowly realized she hadn't misunderstood. He wasn't joking. He was serious. And yet surely he couldn't be—surely he could not possibly want to marry *her*.

'I told you the proposition was an intriguing one,' he said, and there was laughter in his voice.

'That's one word for it,' Ana managed, and took a healthy draught of wine. It went down the wrong way and for a few seconds her eyes watered as she tried to suppress a most inelegant cough. A smile lurked in Vittorio's eyes, in the upward flick of his mouth and he reached out to touch her shoulder, his hand warm even through the thick cloth of her jacket.

'Just cough, Ana. Better out than in.'

She covered her mouth with her hand, managing a few ladylike coughs before her body took over and she choked and spluttered for several minutes, tears streaming from her eyes, utterly inelegant. Vittorio poured her a glass of water and thrust it into her hands.

'I'm sorry,' she finally managed when she had control over herself once more. She wiped her eyes and took a sip of water.

'Are you all right?' She nodded, and he leaned back in his chair. 'I see I've surprised you.'

'You could say that.' Ana shook her head, still unable to believe Vittorio had actually said what she'd thought he had said. And if he had said it, why? What on earth was he thinking of? None of it made sense. She couldn't even *think*.

'I didn't intend to speak so plainly, so quickly,' Vittorio said, 'but I thought you'd appreciate an honest business proposition.'

Ana blinked, then blinked again. She glanced around the room with its flickering candles and half-drunk glasses of wine, the fire burned down to a few glowing embers; the desire still coiled up inside her, desperate to unfurl. What a fool she was. 'Ah,' she said slowly, 'business.' Marriage must, for a man like Vittorio, determined and ambitious, be a matter of business. 'Of course.' She heard the note of disappointment in her own voice and cringed inside. Why should she feel let down? Everything she'd wanted and felt—that had been in her own head. Her own body. Not Vittorio's. She turned to gaze at him once more, her expression direct and a little flat. 'So just how is marriage a business proposition?'

Vittorio felt the natural vibrancy drain from Ana's body, leaving the room just a little bit colder. Flatter. He'd made a mistake, he realized. Several mistakes. He'd gone about it all wrong, and he'd tried so hard not to. He'd seen her look around the room, watched her take in all the trappings of a romantic evening which he'd laid so carefully. The fire, the wine, the glinting crystal. The intimate atmosphere that wrapped around them so suggestively. It was not, he realized, a setting for business. *Fool.* If he'd been intending to conduct this marriage proposal with a no-nonsense business approach, he should have done it properly, in a proper business setting. Not here, not like this. This room, this meal promised things and feelings he had no intention or desire to give. And Ana knew it. That was why she looked so flat now, so...*disappointed.*

Did she actually want—or even expect—that from him? Had she convinced herself this was a *date*? The thought filled Vittorio with both shame and disgust. He could not, he knew, pretend to be attracted to her. He shouldn't even try. He shouldn't have brought her to this room at all. He needed to stop pretending he was wooing her. Even when he knew he wasn't, he still fell back on old tactics, old ploys that had given him success in the past.

Now was the time for something new.

Vittorio leaned forward. 'Tell me, Ana, do you play cards?'

Ana looked up, arching her eyebrows in surprise. 'Cards…?'

'Yes, cards.' Vittorio smiled easily. 'I thought after dinner we could have a friendly game of cards—and discuss this business proposition.'

She arched her eyebrows higher. 'Are you intending to wager?'

Vittorio shrugged. 'Most business is discussed over some time of sport or leisure—whether it is golf, cards, or something else entirely.'

'How about billiards?'

Vittorio's own eyebrows rose, and Ana felt a fierce little dart of pleasure at his obvious surprise. 'You play billiards?'

'*Stecca*, yes.'

'*Stecca*,' Vittorio repeated. 'As a matter of fact, the castle has a five pins table. My father put it in when he became Count.' He paused. 'I played with him when I was a boy.'

Ana didn't know if she was imagining the brief look of sorrow that flashed across Vittorio's face. She remembered hearing, vaguely, that he'd been very close to his father.

It's all right to be sad, rondinella.

She pushed the memory away and smiled now with bright determination. 'Good. Then you know how to play.'

Vittorio chuckled. 'Yes, I do. And I have to warn you, I'm quite good.'

Ana met his dark gaze with a steely one of her own. 'So am I.'

He led her from the cosy little room with the discarded remains of their meal, down another narrow corridor into the stone heart of the castle and then out again, until he came to a large, airy room in a more recent addition to the castle, with long sash windows that looked out onto a darkened expanse of formal gardens. In the twilit shadows Ana could only just discern the bulky shapes of box hedges and marble fountains. The room looked as if it hadn't been used in years; the billiards table was covered in dust sheets and the air smelled musty.

'I suppose you haven't played in a while,' she said, and Vittorio flashed a quick grin that once more caused her insides to fizz and flare. She did her best to ignore the dizzying sensation, pleasant as it was.

'Not here, anyway.' He pulled the sheet off the table and balled it up, tossing it in a corner, then opened the windows so the fresh, fragrant air wafted in from the gardens. 'The cues are over there. Do you want something to drink?'

Ana felt reckless and a little bit dangerous; she knew why Vittorio had asked her if she played cards, why they were here about to play billiards instead of back in that candlelit room. This was business. *She* was business. He could not have made it plainer. And that was fine; she could handle this. Any disappointment she'd felt—unreasonably so—gave way to a cool determination. 'I'll have a whisky.'

Vittorio gazed at her for a moment, his expression thoughtful and perhaps even pleased, his mouth curling upwards into a little smile before he nodded and went to push a button hidden discreetly by the door. Within minutes another servant—this time a man, some kind of butler—appeared at the doorway, silent and waiting.

'Mario, two whiskies please.'

'Yes, my lord.'

Ana selected her cue and carefully chalked the end. She studied the table with its three balls: two cue balls, one white, one yellow and a red object ball. Vittorio was setting up the castle in the middle of the table: five skittles, four white, one red, made into a cross. The object of the game was simple: you wanted to knock your opponent's ball into the skittles for points, or have it hit the red object ball. Her father liked to say it was a grown-up game of marbles.

'So where did you learn to play *stecca*?' Vittorio asked as he stepped back from the table.

'My father. After my mother died, it was a way for us to spend time together.'

'How touching,' he murmured, and Ana knew he meant it. He sounded almost sad.

'And I suppose your father taught you?' she asked. 'Or did you play with your brother?' She leaned over the table and practised a shot, the cue stick smooth and supple under her hands.

'Just my father.'

Ana stepped back, letting the cue stick rest on the floor. 'Would you like to go first?'

Vittorio widened his eyes in mock horror. 'Would a gentleman ever go first? I think not!'

Ana gave a little laugh and shrugged. 'I just wanted to give you the advantage. I warned you I was good.'

Vittorio threw his head back and let out a loud laugh; the sight of the long brown column of his throat, the muscles working, made something plunge deep inside Ana and then flare up again in need. Suddenly her hands were slippery on the cue stick and her mouth was dry. She was conscious of the way her heart had started beating with slow, deliberate thuds that seemed to rock her whole body. 'And I told you I was good too, as I remember.'

'Then we'll just have to see who is better,' Ana returned pertly, smiling a little bit as if she was relaxed, as if her body wasn't thrumming like a violin Vittorio had just played with a few words and a laugh.

The servant entered quietly with a tray carrying two tumblers, a bottle of Pellegrino and another bottle of very good, very old single malt whisky. Ana swallowed dryly. She'd only said she wanted whisky because she'd known what Vittorio was up to; she'd felt reckless and defiant and whisky seemed like the kind of drink men drank when they were playing a business games of billiards.

She, however, didn't drink it. She had a few sips with her father every now and then, but the thought of taking a whole tumbler with Vittorio made her nervous. She was a notorious lightweight—especially for a winemaker—and she didn't want to make a fool of herself in front of him. Especially not with this desire—so treacherous, so overwhelming, so new—still warring within her, making her feel languorous and anxious at varying turns.

'So,' Vittorio said as he reached for the whisky, 'do you take yours neat or with a little water?'

Water sounded like a good idea, a way to weaken the alcohol. 'Pellegrino, please.'

'As you wish.' He took his neat, Ana saw, accepting her tumbler with numb fingers. Vittorio smiled and raised his glass and she did likewise. They both sipped, and Ana managed not to choke as the whisky—barely diluted by water—burned down her throat.

'Now, please,' Vittorio said, sweeping his arm in an elegant arc. 'Ladies first.'

Ana nodded and set her glass aside. She lined up her first shot, leaning over the table, nervous and shy as Vittorio watched blandly. Focus, she told herself. Focus on the game, focus on the business. Yet that thought—and its following one, *marriage*—made her hands turn shaky and the shot went wide.

Vittorio clicked his tongue. 'Pity.'

He was teasing her, Ana knew, but she ground her teeth anyway. She hated to lose. It was one of the reasons she was so good at *stecca*; she'd spent hours practising so she could best her father at the game, which she hadn't done until she was fifteen. It had been five years of practice and waiting.

She stepped back from the table and took another sip of whisky as Vittorio lined up his shot. 'So why *do* you want to marry me?' she asked, her tone one of casual interest, just as he prepared to shoot. His shot went as wide as her own.

He swung around to face her, his eyes narrowed, and Ana smiled sweetly. 'I think you'd make an appropriate wife.'

'Appropriate. What a romantic word.'

'As I said,' Vittorio said softly, 'this is a matter of business.'

Ana lined up her own shot; before Vittorio could say anything else, she took it, banking his ball and missing the skittle by a centimetre. She'd been a fool to mention romance. 'Indeed. And you see marriage as a matter of business?'

He paused. 'Yes.'

'And what about me is so appropriate?' Ana asked. 'Out of curiosity.' Vittorio took his shot and knocked her ball cleanly into a skittle. Ana stifled a curse.

'Everything.'

She let out an incredulous laugh. 'Really, Vittorio, I am not such a paragon.'

'You are from a well-known, respected family in this region, you have worked hard at your own winery business these last ten years, and you are loyal.'

'And that is what you are looking for in a wife?' Ana asked, her tone sharpening. 'That is quite a list. Did you draw it up yourself?' She took another shot, grateful that this time she knocked his ball into a skittle. They were even, at least in billiards.

Vittorio hesitated for only a fraction of a second. 'I know what I want.'

She had to ask it; she had to know. She kept her voice light, even dismissive. 'You are not interested in love, I suppose?'

'No.' He paused. 'Are you?'

Ana watched as he stilled, his head cocked to one side, his dark eyes narrowed and intent as he waited for her answer. What a strange question, she thought distantly. Weren't most people interested in love?

Yet, even as she asked the question, she knew the answer for herself. She was not—could not—be interested in love, the love of a man, romantic, sexual. She'd tried it once and had felt only failure and shame—both feelings had taken years to forget, and even now she remembered the way they'd roiled through her, Roberto's horrified look...

No. Love—that kind of love—Ana had long ago accepted, was a luxury she could neither afford nor access. Yet did she want it? Crave it? *Need* it? Ana knew the answer to that question as well. No, she did not. The risk was simply too great, and the possibility—the hope—too small. 'No,' she said coolly. She leaned over for her next shot, determined to focus completely on the game. 'I'm not.'

'Good.'

She took the shot and straightened. 'I thought you'd say that.'

'It makes it so much easier.'

'Easier?' she repeated, and heard the sardonic note in her voice. When had she become so cynical? From the moment Vittorio had proposed a marriage of convenience, or before? Long before?

'Some women,' Vittorio said carefully, 'would not accept the idea of a marriage based on common principles—'

'Based on business, you mean.'

'Yes,' Vittorio said after a moment, 'but you must realize that I mean this to be a true marriage.' He paused. 'A *proper* marriage, a marriage in every sense of the word.'

Naïve virgin she may be, but Ana still knew what Vittorio was talking about. She could imagine it all too easily. Or almost. She closed her eyes briefly, but if she wanted to banish the image, she failed. It came back clearly, emblazoned on her brain. An antique four-poster, piled high with pillows and cushions. Vittorio, naked, tangled in sheets. Magnificent. Hers.

Ana turned back to the billiards table. 'So,' she said, blindly lining up a shot, 'you mean sex.' She didn't—couldn't—look at him, even as she kept her voice nonchalant. She missed her shot entirely.

'Yes.' Vittorio sounded completely unmoved. 'I'd like children. Heirs.'

'Is that really why you're marrying?'

He hesitated for only a second. 'The main reason,' he allowed and Ana felt a ripple of disappointment, although she hardly knew why. Of course a man like Vittorio wanted children, would marry for an heir. Heirs. He was a count; he had a title, a castle, a business, all to pass on to his child. A hoped-for son, no doubt. Her son. The thought sliced through her, shocking her, not an altogether unpleasant feeling. Vittorio arched his brows. 'Do you want children, Ana?'

There was something intimate about the question, especially when he spoke in that low, husky tone that made her insides ripple and her toes curl. She'd never expected to have such a fierce, primal reaction to him. It was instinctive and sensual, and it scared her. She turned away.

'Yes, I suppose.'

'You only suppose?'

'I never thought to have children,' she admitted with a bleak honesty that turned her voice a bit ragged. 'I never thought to have the opportunity.'

'Then this marriage suits us both.'

She gave a little instinctive shake of her head. He spoke as if it were agreed, the proverbial done deal. It couldn't be that easy. *She* couldn't be that easy. 'No.'

'Why not?' He'd moved closer to her; she could feel him by her shoulder, the heat and the musk of him.

'We're talking about marriage, Vittorio. A lifetime commitment.'

'So?'

'Such a decision requires some thought.'

'I can assure you I have thought of it a good deal.'

'Well, I haven't.' She turned around, suddenly angry. 'I haven't thought about it at *all*.'

He nodded, annoyingly unperturbed. 'You must have questions.'

She didn't answer. Of course she had questions, but they

weren't ones she necessarily wanted to ask. *Why do you want to marry me? What if we hate each other? Do you even desire me at all?*

Why am I so tempted?

She looked up, taking a breath. 'I don't even know what you think of marriage...of a wife. What would you expect of me? How would we...get on...together?' It seemed ridiculous even to ask the questions, for surely she wasn't seriously considering his outrageous proposal. Yet, even so, Ana was curious. She wanted to know the answers.

'We'd get on together quite well, I imagine,' Vittorio replied easily. Ana wanted to scream.

You're not attracted to me, she wanted to shout. *I saw how you looked at me in that first moment—you summed me up and dismissed me! And now you want to marry me?*

She'd convinced herself she could live without love. But desire? Attraction? Could she give her body to a man who looked at her with disdain or, worse, disgust? Could she live with herself, if she did that, day after day?

'Ana, what are you thinking?' Vittorio's voice was gentle, concerned. She almost wanted to tell him, yet she knew she couldn't bear the truth of his confession, or the deception of his denial. She let out a long shuddering breath.

'Surely there are other women who fulfil your criteria,' she said at last.

Vittorio shook his head. 'No. There are few women with your knowledge of wine, Ana, or of this region. And of course your vineyard combined with mine would give us both a legacy for our children. And I appreciate your breeding and class—'

'You make me sound like a horse. I'm as good as, aren't I?' Calm once more, she spoke without rancour, merely stating the rather glum fact.

'Then consider me one as well.'

'A stallion, you mean?' and her mouth quirked upwards

with wry amusement in spite of all the hurt and disappointment she felt.

'Of course.' Vittorio matched her smile. 'If I am considering this marriage a business, there is no reason you cannot as
well. We are each other's mutual assets.'

Ana bit her lip. He made it sound so easy, so obvious. So natural, as if bartering a marriage over billiards in this day and age
was a perfectly normal and acceptable thing to do. Vittorio had
already told her he would not love her. Yet, Ana asked herself
with bleak honesty, would someone else, *if* she were interested
in love, which she'd already told herself she wasn't? Funny how
much convincing that took.

She would be thirty years old in just two months. She hadn't
had a date of any kind in over five years, and the last one had
been appalling, an awkward few hours with a man with whom
she'd shared not one point of sympathy. She'd never had a serious boyfriend. She'd never had *sex*. Was Vittorio's offer the
best she'd get?

And, Ana acknowledged as she sneaked a glance at him from
under her lashes, she could certainly do worse. He'd shed his
jacket and tie and undone the top two buttons of his shirt. Under
the smooth luxurious fabric, his muscles moved in sinuous elegance. His dark hair gleamed in the dimly lit room like polished ebony. The harsh lines of his jaw and cheek were starkly
beautiful... He was beautiful. And he wanted to be her husband.

The thought was incredible. Insane. It couldn't work. It
wouldn't. Vittorio would come to his senses, Ana would feel
that devastating disappointment once again.

He wouldn't desire her. She'd see it in his eyes, feel it in his
body—

And yet. Yet. Even now, she considered it. Even now, her
mind raced to find possibilities, solutions. *Hope.* Some part of
her wanted to marry Vittorio. Some part of her wanted that life.
That, Ana knew, was why she hadn't dismissed him immediately and utterly. It was why she was asking questions, voic-

ing objections as if this absurd and insulting proposal had any merit. Because, to some small suppressed part of her soul, it *did*.

Ana stood up and reached for her cue stick. 'Let's play,' she said, her voice brusque. She didn't want to talk any more. She didn't want to think about any of it. She just wanted to beat the hell out of the Count of Cazlevara.

Vittorio watched as Ana shrugged off her boxy jacket, tossing it onto a chair. She glanced over her shoulder, her eyes dark and smoky with challenge. 'Ready?'

Vittorio felt his insides tighten with a sudden surprising coil of desire. One sharp dart of lust. Without that awful jacket, he could actually see some of Ana's body. She wore a hugging top of creamy beaded silk that pulled taut over her generous breasts as she leaned forward to line up her shot. Vittorio found his gaze fixed first on the back of her neck, where a long tendril of dark hair lay curled against her skin. Her hair wasn't brown, he realized absently, it was myriad colours. Brown and black and red and even gold. His gaze dropped instinctively lower, to her backside. Bent over the billiards table, the fabric of her trousers pulled tightly across her bottom. The realization caused another shaft of lust to slice through him and he found he was gripping his cue stick rather tightly. He'd thought she had a mannish figure because she was tall. Yet, seeing her now, her curves on surprising and provocative display, he realized she wasn't mannish at all.

She still wasn't the kind of woman he normally took to bed, and he would never call her pretty. Even so, that brief stab of lust reassured him, made him realize this could work. He would make it work. Ana was intrigued, interested; she hadn't said no. He'd expected her to say no immediately, a gut reaction. But she hadn't betrayed her own desire—he'd seen it before, at dinner, a flaring in her eyes—as well as, perhaps, her own sense of logic.

When he'd spoken to Enrico about the match, the old man had been surprised but accepting.

'Ana is a practical girl,' he'd said after a moment. 'She will see the advantages.'

Vittorio could see her now, considering those advantages, wondering if the comforts he could give her outweighed the lack of feeling. And yet there would be feeling…affection, respect. He wanted to *like* Ana; he simply didn't want to love her.

And, Vittorio acknowledged with a surprised wryness, he would desire her. Somewhat, at least.

Ana took her shot and then stepped aside so Vittorio could take his. As he passed by her, he inhaled her scent; she wore no perfume and smelled of soap and something else, something impossible to define. Dirt, he realized after a moment and nearly missed his shot. She smelled of sunshine and soil, of the vineyard he'd seen her stride through only days ago, as if she owned the world, or at least all of it that mattered.

It was not a smell he normally associated with a woman.

He straightened, stepping back so Ana could take her shot, making sure to step close enough to her so his elbow brushed her breast, as if by accident, just to see how she reacted. And how *he* reacted. Ana drew her breath in sharply; Vittorio shifted his weight to ease the intensifying ache of need in his groin.

She was untouched, he was sure of it. Untouched and untamed. And, despite the terrible clothes, the complete lack of feminine guile or charm or artifice, at that moment he wanted her. He wanted her, and he wanted to marry her.

He *would*.

She won. Ana knew she should feel triumph at this victory, yet in the light of everything else she found she felt little at all.

'It seems I must concede the game,' Vittorio said as he replaced his cue stick in the holder. 'Congratulations. You did warn me.'

'So I did.' Ana replaced her cue stick as well. She felt awkward now the game of *stecca* was over; a glance at her watch told her it was nearly midnight. They hadn't spoken of the whole wretched business proposition in over an hour, and she wasn't sure she wanted to bring it up now.

'So,' Vittorio said briskly, 'you'll need a few days to think about my business proposition?'

Vittorio obviously did not share her reluctance. 'A few days?' Ana repeated, her voice rising to something close to a squawk. 'Vittorio, I don't think—'

'Surely you won't dismiss it out of hand?' he countered, cutting off the objection she hadn't even known how to finish. He leaned against the billiards table, smiling, at ease, his powerful forearms folded. 'That is not good business, Ana.'

'Perhaps I don't want my marriage to be business,' she replied a bit stiffly.

Vittorio's gaze dropped to her mouth. She could *feel* his eyes there, on her lips, almost as if he were touching her. She could imagine his finger tracing the outline of her lips even though he hadn't moved. *She* had; she'd parted her lips in a silent yearning invitation. Her body betrayed her again and again. 'I think it could be good between us, Ana,' he said softly. 'Good in so many ways.'

His words thrilled her. They shouldn't—words counted for so little—but they did. They gave her hope, made her wonder if Vittorio could see her as a woman. A woman he wanted not just with his mind, but with his body. Unlike Roberto.

'In fact,' he continued, his voice as soft and sinuous as silk, 'as we have just finished a game where you soundly trounced me, we could shake hands.'

Automatically, Ana stuck out her hand, ignoring the tiny flip-flop of disappointment at his sensible suggestion. This was how she did business, had been doing it for years. In a man's world, she acted like a man. It made sense. It made sense *now*.

'I said we *could*,' Vittorio said, his voice so soft, almost languorous, and yet with a little hint of amusement. 'I didn't say we would.' His eyes glittered, his own mouth parting as hers had, and he leaned forward so when she breathed in she inhaled his musky scent. 'Instead, how about a kiss?'

'A kiss?' Ana repeated blankly as if she didn't understand the word. But oh, she did—already she could imagine it, wanted it, *needed* it: the feel of Vittorio's lips on hers, hard and soft at the same time, his hands on her waist or even— 'That's not how I do business, Vittorio.'

'But this business is a little different, is it not? And we should perhaps make sure we suit. That we are,' he clarified in that soft, dangerous voice, 'in fact attracted to one another.'

Again, his words rippled through her with a frisson of excitement and hope; it was a heady, potent mix. Was he actually saying he could be attracted to her? That he *was*? 'I don't think that's a good idea,' Ana said stubbornly, yet she heard the longing in her own voice. So did Vittorio.

He smiled. Although he hadn't moved—he was still leaning against the billiards table, his arms folded—he exuded a lethal grace and Ana could all too easily imagine him closing the distance between them, taking her into his arms and... For heaven's sake, she'd read too many romance novels. Had too many desperate dreams.

That was just what she *wanted* him to do.

'I think it's a very good idea.'

'You don't want to kiss me,' she said, meaning it as a blunt statement of fact. Yet, even as she said the words she was conscious of how Vittorio looked *now*. There was no lip-curl of disdain, no dismissive flick of the eyes. His eyes were dark, dilated, his cheeks suffused with colour. She felt the answering colour rise up in her own cheeks, flood through her own body.

'Oh, but I do,' he murmured, and Ana realized just how much she wanted him to want to kiss her. And she wanted it too; she'd realized that a long time ago, but now she knew she was going to do it. It had become both a challenge and a craving.

'All right, then,' she said and, smiling a little, her heart thudding sickly, she stepped forward, straight into his arms. She'd been moving too fast and Vittorio's hands came up to steady her, gripping her bare shoulders so she didn't smack straight into his chest. Still, she felt the hard length of his body against hers, every nerve and sinew leaping to life in a way they never had before. This was so new, so intimate, so *wonderful*.

His lips were a millimetre from hers as he whispered, 'I like that when you decide to do something, you do it completely, with your whole heart.'

'Yes, I do,' Ana answered, and kissed him. She wasn't a good kisser. She knew that; she'd had too little experience. She was unschooled, clumsy, her lips hard against his, pressing, not knowing what to do. Feeling a fool.

Then Vittorio opened his mouth, somehow softening his lips—how did he do that? Ana wondered fuzzily—before she stopped thinking at all. His tongue slipped into the warmth of her own mouth, surprising her and causing a deep lightning shaft of pleasure to go right through her belly and down to her toes. Her hands came up of their own accord and bunched on his shirt, pulling him closer so their hips collided and she felt the full evidence of his desire; he hadn't been lying. He *had* wanted to kiss her.

That knowledge thrilled her, consumed her with its wonderful truth. This was not a man who had been left cold by her kiss, by her body. His body had betrayed *him*. Right now, at least, he wanted her. As a woman.

A sense of power and triumph surged through her, making her bold. Her hands slid down the slippery fabric of his shirt to the curve of his backside, pulling him towards her. She heard Vittorio's little inhalation of shock and smiled against his lips. He moaned into her mouth.

His mouth remained on hers, exploring the contours of her tongue and teeth, nipping and sliding, the intimate invasion making Ana's head spin and her breath shorten. She'd never known kissing could be like this. The few chaste pecks and stolen smacks at the end of a date didn't compare, didn't even count—

And then it was over. Vittorio released her and Ana took a stumbling step backwards, her fingers flying to her swollen lips.

'Well...' she managed. Her mind was still fuzzy, her senses still consumed by what had just occurred. Then she looked at Vittorio and saw how smug he seemed. He was smiling as if he'd just proved something, and Ana supposed he had.

'I think that quite settles the matter, wouldn't you say?'

'Nothing's settled,' Ana retorted sharply. She wouldn't have her future decided by a simple kiss—even if there hadn't been anything simple about it at all. It had been amazing and affirming and even transforming, the evidence of Vittorio's desire changing everything—or at least it *could* change everything. 'You said I should have a few days to consider.'

'At least you want to consider it now,' Vittorio replied, and Ana knew nothing she said could take away his smug sense of superiority that he'd been able to kiss her senseless. He looked completely recovered, if he had been shaken by that kiss, which Ana suspected he had not. Not like she had. All right, he'd desired her—for a moment—but perhaps any man would react the same way when a woman threw herself at him, which was essentially what Ana had done.

Except Roberto hadn't. When she'd thrown herself at *him*, desperate to prove herself desirable, he'd remained as still and cold as a statue, as unmoved and emotionless as a block of cold marble. And when she'd finished—pressing herself against him, kissing those slack lips, he'd actually stepped back and said in a voice filled with affront, 'Ana, I never thought of you that way.' A pause, horrible, endless, and then the most damning words of all: 'How could I?'

Still, Ana thought, gazing at Vittorio with barely disguised hunger, was that brief stab of desire—that amazing kiss— enough to base a marriage on? Along with the respect and affection and everything else Vittorio had promised?

'I'll consider it,' she said at last. 'I didn't say I would say yes.'

'Of course.'

Ana touched her lips again, then dropped her hand, knowing how revealing that little gesture was. 'I should go home.'

'I'll have my driver take you.' Vittorio smiled wryly. 'I'm afraid I've drunk a bit too much whisky to handle a car myself, and of course I would never jeopardise your safety.'

Ana nodded in acceptance, and Vittorio pressed the button by the door again. Within seconds a servant appeared. He issued some quick instructions, and then turned back to Ana. 'I'll see you to the door.'

They didn't speak as he led her through several stone corridors back to the huge entryway of the castle. The doors were already open and a driver—in uniform, even at this hour—waited on the front step.

'So this is goodbye,' Ana said a bit unevenly.

Vittorio tucked a tendril of hair behind her ear, his fingers trailing her cheek. That smugness had left his eyes and he looked softer now, if only for a moment. 'For now.'

Ana tried not to react to the touch of his hand. She felt incredibly unsettled, uncertain, unable to believe that the kiss they had just shared was real, that it could possibly mean something. At least to her. She had a horrible sick feeling that Vittorio, inflamed by a bit of whisky, had been acting on his baser instincts, trying to prove that this marriage bargain could actually work.

And he'd almost convinced her that it could.

Too tired to think any more, Ana slipped into the interior of the limo—the Porsche, it seemed, was reserved for Vittorio's exclusive use—and laid her head back against the seat as the driver sped away from Castle Cazlevara back to her home.

Vittorio watched the car disappear down the curving drive with a deep, primal sense of satisfaction. He'd as good as branded her with that kiss; she was his. In a matter of days, weeks at the most, she would be his bride. His wife. He felt sure of it.

He couldn't keep the sense of victory from rushing through him, headier than any wine. He'd set out to acquire a wife and, in a matter of days—a week at the most—he would have one. Mission accomplished.

He imagined the look on his mother's face when he told her he was getting married; he leaped ahead to the moment when he held his son, and saw Bernardo's dreams of becoming Count, of taking control of Cazlevara Wines, crumble to nothing. He pictured his mother looking stunned, lost, and then the image suddenly changed of its own accord and instead he saw her smiling into the face of his child, her grandchild. A baby girl.

Vittorio banished the image almost instantly. It didn't make sense. The only relationship he'd ever had with his mother had been one of, at worst, animosity and, at best, indifference. And he didn't want a girl; he needed sons.

Yet still the image—the idea—needled him, annoyed him, because it made a strange longing rise up in a way he didn't understand, a way that almost felt like sorrow.

Vittorio pushed it aside once more and considered the practicalities instead. Of course, there were risks. With any business proposition, there were risks. Ana might not fall pregnant easily, or they might only have girls. Baby girls, all wrapped in pink—Vittorio dismissed these possibilities, too exultant to dwell on such concerns.

He supposed he should have married long ago and thus secured his position, yet he'd never even considered it. He'd been too intent on avoiding his home, on securing his own future. He'd never thought of his heirs.

He'd run away, Vittorio knew, the actions of a hurt child. Amazing how much power and pain those memories still held. His mother's averted face, the way she'd pushed him down when he'd attempted to clamber on her lap. He'd stopped trying after a while. By the time he was four—when Bernardo had been born—he'd regarded his mother with a certain wariness, the way you would a sleeping tiger in a zoo. Fascinating, beauti-

insisted on a full English breakfast every day and, sixteen years after her death, Enrico still continued the tradition.

'Good morning!' he called brightly. 'You were out late last night. I waited up until eleven.'

'You shouldn't have.' Almost reluctantly, Ana came into the dining room, dropping her usual kiss on her father's head. She wasn't ready to talk to her father, to ask him how much he knew. She remembered his lack of surprise at Vittorio's return, or the fact that he'd asked her out to dinner. Had he known—could he possibly have imagined—just what the business proposition was? The thought sent something strange and alarming coursing through Ana's blood. She didn't know whether it was fear or joy, or something in between. Had Vittorio asked her father for his *blessing*? How long had he been planning this?

'Come, have some breakfast. The kippers are especially good this morning.'

Ana made a face as she grabbed a roll from the sideboard and poured herself a coffee from the porcelain pot left on the table. 'You know I can't abide kippers.'

'But they're so delicious,' Enrico said with a smile, and ate one.

Ana sat down opposite him, sipping her coffee even though it was too hot. 'I can only stay a moment,' she warned. 'I need to go down to the offices.'

'But Ana! It's Saturday.'

Ana shrugged; she often worked on Saturdays, especially in the busy growing season. 'The grapes don't stop for anyone, Papà.'

'How was your dinner with Vittorio?'

'Interesting.'

'He wanted to discuss business?' Enrico asked in far too neutral a tone.

Ana looked at him directly, daring him to be dishonest. 'Papà, did Vittorio speak to you about this—this business proposition of his?'

Enrico looked down, shredding a kipper onto his plate with the tines of his fork. 'Perhaps,' he said very quietly.

Ana didn't know whether to be disappointed or relieved or, even, strangely flattered. She felt a confusing welter of emotions, so she could only shake her head and ask with genuine curiosity, 'And what did you think of it?'

'I was surprised, at first.' He looked up, smiling wryly, although his eyes were serious. 'As I imagine you were.'

'Completely.' The single word was heartfelt.

'But then I thought about it—and Vittorio showed me the advantages—'

'What advantages?' What could Vittorio have said to convince her father that he should allow his daughter to marry him as a matter of convenience? For surely, Ana knew now, her father was convinced.

'Many, Ana. Stability, security.'

'I have those—'

'Children. Companionship.' He paused and then said softly, 'Happiness.'

'You think Vittorio Cazlevara could make me happy?' Ana asked. She didn't sound sceptical; she felt genuinely curious. She wanted to know. Could he make her happy? Why was she thinking this way? She'd been happy... Yet at that moment Ana couldn't pretend she didn't want more, that she didn't want the things her father had mentioned. Children. A home of her own. To kiss Vittorio again, to taste him...

Some last bastion of common sense must have remained for she burst out suddenly, 'We're talking about *marriage*, Papà.' Her voice broke on the word. 'A life commitment. Not some... some sort of transaction.' Even if Vittorio had presented it as such.

'What is your objection?' Enrico asked, his fingertips pressed together, his head cocked to one side. He'd always been a logical man; some would call him unemotional. Even after the death of his beloved wife, his calm exterior had barely cracked.

Ana remembered the one time he'd truly shown his grief, rocking and keening on Emily's bedroom floor; as a girl, the sudden, uncontrollable display of emotion had shocked her. He'd closed her off from it, slammed the door and then, with a far worse finality, shut himself off from her rather than let his daughter see him in such a state of emotional weakness. The separation at such a crucial time had devastated her.

It had been two years before they'd regained the relationship they'd once had.

Now she knew she couldn't really be surprised that he was approaching the issue of her possible marriage with such a cool head.

Vittorio's arguments would have appealed marvellously to his own sense of checks and balances. Indeed, she shared his sense of logic, prided herself on her lack of feminine fancy. After living with her father as her lone companion for most of her life, the sentimental theatrics of most women were cloying and abhorrent. She didn't, Ana reflected with a wry sorrow, even know how to be a woman.

Yet Vittorio had treated her as one, when he'd kissed her...

Even so. *Marriage*...

'My objection,' she said, 'is the entire idea of marriage as a business proposition. It seems so cold.'

'But surely it doesn't have to be? Better to go into such an enterprise with a clear head, reasonable expectations—'

'I still don't even understand why Vittorio wants to marry me—' Ana said, stopping suddenly, wishing she hadn't betrayed herself. Just like her father, she hated to be vulnerable. She knew what it felt like to be so exposed, so raw, and then so rejected.

'He needs a wife. He must be in his late thirties, you know, and a man starts to think of his future, his children—'

'But why me?' The words came, as unstoppable as the fears and doubts that motivated them. 'He could have anyone, anyone at all—'

'Why not you, Ana?' Enrico asked gently. 'You would make any man a wonderful wife.'

Ana's mouth twisted. Her father also called her *dolcezza*. Sweet little thing. He was her father, her *papà*; of course he believed such things. That didn't mean *she* believed them, or him. 'Still, there would be no love involved.'

Enrico gave a little shrug. 'In time, it comes.'

She was shredding her roll onto her plate, just as her father had done with his poor little kipper. Her appetite—what little there had been of it—had completely vanished. She looked up at her father and shook her head. 'With Vittorio, I don't think so.' Her throat went tight, and she cursed herself for a fool. She didn't *need* love. She'd convinced herself of that long ago. She didn't even want it, and she couldn't fathom why she'd mentioned it to her father.

Her father remained unfazed. 'Still, affection. Respect. These things count for much, *dolcezza*. More perhaps than you can even imagine now, when love seems so important.'

'Yet you loved Mamma.'

Her father nodded, his face seeming to crumple just a little bit. Even sixteen years on, he still lived for her memory.

'Don't you think I want that kind of love too?' Ana asked, her voice turning raw. Despite what she'd said—what she believed—she needed to know her father's answer.

Enrico didn't speak for a moment. He poured himself another cup of coffee and sipped it thoughtfully. 'That kind of love,' he finally said, 'is not easy. It is not comfortable.'

'I never said I wanted to be comfortable.'

'Comfort,' Enrico told her with a little smile, 'is always underrated by those who have experienced nothing else.'

'Are you saying you weren't…comfortable…with Mamma?' The idea was a novel one, and one Ana didn't like to consider too closely. She'd always believed her parents to have had the grandest of love matches, adoring each other to the end. A fairy tale, and one she'd clung to in those first dark days of grief. Yet now her father seemed to be implying something else.

'I loved her,' Enrico replied. 'And I was happy. But comfortable, always? No. Your mother was a wonderful woman, Ana, be assured of that. But she was emotional—and I'm the one who is Italian!' He smiled, the curve of his mouth tinged with a little sadness. 'It was not always easy to live with someone who felt things so deeply.' Snatches of memory came to her, swirls of colour and sound. Her mother crying, the cloying scent of a sick room, the murmurs of a doctor as her father shook his head. And then her mother pulling her close, whispering fervently against her hair how she, Ana, would be the only one, the only child. Love, Ana thought, did not protect you from sorrow. Perhaps it only softened the blow.

Enrico put down his coffee cup and gave Ana a level look. 'Be careful to realize what you would be giving up by not marrying Vittorio, Ana.'

Ana drew back, stung. 'What are you saying? That I might as well take the best offer—the only offer—I can get?'

'No, of course I am not saying that,' Enrico said gently. 'But it is a very good offer.'

Ana sipped her coffee, moodily acknowledging the truth of her father's words. She'd only given voice to her own fears—that there would be no other offers. Would she rather live alone, childless, lonely—because, face it, she *was*—than attempt some kind of marriage with Vittorio? She didn't know the answer. She could hardly believe she was actually asking herself the question.

'Vittorio is a good man,' Enrico said quietly.

'How do you know?' Ana challenged. 'He's been away for fifteen years.'

'I knew his father. Vittorio was the apple of Arturo's eye. Arturo was a good man too, but he was hard.' Enrico frowned a little. 'Without mercy.'

'And what if Vittorio is the same?' She remembered the steely glint in his eye and wondered just how well she knew him. Not well at all, was the obvious answer. Certainly not well enough to marry him.

And yet…he *was* a good man. She felt that in her bones, in a certain settling of her soul. She believed her father and, more importantly, she believed Vittorio.

It's all right to be sad, rondinella.

'Vittorio needs a wife to soften him,' Enrico said with a smile.

'I don't want him to be my project,' Ana protested. 'Or for me to be his.' She was so prickly, had been so ever since Vittorio had proposed—if you could call it proposing. The word conjured images of roses and diamond rings and declarations of undying love. Not a cold-blooded contract.

'Of course not,' Enrico agreed, 'but you know, in marriage, you are each other's projects. You don't seek to change each other, but it is hoped that you will affect one another, shape and smooth each other's rough edges.'

Ana made a face. 'You make it sound like two rocks in a stream.'

'But that's exactly it,' Enrico exclaimed. 'Two rocks rubbing along together in the river of life.'

Ana let out a reluctant laugh. 'Now, really, Papà, you are waxing far too philosophical for me. I must get to work.' She rose from the table, kissing him again, and went to get her shoes and coat; a light spring drizzle was falling.

Once at the winery, she immersed herself in what she loved best. Business. *Just like Vittorio*, a sly little voice inside her mind whispered, but Ana pushed it away. She wasn't going to think about Vittorio or marriage or any of it until noon, at least.

In fact, she barely lifted her head from the papers scattered over her desk until Edoardo knocked on her door in the late afternoon. 'A package, Signorina Viale.'

'A package?' Ana blinked him into focus. 'You mean a delivery?'

'Not for the winery,' Edoardo said. 'It is marked personal. For you. It was dropped off—by the Count of Cazlevara.'

Ana stilled, her heart suddenly pounding far too fiercely. Vittorio had been here, had sent her something? Anticipation raced through her, made her dizzy with longing. Somehow she managed to nod stiffly, with apparent unconcern, and raised one hand to beckon him. 'Bring it in, please.'

The box was white, long and narrow and tied with a satin ribbon in pale lavender. Roses, Ana thought. It must be. She felt mingled disappointment and anticipation; roses were beautiful, but when it came to flowers they were expected and a bit, well, ordinary. It didn't take much thought to send a woman roses.

Still, she hadn't received roses or any other flowers in years, so she opened the box with some excitement, only to discover he hadn't sent roses at all.

He'd sent grapes.

She stared at the freshly cut vines with their cluster of new, perfect, pearl-like grapes and then bent her head to breathe in their wonderful earthy scent. There was a stiff little card nestled among the leaves. Ana picked it up and read:

A new hybrid of Vinifera and Rotundifolia, from the Americas, that I thought you'd be interested in.—V.

She flicked the card against her fingers and then, betrayingly, pressed it against her lips. It smelled fresh and faintly pungent, like the grapes. She closed her eyes. This, she realized, was much better than roses, and she had a feeling Vittorio knew it.

Was this his way of romancing her? Or simply convincing her? Showing her the benefits of such business?

Did it even matter? He'd done it; he'd known what she'd like, and Ana found she was pleased.

For the rest of the day Ana immersed herself in work, determined not to think of Vittorio or the spray of grapes that remained on her desk, in plain view. Yet she couldn't quite keep the thoughts—the hopes—from slipping slyly into her mind. She found herself constructing a thousand what-ifs. *What if we married? What if we had a child? What if we actually were happy?*

These thoughts—tempting, dangerous—continued to dance along the fringes of her mind over the next week. She caught herself more than once, chin in hand, lost in a daydream that was vague enough to seem reasonable. Possible. She found she was arguing with herself, listing the reasons why a marriage of convenience was perfectly sensible. Why it was, in fact, a good idea.

She didn't see Vittorio all week, but every day there was something from him: a newspaper article on a new wine, a bar of dark chocolate—how did he know that was her secret indulgence?—a spray of lilacs. Ana accepted each gift, found herself savouring them, even as she knew why he was doing it. It was, undoubtedly, a means to an end, a way of showing her how it could be between them.

I think it could be good between us, Ana... Good in so many ways.

Remembering how it had felt to kiss him—how he'd felt, the evidence of his own arousal—made Ana agree with him. Or, at least, want to agree with him. And want to experience it again.

A week after her dinner with Vittorio, as the day came to a close, the sun starting its orange descent, Ana left the winery office and decided to walk the half-kilometre home along the winding dirt track, her mind still brimming with those seductive what-ifs. A new wealth of possibilities was opening up to her, things she'd never hoped to have. A husband, a child, a home, a life beyond what she'd already made for herself, what she'd been happy to have until Vittorio stirred up these latent desires like a nest of writhing serpents. Ana wondered if they could ever be coaxed to sleep again.

If she said no, could she go back to her life with the endless work days and few evenings out among old men and fellow winemakers? Could she lull to sleep those deep and dangerous desires for a husband, a family, a home—a castle, even—of her own? Could she stop craving another kiss and, more than that, so much more, the feel of another's body against hers, that wonderful spiral of desire uncoiling and rising within her, demanding to be sated?

No, Ana acknowledged, she couldn't, not easily anyway and, even more revealingly, she didn't want to. She wanted to feel Vittorio's lips against hers again. She wanted to know the touch of his hands on her body. She wanted to be married, to live and learn together like the two stones her father had been talking about.

Even if there was no love. She didn't need it.

Stopping suddenly right there in the road, Ana laughed aloud. Was her decision already made? Was she actually going to marry Vittorio?

No. Surely she couldn't make such a monumental decision so quickly, so carelessly. Surely her life was worth more than that.

Yet, even as common sense argued its case, her heart and body were warring against it, lost in a world of wonderful—and sensual—possibility.

Slowly, she started walking again; the sun was low in the sky, sending long lavender rays across the horizon. Villa Rosso appeared in the distance, its windows winking in the sunlight, its long, low stone façade so familiar and dear. If she married Vittorio, she wouldn't live there any more. Her father would be alone. The thought stopped her once more in the road; could she do that? Could she leave her father after all they'd shared and endured together? She knew he would want her to do so; this marriage—should it happen—already had his blessing.

Still, it would be hard, painful even. It made her realize afresh just how enormous a decision she was contemplating.

Could she actually say yes? Was she brave—and foolish—enough to do it?

As she came closer to the house, she saw a familiar navy

Porsche parked in the drive. Vittorio's car. He was inside, waiting for her, and the realization made her insides flip right over. She'd *missed* him, she realized incredulously; she'd expected him to come before now.

She'd *wanted* him to come.

At the front step she took a moment to brush the hair away from her face and wipe the dust from her shoes before she opened the door and stepped into the foyer.

It was empty, but she followed the voices into the study, where she checked at the sight of Vittorio and her father in what looked like a cosy tête-à-tête. Enrico looked up and smiled as she entered, and Vittorio stood.

'We were just talking about you,' Enrico said with a little smile and, despite the treacherous beating of her heart, Ana smiled rather coolly back.

'Were you? What a surprise.'

'I came to see if you'd like to have dinner with me,' Vittorio said. He seemed entirely unruffled at being caught gossiping about her with her father.

Ana hesitated. She wanted to have dinner with Vittorio again but suddenly she also felt uncertain, afraid. Of what, she could not even say. She was afraid to rush, to show her own eagerness. She needed time to sort her thoughts and perhaps even to steel her heart. 'I'm not dressed—'

'No matter.'

She glanced down at her grey wool trousers and plain white blouse—which, aggravatingly, had become untucked. Again. 'Really?'

Vittorio arched his eyebrows, a smile playing around his mouth. 'Really.' And, though he said nothing more, Ana knew he was surmising that she had a wardrobe of similarly unappealing clothes upstairs. At least they were clean and freshly ironed.

Still, she accepted the challenge. Why should she change for Vittorio? Why should she attempt to look pretty—if such a thing could be done—for the sake of this business arrangement? She lifted her chin. 'Fine. Let me just wash my face and hands at least.' He nodded, and Ana walked quickly from the room, trying to ignore the hurt that needled her, the little sink of her heart at his indifference to her clothes, her appearance. She wanted Vittorio to care how she looked. She wanted him to *like* how she looked.

Get over it, her mind told her, the words hard and determined. *If you're going to marry him, this is how it is going to be.*

Her heart sank a little further. She wished it hadn't.

Within just a few minutes they were speeding down the darkening drive, away from Villa Rosso, the windows open to the fragrant evening air.

'Where are we going?' Ana asked as the hair she'd just tidied blew into tangles around her face.

'Venice.'

'Venice!' she nearly yelped. 'I'm not dressed for *that*—'

Vittorio's glance was hooded yet smiling. 'Let me worry about that.'

Ana sat back, wondering just how and why Vittorio was going to worry about her clothes. The idea made her uneasy.

She found out soon enough. Vittorio parked the Porsche at Fusina and they boarded a ferry for the ten-minute ride into the city that allowed no cars. As the worn stone buildings and narrow canals with their sleepy-looking gondolas and ancient arched bridges came into view, Ana felt a frisson of expectation and even hope. What city was more romantic than Venice? And just why was Vittorio taking her here?

After they disembarked, he led her away from the Piazza San Marco, crowded with tourists, to Frezzeria, a narrow street lined with upscale boutiques. Most of them had already closed, but all it took was Vittorio rapping once on the glass door of one for the clerk inside, a chic-looking woman with hair in a tight chignon, wearing a silk blouse and a black pencil skirt, to open the door and kiss him on both cheeks.

A ridiculous, totally unreasonable dart of jealousy stabbed

Ana, and fury followed it when the woman swept her assessingly critical gaze over her and said, 'This is the one?'

'Yes.'

She snapped her fingers. 'Come with me.'

Ana turned to Vittorio, her eyes narrowed. 'You talked about me?' she said in an angry undertone, choosing to show anger over the hurt she felt inside, a raw, open wound to the heart. She could only imagine the conversation Vittorio must have had with this woman, talking about her hopeless clothes, her terrible taste, how pathetic and *ugly* she was…

She tasted bile, swallowed. What a fool she'd been.

'She's here to help you, Ana,' Vittorio murmured. 'Go with her.'

Ana could see racks of gorgeous-looking clothes—a rainbow of silks and satins—in the back of the boutique. They beckoned to her, surprisingly, because she'd never been a girly kind of woman. She'd avoided all things feminine, mostly out of necessity. She didn't want to look ridiculous. Yet the enticement of the clothes was no match for the hurt—and fury—she felt now.

'Perhaps I don't want help,' she snapped. 'Did you ever consider that?'

Vittorio remained unfazed. 'Is that true?' he asked calmly, so clearly confident of the answer. Humiliatingly, his gaze raked over her, more eloquent than anything he could have said. Ana's cheeks burned.

The woman appeared once more in the doorway, her lips pursed in impatience. She was holding a gown over one arm, frothy with lace. Ana had never seen anything so beautiful. She could not imagine wearing such a thing, or what she would look like in it. It could not possibly be her size.

'Ana,' Vittorio murmured, 'you will look beautiful in these clothes. Surely you want to look beautiful?'

'Perhaps I just want to be myself,' Ana said quietly. She didn't add that she was afraid she *wouldn't* look beautiful in those clothes, or that she wished he thought she looked beautiful already. It was too difficult to explain, too absurd even to feel. She didn't want Vittorio to want to change her, even if she was willing to be changed. Stupid, unreasonable, perhaps, but true. She shook her head and pushed past him to the door. 'I'm sorry, Vittorio, but I'm not going to be your Cinderella project.'

Vittorio stifled a curse as he called back to Feliciana before following Ana out into the street. He'd thought she would appreciate the clothes, the opportunity to look, for once, like a woman. He'd thought he was giving her a *gift*. Instead, she acted offended. Would he ever understand women? Vittorio wondered in annoyed exasperation. He'd *thought* he understood women; he was certainly good with them. Allow them unlimited access to clothes and jewels and they'd love you for ever—or think they did.

Not that he wanted Ana's love, but her gratitude would have been appreciated at this point. He gazed at her, her arms wrapped around herself, her hair blowing in the breeze off the canal, and wondered if he'd ever understand her. He'd thought it would be simple, easy. He'd thought her an open book, to be read—and discarded—at his own leisure. The realization that she was far more complicated, that he'd managed to dismiss her before even getting to know her, was both annoying and shaming.

'I think perhaps you should take me home.'

'We have reservations at one of the finest restaurants in Venice,' Vittorio said, his voice clipped, his teeth gritted. 'That's why I brought you to this boutique—so you could be dressed appropriately, preferably in a dress!'

'If you want to marry me,' Ana replied evenly, 'then you need to accept me as I am. I won't change for you, Vittorio.'

'Not even your clothes?' He couldn't keep the caustic note out of his voice. The woman was impossible. And, damnation, she was blinking back tears. He hadn't meant to make her cry;

the last thing he needed now was *tears*. He'd hurt her, and his annoyance and shame deepened, cutting him. Hurting *him*. 'Ana—'

She shook her head, half-talking to herself. 'I don't know why I ever thought—hoped, even—that this could work. You don't know me at all. We're *strangers*—'

'Of course I don't know you!' he snapped. Impatience bit at him, the swamping sense of his own failure overtook him. He'd lost control of the situation, and he had no idea how it had happened. When she'd come into the villa this evening and he'd seen how her eyes had lit at the sight of him, he'd felt so confident. So sure that she was going to marry him, that she'd already said yes in her mind, if not her heart. Hearts need not be involved.

Yet, even as Vittorio reminded himself of this, he realized how impossible a situation this truly was. He wanted to be kind to Ana; he wanted affection and respect to bud and grow. He wanted her loyalty; he just didn't want her to fall in love with him.

Yet there seemed no danger of that right now.

'I thought,' he finally said, 'this could be an opportunity for us to get to know one another.'

'After you've changed me.'

'After I bought you a dress!' Vittorio exploded. 'Most women would have been thrilled—'

'Well, I'm not most women,' Ana snapped. Her cheeks glowed with colour and her eyes were a steely grey. She looked, Vittorio thought with a flash of surprise, magnificent. Like a woman warrior, Boadicea, magnificent in her self-righteous anger, and all that vengeful fury was directed at him. 'And *most* women I know,' she spat, 'wouldn't entertain your business proposition for a single minute!' With that, her eyes still shooting angry sparks at him, she turned on her heel and stormed down Frezzeria towards the Piazza.

This time Vittorio cursed aloud.

* * *

Standing alone, crowds of tourists pushing past her, Ana wondered if she should have gone back with that stick-thin saleswoman and tried on those gorgeous clothes. In one part of her mind—the part that still managed to remain cool and logical—she knew Vittorio had been trying to please her. Surprise her with a gift. It would have been the kind thing—the sensible thing—to accept it and go back into that dressing room. Part of her had even wanted to.

And part of her had been afraid to, and another part had wished Vittorio didn't want to improve her. No matter what her father had said about smoothing stones and that ridiculous river of life, she didn't want Vittorio to improve her. She wouldn't be his little project.

And if he was thinking of marrying her—if she was actually still considering marrying him—then she knew he needed to accept that. Accept *her*.

She'd only walked a few metres before Vittorio caught up, grabbing her by the arm none too gently. 'How are you planning on returning home?' he asked, his voice coldly furious and, angry again, Ana shrugged off his arm.

'Fortunately, there are such things as water taxis.'

'Ana—' Vittorio stopped helplessly and Ana knew he was utterly bewildered by her behaviour. Well, that made two of them. She stopped walking, her head bowed.

'I know you think you meant well,' she began, only to stop when Vittorio laughed dryly.

'Oh, dear,' he said. 'I've *really* botched it then, haven't I?'

She looked up, trying to smile. 'I just—' She took a breath, trying to explain without making herself utterly vulnerable. It was impossible. 'I don't wear dresses for a reason, Vittorio. It's not simply that I have appalling taste in clothes.' He looked so surprised, she almost laughed. 'Is that what you thought? That I don't know a designer gown from a bin bag?'

'I didn't—' he began, and now she did laugh. She'd never expected to see the Count of Cazlevara so discomfited.

'I'm a full-figured five foot eleven,' she said flatly. 'Designer gowns generally don't run in my size.'

Surprise flashed briefly in Vittorio's eyes. 'I think,' he said quietly, 'you are selling yourself a bit short.'

'I prefer not to sell myself at all,' she returned rather tartly.

Someone tapped her on the shoulder and Ana turned. 'Would you mind moving? I'm trying to get a snap of San Marco,' a camera-toting tourist explained and, muttering an oath, Vittorio took Ana by the arm once more and led her away from the crowded piazza.

'We can't have a conversation here—let's go to dinner, as I originally suggested.'

'But I'm not dressed appropriately—'

Vittorio gave her an arch look. 'And whose fault is that?'

'Yours,' she replied but, instead of sounding accusing, her voice came out pert, almost as if she were flirting. Except, Ana thought, she didn't know how to flirt. Yet Vittorio was smiling a little and so was she. 'If you'd let me change,' she continued in that same pert voice, 'instead of trying to turn a sow's ear into a—'

'Don't.' Suddenly, surprisingly, his hand came up to cover her mouth. Ana could taste the salt on his skin. 'Don't insult yourself, Ana.' His expression had softened, his mouth curved in something close to a smile, except it was too serious and even sad. She tried to speak, her lips moving against his fingers, but he wouldn't let her. 'I'm taking you to dinner,' he stated, 'no matter what you're wearing. Anyone who is with the Count of Cazlevara doesn't need to worry about clothes.' He smiled and his thumb caressed the fullness of her lower lip, the simple touch sending shockwaves of pleasure down into her belly. 'You'll find that's one of the advantages of becoming a Countess,' he said, and dropped his hand.

CHAPTER FIVE

ONCE SEATED AT the best table at the Met, one of Venice's finest restaurants, Ana took in the glamorous couples all around them, the women all in designer gowns like the one she could have worn, and she felt another shaft of regret that she'd spurned Vittorio's generous offer of a dress. Even if it had been the safe—and even the right—thing to do.

Still, Vittorio seemed utterly unperturbed by the difference between her own attire and that of every other woman in the room. He gazed down at the menu, tapping it with one finger. 'The mussels are particularly good.'

'I'll keep that in mind.' Now that she was here, seated across from Vittorio, contemplating actually *marrying* him... Ana swallowed. Her throat felt bone-dry. She felt as if she were poised to jump off a cliff and she had no idea what waited underneath her, water or rocks, life or death.

They chose from the menu—Ana decided on chicken over fish—and Vittorio ordered the wine, a local vintage, of course, although not one of either of theirs. 'Always good to consider the competition,' he said with a smile, and Ana nodded. She did the same when she dined out, which admittedly wasn't all that often.

When their first courses arrived and the wine had been

poured, Ana gave Vittorio as direct a look as she could and said, 'I have some questions.'

Vittorio took a sip of wine. 'Very well.'

Nerves made her hands slippery around her wine glass and her voice came out a little breathless. 'What would you expect of...of a wife?'

Vittorio's expression was annoyingly inscrutable. He took another sip of wine, cocking his head to regard Ana thoughtfully. 'I'd expect my wife to be a life partner,' he said finally. 'In every sense.'

The answer, so simple, so honest, made Ana feel even more breathless and her cheeks heated. She looked down. 'Without knowing me, that's quite a big gamble.' She looked up at him again, searching for some clue to his emotions, trying to discover just why he had, over all women, chosen her in this surely coveted role.

'It's not,' Vittorio said after a moment, 'as big a gamble as you think.'

'What do you mean?'

He shrugged. 'I'm not about to embark on one of my life's major decisions without any knowledge at all, Ana. I did some research.'

'Research?' she practically spluttered. 'On me?'

'Of course.' He smiled, amused by her outrage. 'And you can research me if you like. As I said, we are each other's best assets.' He sat back, still smiling, and Ana found she was annoyed at his smug confidence. He was so very sure that any research she did would show him to advantage and, annoyingly, she was quite sure of it too.

'What did you learn?' she finally asked, her voice stiff with dignity.

'That you are a hard worker. That you are healthy—'

'You accessed my medical records?' Ana squawked, wondering how he had managed to do *that*, and Vittorio gave a negligent shrug. Nothing, apparently, was beyond the power—or the pale—for the Count of Cazlevara.

'Now I really feel like a horse,' she muttered. 'Would you like to see my teeth as well?'

'I see them when you speak,' Vittorio replied with a little smile. 'They're very nice.'

Ana just shook her head. Was there any aspect of her life—her body—that he had not researched and inspected? Should she be honoured that she'd passed all these nameless tests? She wasn't. She was furious and, worse, she felt horribly vulnerable, as if Vittorio had spied on her when she was naked. At least he seemed to have liked what he'd seen.

'I also learned,' Vittorio continued blandly, 'that you are passionate about wine and this region. That you are a good friend to those who know you. And, most importantly, that you are loyal.'

She looked up in curiosity and surprise, remembering how he'd spoken of loyalty the other night. 'And loyalty is so important to you?'

'It is,' Vittorio said and his voice, though still low and modulated, seemed suddenly to vibrate with intensity, 'paramount.'

Ana stared, trying to digest this new bit of information. Loyalty was surely so important mainly to those who had once been betrayed. What had happened to Vittorio? 'Are you speaking of fidelity?' she asked.

'No, although of course I would expect you to be faithful to me and our marriage vows. I speak of another kind of loyalty. I would expect you to stand by me and the decisions I make, never to take another's position against me.' His dark eyes caught and held hers. 'Can you do that, Ana? It will not always be easy.'

The conversation that had started so matter-of-fact had suddenly become emotional, intense. Dark. 'If you mean will I never question you—'

His hand slashed through the air. 'I'm not asking for blind obedience. I want a wife, not a lapdog. But you must realize that, because of my position and my wealth, there are those who seek to discredit me. They would even enlist your aid, attract your sympathy by the foulest and most devious motives. Can you—will you—be loyal to me against those enemies?'

Ana suppressed a shiver. She wanted to make a joke of it, tell Vittorio to stop being so melodramatic, yet she had the terrible feeling that he was deadly serious. 'Vittorio—'

'I mean all that I say, Ana,' he said quietly. He reached across the table to encircle her wrist with his hand, his fingers pressing against her bare skin. Nerves jumped at the touch. 'I can tell you think I exaggerate, that I am seeing shadows where there is only light. But I will tell you that the quality that attracted me to you most of all was your sense of loyalty. You've lived with your father for nearly ten years, ever since you returned from university. You've helped him and taken care of him in a way that is gentle and beautiful. Of course, he is your father and he commands your loyalty because of his role. I will ask you now—do you think you can give such allegiance to me?'

'If I were married to you,' Ana said slowly, 'then, yes.'

Vittorio released her wrist and sat back with a deeply satisfied smile. 'Then I know all I need to know. Now it is your turn to ask questions of me.'

'All right,' Ana said, still a bit shaken by the intensity of their exchange. 'If we were married, I would still expect to work for Viale Wines. Would that be acceptable to you?'

Vittorio lifted a shoulder in assent. 'Of course. Naturally, I would expect our children to take the reins of both the Cazlevara and Viale labels. Truly, an empire.'

Ana nodded slowly. *Children.* Under the table, she pressed a hand against her middle. 'And my father,' she said after a moment. 'Of course, he would still live at Villa Rosso, but I would want to see him often, and invite him to be with us whenever possible.'

'Naturally.'

A bubble of sudden nervous laughter escaped her and she shook her head. 'This is so crazy.'

'It seems so, I agree, but actually it makes wonderful sense.'

And she was a sensible person, which was why she was considering it all. Because it was so logical. It just didn't feel that way at the moment. It didn't feel logical when he kissed her.

It felt wonderful.

'I'm scared,' she whispered, her voice so low she didn't know if Vittorio had heard her. She didn't know if she wanted him to.

In fact, she thought he hadn't heard her, for he didn't reply; then she felt his hand on hers, his fingers warm on her skin, curling around her own fingers, squeezing slightly. She took a deep breath and let it out in a shuddering sigh. 'I never thought I'd marry, you know.'

'Why not?' Vittorio asked, his voice as quiet as hers.

Ana shrugged, not wanting to explain. Vittorio squeezed her fingers again, and she felt a lump at the back of her throat. 'What if we end up hating each other?'

'I have too much faith in both of us for that.'

'But we might—' she persisted, her mind coming up with every possibility, every consideration, now that she was actually at the moment of decision. Now that she was ready to jump.

'All good business decisions require a certain amount of risk, Ana. They also take courage and determination.' He smiled and released her hand to take a sip of wine. 'I recently closed a deal with several major hotels in Brazil. South America has never imported much Italian wine, and some would have said I was wasting time and money going there.' He leaned forward. 'But, when I went there, I did so knowing I would do anything to make it succeed. Once the decision is made, all it requires is a certain amount of persistence and follow-through.'

What clinical terms, Ana thought. Although she knew Vittorio meant them to be comforting, she found a certain coldness settling inside her instead. 'This really is…business.'

'Of course.' He glanced at her sharply. 'I told you last week, I'm not interested in love. You agreed with me. If you were not telling the truth—'

'I was.' Ana swallowed. 'Why?' she whispered. When Vittorio simply looked nonplussed, she continued, her voice only a bit ragged, 'Why do you not want to fall in love?'

He didn't answer for a long moment. 'Love,' Vittorio finally said, his voice flat, 'is a destructive emotion.'

'It doesn't have to be—'

'Invariably, because we are all imperfect people, it becomes so. Trust me, Ana, I have seen it happen.' He swivelled his glass between his palms. 'Time and time again.'

'You've been in love, then?' Ana asked, her voice small, far too small and sad. Vittorio shook his head and she felt an absurd leap of relief.

'No. Because I have never wanted to be. But don't think that a loveless marriage must therefore be joyless. We will have affection, respect—'

'You sound like you've been speaking to my father.'

'He is a wise man.'

'He loved my mother,' Ana countered a bit defiantly.

'And yet he recommends you marry me?' There was only the faintest questioning lilt to Vittorio's voice and he smiled, leaning back once more, utterly confident. He arched an eyebrow. 'Why are you not interested in love, then?'

'I was in love once,' Ana said after a moment. She saw shock ripple across Vittorio's features before it was replaced by his usual bland composure. She wondered at her own answer. She didn't think she'd actually *loved* Roberto, but he had hurt her. 'I decided not to experience it again.'

'This man—he hurt you?'

'Yes. He…he decided he…' She faltered, not wanting to spell it out. *I never thought of you that way. How could I?* She'd left Roberto utterly cold, and Ana felt cold herself just remembering it. At least Vittorio desired her, to some degree. She could not deceive herself that he felt even an ounce of the overwhelming attraction she experienced with him, but at least he felt *some-*

thing. He wouldn't have kissed her otherwise. He wouldn't have responded to her own clumsy kiss.

That, at least, was something. Something small, pathetically so, perhaps, but it was more than Ana had ever had with a man before.

'We need not discuss it,' Vittorio said, covering her hand briefly with his own. Ana heard a hardness in his voice and his eyes flashed darkly. 'That man is in the past. We are forging something new, something good.'

'You sound so sure.'

'I am.' Ana just shook her head, still too overwhelmed by the speed with which these negotiations had been conducted. 'Why is it so difficult?' Vittorio asked. His voice remained bland, reasonable, yet Ana thought she heard the bite of impatience underneath. He'd made up his mind ages ago; he'd decided he wanted a wife and so he immediately went out and acquired one. For Vittorio, without the complications of any emotions, it was easy. Simple. 'There is no one else now,' he asked sharply, 'is there?'

She looked up, surprised. 'You know there isn't.'

'Then surely I am the best candidate.'

'If I even want a candidate,' she returned, her tone sharpening too. 'Perhaps living alone would be better.'

Vittorio's lips twisted wryly. 'Ouch.'

Ana's own mouth curved in a reluctant smile; even now he could make her laugh. 'What's your favourite colour?' she asked suddenly, and Vittorio raised his brows.

'Blue.'

'Do you like to read?'

'Paperback thrillers, my secret weakness.' He leaned back, seeming to enjoy this little exchange. Ana searched her mind for more questions; she should have dozens, hundreds, yet in the face of Vittorio's sexy little smile her mind was blanking horribly.

'Do you like dogs?'

'Yes, but not cats.'

'What food do you like?'

'Seafood. Chocolate. I keep a bar of dark chocolate in the kitchen freezer for my own personal use.' He was still smiling that incredible little smile that melted Ana's insides like that bar of dark chocolate left out in the sun.

'What food could your mother never get you to eat?'

His smile faltered for the merest of seconds, barely more than a flash, yet Ana saw it. Felt it. 'Broccoli.' He loosened his collar with one finger. 'Now I'm almost embarrassed.'

'For not liking broccoli?' Ana returned, smiling too. 'Surely you have more secrets than that.'

Vittorio's lips twitched even as his eyes darkened. 'A few.'

She thought about asking other questions. *What makes your expression change like that, darkening as if the sun has disappeared? What memories are you hiding? How many lovers have you had? Why do you think love is destructive?* She swallowed, forcing them away, knowing that now was not the time. 'Tell me something about you that I'd never guess.'

'I play the trombone.'

She laughed aloud, the sound incredulous and merry. 'Really?'

Vittorio nodded solemnly. 'You had to take music lessons at school, and the trombone was the only instrument left in the music cupboard.'

'Were you any good?'

'Awful. I sounded like a dying sheep. My music teacher begged me to stop eventually, and I played football instead, thank God.'

Ana pressed her lips together against another laugh, and shook her head a little bit. *Don't make me fall in love with you.* She pushed the thought aside. 'If you could go anywhere or do anything, what would it be?'

His little smile widened into something almost feral, his eyes glinting in the candlelight. 'Marry you.'

Her heart leaped and she shook her head. 'Be serious.'

'I am.'

'Only because I tick the right boxes.'

'I have a lot of boxes.'

'Just when did you decide I was such a suitable candidate?' Ana asked. She looked up to see Vittorio tilt his head and narrow his eyes; it was a look she was becoming used to. It meant he was thinking carefully about what to say...and what he thought she wanted to hear.

'Does it matter?'

'I'm curious.'

He gave a tiny shrug. 'I've already told you, I first read about you in the in-flight magazine. It was a short article, but it piqued my interest.'

'Enough to dig into my background?' Ana guessed, and Vittorio's mouth tightened. He gestured to the waiter to take their plates, and the man scurried forward.

'I don't particularly like your tone or your choice of words,' he said calmly. 'I've been honest from the beginning.'

'That's true.' Yet, for some reason, his honesty hurt all the more. 'It's just so...cold-blooded.'

'Funny,' Vittorio said, taking a sip of wine, 'I thought you said you weren't a romantic.'

'I'm not,' Ana said quickly. She wondered whether she was lying. Had she actually been waiting for her knight in shining armour all this time? Was she really such a lovelorn fool?

No. She would not allow herself the weakness.

'Then what is the trouble?'

'It is a big decision, Vittorio,' Ana replied, a hint of sharpness to her tone. 'As you said before. I don't make such decisions lightly.' She took a breath. If he wanted businesslike, then that was what he would get. 'What about a pre-nuptial agreement?'

Vittorio arched his eyebrows. 'Are you worried I'll take your fortune?' he asked dryly, for the Viale wealth was a fraction of his.

'No, but I thought you might have that concern.'

Vittorio's mouth hardened into a thin line. 'Divorce is not an option.'

Ana swallowed. 'What if you meet someone else?'

'I won't.' The steely glint in those dark eyes kept Ana from even asking the question about whether she would.

'Children?' she finally managed. Vittorio regarded her coolly, waiting. 'You said you needed an heir. How many?'

'Several, if God wills it.' He paused. 'You intimated you wanted children. Will that be a problem?'

'No.' The ache for a baby had only started recently, her biological clock finally having begun its relentless tick. Yet right now she couldn't think of babies, only how they were made.

Her and Vittorio. Her mind danced with images and her body ached with longing. She'd never realized how much desire she could feel, how it caused a sweet, sweet pain to lance through her and leave her breathless with wanting. The knowledge that Vittorio surely did not share it, or at least feel it as she did, that he could talk about the consummation of their marriage—the joining of their bodies—without so much as a flicker of emotion or longing made Ana ache, not just with desire, but with disappointment.

She wished he desired her the way she desired him, a wonderful consuming ache that longed only to be sated. Yes, she knew she could stir him to sensuality, but surely any man—well, *almost* any man—would have such a response.

Was it enough?

'Ana, what are you thinking?' Vittorio asked. His voice was gentle, and Ana saw a wary compassion in his eyes.

'I'm thinking I don't want to marry a man who doesn't find me attractive,' she said flatly. The words seemed to lie heavily between them, unable to be unsaid. Vittorio's face was blank, but Ana sensed his withdrawal, as if he'd actually recoiled from the brutal honesty of her words.

'I think you are being too harsh.'

The fact that he did not deny it completely made her heart sink a little. 'Am I?' she asked, and heard the hurt in her own voice.

'You felt the evidence of my desire for you the other night,' Vittorio told her in a low voice. A smile lurked in his eyes. 'Didn't you?'

Ana flushed. 'Yes, but—'

'Admittedly, you are different from the other women I've... known. But that doesn't mean I can't find you attractive.'

Having drunk enough whisky and given the right inducements, Ana silently added. 'Have you had many lovers?' she asked impulsively, and almost laughed at Vittorio's expression of utter surprise.

'Enough,' he said after a moment. 'But there is no point raking over either of our pasts, Ana. As I said before, we should look now to the future. Our future.'

Ana tossed her napkin on the table, suddenly restless, needing to move. 'I've finished. Shall we? The last boat back to Fusina leaves before midnight.'

'So it does.' Vittorio raised one hand with easy grace to signal for the bill, and within minutes they were winding their way through the tables and then outside, the spring air slightly damp, the heady scent of flowers mixing with the faint whiff of stagnant water from one of the canals, an aroma that belonged purely to Venice. 'Shall we walk?' Vittorio asked, taking her arm; it fitted snugly into his and her side collided not unpleasantly with his hip. She could feel the hard contours of his leg against hers.

The piazza outside San Marco had emptied of tourists and now only a few people lingered over half-drunk glasses of wine at the pavement cafés; Ana saw a couple entwined in the shadows by one of the pillars of the ancient church. She found herself hurrying, needing to move, to get somewhere. Her thoughts—her hopes, her fears—were too much to deal with.

They didn't speak as they made their way back to the ferry

and, even once aboard the boat, they both stood at the rail, silently watching the lights of Venice disappear into the darkness and fog.

Ana knew she should have a thousand questions to ask, a dozen different points to clarify. Her mind buzzed with thoughts, concerns flitting in and out of her scattered brain.

'I don't want my children to be raised by some nanny,' she blurted and Vittorio glanced sideways at her, his hands still curved around the railing of the ferry.

'Of course not.'

'And I refuse to send them to boarding school.' Her two years at a girls' school near Florence had been some of the darkest days she'd ever known. Even now, she suppressed a shudder at the memory. Vittorio's expression didn't even flicker, although she sensed a tension rippling from him, like a current in the air.

'On that point we are of one accord. I did not enjoy boarding school particularly, and I am presuming you didn't either.'

'No.' She licked her lips; her mouth was suddenly impossibly dry. 'You can't expect to change me.' Vittorio simply arched an eyebrow and waited. 'With make-up and clothes and such. If you wanted that kind of woman, Vittorio, you should have asked someone else.' She met his bland gaze defiantly, daring him to tell her—what? That she needed a little polish? That her shapeless trouser suits—expensive as they were—would have to go? That she wasn't beautiful or glamorous enough for him? Or was that simply what *she* thought?

'There would be little point in attempting to change you,' he finally said, 'when I have asked you to marry me as you are.' Ana nodded jerkily, and then he continued. 'However, you will be the Countess of Cazlevara. I expect you to act—and dress—according to your station.'

'What does that mean exactly?'

Vittorio shrugged. 'You are an intelligent adult woman, Ana. I'll leave such decisions to you.'

Ana nodded, accepting, and they didn't speak until they were off the boat and back in Vittorio's Porsche, speeding through the darkness. A heavy fog rested over the hills above Treviso, lending an eerie glow to the road, the car's headlights barely penetrating the swirling mist. The air was chilly and damp and Ana's mind flitted immediately to the vineyards, the grapes still young and fragile. She didn't think it was cold enough to be concerned and she leaned her head back against the seat, suddenly overwhelmingly exhausted.

Vittorio turned into Villa Rosso's sweeping drive, parking the car in front of the villa's front doors and killing the engine. The world seemed impossibly silent, and Ana felt as if she could nearly fall asleep right there in the car.

'Go to bed, *rondinella*,' Vittorio said softly. His thumb skimmed her cheek, pressed lightly on her chin. 'Sleep on it awhile.'

Ana's eyes fluttered open, his words penetrating her fogged mind slowly. 'What did you say?' she asked in a whisper.

Vittorio's mouth curved in a small smile, yet Ana saw a shadow of sorrow in his eyes, lit only by the lights of the villa and the moon, which had escaped from the clouds that longed to hide it from view. 'I told you to sleep. And preferably in a bed, I think.'

'Yes, but—' Ana swallowed and struggled to a more upright position. 'What did you call me?'

'Rondinella.' His smile deepened, as did the sorrow in his eyes. 'You think I don't remember?'

Ana stared at him, her eyes wide, thoughts and realizations tumbling through her now-clear mind. He remembered. Suddenly she was back at her mother's graveside, her hand still caked with mud, tears drying on her cheeks. Suddenly she was looking at the only person who had shown her true compassion; even her own father had been too dazed by grief to deal with his daughter. And suddenly the answer was obvious.

'I don't need to sleep on it,' she said, her words no more than a breath of sound.

Hope lit Vittorio's eyes, replacing the sorrow. His smile seemed genuine now and he touched her cheek again with his thumb. 'You don't?'

'No.' She reached up to clasp his hand with her own, her fingers curling around his. 'The answer is yes, Vittorio. I'll marry you.'

CHAPTER SIX

EVERYTHING HAPPENED QUICKLY after that. It was as if her acceptance had set off a chain reaction of events, spurring Vittorio into purposeful action that left Ana breathless and a little uncertain. It was all happening so *fast*.

The morning after she'd accepted his proposal—his proposition—he came to the winery offices. Seeing him there, looking official and elegant in his dark grey suit, the only colour the crimson silk of his tie, Ana was reminded just how businesslike this marriage really was. Vittorio hardly seemed the same man who had caressed her cheek and called her swallow only the evening before. The memory of his touch still lingered in her mind, tingled her nerve-endings.

'I thought we should go over some details,' Vittorio said now. 'If you have time?'

Ana braced her hands on her desk, nodding with swift purpose, an attempt to match Vittorio's own brisk determination. 'Of course.' He paused, and Ana moved from behind the desk. 'Why don't we adjourn to the wine-tasting room? I'll order coffee.'

He smiled then, seeming pleased with her suggestion. Just another business meeting, Ana thought a bit sourly, even as she reprimanded herself that she had no right to be resentful of Vittorio's businesslike attitude. She was meant to share it.

Once they were seated on the leather sofas in the wine-tasting room, a tray of coffee on the table between them, Vittorio took out a paper that, to Ana, looked like a laundry list. He withdrew a pair of wire-rimmed spectacles and perched them on the end of his nose, making an unexpected bubble of laughter rise up her throat and escape in a gurgle of sound. 'I didn't know you wore specs.'

He arched his eyebrows, smiling ruefully. 'I started needing them when I turned thirty-five, alas.'

'Is that in your medical file?' Ana couldn't help but quip. 'I should have a full report, you know.'

'I'll have it sent to you immediately,' Vittorio returned, and Ana realized she didn't know if he was joking or not. To cover her confusion she busied herself with preparing the coffee.

'I realize I don't know how old you are,' she commented lightly. 'At my mother's funeral, you were—what? Twenty?'

'Twenty-one.'

The mood suddenly turned sober, dark with memories. Ana gazed at him over the rim of her coffee cup. 'Your father died when you were around my age then, didn't he?'

'Yes. I was fourteen.'

'A heart attack, wasn't it? Sudden.'

Vittorio nodded. 'Yes, as was your mother's death, if I remember correctly. A car accident?'

Ana nodded. 'A drunk driver. A boy no more than seventeen.' She shook her head in sorrowful memory. 'He lost his life as well.'

'I always felt like the death of a parent skewed the world somehow,' Vittorio said after a moment. 'No matter how happy you are, nothing seems quite right after that.' Ana nodded jerkily; he'd expressed it perfectly. He understood. Vittorio looked away, sipping his coffee before he cleared his throat and consulted his list. 'I thought we could have a quiet ceremony in the chapel at Castle Cazlevara. Unless you object?'

'No, of course not. That sounds…fine.'

'If you envisioned something else—'

'No.' She'd stopped dreaming of any kind of wedding years ago. The thought of a huge spectacle now seemed like an affront, a travesty, considering the true nature of their marriage. The thought was an uncomfortable one. 'A quiet ceremony will be fine,' she said a bit flatly, and Vittorio frowned.

'As long as you are sure.' He turned back to his list, a frown still wrinkling his forehead, drawing those strong, straight brows closer together. 'As for dates, I thought in two weeks' time.'

Ana nearly spluttered her mouthful of coffee. 'Two *weeks*!'

'Three, then, at the most. There is no reason to wait, is there?'

'No, I suppose not,' Ana agreed reluctantly. 'Still, won't it seem…odd? People might talk.'

'I am not interested in gossip. In any case, the sooner we marry, the sooner we become…used to one another.' He gave her the glimmer of a smile. 'Of course, we can wait—a while— before we consummate the marriage. I want you to feel comfortable.'

Ana blushed. She couldn't help it. Despite his tone of cool, clinical detachment, she could imagine that consummation so vividly. Wonderfully. And she didn't want to wait. She took another sip of coffee, hiding her face from Vittorio's knowing gaze. She wasn't about to admit as much, not when Vittorio was all too content to delay the event.

'Thank you for that sensitivity,' she murmured after a moment, and Vittorio nodded and returned to his list.

'I thought a small wedding, but do let me know if there is anyone in particular you would like to invite.'

'I'll have to think about it.'

'I realize if we invited only some of the local winemakers, others will be insulted at not being included,' Vittorio continued. 'So I thought not to invite any… We'll have a party at the castle a few days after the wedding. Everyone can come then.'

'All right.' Ana wished she could contribute something more coherent to this conversation other than her mindless murmured agreements. Yet she couldn't; her mind was spinning with these new developments, realizations. Implications.

In a short while—as little as two weeks—they could be married. *Would* be married. Her hand trembled and she put the coffee cup back in its saucer with an inelegant clatter.

'We will need witnesses, of course, for the ceremony,' Vittorio said, reaching for his own cup. If he noticed Ana's agitation, he did not remark on it. 'Is there a woman friend in particular you would like to stand witness?'

'Yes, a friend from university.' Paola was still her best friend, although they saw each other infrequently ever since her friend had married a Sicilian. She'd moved south and had babies. Ana had moved home, caring for her father and the winery. 'She'll be surprised,' Ana said a bit wryly. She could only imagine Paola's shock when she told her she was getting married, and so suddenly. 'And what about you? Who will you have as your witness?'

'I thought your father.'

'My father!' Ana couldn't keep the surprise from her voice; she didn't even try. 'But…'

'He is a good man.'

'What about your brother?'

'No.' Vittorio's voice was flat and when his gaze met Ana's his eyes looked hard, even unfriendly. 'We are not close.'

There was a world of knowledge in that statement, Ana knew, a lifetime of memory and perhaps regret. She longed to ask why—what—but she knew now was not the time. 'Very well.'

Vittorio finished his coffee and folded his list back into his breast pocket. 'I assume I can leave the details of your dress and flowers to you?' he asked. His eyebrow arched, a hint of a smile around his mouth, he added, 'You will wear a dress?'

Ana managed a smile back. 'Yes. For my own wedding, I think I can manage a dress.'

'Good. Then I'll leave you to work now. I thought you could come to dinner this Friday, at the castle. You will need to meet my family.' Again that hardness, that darkness.

Ana nodded. 'Yes, of course.'

And then he was gone. He rose from the table, shook her hand and left the office as if it had just been another business meeting, which, Ana recognized, of course it had.

That evening, over dinner, she told her father. She could have told him that morning, but something had held her back. Perhaps it was her own reluctance to admit she'd done something that seemed so foolhardy, so desperate. Yet, now the wedding was a mere fortnight away, she could hardly keep such news from her father, especially if Vittorio intended for him to stand as witness.

'I said yes to Vittorio, Papà,' Ana said as they finished the soup course. Her voice came out sounding rather flat.

Enrico lowered his spoon, his eyes widening in surprise, a smile blooming across his dear wrinkled face. 'But Ana! *Dolcezza!* That is wonderful.'

'I hope it will be,' Ana allowed, and Enrico nodded in understanding.

'You are nervous? Afraid?'

'A bit.'

'He is a good man.'

'I'm glad you think so.'

Enrico cocked his head. 'You aren't sure?'

Ana considered this. 'I would hardly marry a bad man, Papà.' Vittorio was a good man, she knew. Honourable, just, moral. She thought of that hardness in his eyes and voice when he spoke of his family. He was a good man, but was he a gentle man? Then she remembered the whisper of his thumb on her cheek, the soft words of comfort. *It's all right...rondinella.*

She didn't know what to think. What to believe or even to hope for.

'I am happy for you,' Enrico said, reaching over to cover her hand with his own. 'For you both. When is the wedding?'

Ana swallowed. 'In two weeks.'

Enrico raised his eyebrows. 'Good,' he said after a moment. 'No need to waste time. I will telephone Aunt Iris today. Perhaps she can come from England.'

Ana nodded jerkily. She'd only met her aunt a handful of times; she'd disapproved of her sister marrying an Italian and living so far away. When Emily had died, she'd withdrawn even more. 'I hope she'll come,' Ana said, meaning it. Perhaps her wedding could go some way towards healing such family rifts.

Even when at work in the winery on Monday she found her thoughts were too hopelessly scattered to concentrate on much of anything. She jumped at the littlest sound, half-expecting, hoping even, to see Vittorio again. He did not make an appearance.

In the middle of a task or phone call she would catch herself staring into space, her mind leaping ahead... *I'll be the Countess of Cazlevara. What will people say? When will Vittorio want to—?*

She forced her mind back to her work, even as a lump of something—half dread, half excitement—lodged in her middle and made it impossible to eat or even to swallow more than a sip of water. She was a seething mass of nerves, wondering just what insane foolishness she'd agreed to, longing to possess the cool business sense Vittorio had credited her with. She couldn't summon it for the life of her.

On Thursday evening, as she headed back to the villa, she compiled a list in her head of all the things she needed to do. Tell the winery staff. Ring Paola. Find an outfit—a dress?—for her dinner with Vittorio and his family tomorrow.

The downstairs of the villa was quiet and dark when Ana entered.

'Papà?' she called, and there was no answer. She headed upstairs, pausing in the doorway of one of the guest bedrooms they never used. Her father, she saw, was seated on the floor, his head bowed. Ana felt a lurch of alarm. 'Papa?' she asked gently. 'Are you all right?'

He looked up, blinking once or twice, and smiled brightly. 'Yes. Fine. I was just looking through some old things.'

Ana stepped into the room, now lost in the gloom of late afternoon. 'What old things?' she asked.

'Of your mother's…' The words trailed off in a sigh. Enrico looked down at his lap, which was covered by a heap of crumpled white satin. 'She would be so pleased to know you were getting married. I like to think that she does know, somehow. Somewhere.'

'Yes.' Ana couldn't help but remember Vittorio's words: *tua cuore*. 'What's that on your lap?'

'Your mother's wedding dress. Have I never shown it to you?'

Ana shook her head. 'In photographs…'

Enrico held it up, shaking it out as he smiled tremulously. 'I know it's probably out-of-date,' he began, his voice hesitant. 'And it needs to be professionally cleaned and most likely altered, but…'

'But?' Ana prompted. She felt moved by her father's obvious emotion—unusual as it was—but it saddened her too. This enduring love was something she'd agreed never to know.

'It would give this old man great joy for you to wear your mother's gown on your wedding day,' Enrico said, and Ana's heart sank a little bit.

'You're not an old man, Papà,' she protested, even as she scanned his face, noticing how thin and white his hair was, the new deeper grooves on the sides of his mouth. He'd been forty when he'd married; he was just past seventy now. It seemed impossible, and her heart lurched as she reached for the gown.

'Let me see.' She shook the dress out, admiring the rich white satin even as she recognized the style—over thirty years old—was far from flattering for her own fuller figure. The round neckline was bedecked with heavy lace and the skirt had three tiers of ruffles. Not only would she look like a meringue in it, she would look like a very large meringue. She'd look *awful*. Ana turned back to her father; tears shimmered in his eyes. She smiled. 'I'd be honoured to wear it, Papà.'

The next day Ana stood outside Castle Cazlevara. The torches guttered in a chilly spring breeze and lights twinkled from within. Even before she stepped out of her car—she'd insisted on driving herself—a liveried footman threw open the double doors and welcomed her inside.

'Signorina Viale, welcome. The Count and his mother, the Countess, are in the drawing room awaiting your arrival.'

Ana swallowed past the dryness in her mouth; her heart had begun to thump so loudly she could feel it in her ears. She straightened, her hands running down the silvery-grey wide-legged trousers she wore. She'd taken great pains over her outfit, and yet now she wondered if it was as plain as the other trouser suits she donned as armour. Only yesterday she'd taken the ferry to Venice, had even ventured down Frezzeria to the chic boutique Vittorio had led her to just the other night. She'd stood in front of the window like a child in front of a sweet shop; twice she'd almost gone in. But the stick-thin sales associate with her black pencil skirt and crisp white blouse looked so svelte and elegant and forbidding that after twenty minutes Ana had crept away. The thought of trying on such beautiful clothes—of looking at herself in such beautiful clothes—in front of such a woman was too intimidating. Too terrifying.

So she'd scoured her closet, finding a pair of trousers she'd never worn; the fabric shimmered as she moved and even though it was still a pair of trousers, the legs were wide enough to almost pass for a skirt. She chose the beaded top she'd worn the last time she'd come to the castle and she'd pulled back her hair loosely so a few loose tendrils framed her face, softening the effect. She'd even put on a little lipstick.

Now as she made her way to the drawing room, she wondered if Vittorio would notice. If he would care. And, if he did, would she be glad? She couldn't decide if she would feel more of a fool if he did notice or if he didn't.

All these thoughts flew from her head as she stood in the doorway of the drawing room and a slim, petite blonde—the kind of woman who made Ana feel like an ungainly giant—swivelled to face her. Constantia Ralfino, the Countess of Cazlevara. Soon to be the *Dowager* Countess.

The moment seemed suspended in time as they both stood there, the Countess taking in Ana with one arctic sweep of her eyes. Ana quailed under that gaze; she felt herself shrivel inside, for Constantia Cazlevara was looking at her as so many people had looked at her, beginning with most of the girls at the boarding school her father had sent her to after her mother had died.

It was a look of assessment and then disdain, followed swiftly by dismissal. It was a look that hurt now, more than it should, because it made Ana feel like a gawky thirteen-year-old again, awkward and still stricken with grief.

'So,' Constantia said coolly. She lifted her chin and met Ana's humble gaze directly. 'This is your bride.' Her tone was most likely meant to be neutral, but Ana heard contempt. She lifted her chin as well.

'Yes. We met many years ago, my lady. Of course, I am pleased to make your acquaintance once more.'

'Indeed.' Constantia did not make any move to take Ana's proffered hand, and after a moment she dropped it. Constantia turned to Vittorio, who was watching them both in tight-lipped silence. 'Aren't you going to introduce us, Vittorio?'

'Ana seems to have accomplished the introductions better than I ever could,' he said in a clipped voice. 'However, if you must.' He waved one hand between the pair of them. 'Mother, this is Ana Viale, one of the region's most promising winemakers, daughter of our neighbour Enrico Viale, and my intended bride.' His lips, once pursed so tightly, now curved in a smile that still managed to seem unpleasant. 'Ana, this is my mother, Constantia.'

The tension almost made the air shiver; Ana imagined she could hear it crackle. Constantia shot her son a look of barely veiled resentment before she turned back to Ana. 'So was it love at first sight, my dear?'

Ana couldn't tell if the older woman was baiting her or genuinely interested in knowing. She glanced at Vittorio, wondering what to say. How to dissemble. Did he want people to know just how convenient their marriage was meant to be? Or was he intending to deceive everyone into thinking they were in love? Such a charade would be exhausting and ultimately pointless, Ana was sure.

Before she could frame an answer, Vittorio cut in. 'Love at first sight? What a question, Mother. Ana and I both know there is no such thing. Now, dinner is served and I don't enjoy eating it cold. Let's withdraw to the dining room.' He strode from the room, pausing only to offer Ana his arm, which she accepted awkwardly, her elbow crooked in his, her strides made awkwardly longer than normal in order to match his.

Dinner was, of course, interminable. Vittorio and Constantia both spoke with that chilly politeness that managed to be worse than outright barbs or even insults. Ana felt her whole body tense and she had the beginnings of a terrible headache. It was impossible to know what to say, how to act. Vittorio gave her no clues.

A thousand questions and, worse, doubts, whirled in her head, demanding answers. What was the source of the antipathy between Vittorio and his mother? How could two people in the same family seem to dislike each other so much? And how could she possibly fit into this unhappy picture? The thought of living in Castle Cazlevara with Constantia's continual scorn and disdain was unendurable. An hour into the evening, Ana was just beginning to realize how much she'd agreed to when she'd accepted Vittorio's proposal. Not just a marriage, but a family. Not just a business proposition, but a lifestyle. A *life*.

She felt fraught with nerves, sick with dread by the time the miserable meal came to an end. There had been some sort of conversation, she supposed, desultory remarks that still managed to be pointed, poised to wound. Ana had contributed very little; she'd eaten less, merely toying with her food.

Constantia rose from the table in one graceful movement. She was a slender slip of a woman, still strikingly beautiful despite the wrinkles that lined her face like a piece of parchment that had been crumpled up and smoothed out again. 'I'm afraid I'm too weary from my journey to stay for coffee,' she said, offering Ana a cool little smile. 'I do hope you'll forgive me, my dear.'

'Of course,' Ana murmured. She was relieved to be able to avoid any further awkwardness with her future mother-in-law— if she was even going to marry Vittorio. A single evening had cast everything into terrible doubt.

'Well, then.' She turned to Vittorio, her haughty expression seeming to turn sad, the cool little smile softening into something that looked weary and lost. Before Ana could even register what that look meant, it had cleared, leaving Constantia distant and regal once more, and with one last haughty look she swept from the room and left Vittorio and Ana suspended in a tense and uneasy silence.

'Vittorio—' Ana began, the word bursting from her. She stopped, unable to continue, afraid to frame the thoughts pounding through her head.

'What is it, Ana?' His tone was sharp, his look assessing. Knowing. 'You're not having second thoughts already?' he asked, his voice soft now and yet still faintly menacing. He rose from the table, coming around to help Ana from her chair. His hands slid down her bare shoulders in what was surely no more than a pretext to touch her; she shivered noticeably. 'Cold feet, *rondinella*?' he whispered and she shook her head, sudden pain lancing through her.

'Don't call me that.'

'Why not?'

'Because—' She pressed her lips together. It would sound foolish—pathetic, even—to admit the endearment was special. That it *meant* something. Yet still she couldn't stand Vittorio using it now, when his expression was so forbidding, his voice faintly mocking. When there suddenly seemed so much she didn't know about him, so much she was afraid of.

'Because why?' Vittorio asked. He'd trailed his hand down Ana's bare arm so now their fingertips were touching. Smiling faintly, he laced his fingers with her own and drew her from the table, out into the foyer with its flickering torches, the ancient stones dancing with shadows. 'We are about to be married, after all.'

Ana let him lead her. His touch was mesmerizing, her thoughts and even doubts seeming to fly from her head as she followed him slowly, knowing each step was taking her closer to danger. Danger, and yet such exquisite danger it was. All she could think or feel was his fingers on her skin. Wanting more. Needing more.

'I don't—' she began, and then simply shook her head, at a loss for words. Feeling was too much, taking over every sense.

'You don't...?' Vittorio prompted. She thought she heard laughter in his voice; he *knew*. He knew how much his simple touch affected her, reduced her. He used it as a weapon. His fingers still laced with hers, he pulled her towards him. She came, unresisting, until their bodies collided and she had to tilt back her head to look up into his face, his onyx eyes glittering as he gazed down at her. 'Don't be afraid, Ana,' he murmured, his lips inches from hers.

Her own lips parted instinctively, yet also in anticipation. *Hope*. Even so, she summoned one last protest; it was both an attack and a defence. 'There's so much I don't know about you, Vittorio.'

'Mmm.' Vittorio's fingers trailed up and down her arm, playing her skin like an instrument, his lips now a scant inch from hers so his breath feathered her face. She knew what he was doing. He was distracting her, keeping her from asking the questions whose answers she needed to know, whose answers, she realized fuzzily, might keep her from marrying him. And, even as she knew this, she couldn't help her overwhelming response to his touch, blocking out all rational thought, all sense of reason.

And so another damning thought followed on the heels of the first: that *nothing* could keep her from marrying Vittorio, from possessing him, or having him possess her. She knew that as, with his free hand, he cupped her cheek and brought her face closer to his, their lips now no more than a breath apart.

He was going to kiss her. She needed him to kiss her, craved it, knew that her body and mind and soul could not be satisfied until she'd felt his lips on hers once more. Later, she knew, she would be humbled and perhaps ashamed by her own helpless desire. For now, it remained only an unstoppable force, an overwhelming hunger. So much so, in fact, that in barely a breath of sound, she whispered, *begged*, 'Kiss me.'

Vittorio's mouth curved in a smile tinged with triumph. Ana didn't care. She didn't care if she was humiliating herself, if Vittorio would gloat in his sensual power over her. She *couldn't* care, because the need was too strong. 'Kiss me,' she said again, and then, because still he just smiled, she closed the gap between their lips herself, her eyes closing in blissful relief as their mouths connected and her whole body flooded with both satisfaction and yet more need.

Her hands found their way to his hair, fisting in its softness, her body pressing against the full length of his. She let her mouth move slowly over his, let her tongue slide against his lips, knowing she was inexpert, clumsy even, and not caring because it felt so good. She lost herself in that kiss, sank into it like she would a big feather bed, revelling in its softness, its wonder and pleasure, until she realized—slowly—that Vittorio had not moved, had not responded at all. Dimly, distantly, she became aware that his body was rigid against hers, his hands only loosely on her shoulders, his lips unresponsive and even slack under hers.

Desire had swamped her senses, flooded her reason, and yet Vittorio barely seemed affected at all.

In a sickening flash she remembered how she'd kissed Roberto—just as clumsily, no doubt—and how he had not moved either. He had remained still, enduring her touch, relieved when it was over. He'd felt disgust, not desire. And—oh, please, no—was Vittorio the same? She took a stumbling step backwards, shame pouring through her, scalding her senses, making her eager for escape.

Yet Vittorio would not let her flee. His hands came up to encircle her arms and he pulled her towards him as he deepened the kiss and made it his own. His hands moved to her hips, rocking her so their bodies collided in the most intimate way, and her lips curved in a triumphant, incredulous smile when she heard his sharp intake of breath and felt the evidence of his arousal.

Yet if Ana felt she was in control—even for a second—she soon realized she was sorely mistaken. Vittorio had taken command, pulling her into even closer contact, keeping her there, trapped between his powerful thighs. His mouth, at first so still and unresponsive under hers, now moved with deliberate, languorous ease, travelling from her lips to the sensitive skin under her ear so she was the one gasping aloud, and then to the intimate curve of her neck, and finally to the vee between her breasts.

Ana threw her head back, her eyes clenched shut, her breath coming in audible moans. She'd never been touched so intimately, so *much*. Her head spun and her body felt as if every nerve-ending had blazed to life; it almost hurt to feel this much, to know such pleasure.

She'd never known that *anything* could be like this.

Then Vittorio stepped away, leaving Ana reeling and gasping, the aftershocks of exquisite sensation still rocking her, and he smiled rather coolly. 'See, Ana?' he said, reaching behind her to open the front door of the castle; a cool breeze blew over her heated body. 'I think you know me well enough.'

Vittorio waited until Ana was safely in her car, making her way down the curving drive, before he let out a long, low shudder.

He had not expected that. He'd been planning to seduce Ana, to sweep away her doubts with a kiss—or two. Instead, *she'd* kissed *him*. He'd been shocked by her audacity as well as his response. For, in that kiss, he'd realized that Ana was more than this thing he wanted, this possession he meant to acquire, his goal achieved. *Wife*.

She was a person, a being with hopes and needs and oh, yes, desires—and, even as he'd sent his little gifts and said the right words and kissed her, he'd somehow managed to forget this fact. Had he ever really known it?

Why he should realize that when she'd been kissing him, pressing against him, stirring him to a sudden desperate lust, he had no idea. He wished he hadn't realized; it was easier not to know, or at least to pretend not to know.

To hold someone's happiness in your hand, to take responsibility for her life—

It was monumental. Frightening, too.

'Why, Vittorio?'

Vittorio stilled, his mother's accusing voice ringing in his ears. He turned slowly, his gaze sweeping over her in one dismissive glance. She stood poised on the bottom step of the ornate marble staircase—a nineteenth-century addition to the castle—her eyes blazing blue fire and her mouth twisted into a contemptuous sneer. It was an expression he'd become accustomed to.

'Why what, Mother?' he asked, his words holding only a veneer of icy politeness.

'Why are you marrying that poor girl?'

Vittorio's eyes narrowed. 'I don't appreciate the way you refer to my bride. There is nothing poor about Ana.'

Constantia let out a crow of disbelieving laughter. 'Come, Vittorio! I know the women you've taken to your bed. I've seen them in the tabloids. They would eat Anamaria Viale alive.'

He just kept himself from flinching. 'They will never have the opportunity.'

'No?' Constantia took a step towards him, incredulity lacing the single word. 'You think not? And how will you manage that, my son? Will you keep your precious wife locked away in a glass case? Because, I assure you, that is not a pleasant place to be.'

'I have no intention of putting Ana anywhere,' Vittorio said flatly, 'that she does not wish to be.'

'She loves you,' Constantia said after a moment. Her voice was quiet. 'Or at least she could.'

Vittorio's jaw tightened. 'That is no concern of yours, Mother.'

'Isn't it?' Constantia lifted her chin, her expression challenging and obdurate. 'Do you know how it feels to love someone and never have them love you back? Do you know what that can drive you to think, to *do*?' Her voice rang out, raw and ragged, and Vittorio narrowed his eyes. Her words—her tone—made no sense to him; was her obvious distress another ploy?

'What are you talking about?'

Constantia pressed her lips together and shook her head. 'Why are you going to marry her, Vittorio? Is it simply to spite me?'

'You give yourself too much credit.'

'You had no interest in marriage until I spoke of it.'

Vittorio lifted one shoulder in a careless shrug. 'You simply reminded me to do my duty as Count of Cazlevara and CEO of Cazlevara Wines,' he said. 'It is my duty to provide an heir.'

'So Bernardo cannot take your place,' she finished flatly.

Vittorio's eyes narrowed. She didn't even hide her true ambition, but then she never had. 'Every man wants a son.'

'Why her?' Constantia demanded. 'Why marry a woman you could not love?'

'I'm not interested in love, Mother.'

'Just like your father, then,' she spat, and again Vittorio felt a confused lurch of unease which he forced himself to dismiss.

'I'm finished with this conversation,' he said shortly and he turned away, walking quickly from the room. It was only later, when he was preparing for bed, that he remembered and reflected on his mother's words. She'd called Ana a woman he could not love, as if such a thing—to love Ana—was an impossibility.

His hands stilling on the buttons of his shirt, Vittorio wondered if his mother spoke the truth. He'd never *wanted* to love, that was true; was he even capable of it?

CHAPTER SEVEN

TODAY WAS HER wedding day. Ana stared at her reflection in her bedroom mirror and grimaced. She looked awful. Although she couldn't regret the decision to wear her mother's wedding gown, neither could she suppress the natural longing to look better in it.

The gown had been professionally cleaned and altered, but it was still befrilled and belaced to within an inch of its life—and hers. The thought of Vittorio seeing her looking like Little Bo Beep from a bad pantomime made her cringe. Sighing, she stroked the rich satin—no matter what the style, the dress was of the highest quality—and forced such negative thoughts from her mind. Today was her wedding day. She wanted to enjoy it.

Yet other negative thoughts—the doubts and fears that had dogged her since her dinner with Vittorio and Constantia—crept in and gnawed at her already struggling sense of happiness.

She'd seen Vittorio many times in the last fortnight; he'd made a point of stopping by the winery office, whether it was for a simple hello, or to show her a magazine article on the latest growing techniques, or to stroll through the Viale vineyards with her, the sun blazing benevolently down on them as they walked. Ana appreciated his attempts to make their relationship at least appear normal and pleasant, yet she couldn't quite stop the creeping doubt that, even though she enjoyed them, the visits seemed a little...*perfunctory*. Another item ticked off on her husband-to-be's to-do list. He'd acquired his bride; now he was maintaining her.

She knew she shouldn't begrudge Vittorio the time he spent with her, and she shouldn't expect more. She shouldn't even *want* more. She'd agreed to a business-minded marriage, she reminded herself, not nearly for the first time. She had to stick to her side of the bargain.

Someone tapped on the door and then a dark curly head peeked round the frame. 'Are you ready?' Paola asked. Ever since Ana had told her friend about her upcoming wedding, Paola had been wonderfully supportive. Ana had not yet told her the truth of her marriage. 'The car is here to take you to the castle.'

Ana nodded. 'Yes, I just need my veil.'

Smiling, Paola reached for the gossamer-thin veil of webbed lace and settled it on Ana's head. She wore her hair up in a chignon, clusters of curls at the corners of her brow. 'You look...' Paola began, and Ana smiled wryly.

'Terrible.'

Paola smiled back at Ana, their eyes meeting in the mirror. 'I wasn't going to say that.'

'The dress doesn't suit me in the least.'

Paola gave a little shrug. 'I think it's wonderful you're wearing your mother's gown and anyone with any sense will think the same, no matter what it looks like. Anyway,' she continued robustly as she twitched the veil so the lace flowed down Ana's back, 'I think a bride could wear a bin bag and it wouldn't matter at all. When you're in love, you glow. No one looks better than a bride on her wedding day.'

'You think so?' Ana asked, her voice pitched just a little too shrill. She didn't glow, and it was no wonder. She wasn't in love. She looked, in fact, rather pasty.

Paola laid a hand on Ana's shoulder. 'Is everything all right,

Ana? I know we haven't been in touch in a while, but—' she paused, chewing her lip '—you seem so nervous. Everyone has cold feet, of course. I was nearly sick the morning of my own wedding, do you remember? But…are you sure this is what you want?' She softened the question with a smile, adding, 'It's my duty as your bridesmaid and witness to ask that, you know.'

'I know.' Ana made herself smile back, despite the nerves that were fluttering rather madly in her stomach and threatening to make their way up her throat. 'Yes, Paola, this is what I want.' No matter how nervous she was now, Ana knew she couldn't go back to her old life, her old ways. She couldn't walk out on Vittorio, and what marriage to him would—could—mean. She let out her breath slowly. 'If I seem particularly nervous, it's because this marriage isn't—isn't really a normal marriage.'

Paola frowned. 'What are you talking about?'

'Vittorio and I only agreed to get married a fortnight ago,' Ana explained in a rush. She felt better for admitting the truth she hadn't been brave enough to reveal since Paola's arrival two days ago. 'We're not in love, not even close. It's a marriage… of convenience.'

'Convenience?' Paola echoed. She gave a disbelieving laugh. 'Just what is convenient about marriage?'

Ana tried for a laugh as well; the sound came out shaky. 'Vittorio and I have common goals. We're both ambitious and we have similar ideas about…things…' She trailed off, realizing how absurd she sounded. She didn't even know if she believed half of what she said. From the look in Paola's narrowed eyes, neither did her friend.

'Ana, are you really sure—'

A knock sounded at the door and the muffled voice of her father could be heard from behind it. 'Ana, *dolcezza*, are you ready? The car is here and if we are to be on time…'

Ana took a deep breath. Her wedding day was here; the moment had arrived. In less than an hour she would be married to Vittorio, she would be the Countess of Cazlevara. A thousand thoughts and memories flitted through her dazed mind: the moment when she'd learned her mother had died, and her whole world fell away. Her father's refusal even to see her, hiding his grief behind locked doors, insisting she attend boarding school. The hellish days at that school, alone, grief-stricken, awkward and miserable, teased and ignored. Then, later, her years at university, slowly learning how to be confident, what it would take to be successful, only to have her frail self-esteem obliterated by that awful moment in Roberto's arms. The nights spent gazing out of her window, wondering if life would ever offer more, if love could be found. The decision to stop looking for love and enjoy what she already had, to live for what life offered her rather than seeking more, always more… All of it, every second, it seemed then, had led up to this moment and her decision to marry Vittorio.

And then new, fresh memories raced through her: the gentle touch of Vittorio's hand on her cheek, both when she was thirteen and when she was nearly thirty. The feel of his lips on hers, his hands on her body, so deft, so desirable. The kindnesses he'd shown her in the last fortnight—calculated, perhaps—whether it was a spray of new grapes or the offer of a new gown. The tension with his mother, the hope they both had for the future.

And then, to her surprise, as the memories faded and she blinked the room back into focus, she realized she was no longer afraid. Her nerves had fled and in their place a new, serene determination had emerged. She smiled at Paola.

'This is what I want, Paola. I am sure.' Turning, Ana called to her father, 'Papà! I'm ready.'

As she opened the door, Enrico blinked tears from his eyes as he saw her in her mother's gown. 'Oh, *dolcezza! Magnifica!*'

Ana smiled.

She didn't quite manage a smile as she saw Vittorio's expression when she came down the aisle of the chapel attached to Castle Cazlevara. Only a dozen guests were scattered among the dark wood pews, a few relatives and friends. Paola, Vittorio and her father all stood at the front as Ana walked down the aisle alone in her mother's ruffled gown.

Vittorio, for a single second, looked horrified. Then his expression smoothed out as if an iron had been applied to it and he gave her the barest flicker of a smile; his eyes remained dark. Ana remembered what she'd once said about her own fashion sense and knew Vittorio was doubting her now. He was probably wondering just what kind of woman he was marrying, when she came down the aisle in a gown thirty years out of date, a gown that made her look like a melting meringue.

Ana lifted her chin and found her smile.

The ceremony only lasted a few minutes, or so it seemed, for, after a blur of words and motions, Vittorio was sliding the heavy band of antique gold on her finger and then his lips, cool and somehow remote, were pressing her cheek in the chastest of kisses. Even so, Ana's blood stirred and desire leapt low in her belly.

Vittorio stepped away.

Ana heard a spattering of applause from the paltry crowd as if from a great distance, and then Vittorio was leading her down the aisle, away from the chapel and towards the great hall of the castle where their wedding feast would be held.

She sneaked a glance at his profile; his jaw was tight, his gaze staring straight ahead. Ana realized afresh just how much of a stranger her husband was.

Her husband. The thought was incredible, bizarre, ridiculous. Exciting. She swallowed past the fear and remembered her earlier certainty, tried to feel it again.

A servant opened the doors to the great hall, the long table now laid for a meal for twenty. Vittorio turned to her.

'A small wedding reception, and then we can retire. I'm sure you're tired.' He spoke with a careful politeness that managed to make Ana feel even more awkward and strange. She nodded jerkily.

'Thank you.'

Vittorio nodded back, and Ana wondered if this kind of stilted conversation was what she had to look forward to for the rest of her life.

What had she just done? What had she agreed to?

Like the ceremony, the wedding reception passed in a blur that still managed to make Ana both uncomfortable and exhausted. It wasn't a normal marriage, and people seemed to sense that, so it wasn't a normal wedding reception either. Her friends regarded her a bit quizzically; everyone she'd told had been utterly surprised by her abrupt engagement, although too polite perhaps to show it. Even her Aunt Iris, a distant stranger, scrutinized her with pursed lips and narrowed eyes, as if she suspected that something was amiss. Vittorio's brother, Bernardo, shook her hand; his fingers were cold against hers and his smile didn't reach his eyes. Constantia didn't speak to her at all.

Ana did her best to chat and smile with those who did want to talk to her; she ate a few mouthfuls of the delicious *cicchetti*, meatballs and fried crab, as well as one of the region's specialities, a lobster risotto. And of course there was wine: a rich red wine with the pasta, and crisp white wine with the fish, and prosecco with lemon sorbet for dessert.

By the time the plates had been cleared, Ana felt both exhausted and a bit dizzy. She saw Vittorio signal to a servant, and then moments later felt someone's hand on her shoulder. She turned and saw Paola smiling at her.

'Come, the wedding feast is nearly over. I'll help you out of your dress.'

'Out of...?' Ana repeated blankly, her mind fuzzy from the food and wine. Of course; the wedding was over, it was now her wedding night.

Vittorio had been vague about what he expected—what he *wanted*—from their first night together as husband and wife. He'd mentioned that he would give her time; there was no need to consummate their marriage on the very first night.

Yet what did he want? What did she want?

She knew the answer to the second question: *him*.

Ana let Paola lead her away from the reception, up to an unfamiliar corridor—she'd never even been upstairs before—and finally to a bedroom suite. Ana took in the massive stone fireplace, a fire already laid, the huge four poster bed piled high with velvet and satin pillows and the dimmed lighting. It was a room for seduction. It was a room for love.

'How did you know where to go?' she asked Paola, who had already closed the door and was reaching for the back of Ana's dress, and the thirty-six buttons that went from the nape of her neck to the small of her back.

'One of the servants showed me. Vittorio has a timetable, apparently. It's all very organized, isn't it?'

'That's a good thing,' Ana replied. She couldn't help but feel just a little defensive; she heard a note of censure in her friend's voice.

'So,' Paola asked as she finished with the buttons and the dress sank around Ana's ankles in a pool of satin, 'just how convenient is this marriage, anyway?' She gestured towards the room with its candlelight and pillows with a wry smile.

'Not that convenient, I suppose.' Ana smiled, felt the leap of anticipation in her belly, the tightening of her muscles and nerves in heady expectation. She was ready. She *wanted* this. So terribly, dangerously much.

'Do you love him, Ana?' Paola asked quietly. Ana stepped out of her dress, standing in just a thin slip, and reached for the pins that held her hair in its fussy chignon. Her back remained to Paola.

'No,' she said after a moment, 'but that's all right.'

'Is it?'

Ana turned around. 'I know you married for love, Paola, but that doesn't mean it's the only way. Vittorio and I want to be happy together, and I think we will be.' Brave words. She'd believed them once, when she'd accepted his proposal, when she'd agreed with all of his logical points. It had made *sense*.

Yet, looking at that bed piled high with pillows and flickering with candlelit shadows, there was nothing sensible about it.

'I almost forgot,' Paola said. 'Your husband left this for you.' She gestured to a plain white box, wrapped with a ribbon of ivory silk.

'Oh?' Ana reached for it; the ribbon fell away with a slither and she opened the box. Inside was the most exquisite nightdress she'd ever seen; the silk was whisper-thin and delicately scalloped lace embroidered the edges. It was held up by two gauzy ribbons, to be tied at each shoulder.

'It's gorgeous,' Paola breathed, and Ana could only nod. Then she caught sight of the tag, and her heart sank straight down to her feet.

'It's also three sizes too big.'

'Men are terrible with things like that—' Paola said quickly, too quickly.

Ana nodded, tossing the gorgeous gown back into its box. 'Of course. It doesn't matter.' Yet it did. She felt hurt, ridiculously near tears, horribly vulnerable, and suddenly she wanted—needed—to be alone. 'I'm fine, Paola. Vittorio will most likely arrive soon. You can leave me.'

'Ana—'

'I'm fine,' she said again, more firmly, and then she gave her friend a quick kiss on the cheek. 'Thank you for all you've done, and for coming to be my bridesmaid. I know how sudden it all was—'

'That doesn't matter.' Paola hugged her tightly for a moment before releasing her and stepping back. 'Are you sure you'll be all right? I can wait—'

'No, I'd like a few moments alone.' Ana smiled, straightening her spine, throwing her shoulders back. When she spoke, her voice came out firm. 'Don't worry about me, Paola. I'll be fine.' If she kept saying it, perhaps she would believe it.

When she was alone, Ana spared that gown one more accusing glance and then she moved around the room, pacing, anxiety taking the place of her earlier resolve. She told herself it hardly mattered that the gown was three sizes too big, yet no matter how many times she repeated the words, a desperate litany, she couldn't believe it.

She felt that it did matter. She felt that Vittorio must secretly think she was plain and overweight and he couldn't possibly desire her at all, unless fortified with a great deal of very good whisky. Each thought, each realization, was like a direct hit to her self-confidence, a dagger wound to her heart.

An hour passed in agonizing slowness. She wanted him to come; she didn't want him to come. She wanted to confront him; she wanted to hide. She was annoyed with herself and her own absurd indecision. For ten years she'd been in control of things—of the winery, of her life, of her own emotions. Admittedly, it hadn't been a very exciting life, but she'd been purposeful and determined and *happy*.

Now she felt completely lost, adrift in the bewildering sea of her emotions. It was a sensation she did not enjoy at all.

When a light knock sounded on the door, Ana was almost relieved. Anything at that point was better than waiting. She'd found a thick terry cloth dressing gown in the wardrobe and she'd thrown it on, belting it tightly around her waist so she was covered nearly from her neck to her ankles.

'Where have you been?' she demanded before she'd even laid eyes on him properly; too late, she realized she sounded rather shrewish.

'I thought you'd appreciate a bit of time alone,' Vittorio replied mildly.

Ana swallowed all the hurt and disappointment and nodded stiffly. 'Yes, well. Thank you.'

'Apparently I thought wrong?' he asked, moving past her into the bedroom.

'I just wondered where you were.'

Standing in the middle of the sumptuous bedroom, Vittorio looked utterly in his element. He'd removed his tie and jacket and the top two buttons of his crisp white shirt were undone. His hair was a little rumpled, and Ana could see the shadow of stubble on his strong jaw. He looked unbearably sexy and suddenly, despite everything, she felt faint with longing. She sagged against the door.

Vittorio held up a bottle he was carrying. 'I brought you a wedding present.'

'Oh?' Ana glanced at it. 'Whisky,' she said a bit flatly, and tried to smile. 'Thank you.'

'You did express a preference for it,' Vittorio replied in that same mild voice that Ana wasn't sure she liked. It was so damn unemotional, and here she was, feeling utterly fraught.

'Actually,' she told him, 'I lied.' She enjoyed the look of surprise on his face, his jaw slackening for a second. 'I don't really like whisky. That is, I haven't tried it very much.'

'Really.'

'Really.' Ana strode across the room and plucked the bottle from Vittorio's hand. 'I only said that because I could see how intent you were on manufacturing some kind of businesslike atmosphere, and it seemed like a bottle of whisky would help that.'

'Or we could have just had coffee,' Vittorio replied with the flicker of a smile.

'Coffee over billiards?' Ana arched an eyebrow. 'I don't think so. Anyway, since you brought it, why don't we have a glass now?'

'I thought you said you didn't like it.'

'Oh, didn't I tell you?' Ana gave him a wicked little smile. 'I've developed a taste for it, after all.'

Vittorio paused; Ana could see he was trying to gauge her mood, to decide what was the best—the most efficient and effective—thing to do now. Well, she was tired of that kind of attitude. Just like the last time they'd drunk whisky together, she felt reckless and defiant and even a little dangerous; it was not a pleasant feeling but it made her feel *alive*. She raised the bottle. 'Are there any glasses around?'

'I'm sure I can find some,' Vittorio murmured and moved past her to the en suite bathroom. He returned with two water tumblers and handed them over. 'No ice, I'm afraid.'

'That's all right. I've found I prefer it straight.'

'As do I,' he murmured. He was standing close to her so his breath tickled her ear, making her want to shiver. She just barely suppressed the urge and unscrewed the bottle, pouring two rather large whiskies. She handed Vittorio one of the glasses.

'Cento anni di salute e felicità,' he said with a wry twist to his mouth; it was the traditional wedding toast. A hundred years of health and happiness.

Ana nodded jerkily, and they drank at the same time.

In the aftermath of the alcohol her eyes burned and watered. She just barely kept herself from choking.

'All right?' Vittorio asked, putting his glass aside, and Ana smiled defiantly.

'Never better.'

For a second, his expression flickered. 'Ana—'

'Thank you for the gown, by the way. It's gorgeous.'

'Gown?' Vittorio repeated a bit warily and Ana smiled, the curve of her mouth forced and overbright.

'This.' She reached for the box with its rather large scrap of silk. 'Am I meant to wear it tonight? Because I'm afraid it's a bit too big.' She gave a little laugh. 'I'm not actually as large as you think I am, I suppose.'

Vittorio took the gown without speaking, shook it out and gazed at it with a rather clinical eye. 'I see. It is a beautiful gown, Ana, but I'm afraid I didn't give it to you. I've learned my lesson with you where clothes are concerned.'

Now Ana's jaw slackened, the wind leaking right out of her self-righteous sails. 'You didn't send it?'

'No. But I can guess who did.'

'Who?'

'My mother. To send you a gown several sizes too big—this is the kind of thing she would do. Her little attempt to wound. It stings, *si*?' His eyes hardened. 'Trust me, I know.'

Suddenly the gown didn't matter at all. 'Vittorio—what has happened between you and your mother? And your brother too? Why are you all so—so terrible to one another? So cold.'

Vittorio was silent for a moment, before he shook his head. 'It is past, Ana, past and forgotten. There is nothing you need to know.'

'But it isn't really forgotten, is it? I can tell by the way you talk about it, even now—'

'It's late—' he cut her off '—and you need your sleep. I'll see you in the morning.'

Disappointment opened up inside her, a vast looming pit. She wanted to ask him to stay, but she knew she wouldn't. Couldn't begin their marriage this way, with her begging for him, for his touch. Yet why was he leaving? Was this his so-called sensitivity or merely his indifference? 'All right,' she whispered, her voice catching on the words.

He reached out with one hand and touched her cheek, his thumb finding that secret place where a tear had once sparkled. Ana closed her eyes and nearly swayed where she stood. 'It will be all right, *rondinella*,' he murmured. 'I know this is hard now—awkward too, for both of us, but it will be all right.'

Ana swallowed and nodded, her throat too tight to speak. She didn't open her eyes for a moment and, when she did, Vittorio had already gone.

Alone in the hallway, Vittorio cursed under his breath. Of course his mother would seek to discredit him with Ana from the first moment of their marriage. Of course she would find ways to weaken the tenuous link he'd forged with his bride. And, if Constantia stayed here, she would continue to poison Ana's mind and pare away her self-confidence.

Yet he knew he would not ask his mother to leave. He'd never asked her to leave. He'd been the one to leave, all those years ago; he'd felt like an interloper in his own home, unwanted and undesired, and it had been easier simply to walk away.

Vittorio thought of the disappointment he'd seen in Ana's eyes. She'd wanted him to stay; she'd even wanted him to make love to her. And he'd wanted it, too; his body even now stirred to lust. Yet he'd balked, like a shy virgin! The thought almost made him laugh in exasperation at his own reticence. All too easily he could imagine taking her in his arms, unwrapping her from that thick, bulky robe like a parcel from its paper.

Yet she wasn't merely a parcel, a thing, this wife of his, and it was this uncomfortable new knowledge that kept him from staying. From consummating their marriage, for surely that was all it would be. A consummation, a soulless act, and he was—suddenly, stupidly too—afraid of hurting her.

Vittorio cursed aloud. Now was not the time to develop some kind of stupid sensitivity. He stopped, almost turned around, even if just to prove a point to himself. Then he remembered the way Ana's grey eyes, so wide and luminous and somehow soft, had darkened with disappointment when he'd said he was leaving, how her breath had shortened when he'd touched her cheek and, furious with himself, at a loss for what he should do now, he kept on walking.

CHAPTER EIGHT

THE NEXT FEW days were some of the most depressing Ana had ever known, simply by reason of their utter sameness. Except for the fact that she drove back to Castle Cazlevara every night after work, Ana would not know she was married. Her days had not changed at all; after an impersonal breakfast with Vittorio, she left for the winery offices, spent the day there and returned to the castle for another impersonal and often silent meal.

Vittorio seemed to have retreated into himself; they hardly talked, and the little gifts he'd showered her with before their marriage had stopped completely. Ana couldn't tell if Vittorio was simply satisfied now he'd married her, or if he actually regretted the deed. As far as periods of adjustment went, theirs was an utter failure. There was no adjusting; there was only enduring.

Ana saw Constantia and Bernardo on occasion; they were currently residing at the castle, although they seemed to avoid both her and Vittorio. Bernardo ate out, and Constantia took her meals in her rooms. It was, Ana reflected, an unhappy household, shrouded in its own misery.

After three days of this, Ana could take it no longer. She found Vittorio at the breakfast table, reading the newspaper and drinking his espresso. He barely glanced up when she entered.

'You'd think,' Ana said, hearing the acid in her own voice, 'that we'd been married three decades rather than three days.'

She saw Vittorio's fingers tense and then he lowered the newspaper. 'What do you mean, Ana?' he asked in that careful, mild voice he seemed to save just for her. It was so neutral, so *irritating*, for it made Ana feel as if he was dealing with a child or a puppy that needed training.

'I mean,' she retorted, as Giulia, the morning maid, came bustling forth with her own latte, 'that for the last three days—the only three days we've been married—you have been ignoring me. Are you regretting your decision, Vittorio? Because of course you know we can still get the marriage annulled.'

The only change in Vittorio's expression was a tightening of his lips and a flaring of his nostrils. 'I have no wish to annul this marriage.'

'You have no wish to act as if you were married, either.'

Vittorio folded his paper and dropped it on the table. He picked up his tiny cup of espresso and took a sip, studying Ana from over its rim. 'I wanted to give you time,' he finally said quietly. 'I thought…to rush into things might be difficult.'

'To feel like I don't belong—that we're not even married—is difficult too,' Ana countered. His words had comforted her, given her hope, but she wasn't about to give up any ground quite yet.

Vittorio nodded slowly. 'Very well. I was drawing up the guest list for the party I mentioned earlier. I thought we could have it on Friday, in two days' time. If you have anyone you'd like to add to the list, just tell me, or email me the particulars.' He paused before adding only a bit acerbically, 'Perhaps when we announce to the world we are married, you will feel it yourself.'

Or, Ana thought a bit savagely as Vittorio rose and took his leave, perhaps she would feel married when Vittorio treated her like a wife, a proper wife, a wife in every sense of the word as he'd told her he would.

Alone in the dining room, she drummed her fingers on the burnished mahogany table top and moodily sipped her latte. All around her the castle was quiet; even though Giulia was undoubtedly hovering just outside the door, Ana could hear nothing. She felt very alone.

I didn't think it would be like this.

Annoyed with herself, Ana pushed the traitorous thought aside and rose from the table. The dining room, like many other rooms in the castle, had been refurbished some time in the last century and now possessed long elegant windows overlooking the terraced gardens that led down to the drained moat. Under a fragile blue sky, it was austerely beautiful, yet it hardly felt like home. And she still couldn't see or hear another living soul.

Without even realizing she was doing it, Ana brushed at the corner of her eye and her fingertip came away damp. She was crying. She never cried, not since her mother had died. Even during those miserable years at boarding school, that first seeming rejection of her father and, later, Roberto's worse rejection, she'd always choked her sorrow down and soldiered on so it remained a hot lump in her chest, pushing it further and further down until she couldn't feel it at all. Almost.

Now she felt it deeply, all the sorrow and anger and fear, rising up in a red tide of emotion she didn't have the time or energy to deal with.

She'd accepted that Vittorio didn't love her. She'd been prepared that he might not desire her the way she desired him. She hadn't counted on the fact that he'd actually avoid her.

How was this meant to make her life easier?

'Has Vittorio left you alone?'

Ana whirled around at the sound of her mother-in-law's clipped voice. The ageing beauty stood framed in the doorway of the dining room, poised as ever to make an entrance. Ana forced a small smile. She really didn't feel like dealing with Constantia just now.

'He went to work, and I'm off in a moment too,' she said,

trying to sound cheerful even as she attempted some kind of regretful look that she wouldn't be able to spend breakfast with her mother-in-law. 'We're both very busy.'

'Of course you are.' Constantia glided into the room, followed by Giulia, who brought a separate tray of espresso and rolls. The Dowager Countess clearly deserved special service. 'Tell me, Anamaria,' Constantia asked as she sat down and neatly broke a roll in half, 'how is marriage suiting you?' She glanced up, her eyes narrowed only slightly, so Ana couldn't tell if her mother-in-law knew just what kind of marriage she and Vittorio had, or if she genuinely wanted to know the answer to that thorny question. Constantia never gave anything away.

Ana's mouth widened into a bright false smile. 'Wonderfully.'

Constantia nodded thoughtfully and nibbled a piece of her roll. 'Vittorio is so much like his father. A hard man to be married to.'

In a flash Ana remembered her own father's assessment of Arturo Cazlevara: *Arturo was a good man too, but he was hard. Without mercy.*

She glanced at Constantia, now composedly sipping her espresso, with genuine curiosity. 'What do you mean?'

Constantia shrugged one shoulder. 'Surely you know what I mean? Vittorio isn't…affectionate. Emotional.' She paused, and when she spoke her voice sounded almost ragged. 'He will never love you.'

Something sharp lanced through Ana; she didn't know whether it was fear or pain. Perhaps both. She turned back to the window. 'I don't expect him to love me,' she said quietly.

'You may have convinced yourself of that once, my dear,' Constantia said. 'But can you continue to do so? For years?'

There was too much knowledge, too much sorrowful experience in the older woman's voice for Ana not to ask. 'Is that what happened to you?' Ana turned around; for a moment Constantia looked vulnerable, and her fingers shook a little bit as she replaced her cup in its saucer.

'Yes, it is. I loved Arturo Cazlevara from the time I was a little girl. We were neighbours, you know, just like Vittorio and you are—were. Everyone approved of the marriage, everyone thought it was a great match. Arturo never said he didn't love me, of course. And on the surface he was considerate, kind. Just like Vittorio, *si*? Yet here—' Constantia lightly touched her breastbone '—here, I knew.'

Tua cuore. Sudden tears stung Ana's eyes and she blinked them away. She was *not* going to cry. 'Consideration and kindness,' she said after a moment, 'count for much.'

Constantia laughed once, the sound sharp with cynicism. 'Oh, you think so? Because I happen to believe those agreeable sentiments make you feel like a puppy that has been patted on the head and told to go and lie down and stop bothering anyone anymore. Not a nice feeling all these years, you know? To feel like a dog.' She paused, and something hardened in both her face and voice. 'You would be amazed to know the things you can be driven to, the things you do even though you hate them—hate yourself—when you feel like that.' She drained her espresso and rose from the table, giving Ana one last cool smile. The haughty set of her shoulders and the arrogant tilt of her chin made Ana think Constantia regretted her moment of honesty. 'Perhaps it is different for you, Ana.'

'It *is* different,' Ana replied with sudden force. 'I don't love Vittorio either.'

Constantia's smile was pitying. 'Don't you?' she said, and walked from the room.

Constantia's words echoed through Ana's mind all morning as she tried to focus on work. She couldn't. She argued endlessly with herself, trying to convince herself that she didn't love Vittorio, she didn't love the way his eyes gleamed when he was amused, the way they softened when he spoke quietly, the broad set of his shoulders, the feel of his lips—

Of course, those were all physical attributes. You couldn't love someone based on how they *looked*. Yet Ana knew there was more to Vittorio than his dark good looks. When she was in his presence, she felt alive. Amazed. As if anything could happen, good or bad, and the good would be wonderful and even the bad would be all right because she still would be with him. She wanted to know more about him, not just to feel his body against hers, but his heart against hers also. She wanted to see him smile, just for her. To have him whisper something just meant for her.

She wanted him to love her. She wanted to love him.

She wanted love.

'No!' The word burst out of her, bounced around the walls of her empty room. 'No,' she said again, a whisper, a plea. She couldn't want love. She couldn't, because Vittorio would never give it. She thought of Constantia, her face a map of the disappointments life had given her. Ana didn't know all the history between Constantia and Vittorio, or Constantia and her own husband, but she knew—it was plain to see—that the woman was bitter, angry, and perhaps even in despair. She didn't want that. Yet, if she wanted Vittorio's love—which she was still trying to convince herself she didn't—it seemed like only a matter of time until she was like Constantia, unfulfilled and unhappy, pacing the rooms of Castle Cazlevara and cursing other people's joy.

That afternoon Ana left work early—a rare occurrence—and drove to the Mestre train station that crossed the lagoon into Venice. As she rode over the Ponte della Libertà—the Bridge of Liberty—Ana wondered what she was doing...and why. Why had she summoned all her courage and rung the boutique Vittorio had taken her to before their marriage, why had she made an appointment with the pencil-thin Feliciana to be fitted for several outfits, including a gown for the party on Friday night?

Ana told herself it was because she needed some new clothes, now that she was the Countess. Part of her arrangement with Vittorio was that she would dress appropriately to her station, as he'd said. Naturally, it made sense to visit the boutique he'd chosen above all others for this purpose.

Yet, no matter how many times Ana told herself this—mustering all her logic, her common sense—her heart told her otherwise. She was doing this—dressing this way—because she wanted Vittorio to see her differently. She wanted him to see her as a wife, and not just any wife, but a wife he could love.

The thought terrified her.

'Contessa Cazlevara!' Feliciana started forward the minute Ana entered the narrow confines of the upscale boutique. Ana smiled and allowed herself to be air-kissed, even though she felt awkward and cloddish and, well, *huge* in this place. Feliciana had to be a good eight inches shorter than her, at the very least.

'I've put some things aside for you,' Feliciana said, leading her to a private salon in the back of the boutique, 'that I think will suit you very well.'

'Really?' Ana couldn't keep the scepticism from her voice. Feliciana had only glimpsed her once before; how on earth could she know what suited her? And a little mocking voice asked, how could *anything* suit her?

Ana commanded that voice to be silent. Yet other voices rose to take its place: the locker room taunts of the girls at boarding school, the boys who had ignored or teased her, the helpless sigh of the matron who had shaken her head and said, 'At least you're strong.' And then, most damning of all, Roberto's utter rejection. *How could I?*

Over the years she'd avoided places like this, dresses like these, for a reason. And now, standing in the centre of a brightly lit, mirrored dressing room while Feliciana bustled over with an armful of frocks, she felt horribly exposed and vulnerable.

'Now, first I thought, a gown for the party, *si*?' Feliciana smiled. 'Most important.'

'Yes, I suppose,' Ana murmured, looking dubiously at a white lace gown she'd glimpsed on her last visit to the boutique. It now hung over Feliciana's arm, exquisite and fragile.

'A formal occasion, is it not? I thought we'd try this.' Feliciana held up the gown.

Ana shook her head. 'I don't think…'

'You'll see,' Feliciana said firmly. She gestured to Ana's trouser suit with a tiny grimace of distaste. 'Now, you hide yourself in these clothes, as if you are ashamed.'

Ana flushed. 'I'm just not—'

'But you *are*,' Feliciana interjected. She smiled, laying a hand on Ana's arm. 'It is not my job to make women look awkward or ugly, *si*? I know what I am doing. Right now, you walk with your shoulders stooped, your head bowed as if you are trying not to be tall.'

'I don't—' Ana protested.

'You are tall,' Feliciana said firmly. 'With a beautiful full figure. And don't you know many women long to be so tall? You are strikingly beautiful, but I know you don't think you are.' She let go of Ana's shoulders and gestured to the lace confection of a dress. 'In this, you will see.' She smiled again, softly. 'Trust me.'

So Ana did. She took the dress and let Feliciana take her trouser suit, slipping into the lacy sheath with some foreboding and also a building excitement. The dress fitted like a second skin, hugging her hips, the dip of her waist and the swell of her breasts. Its plunging neckline was made respectable by the handmade Burano lace edging it, and the material ended in a frothy swirl around her ankles. Ana sucked her stomach in as Feliciana did up the hidden zipper in the back, but there was no need as the dress fitted perfectly. They *did* make gowns like this in her size.

Ana didn't dare look in the mirror. She wasn't afraid, precisely, but neither did she want to be disappointed.

'Uno minuto…' Feliciana muttered, surveying her, her hands on her hips. She reached out and tugged the clip from Ana's hair; it cascaded down her back in a dark swirl. 'Ah…*perfectto!*'

Perfect? Her? Ana almost shook her head, but Feliciana

steered her towards the mirror. 'Look. You've never seen yourself in something like this before, have you?'

No, she hadn't. Ana knew that the minute she gazed at her reflection, because for a second at least she couldn't believe she was staring at herself. She was staring at a stranger, a woman—a gorgeous, confident, sexy woman. She shook her head.

'No...'

Feliciana clucked in dismay. 'You don't like it?'

'No.' A bubble of laughter erupted, escaping through her lips as Ana turned around. 'I don't like it. I love it.'

Feliciana grinned. '*Buon*. Because I have at least six other gowns I want you to try.'

By the time Ana left the boutique, she'd purchased four gowns, several skirts and tops, three pairs of shoes, including a pair of silver stilettos that she'd balked at until Feliciana had told her sternly, 'Your husband must be almost five inches taller than you. You can wear heels.'

She'd never worn heels in her life. She'd probably fall on her face. Ana giggled; she wasn't used to making such a girlish sound. Yet right now she felt girlish, feminine and frivolous and *fun*. She'd enjoyed this afternoon and, best of all, she couldn't *wait* until Vittorio saw her in the lace gown on Friday night.

Yet, when Friday night actually came and she stood at the top of the sweeping staircase that led down to the castle's foyer and its waiting master, Ana didn't feel so confident. So *fun*. She felt sick with nerves, with a queasy fear that Vittorio wouldn't like how she looked or, worse, that he wouldn't even care how she looked. They'd barely seen each other outside meals and Ana spent her nights alone. She was a wife in name only, and she longed to change that tonight.

From the top of the stairs she could see him waiting at the bottom, could feel his impatience. He wore a perfectly cut suit of grey silk and he rested one long tapered hand on the banister railing.

'Ana?' he called up, a bit sharply. 'Are you ready? The guests will be here very soon.'

'Yes,' she called, her own voice wavering a little. 'I'm ready.'

Vittorio heard Ana coming down the stairs behind him, but he didn't turn around right away. He needed to steel himself, he realized, for however his wife might look. So far he had not been impressed with her clothes; her wedding dress had been an unmitigated disaster. She'd told him she knew the difference between a designer gown and a bin bag, but Vittorio had yet to be convinced. Not, he reflected, that he'd taken Ana's dress sense into consideration when he'd chosen her as his bride.

Why *had* he chosen her as his bride? Vittorio wondered rather moodily. All the businesslike reasons about merging wineries and knowing the region seemed utterly absurd to base a marriage on. Of course, when his mother had spoken to him about heirs, his logical mind had not thought about a *marriage*; it had simply fastened on the one necessity: wife. Object. Then he'd seen the vulnerability in Ana's eyes, had felt her softness against him, had breathed in the earthy scent of her desire and known that *wife* and *object* were not two words ever to string together.

Ana was a person, and not just a person, but his *wife*. His beloved. The person he should protect and cherish above all others. The person, he realized bleakly, he was meant to love. And he had no idea what to do with her.

It was why he'd avoided her since their wedding; why he still had not come to her bed. He'd thought he could live with a business arrangement. That was what he had wanted. Yet now, bizarrely, he found the cold-blooded terms of their arrangement to be…distasteful. Yet he didn't love Ana, didn't know if he was even capable of such an emotion. He hadn't loved anyone in years. His entire adult life had been focused on *not* loving, on building Cazlevara Wines, maintaining his reputation and influence as Count, trying to forget the fractured family he'd left behind. The women he'd involved himself with hadn't even come close to touching his heart.

Yet *Ana*… Ana with her blunt way of speaking and her soft grey eyes, her brash confidence and her lurking vulnerability, her tall, lush figure and her earthy scent… Ana somehow slipped inside the defences he'd erected around himself, his heart. He'd prided himself on being logical, sensible, perhaps even cold. Yet now he wouldn't even go to his wife's bed for fear of—what? Hurting her?

He'd told his bride very plainly that he never intended to love her. Love, he had said, was a destructive emotion. And perhaps that was what made him afraid now; he was afraid that his love would destroy Ana, would ruin their marriage.

His love was destructive.

'Vittorio…?' He felt Ana's hand on his sleeve, her voice no more than an uncertain whisper. She must have been standing there for some moments, waiting for him to notice her while he was lost in his gloomy reflections. Vittorio turned around.

'Good even—' He stopped, the words dried in his mouth, his head suddenly, completely empty of thoughts. The woman in front of him was stunning, a vision of ethereal loveliness in white lace. No, he realized distantly, she wasn't ethereal. She was earthy and real and so very beautiful. And she was his wife. 'You look…' he began and, though she tried to disguise it, he saw Ana's face fall, the disappointment shadowing her eyes and making her shoulders slump just a fraction. He let himself touch her, holding her by the shoulders. Her skin was warm and golden. The dress clung to her figure; he'd never realized how perfectly she was proportioned, the swell of her breasts and the curve of her hips. He'd once considered her mannish; the thought was now laughable. He'd never seen a more feminine woman. 'You look amazing,' he said, his voice low, heartfelt, and Ana smiled.

She had the most amazing smile. He'd noticed her teeth before, straight and white, as one might notice a piece of workmanship. Now he saw the way the smile transformed her face, softened the angles and made joy dance in her eyes in golden glints.

Amazing. His wife was amazing.

'Thank you,' she said, her voice just as heartfelt, and Vittorio did the only thing he could do... He kissed her. As he drew her close, he was conscious of her generous curves fitting so snugly against his own body, amazed at the way her length lined up to his. How had he ever stooped to kiss a shorter woman before? His back ached just to think of it.

And Ana's lips... They were soft and warm and as generous as the rest of her, open and giving and so very sweet. Vittorio had meant only to kiss her briefly—something between a peck and a brush—but once he tasted her he found he couldn't get enough. The kiss went on and on, her arms snaking up around his shoulders, her body pressing against his—she'd never been shy—until someone behind him cleared his throat in a pointed manner.

'Pardon me for breaking up this rather touching scene,' Bernardo drawled, 'but the guests are starting to arrive.'

'Good.' Vittorio stepped away from Ana, his arm still around her waist. She *fitted* against him, nestled near him in a way that was neither cloying nor coy. It was, he knew, as genuine as the rest of her was.

Bernardo eyed Ana with obvious surprise. 'You cleaned up rather well.'

'Bernardo,' Vittorio said sharply, 'that is no way to speak to my wife the Countess.'

Bernardo turned back to Vittorio, his eyebrows raised. 'Isn't it what you were thinking?' he countered. Vittorio pressed his lips together; he didn't want to argue with his brother now. He wouldn't spoil this evening for Ana. Bernardo turned to Ana and made a little bow. 'Forgive me, Ana. I meant no insult. You look very beautiful.'

Vittorio said nothing. This was how his brother always acted;

he'd deliver the sting with one hand and the sweetness with the other. It made it impossible to fight him, or at least to win. Vittorio had learned this long ago, when his parents had drawn the battle lines. Constantia got Bernardo and his father took him. They had been his parents' most potent weapons. It had, Vittorio reflected, been a long drawn-out war.

'No offence taken, Bernardo,' Ana said, smiling. 'I was thinking the same thing myself.'

Bernardo gave her an answering flicker of a smile and bowed again. Vittorio squeezed Ana's waist and the first guests came towards them before he could thank his wife for being so gracious.

Ana moved through the party in a haze of happiness. She never wanted to forget the look on Vittorio's face when he'd turned around and seen her. She'd expected the disbelief, of course, but not the joy. He'd been *happy* to see her. He'd wanted her by his side. And when he'd kissed her… Every secret hope and latent need had risen up inside her on newly formed wings, and she hadn't suppressed them or forced them back to the ground. For years she'd refused to entertain such dreams, knowing they could only lead to disappointment, yet when Vittorio had looked at her, she'd felt like the woman she'd always longed to be. The woman she was meant to be. It was a wonderful feeling.

She stayed by Vittorio's side for most of the party. He wanted her there, kept his arm around her, her hip pressed against his. She laughed and chatted and listened and nodded, but none of it really penetrated. The need—the desire—was building within her slowly, a force rising up and needing to be reckoned with. To be satisfied.

Tonight, she told herself. *Tonight, he will come to me.* As the evening wore on, her certainty—and her happiness—only grew.

Vittorio had been so proud, so happy to have Ana by his side. He'd drifted through the party in a haze, on a cloud. He couldn't wait to get Ana alone, to touch her—

Yet now she'd gone to see her father off and, alone, he felt strangely flat, indifferent to all he'd achieved. He wanted her to come back to him and yet, even so, he didn't go in search of her. He didn't even know what he would say.

He thought of how Enrico Viale had stopped him in the middle of the party, one hand on his sleeve. 'She looked beautiful, our Ana, *si*?' the older man had said, pride shining in his eyes. Vittorio had been about to agree when he realized Enrico was not talking about how Ana looked tonight. 'It was her mother's wedding dress, you know. I asked her to wear it.'

Vittorio had been left speechless, amazed and humbled by Ana's selflessness, by her loyalty. And he'd demanded that same loyalty of her for *him*? When he didn't even know what to do with her, how to treat her, how to *love* her?

Love. But he didn't *want* love.

As the last guests trickled outside, the cars heading down the castle's steep drive in a steady stream of light, Vittorio wondered what on earth he'd been trying to accomplish by setting out to acquire a wife like so much baggage. What had been the point, to take another being into his care, another life into his hands? Who was meant to notice, to know?

Who cared?

Of course, most of his neighbours and fellow winemakers were curious about the Count of Cazlevara's sudden return and even more sudden marriage. He'd felt their implicit approval that he'd returned to where he belonged, was now taking his rightful place, esteemed winemaker and leader of the community.

Yet he hadn't been trying to gain *their* approval. At that moment, their approval hardly mattered at all.

'So, Vittorio. A success.'

Vittorio turned slowly around; his mother stood in the doorway of the drawing room. She looked coldly elegant in a cream satin sheath dress, her expression unsmiling. This was the person whose approval he'd been trying to gain, Vittorio realized, and how absurd that was, considering his mother had not had a moment of interest or affection for him since he was four. When his brother had been born.

He was jealous, Vittorio realized, incredulous and yet still somehow unsurprised by this. All these years, his desire to return to his home and show his brother and mother his success, his self-sufficiency—it had just been jealousy. Petty, pathetic jealousy.

He turned back to the window. The last cars had disappeared down the darkened drive. 'So it appears.'

'You're not pleased?' she asked, moving into the room. He heard a caustic note in her voice that still made his shoulders tense and the vulnerable space between them prickle.

Go away, Vittorio. Leave me alone.

At that moment he felt like that confused child who had tugged his mother's sleeve, desperate to show her a drawing, receive a hug. She'd turned away, time and time again, forever averting both her face and her heart. When she'd welcomed Bernardo, adored and doted on and spoiled him utterly, it seemed obvious. She simply preferred his brother to him.

Vittorio made an impatient sound of disgust; he was disgusted with himself. Why was he remembering these silly, childish moments now? He'd lived with his mother's rejection for most of his life. He'd learned not to care. He'd steeled himself against it, against the treachery she'd committed when his father had died—

Except obviously he hadn't, for the emotions were still present, raked up and raw, and they made him angry. What kind of man was still hurt by his *mother*? It was ridiculous, pathetic, shaming.

'On the contrary, Mother. I am very pleased.' His voice was bland with just a hint of sharpness; it was the tone he always reserved for her.

She gave an answering little laugh, just as sharp. 'Oh, Vittorio. Nothing is ever enough, is it? You're just like your father.' The words were meant to be an accusation, a condemnation.

'I'll take that as a compliment.'

His mother's lip curled in a sneer. 'Of course you will.'

Impatient with all her veiled little barbs, Vittorio shrugged. 'Where's Ana?'

Constantia arched her eyebrows in challenge. 'Why do you care?'

His temper finally frayed. 'Because she is my *wife*.' And he wanted to know where she was, he wanted to see her now, to feel her smile, her sweetness—

'A wife you won't love.'

Vittorio stiffened. 'That is no concern of—'

'Isn't it?' She stepped closer and he saw the anger in her eyes, as well as something else. Something that looked strangely like sorrow. It was unfamiliar. He was used to his mother angry, but sad—?

'You don't know what it is like to love someone, Vittorio, who will never love you back—'

He laughed in disbelief; he couldn't help it. 'Don't I?'

Constantia looked utterly nonplussed. 'No—'

He shook his head, too weary to explain. 'Do you know where Ana is?'

'You will bring heartache to that girl. You will destroy her—'

Vittorio tensed, steeling himself once more, but this time he couldn't. *Love is a destructive emotion.* The thought of bringing such pain and misery to Ana made his head bow, his shoulders shake. 'Why do you care?' he asked in a low, savage voice.

'She is a good woman, Vittorio.'

'Too good for me, obviously.'

Constantia sighed impatiently. 'I have made many mistakes with you, I know. I have many regrets. But this marriage—it can only lead to more despair. And surely our family has had enough unhappiness?'

She was pleading with him, as if their family's misery was his fault? Vittorio turned around, his body rigid with rage. 'On that point we agree, Mother. Yet it seems odd that the instrument of so much unhappiness should then seek to end it.'

Constantia blinked as if she'd been struck. 'I know you blame me—'

'Blame you?' Vittorio repeated silkily. 'Are you referring to your attempt to take my inheritance, my father only *hours* in the grave? Your desperate desire to drag the family into the law courts and give my brother my title?'

Constantia straightened and met his hostile gaze directly. 'Yes, Vittorio, I am referring to that. God knows you will never let me forget it.'

'One hardly forgets the dagger thrust between one's shoulders,' Vittorio returned, every word encased in ice. He still remembered how he had reeled with shock; he'd come back from his father's funeral, devastated by grief, only to find that in his absence his mother had met a solicitor and attempted to overturn the contents of his father's will, disinheriting him completely and giving everything to Bernardo. All the childhood slights had led to that one brutal moment, when he'd understood with stark clarity that his mother didn't just dislike him, she *despised* him. She'd do anything to keep him from inheriting what was rightfully his.

He would never forget. He couldn't.

'No,' Constantia agreed softly, her eyes glittering, 'one does not forget. And I will tell you, Vittorio, that for a woman to be denied love—by her own husband—is not a dagger between the shoulders, but one straight to the heart. For your wife's sake, if not my own, do not hurt her.'

'Such pretty words,' Vittorio scoffed. The rage had left him, making him feel only weary. 'You have come to care for my wife then, Mother?'

'I know how she feels,' Constantia said bleakly and, with one last shake of her head, she left the room.

Her words rang in his ears, and yet Vittorio still made himself dismiss them. *I know how she feels.* Was his mother implying she'd loved his father? To Vittorio's young eyes, his parents had agreed on a polite marriage of convenience. Just like the one he'd meant to have. Yet his parents' marriage had descended into anger and even hatred, and at the thought of that happening to him—to Ana—Vittorio swore aloud. All the old feelings, hurt memories, had been raked up tonight and Vittorio knew why.

Ana.

Somehow she'd affected him, touched him in a way he had never been touched. Made him open and exposed and, more than that, she made him want. Made him need.

Love.

He swore again.

'Vittorio?'

He whirled around. Ana stood in the doorway, her face nearly as white as her lace gown.

'How much did you hear?' he asked, his tone brusque, brutal.

Ana flinched. 'Enough. Too much.'

'I told you my family's history was not worth repeating,' Vittorio replied with a shrug. He moved to the drinks table and poured himself a whisky.

'Don't—' Ana said inadvertently and he turned around, one eyebrow arched.

'I'm having a *drink*, Ana,' he said, the words a taunt. 'Whisky. Your favourite. Don't you want to join me?'

'No. Vittorio, I want to talk.'

He took a healthy swallow and let the alcohol burn straight to his gut. 'Go ahead.'

Ana flinched again. Vittorio knew he was being callous, even cruel, but he couldn't help it. The exchange with his mother, the emerging feelings for Ana—it all left him feeling so exposed. Vulnerable.

Afraid.

He hated it.

Turning away from her, he kept his voice a bored drawl. 'So what do you want to talk about?'

* * *

Ana watched her husband as he gazed out of the window, affecting an air of bored indifference, yet she knew better now. He was hurting. She didn't understand everything he'd referred to in his conversation with Constantia, didn't know the source of all the pain, but she did know her marriage had no chance if Vittorio was going to remain mired in his painful past.

'Tell me what went wrong,' she said quietly.

Vittorio must not have been expecting that, for he bowed his head suddenly, his fingers clenched around his whisky glass.

'Everything,' he finally said in a low voice. 'Everything went wrong.'

Cautiously Ana approached him, laid a hand on his shoulder. 'Oh, Vittorio—'

He jerked away. 'Don't pity me. I could not stand that.'

'I just want to understand—'

'It's simple, Ana.' He turned to face her, his expression hard and implacable once more. 'My mother didn't love me. What a sad story, eh? Pathetic, no? A thirty-seven-year-old man whingeing on about his mean *mamma*.'

'There's more to it than that,' Ana said quietly.

'Oh, a few trite details.' He gave a negligent shrug and drained his glass. 'You see, my parents hated each other. Perhaps there was once love or at least affection, but not so I could remember. By the time Bernardo came along, the battle lines were drawn. I belonged to my father and Bernardo was my mother's.'

'What do you mean?'

'Simple. My father had no time or patience for Bernardo, and my mother had none for me. They used us like weapons. And my father was a good man, he trained me well—'

'But he was a hard man,' Ana interjected, remembering.

Vittorio glanced at her sharply. 'Who told you that?'

'My father. He said Arturo was a good man, but without mercy.'

Vittorio let out a little breath of sound; Ana wasn't sure if it was a laugh or something else. Perhaps even a sob. 'Perhaps that is true. But he knew I was to inherit, and he wanted to train me up for the role—'

Ana could just imagine what that must have felt like, especially if Bernardo was not receiving the same harsh treatment. 'And Bernardo?' she asked softly.

'My mother lavished all her love on him. He was like a spoilt poodle.'

Ana flinched at the contempt in his voice. Surely being spoiled was just as bad as being disciplined, just in a different way. 'It sounds like both of you had difficult childhoods.'

'Both of us?' Vittorio repeated in disbelief, then shrugged. 'Maybe.' He sounded bored, and Ana clung to her belief that it was merely a cover for the true, deeper emotions he was too afraid to expose.

She knew all about being vulnerable. Physically and emotionally. Even wearing this dress—opening herself to scorn—made her feel exposed, as exposed as Vittorio did raking through his unhappy childhood. No one liked to talk about such dark memories, admit how they hurt.

'What happened when your father died?' Ana asked.

'My mother did what she'd undoubtedly been planning to do ever since Bernardo was born. She went to court to have his will overturned—and Bernardo made heir.'

Ana gasped. Even though she'd suspected as much, it still surprised her. Why would Constantia do such a vindictive thing? Yet, even as she asked the question, Ana thought she knew the answer. Hadn't Constantia explained it herself? *You would be amazed to know the things you can be driven to...when you feel like that.* And then, her words tonight: *You're just like your father.* Had she transferred all the bitterness and anger she'd felt towards her husband to her son? It seemed perfectly possible, and unbearably sad.

'Oh, Vittorio,' Ana whispered. 'I am sorry.'

'Well, don't be,' he replied, his voice turning harsh again. 'She didn't have a prayer of succeeding. My father was too smart for that. Perhaps he suspected what she was up to, what she could be capable of. His will remained intact, and Bernardo didn't inherit a single *lira*.'

Ana gasped again. 'Not…anything?'

'No, and rightly so. He would have squandered it all.'

'But then,' Ana said slowly, realization dawning, 'he lives here only on your sufferance. Doesn't he work at the winery?'

Vittorio shrugged. 'I let him work as the assistant manager.'

'You let him,' Ana repeated. 'As an assistant.'

'Are you saying it is not enough?' Vittorio demanded raggedly. 'This brother who would have taken everything from me? Do you think he would have been so merciful?'

Ana shook her head. 'But if your mother attempted all this with the will when your father died, you were only—'

'Fourteen.'

'And Bernardo was a child—nine or ten at the most—'

'Ten,' Vittorio confirmed flatly. Anger sparked in his eyes; his face had become hard again, a stranger's. 'Are you taking his side, Ana? Don't you remember what I told you, what I warned you about?'

His tone was so dangerous, so icy, that Ana could only blink in confusion, her mind whirling with all these revelations. 'What—?'

Vittorio closed the space between them, circling her wrist with his hands, drawing her to him. The movement was not one of seduction, but possession, and Ana came up hard against his chest. 'Loyalty, Ana. I told you those closest to me would try to discredit me. You swore you would be loyal to me—'

She could hardly believe he was bringing up loyalty now. This was his *family*. 'Vittorio, I am simply trying to understand—'

'Maybe I don't want you to understand,' Vittorio said harshly. 'Maybe if you understood—' He stopped, shaking his head, a look of what almost seemed like fear flashing across his face before he muttered an oath and then, with a sudden groan, claimed her mouth in a kiss.

It wasn't a kiss, Ana thought distantly, so much as a brand. He was punishing her for her curiosity and reminding her of her vow. And, in that kiss she felt all his anger, his hurt and even his fear. And despite her own answering anger—that he would kiss her this way—she felt the traitorous flicker of her own desire and she pressed against him, let her hands tangle in his hair, wanting to change this angry embrace into something healing and *good*—

'No!' With a bellow of disgust, Vittorio pushed her away. Ana stumbled and reached out to steady herself; both of them were gasping as if they'd run a race. And lost.

'Vittorio—'

'No,' he said again. He raked a hand through his hair, let out a ragged sob. 'Not like this. God help me, I never wanted this.'

'But—'

'I told you,' he said in a low voice, 'love is a destructive emotion.'

Ana shook her head, wanting to deny what he said, wanting to fight—and wondering if he was actually telling her, in a terribly twisted way, that he loved her.

Was this love? This confusion and sorrow and pain?

No wonder they'd both agreed to live without it.

'It doesn't have to be destructive,' Ana said quietly but, his back now to her, Vittorio just shook his head.

'With me,' he said in a voice so low Ana strained to hear, 'it is.' He let out a shuddering sigh. 'Leave me, Ana. Just leave me.'

Ana stood there uncertainly, knowing to slink away now was surely the worst thing to do. 'No,' she said finally. 'I don't want to.'

Vittorio swung around, incredulous. 'What—'

'We're married, Vittorio. I'm not going to run away like some frightened child.' He flinched, and she raised her chin. 'And

I'm not going to sleep alone tonight, either. I'm your wife and I belong in your bed.'

Vittorio's disbelief turned to disdain. *'Now—'*

She stepped closer to him, reached out with one hand to touch his lapel. 'Just hold me, Vittorio.' She saw his mouth tremble and she touched his lips. 'And let me hold you. And maybe, together, for a few moments, we can forget all this bitterness and pain.'

Vittorio shook his head slowly and Ana's heart sank. She'd thought she'd reached him, managed to get past the barrier he'd constructed to keep her—and anyone important—out. She could not bear his rejection now, not when she'd made herself so vulnerable, so exposed—just as he had—

Then, to her amazement and joy, he slowly reached for her hand, lacing his fingers tightly with hers, and silently, accepting, he led her from the darkened room.

CHAPTER NINE

ANA WOKE TO SUNLIGHT. Even better, warming her deep inside, she woke with Vittorio's arm around her, her head nestled against his shoulder. She breathed in the scent of his skin, loving it, loving him.

Yes, she loved him. It seemed so obvious, so simple, in the clean, healing light of day. Yes, love was confusing and scary and full of sorrow and pain; it was *love*. Opening your heart and your body and even your soul to another person. Risking everything, your own health and happiness and well-being. And yet gaining so much.

Maybe.

She pulled away from Vittorio a little so she could look at him; he remained asleep, his features softened, almost gentle in repose. She touched the dark stubble on his chin, felt her heart twist painfully. Yes, love hurt.

This love hurt—for, if she loved him, she had no idea if he loved her.

Love is a destructive emotion.

She was starting to understand why he believed such a thing. Constantia's love for her husband had been destructive, her unhappiness and despair leading her to unhealthy relationships with both of her sons. And, as the one who felt unloved by his mother—and harshly loved, no doubt, by his father—Ana could almost understand why Vittorio wanted no more of it.

My love wouldn't be destructive. My love would heal you.

She touched his cheek, let her fingers feather over his eyebrow. He stirred and she stilled, holding her breath, not wanting him to wake up and ruin this moment. She was afraid when he opened his eyes the distance would be back, the cold, logical man who had insisted on a marriage of convenience, a marriage without love.

And she had agreed. She had, somehow, managed to convince herself that that was the kind of marriage, the kind of life, she wanted. Lying there, half in his arms, Ana knew it was not and never had been. She'd accepted such a poor bargain simply because she was afraid she'd find nothing else—and because it had been a bargain with Vittorio.

A life with Vittorio.

When had she started loving him? The seeds had surely been sown long ago, when he had touched her cheek and called her swallow. Such a small moment, yet in it she'd seen his gentleness, his tender heart, and she hoped—prayed—that she could see them again now. Soon.

She wouldn't let Vittorio push her away or keep their marriage as coldly convenient—and safe—as he wanted it to be.

Ana eased herself out of Vittorio's embrace, wondering just how she could accomplish such a herculean task. She'd agreed to a loveless marriage, very clearly. How could she now change the terms and expect Vittorio to agree?

Lying there in a pool of sunlight, still warmed by Vittorio's touch, the answer was obvious. By having him fall in love with her.

And Ana thought she knew just how to begin.

Vittorio awoke slowly, stretching languorously, feeling more relaxed and rested than he had in months. Years. He blinked at the sunlight streaming in through the windows and then shifted his weight, suddenly, surprisingly, *alarmingly* conscious of the empty space by him in the bed.

Ana was gone.

It shouldn't bother him—hurt him—for, God knew, he was used to sleeping alone. Even when he was involved with a woman, he left her bed—or made her leave his—well before dawn. It had been his standard practice, and he neither questioned it nor chose to change it.

Now, however, he realized how alone he felt. How lonely.

'Good morning, sleepy-head.'

Vittorio turned, his body relaxing once more at the sight of Ana in the doorway of his bedroom, wearing nothing but his shirt from last night. He could see the shadowy vee of her breasts disappearing between the buttons, the shirt tails just skimming her thighs. She looked wonderfully feminine, incredibly sexy. Vittorio felt his own desire stir and wondered how—and why—he'd kept himself from his wife's bed for so long.

'Where did you go?' he asked, shifting over so she could sit on the bed.

'To the loo.' She gave a little laugh. 'I drank quite a bit of champagne last night. Dutch courage, I suppose.'

'Were you nervous?' He found he was curious to hear what she said, to know what she thought. About everything.

Ana shrugged. 'A bit.' She paused. 'You can't say that our marriage is usual, or normal, and I don't want people...saying things.'

'What kinds of things?'

She gave another shrug, the movement inherently defensive. 'Unkind things.'

Vittorio nodded, realizing for the first time how their marriage bargain might reflect on her, as if she wasn't good enough—or attractive enough—for a proper marriage. For love.

I'm not interested in love.

What he was interested in, Vittorio decided, was getting his wife into bed as quickly as possible, and then taking his own sweet time in making love to her. Whatever the guests from the party might think, their marriage would certainly be wonderfully normal in at least one respect.

'I know it's Saturday,' Ana said, rising from the bed before Vittorio could even make a move towards her, 'but it was quite cool last night and I wanted to go to the vineyards and check—'

'We have managers for that, Ana.'

She gave a low throaty chuckle that had Vittorio nearly leaping out of bed and dragging her back to it with him. Had she ever laughed like that before? Surely he would have noticed—

'Oh, Vittorio. I don't leave such things to managers. You might, with your million bottles a year—'

'Nine hundred thousand.'

Her eyebrows arched and laughter lurked in her eyes, turning them to silver. 'Oh, pardon me. Well, considering that Viale only has two hundred and fifty—'

'What does it matter?' Vittorio asked, trying not to sound as impatient as he felt. His wife was wearing his shirt and he was half-naked in his own bed; their marriage was still unconsummated nearly a week after the wedding. Why the hell were they talking about wine production?

'It matters to me,' Ana said, a smile still curving that amazingly generous mouth. Vittorio wondered if she knew how she was teasing him. Seducing him. He'd thought she was insecure, unaware of her own charms, but at the moment his wife looked completely sexy, sensual and as if she knew it. Vittorio felt as if he'd received a very hard blow to the head.

Or to the heart.

Either way, he was reeling.

'It's a beautiful day—' he started again, meaning to end the sentence with *to spend in bed*.

Ana's smile widened. 'Exactly. And I wanted you to show me the Cazlevara vineyards, or at least some of them. It's too nice to be inside.'

Enough, Vittorio thought. Enough talking. He smiled, a

sleepy, sensual smile that left no room for Ana to misunder-
stand. 'Oh, I think we could be inside for a little longer.' Her
eyes widened and she hesitated, clearly uncertain. Vittorio extended a hand. 'Come here, Ana.'

'What—' she began and nibbled her lower lip, which was
just about the most seductive thing Vittorio had ever seen. He
groaned aloud.

'Come *here*.'

She came slowly, hesitantly, perching on the edge of the
bed so her shirt rode even higher on her thighs. God give him
patience, Vittorio thought, averting his eyes. 'What is it?' she
asked, and he heard the uncertainty and even fear in her voice.
His wife, Vittorio realized, didn't think he desired her.

He smiled and reached out to brush a strand of silky hair
away from her eyes, his fingers skimming the curve of her ear.
'Don't you think,' he murmured, 'we've waited long enough to
truly become man and wife?'

Ana's breath hitched. 'Yes, but—'

'But what?'

Again she nibbled her lip. 'You seemed content to wait.'

'Only because I didn't want to hurt you.' Vittorio paused,
the moment turning emotional, scaring him. Even now he shied
away from the truth of his own feelings. 'I wanted to give you
time.'

A smile lurked in Ana's eyes, in the generous curve of her
mouth. 'And now you feel you've given me enough time?'

'Oh, yes.' He reached out to stroke her leg; he couldn't help
himself, her skin looked so silky. And it felt silky, too. Vittorio
suppressed a shudder. 'Do you feel you've had enough time?'

'Oh, yes,' Ana said, and he chuckled at her fervent reply.

'Good.'

Ana sat there in shock, unable to believe Vittorio was saying
these things, touching her this way, his fingers skimming and
stroking her thigh, sending little shocks of pleasure through

her body. His other hand tangled in her hair and he drew her to him, his lips fastening on hers with hungry need; as he kissed her he let out a low groan of relief and satisfaction, and Ana felt another deeper shock: that he seemed so attracted to her, wanted her so, that he couldn't help but touch her, right here in the middle of the morning, in the sunshine, without her having done anything at all. She'd meant to seduce him, to wear a sexy nightdress and have champagne—but this was so much better. So much more real.

'Ana...' Vittorio murmured, his lips now on her ear, her jaw, her neck, 'Ana, you're going on about grapes and vineyards and all I can think about is...this...'

And then it was all Ana could think about too, for Vittorio claimed her lips in a kiss so consuming, so fulfilling, she felt replete and satisfied—as if this kiss could actually be enough—instead of the endless craving she normally felt when they touched.

Vittorio pulled away, just a little bit, but it was enough to make Ana realize that actually she wasn't satisfied at all. She wanted more...and more...and oh, please, a little more than that.

She must have made her need and frustration known, for he chuckled and traced a circle on her tummy with his tongue, making Ana moan aloud, the sound utterly foreign to her. She could hardly believe she was making these sounds, feeling these things.

So *much*.

Vittorio's mouth hovered over her skin. 'I'm going to take my time,' he promised her, and then did just that, while Ana closed her eyes in both surprise and pleasure.

Yet Ana wasn't willing to be a passive recipient, as wonderful as it was. As Vittorio teased her with his mouth and hands, she finally could take no more and flipped him over on his back, straddling his powerful thighs. Vittorio looked so surprised, she laughed aloud.

'You seem to be wearing too many clothes,' she remarked in a husky murmur, and Vittorio nodded.

'I completely agree.'

'Let's do something about that, then.'

'Absolutely.'

She tugged at his pyjama shirt and bottoms, laughing a little bit as buttons snagged and caught, but soon enough he was naked, and Ana pushed back on her elbow to take in his magnificent body, sleek and powerful, all for her. She ran one hand down the taut muscles of his chest.

'I've been wanting to do that for a while,' she admitted a bit shyly, for now that they were both naked, his arousal hard against her thigh, she felt a little uncertain. A little afraid.

'There's a lot I've been wanting to do,' Vittorio admitted, his voice low and a little ragged. 'And I can't take much more waiting, Ana—' True to his word, Vittorio rolled her onto her back, his hands and lips finding her secret sensitive places once again, until Ana found that waiting was the last thing she could think of doing. The wanting took over.

When he finally entered her, filling her up to the very brim with his own self, and with the knowledge of their bodies, fused, joined as *one*, Ana felt no more than a flicker of pain and then the wonderful, consuming certainty that this was the very heart of their marriage, the very best thing that could have ever happened, that they could have ever shared.

Afterwards, as they lay in the warm glow of the sun, their limbs still entangled, she wondered how she'd lived so long without knowing what sex was about. What love was about. For surely the two were utterly entwined, as entwined as her body was now with Vittorio's. She couldn't imagine loving a man she hadn't felt in her own body, and neither could she imagine sharing this with anyone but a man she loved—and that man was Vittorio.

Vittorio ran his hand down her stomach and across the curve

of her hip. 'Ana, if I'd known—' he said softly, and she turned to him.

'Known?'

'Known you were a virgin,' he explained. 'I would have—' he smiled ruefully '—I would have taken *more* time, I suppose.'

'You didn't know I was a virgin?' Ana couldn't keep the amusement from her voice. 'Goodness, Vittorio, I thought it was rather obvious.'

'Obvious to you, perhaps,' Vittorio returned. 'But you mentioned a relationship—a man—'

'It never got that far,' Ana replied. The hurt she usually felt when she remembered Roberto's rejection seemed distant, like an emotion she knew intellectually but had never truly felt. It hardly mattered now.

'I'm sorry he hurt you,' Vittorio murmured.

'It's long past,' Ana told him. She pressed her lips to his shoulder; his skin was warm. 'I've completely forgotten it.' She kissed the hollow of his throat, because now that he was truly hers she just couldn't help herself.

It was several hours later when they finally rose from that bed. Ana was sweetly sore all over, her body awakened in every sinew and sense. 'Now the vineyard,' she said and, still lounging among the pillows, Vittorio threw his head back and laughed.

'The vineyard will always be your first love,' he said, his words giving Ana a tiny pang. She wanted to say, *You're my first love*, but she found she could not. The words stuck in her throat, clogged by fear. Instead, she reached for her clothes.

'Absolutely.'

An hour later Ana followed Vittorio from the estate office to one of Cazlevara's finest vineyards. Since Vittorio owned a much bigger operation than she, he had hectares of vines all over Veneto, but the one closest to the castle—on the original estate—was still reserved for the label's most prized grapes.

The sun beat down hot on her head and her shirt was already sticking to her back as Ana walked between the grape plants in their neatly staked rows. She wished she'd worn a hat, or make-up. Instead, without thinking, she'd donned dusty trousers and an old shapeless button-down shirt, her standard field clothes. Hardly an outfit to impress her husband. And just why did she want to impress him? Ana wondered. The answer was painfully clear. Because she still felt a little uncertain, a little worried.

Because she loved him, and she didn't know if he loved her.

If she'd had any sense, she would have worn one of Feliciana's carefully selected outfits—something sexy and slimming—and asked Vittorio to take her to Venice or Verona, even one of the sleepy little villages nestled in one of the region's valleys, somewhere where they could laugh and chat over antipasti and a jug of wine.

She should not have taken him to his work place and donned her own well-worn work clothes to do it! What had she been thinking? Yet, even as she ranted at herself, Ana knew the answers. She loved the vineyards. She loved the grapes, the earth, the sun. The rich scent of soil and growing things, of life itself.

It was the place she loved most of all, and she'd wanted to share it with Vittorio.

Yet, as perspiration beaded on her brow and her boots became covered in a thin film of dust, she wondered if sharing a meal might have been the better choice. She stopped to touch a vine, its cluster of *Nebbiolo* grapes so perfectly proportioned. The grapes were young, firm and dusky, and this breed wouldn't be harvested until October. She bent to inhale the grapes' scent, closing her eyes in sensual pleasure at the beauty of the day: the wind ruffling her hair, the sun on her face, the earthy aroma all around her.

After a few seconds she opened her eyes, conscious of Vittorio's gaze on her. His expression was inscrutable, save for the faintest flicker of a smile curling his mouth.

'I like the smell,' she said, a bit self-consciously. 'I always did. When I was little, my mother found me curled under the bushes asleep.'

Vittorio had, Ana thought, a very funny look on his face now. Almost as if he were in pain. 'You looked like you were enjoying yourself very much,' he said. His voice sounded strangely strangled.

'It was a safe place for me,' Ana acknowledged. 'And, more than that—a bit of heaven.'

'A bit of heaven,' Vittorio repeated. He was standing surprisingly awkwardly, his hands jammed into the front pockets of his trousers, and his voice still sounded—odd.

'Vittorio?' Ana asked uncertainly. 'Are you all right—?'

'Ana.' He cut her off, smiling now, her name coming out in what sounded like a rush of relief. 'Come here.'

Ana didn't know what he meant. They were standing a foot apart; where was she meant to *go*?

Then Vittorio took his hands out of his pockets and, in one effortless movement, he pulled her towards him and buried his head in her hair, breathing in deeply.

'It's the smell of your hair *I* love,' he murmured. His hand had gone under the heavy mass of her hair to her neck. 'I want you,' Vittorio confessed raggedly, 'so much. Come back to the castle with me. Make love to me, Ana.'

Love. Ana couldn't keep the smile from her voice. 'Again?'

'You think once—or twice—is enough?'

She could hardly believe he wanted her so much. It shook her to her very bones, the heart of herself. 'No, definitely not,' she murmured.

'Come back—'

'No.'

Vittorio's face fell in such a comical manner that Ana would have laughed if she wasn't half-quivering with her own reawakened desire. 'Not at the castle, Vittorio. Here.'

He stared down at the dusty ground. 'Here?' he repeated dubiously.

'Yes,' Ana said firmly, tugging on his hand, 'here.' Here, where he'd found her desirable—sexy—even in her work clothes and wind-tangled hair. Here, where she'd felt safe and heaven-bound all at once, and wanted to again, in Vittorio's arms. Here, because among the grapes and the soil she was her real self, not the woman who wore fancy dresses and high heels and tried to seduce her husband with tricks she couldn't begin to execute with any skill or ease.

Here.

And Vittorio accepted that—or perhaps he couldn't wait any longer—for he spread his blazer, an expensive silk one that was soon covered in dust—on the ground and then lay Ana on it, her hair fanning out around her in a dark silken wave.

Vittorio touched her almost reverently, a look of awe on his face Ana had never expected to see. To know. The ground was hard and bumpy; pebbles dug into her back and the dust was gritty on her skin, but Ana didn't care. She revelled in it, in this. In him.

Vittorio reached for the buttons of her old shirt. 'I never thought white cotton could be so...inflaming,' he murmured, and bent his head to the flesh he'd exposed.

And, as Ana's hand clutched at his hair, she realized she had no idea that she could *feel* so inflamed, as if the very fires of passion were burning her up, turning her craving to liquid heat.

'Vittorio...'

'We may be lying in a field like some farm hand and his dairymaid,' Vittorio murmured against her skin—somehow, all her clothes had been removed, 'but I'm not going to have you like that, with your skirts rucked up around your waist, over in a few pathetic seconds.'

'No, indeed, since I'm not wearing any clothes.'

And, as he smiled against her skin, Ana found she had no thoughts or words left at all. Later, as they lay entangled in a sleepy haze of satisfaction, she murmured, 'We're going to have the most interesting sunburn.'

'Not if I can help it.' In one fluid movement, Vittorio rose from the dusty ground, Ana in his arms. She squealed; she *never* squealed, and yet somehow that ridiculously girlish sound came out of her mouth. Vittorio grinned. 'Put your clothes on, wife,' he said, depositing her on the ground. 'We have a perfectly good bed at home, and I intend to use it...all day.'

'All day?' Ana repeated, still squealing, and then she hurried to yank her clothes back on.

The next few weeks passed in a haze of happiness Ana had never dreamed or even hoped to feel. Although they never spoke of love, her uncertainty melted away in the light of Vittorio's presence and affection, and she hardly thought they needed to. Why speak of love when their bodies communicated far more eloquently and pleasurably? The days were still taken up with work; Ana found herself smiling at the most ridiculous moments, while signing a form or reading a purchasing order. Sometimes, spontaneously, she even laughed aloud.

Vittorio seemed just as happy. His happiness made her happy; his countenance was light, a smile ready on his lips, those onyx eyes lightened to a pewter grey, glinting with humour and love—surely love, for Ana had little doubt that he loved her.

How could he not, when they spent night after night together, not just in passion but in quiet moments afterwards, talking and touching in a way that melted both her body and heart?

He told her bits of his childhood, the hard memories which she'd guessed at, as well as some of the good times: playing *stecca* with his father, going to Rome on a school trip when he was fifteen and getting outrageously drunk.

'It's fortunate I was not expelled.'

'Why weren't you?'

'I told you, I played the trombone,' he replied with a wicked little smile. 'They needed me in the orchestra.'

And Ana told him things she'd never told anyone else, confessed the dark days after her mother's death.

'My father was overwhelmed with grief. He refused to see me for days—locked himself in her bedroom.'

'It's so hard to believe.' Vittorio let his fingers drift through her hair, along her cheek. 'He is so close to you now.'

'It took work,' Ana replied frankly. 'In fact, a week after she died, he sent me to boarding school—he thought it would be easier. For him, I suppose.' It was good, if still hard, to speak of it; bringing light to the dark memories. 'Those two years were the worst of my life.'

Vittorio pressed his lips against the curve of her shoulder. 'I'm sorry.'

'It doesn't matter now.' And it didn't, because in Vittorio's arms she didn't feel big and mannish and awkward; she felt beautiful and sexy and loved.

Loved.

No, she had no doubt at all that Vittorio loved her, no sense that there was anything but happiness—that bit of heaven—ahead of them, shining and pure, stretching to a limitless horizon.

CHAPTER TEN

SIX WEEKS AFTER their wedding, Vittorio came to see Ana at the
Viale offices. She looked up from her desk, smiling in pleased
surprise as he appeared in the doorway.

'I didn't expect to see you here,' she said, rising to embrace
him. Vittorio kissed her with a distracted air, his face troubled
before relaxing into a smile that still didn't reach his eyes.

'I have to go to Brazil again. There has been trouble with
some of the merchants there.'

'What kind of trouble?' Ana asked, her smile turning to a
frown. Her heart had already sunk a bit at the thought: *Brazil*.

Vittorio gave a little shrug. 'It's not worrisome, but important
enough that I should go soothe a few ruffled feathers, murmur
encouragement in the right ears.'

'You're good at that,' Ana teased, but Vittorio missed the
joke entirely.

'I came here because I am leaving this afternoon, before
you return. If I take the private jet to Rio, I can return within
a week.'

'A week!' Disappointment swamped her. It seemed like a
horribly long time.

'Yes, this is business,' Vittorio said a bit sharply, and his tone as well as his words were like ice water drenching her spirit. Her happiness.

Business. Was Vittorio actually reminding her that business was what their marriage was all about? *Just* business? Ana swallowed dryly. 'Yes, of course.'

'I'll ring you,' he said, pressing a quick kiss against her cold cheek, and then he was gone.

Ana stood in the middle of the office for a few moments, listening to the sounds around her: Vittorio slamming the front door of the building, the purr of the Porsche's engine starting up again, the murmur of voices from other offices. And, the loudest sound of all, the sick thudding of her own frightened heart.

Had she been deceiving herself these last few weeks? Lost in a haze of happiness, mistaking lust for love? Ana moved back to her desk and sat down hard in her chair, her head falling into her hands. She couldn't believe how unsure she felt, how afraid. Her serene certainty that Vittorio loved her had been swept away by one careless remark.

Clearly she hadn't been so certain after all.

The castle felt lonely and quiet when she returned that evening, its endless rooms lost in shadow. Ana told the cook she'd have something in her room rather than face the elegant dining room alone; Constantia had returned to Milan last week and Bernardo, as he so often was, appeared to be out. She didn't want to see anyone.

Marco, the cook, however, looked surprised. 'Ah, but I've made dinner! For two—it is all prepared.'

'For two?' Ana repeated, hope leaping absurdly inside her. Had Vittorio come back? But of course not; he was halfway to South America by now.

'Yes, Signor Bernardo wishes to dine with you.'

Ana felt a finger of foreboding trail along her spine, then shrugged the shivery sensation away. Whatever had passed between Bernardo and Vittorio was long ago, and didn't concern her. Perhaps getting to know her husband's younger brother would go some way in helping to heal his family's rift. Despite the happiness of the last few weeks, Ana knew Vittorio was still snared by the dark memories of his childhood. She saw it when he didn't think anyone was looking, a moment alone lost in sorrowful thought, the shadow of grief in his eyes.

'All right,' she told Marco. 'Thank you.'

As Ana entered the dining room, the setting rays of the sun sending long golden beams of light across the elegant room, she saw the table set cosily for two at one end and Bernardo standing by the window. He started forward as soon as he saw her.

'Ana! Thank you for joining me.'

'Of course, Bernardo. I am happy to dine with you.' Yet, as he took her hands and pressed his cheek against hers in a brotherly embrace, Ana couldn't shake the feeling that Bernardo had an agenda for this meal.

She stepped back, surveying him as he moved to the table to pull out her chair. He was a slighter, paler version of Vittorio, still handsome, with the same dark hair and eyes, yet he lacked his brother's strength and vitality. If they stood next to each other, there could be no doubt as to who was the more dynamic, charismatic and frankly attractive brother. How could Bernardo fail to be jealous?

'Thank you,' she murmured, and sat in the chair Bernardo had drawn for her. He sat opposite and reached for the bottle of red he'd left breathing on a side table.

'One of the vineyard's own?' Ana asked as she watched the rich ruby liquid being poured into her glass.

'In a way. I've been experimenting a bit with mixed grapes.' His expression turned wary, guarded. 'Vittorio doesn't know.'

Ana took a sip of wine. 'But this is delicious.' It was rich and velvety, with a hidden aroma of fruit and spice. She set the glass down and gave Bernardo a frank look. 'Why doesn't Vittorio know you've been experimenting with hybrids? Especially as the result is so pleasing.'

Bernardo gave her a faint smile and took a sip from his own

glass. 'Surely you've seen by now that Vittorio and I...' He paused, cocking his head thoughtfully. 'We are not like normal brothers.'

'Of course I've noticed that,' Ana returned. 'In fact,' she added, a bit sharply, 'I even wondered if he would want us to dine like this together, alone.'

'He wouldn't. Not because he thinks it is inappropriate, but because he is afraid I will whisper poison in your ear.'

Ana gestured to her glass. 'Is this poison?' She asked the question lightly, yet Benardo regarded her with grave eyes.

'It is, as far as Vittorio is concerned. He is not interested in anything I have to do with Cazlevara Wines.'

Ana felt a stab of pity. 'Why? Is it simply because of what happened so long ago, when your father died?' Bernardo looked surprised and Ana said quickly, 'I know Constantia tried to take his inheritance, and make you Count. Vittorio told me. Yet that happened so long ago, and you were only a boy—'

'That was merely the beginning,' Bernardo replied. 'I suppose he told you what our childhood was like? We were forced to take sides, Vittorio and I. At first we resisted it. We resented our parents drawing us into their battles. But after time...' He shrugged and spread his hands. 'I admit, I was not a sensible boy. My mother's attention went to my head. When she so clearly preferred me to Vittorio—and my own father did not have so much as a glance for me—well, I flaunted it. I rubbed Vittorio's nose in it. Special presents, trips...these things turn a boy's head. They turned mine.' His mouth twisted in a bitter smile of regret. 'Vittorio saw it all, and said nothing. That only made me angrier. He had my papà's attention and praise, all of it, and I wanted to make him jealous.'

'And of course he was,' Ana cut in. 'Nothing can take the place of a mother's love.'

'Or a father's. I don't know which of us got the better bargain. Vittorio was my father's favourite, but he didn't get spoiled and cosseted like I did. He was whipped into shape.' He held up a hand. 'Not literally. But my father was a hard taskmaster. I remember one time he called Vittorio out of bed—he must have been ten or so, home from boarding school. I was but six at the time. It wasn't even dawn, but my father saw that Vittorio had done poorly on a maths exam. He sat him down at the dining room table and made him write the exam all over again. He didn't stop until every problem was correct. Vittorio worked for hours. He didn't even have breakfast.' Bernardo made a face. 'I remember because I smacked my lips and slurped my juice and he didn't even look up, though he must have been hungry.' Bernardo shook his head, his mouth twisting in a grimace. 'I am not proud of how I behaved over the years, Ana. I freely admit that.'

Ana let out a sorrowful little sigh. It was such a sad, pointless story. Why had Constantia rejected Vittorio so utterly? Couldn't she see how her behaviour had affected him, how her love could have softened her husband's harsh treatment? She'd been so blinded by her own misery, Ana supposed. Arturo's lack of love for his wife had been the rotten seed of it all.

The food had been served, but she found she had no appetite. 'And when your father died? What happened then?'

Bernardo steepled his fingers under his chin. 'By that time the lines were well and truly drawn. Vittorio hated both my mother and me, or at least acted as if he did. He was only fourteen, and he had not one word of kindness for either of us. Oh, he was polite enough, icily respectful, and it drove my mother mad. I suppose Vittorio was so like our father—and my father had never had a true moment of empathy or love for my mother. He was polite, courteous, solicitous even, but there was no love behind it. He was a cold man.'

'Even so, why did your mother try to have the will overturned and disinherit Vittorio? Simply because you were her favourite?' Ana heard the accusation in her own voice. What could justify such cruel, callous behaviour?

Bernardo shrugged. 'Who knows? She has told me she did

it because she thought if Vittorio became Count, he would be too hard a man, like my father was. She said she could not bear to see Vittorio become like Arturo.' He smiled sadly. 'I rather thought she believed she was saving him—from himself.'

Ana raised her eyebrows. 'He certainly didn't view it that way.'

'It made things worse, of course,' Bernardo agreed. 'The plan failed, and Vittorio's enmity was cemented. Over the years we have had nothing to say to one another and—' he paused, his gaze sliding from hers '—I have not always acted in a way I could be proud of.' He turned back to face her resolutely. 'And so it continues even now, as you've undoubtedly seen. Which is why I am here.'

Ana met his gaze levelly. 'You have something to ask me.'

'Yes.' Bernardo took a breath and gestured to the wine he'd poured, glinting in their crystal goblets. 'You have tasted my own vintage, Ana, and as an experienced vintner you know it is good. Vittorio is determined never to let me have any control or authority in Cazlevara Wines. God knows, I can understand it. I have not proven myself worthy. I have done things I regret, even as a grown man. But I cannot live like this, under my brother's thumb. Everything is a grudging favour from him. It wears me down to nothing. And to know he would never market this vintage simply because it is mine—'

'Surely Vittorio wouldn't be so unreasonable,' Ana interjected. 'He is a man of business, after all.' How well she knew it.

'When it comes to me and my mother, he is blind,' Bernardo stated flatly. 'Blind and bitter, and I can hardly blame him.'

'So what are you asking of me?'

'You've done some experimenting with hybrids, yes?'

'A little—'

'If you passed this wine off as your own creation, he would accept it.'

'And I would take the credit?'

Bernardo lifted one shoulder in a tiny shrug. 'That does not matter so much to me. It cannot.'

Ana stared at Vittorio's brother, saw the weary resignation on his pale face. She had no doubt that he'd been petted and spoiled as a child, and he'd made his brother's life miserable— more miserable than it already was—well into young adulthood. Yet now she saw a man who was over thirty and resigned never to prove himself, never to have the satisfaction of excelling in a job he was created to do. The injustice and sorrow of it twisted her heart.

'I will not take credit for your own hard work, Bernardo.' He nodded slowly, accepting, his mouth pulled downwards. 'This wine is excellent, and you deserve to be known as its creator.' Ana took a breath. 'So you can either market it under the Viale label or, as I'm sure would be much more satisfying, under the Cazlevara one. This bitter feud between you and Vittorio must end. Perhaps, if he sees how well you have done, he will be convinced.'

Bernardo leaned forward. 'What do you suggest?'

'Why don't you prepare to market the vintage? Vittorio has given me authority over the vineyards while he is gone.' Ana knew her authority was more perfunctory than anything else; he hardly expected her to change things, or implement strategies such as the one she was suggesting. 'I can arrange a meeting with some merchants in Milan. Start there, and see what happens. By the time Vittorio comes home, God willing, you will have something to show him.' And, Ana added silently, God willing, Vittorio wouldn't be too angry with her. God willing, this feud would finally end and their marriage could continue, grow, work. If he loved her—and she was desperate now to believe he did—his anger would not rule the day.

His love would.

Hope had lit Bernardo's eyes, erasing the resigned lines from his face. He looked younger, happier already. 'What you are doing is dangerous, Ana. Vittorio might be furious. In fact, I know he will be.'

'This feud must end,' Ana said firmly. 'It is the only way forward for any of us. I am not biased by childhood slights the way he is. And I'm sure,' she added with more confidence than she felt, 'my husband will see reason once I have spoken to him.'

It had been a long, hard week, courting the South American merchants. They wanted to rely on their own wines; they were dubious of a European import. Yet, finally, with honeyed words and persuasive arguments, meetings and dinners and tastings, Vittorio had convinced them.

Now he was home and eager—desperate—to see Ana. As his limo pulled up to the castle, Vittorio nearly laughed at himself. He was acting like a besotted boy. He *was* besotted, utterly in love with his wife, and it had taken a week apart to realize just what he was feeling.

Love.

He loved Ana, and he'd felt it in every agonising second he'd spent apart from her, when he'd kept looking for her, even though he knew she was thousands of miles away. He'd felt it when he'd reached for her at night, and both his body and heart had ached when his arms remained empty. It didn't even surprise him, this new-found love; it simply felt too right. He felt completed, whole, and he hadn't realized how much he'd been missing—in and of himself—until he knew that sense of fulfilment, of rightness, caused by loving Ana.

He knew she loved him. He knew it, he'd seen it in her eyes and felt it in her body, yet it still filled him with wonder and incredulous joy. How could he have been so blind to think he didn't want this, didn't need it? Now he could not imagine life without it, without Ana. The very thought left him cold and despairing. But now he didn't despair; now he felt hope. Wonderful, miraculous hope. And he couldn't wait to tell Ana.

The castle was quiet as he entered; it was four o'clock in the afternoon and he had no doubt Ana was at her own office. He thought of surprising her there; he'd make love to her right on her own desk. His mouth widened into a grin at the thought of it. First, he would check in at the Cazlevara office and then... Ana. He could hardly wait.

He was just sorting through the post left by his secretary when his vineyard manager knocked on the door.

Vittorio barely glanced up. 'Yes, Antonio? Everything went well while I was gone?' He tossed another letter aside, only to pause when he realized his manager had not spoken. He glanced up, saw the man twisting his hands together, looking uncertain. Afraid, even. Vittorio's eyes narrowed. 'Antonio? Has something happened?'

'It's Bernardo, Lord Ralfino... Bernardo and the Contessa.'

Vittorio stilled. He felt as if his blood had turned to ice water; the sense of coldness gave him a chilling clarity, a freezing resolve. He'd been expecting this, he realized. He wasn't surprised. 'Has my mother been plotting again?' he asked levelly. 'Now that I am married, she seeks to disinherit and discredit me once more?'

Antonio shook his head, looking wretched. 'Not the Dowager Contessa, my lord. Your wife.'

For a moment Vittorio couldn't speak. Couldn't think. The words made no sense. What his manager was saying was impossible, ridiculous—

Vittorio drew a breath. 'Are you saying my wife is acting with Bernardo?'

'She told me not to ring you,' Antonio confessed unhappily.

'What?' Vittorio could barely process it. His wife had been attempting to deceive him? To scheme against him? The shock left him senseless, reeling, nearly gasping in pain.

'I know you do not wish Bernardo to—well, I knew you'd want this approved,' Antonio continued, 'but since she said— and you'd given her authority—'

Vittorio laid one hand flat on his desk, bracing himself. He would not jump to conclusions. He would *not*. He kept the rage and fear down, suppressing it, even though it fermented and bubbled, threatened to boil over and burn them all. He would not let it. He would listen to Antonio, he would hear Ana's side of the story. He would be fair. 'What has happened, Antonio?'

'Bernardo went to Milan,' the manager confessed. 'He is marketing his own label. I didn't know of it until yesterday, but the Contessa approved it, arranged the meeting—'

'His own label?' Vittorio repeated blankly. Was his brother actually trying to take over the family winery, to make it his own? And Ana was *helping* him? Had they been planning this—this *takeover*—together while he was gone? Or even before? He could hardly make sense of it, his heart cried out its innate, desperate rejection of such lies, even as his mind coolly reminded him that this was exactly how he'd felt returning from his father's funeral, hoping—desperately hoping—that now his father was dead his mother might turn to him, if not with open arms, then at least with a smile.

She'd turned her back instead. Something had died in Vittorio then, that last frail hope he'd never realized he'd still clung to. The desire for love. The hope it would find him. He'd lost it then, or thought he had, only to find the desire and the hope—the need for love—inside him, latent, and with Ana it had begun to grow, young and fragile, seeking her healing light.

Now he felt as if it had been felled at its tender root. His heart had become a barren wasteland, frozen and unyielding. He turned back to Antonio. 'Thank you for telling me. I will deal with it now.'

'I would have rung you, but since the Contessa was meant to be in charge—'

'I completely understand. Do not think of it again.' Vittorio dismissed the man with a nod, then turned to stare blindly out of the window. Rows upon rows of neat growing grapes stretched to the horizon, Cazlevara's fortune, his family's life blood. He'd made love to Ana out there, among those vines. He'd held in her arms and loved her.

Loved her.

And now she'd betrayed him. He tried to stay reasonable, to keep the anger and hurt and oh, yes, the fear from consuming him, but they rose up in a red tide of feeling until he couldn't think any more. He could only feel.

He felt the hurt and the pain and the sorrow, the *agony* of his mother and brother's rejection, over and over again. Day after day of trying to please his father, only to strive more and more; nothing he'd ever done was enough. And then when his father had died, torn between despair and relief, he'd wanted to turn to his mother, thinking that now she would accept him, love him even, only to realize she'd rejected him utterly.

And now. This. Ana had somehow been working against him with his brother, waiting until he was gone to use the authority he'd given her on *trust* to discredit him. This, he acknowledged, was the worst betrayal of all.

'Lord Cazlevara is here to see you, Signorina Vi—Lady Cazlevara.'

Ana half-rose from the desk, smiling at Edoardo. 'You don't need to stand on ceremony, Edoardo. Send him in!' Yet, even as a smile of hope and welcome—how she'd missed him!—was spreading across her face, another part of Ana was registering the look of wariness on her assistant's face and wondering why he seemed so uncomfortable.

'Good afternoon, Ana.'

'Vittorio!' The word burst from Ana's lips and, despite his rather chilly greeting, she couldn't keep from smiling, from walking towards him, her arms outstretched, needing his touch, his kiss—

Vittorio didn't move. Ana dropped her arms, realization settling coldly inside her. He'd heard about Bernardo, obviously. He knew what she'd done. And he hadn't liked it.

'You're angry,' she stated, and Vittorio arched one eyebrow.

'Angry? No. Curious, perhaps.' He spoke with arctic polite-ness that froze Ana's insides. She hadn't heard that voice in such a long time; she'd forgotten just how cold it was. How cold it made her feel. Vittorio leaned against the door frame, hands in his pockets, and waited.

Ana took a breath. She'd been preparing for this conversation, had known that Vittorio, on some level, would not be pleased. He'd try to distance himself; that was how he stayed safe. She *knew* that, yet she'd trusted what she felt for him—and what she believed and hoped he felt for her—that their love would make him see reason. She'd told herself so hundreds of times over the last week, yet now that the time had come and Vittorio was standing here looking so icy and indifferent, all the calm explanations she'd come up with seemed to have vanished, leav-ing her with nothing but a growing sense of panic, a swamp-ing fear. She didn't want her husband looking at her this way, talking to her as if she were a stranger he didn't really like. She couldn't bear it. 'Vittorio,' she finally said, and heard the plea in her voice even though her words sounded firm, 'Bernardo showed me the vintage he's created. He's been working with hybrids—you didn't know—'

'Funny, I thought I knew everything that happened in my company. And, as I recollect, my brother was assistant man-ager, not head vintner. Or did you give him a promotion in my absence?' He spoke pleasantly, yet Ana heard and felt the ter-rible coldness underneath. It crept into her bones and wound its icy way around her heart. She felt like shivering, shudder-ing, crying out.

This was what Constantia had lived with day in, day out. This was what Vittorio had been to her, a man who refused to be reached, whose heart was enclosed in walls of ice. No won-der the woman had gone half-mad. She already felt perilously close to the edge of reason after just a few minutes under his freezing stare.

'No, I didn't give him a promotion,' Ana replied as levelly as she could. 'I wouldn't presume to do such a thing—'

'Wouldn't you?'

Ana forced herself to ignore the sneering question. 'But I did allow him to market his own wine. He's in Milan right now, talking to some merchants about it. I thought we could put it in the catalogue this autumn—'

'Oh, you did, did you?' Vittorio took a step into the room, his pleasant mask dropped so Ana saw the icy rage underneath. 'You didn't waste much time, did you, Ana?' he asked, fairly spitting the words. 'The moment I'd gone, you were plotting and planning behind my back.'

Ana quelled beneath the verbal attack. Did he think so little of her? 'It wasn't a plot, Vittorio,' she insisted, 'though I can understand why you might think that way. But I am not your mother, and Bernardo has changed—'

Vittorio gave a sharp laugh. 'Nothing has changed. Don't you think I have a reason for keeping him on as short a leash as I do?'

Ana struggled to keep her calm. 'Vittorio, your brother was ten when your mother tried to disinherit you—'

'And he was twenty when he tried to sabotage the winery and discredit me to my customers, and twenty-five when he embezzled a hundred thousand euros. Don't you think I know my own brother?'

Ana stared at him in shock, her mouth dropping open before she had the sense to snap it shut. Realization trickled icily though her. 'I didn't know those things,' she finally said quietly. Vittorio gave another disbelieving laugh and she thought of Bernardo's words: *I have done things I regret, even as a grown man.* She almost felt like laughing hysterically, despite the panic and the fear. Perhaps she should have asked Bernardo to clarify what he'd meant. Perhaps she shouldn't have leapt in so rashly, thinking she could heal old wounds, hurts that had never scarred over, just festered and bled—

Still, Ana knew there was more going on here, more at risk than Vittorio's sour relationship with his brother. There was his relationship with *her*, a fundamental issue of trust and love. She had to ask crucial questions, and now she was afraid of their answers.

'I really didn't know everything he'd done,' she said, trying to keep her voice steady. 'Still, I believe Bernardo has changed. If you just give him a chance—'

'So he's convinced you,' Vittorio stated quietly. He turned away so she couldn't see his face. 'He's turned you from me.'

Ana suddenly felt near to tears. Vittorio's voice sounded so final, so *sad*. 'Vittorio, it's not like that! I just wanted to give Bernardo a chance, not only for his sake, but for *ours*.'

'Ours,' Vittorio repeated, the word dripping sarcasm.

'Yes, ours, because your hatred of him poisons everything! Poisons—' She stopped, not wanting to expose herself so utterly and admit she loved him. 'And he could be a credit to you,' she continued quietly. 'He rang me from Milan this morning, and the meetings went well. He's not trying to take some kind of control—'

'So he says.'

'This bitterness must end,' Ana stated. Her voice trembled and she forced herself to go on, to say the words she'd shied away from. The truth was the only thing that had the power to heal. 'It poisons you, and it poisons our love.'

She felt as if she'd laid down a live wire; the room crackled with uncontained energy. *Love*. She'd said it, admitted to that most dangerous forbidden feeling.

Vittorio turned around; his eyes were like two pools of black ice. 'Love?' he enquired silkily. 'What are you talking about, Ana?'

Ana blinked, forcing back the tears. She would be strong now, even if that strength meant being more vulnerable than she ever had before. 'I love you, Vittorio. I gave Bernardo a chance for love of you—'

'Just like my mother took my inheritance, claiming she did it out of love for me?' Vittorio mocked.

'Is that what she said?'

'Or something like it. I found it rather hard to believe.'

Yet Ana didn't. She could see Constantia's twisted reasoning now, understand how she might do anything—*anything*—to keep Vittorio from becoming the cold, hard man his father had been, and had wanted to make him. Yet, right now before her eyes, he was changing, hardening, the last weeks of love and gentleness falling away as if they'd never been, leaving her with a man she didn't like or even know.

'It's true, Vittorio. I don't doubt Bernardo has hurt you, as has Constantia, but this cannot go on. You are all poisoned by it—all three of you. I thought if Bernardo proved himself to you, you could see each other as equals. Forgive each other and learn to—'

'Oh, Ana, this is all sounding very cosy,' Vittorio drawled. 'And completely unrealistic. I didn't marry you to play therapist to my family. I married you to be loyal to *me*.'

Ana blinked. 'And does that loyalty mean blind obedience? I can't take any decisions for myself? You didn't want a lapdog, you said. You rather touchingly referred to our marriage as one of *partnership*—'

'A business partnership,' Vittorio corrected. 'That is what I meant.'

Ana swallowed, struggling to stay reasonable, as if her heart and soul hadn't been shredded to pathetic pieces as they spoke. 'Yet you do not want me to have any concern with your business—'

'I do not want you to use your influence to put my brother's concerns forward!' Vittorio cut her off, his voice rising to a near-shout before he lowered it again to no more than a dark whisper. 'You have betrayed me, Ana.'

'I love you,' Ana returned. Her voice shook; so did her body. 'Vittorio, I *love* you—'

He shook his head in flat dismissal. 'That wasn't part of our bargain.'

She searched his face, looking for any trace of compassion or even regret. Every line, every angle was hard and implacable. He had become a stranger, a terrible stranger. 'I know it wasn't,' she said quietly. 'But I fell in love with you anyway, with the man you…you seemed to be. Yet now—' she took a breath '—you are so cold to me. Vittorio, do you not love me at all?'

A muscle jerked in Vittorio's cheek and he didn't answer. He gazed down at her, his eyes hard and unrelenting, and suddenly Ana could stand it no more. She'd felt this exposed only once before in her life, when she'd flung herself at Roberto, hoping he would take her into his arms and admit he was attracted to her, to make his love physical as well as emotional. She'd been rejected then, utterly, or so she'd thought. Yet that moment was nothing—*nothing*—compared to this. Now Vittorio was rejecting her emotionally; he was rejecting her heart rather than her body and it hurt so much more.

It hurt unbearably.

'I see you don't,' she said quietly and, when Vittorio still didn't answer, Ana did the only thing she could think of doing, the only option left to her. She fled.

In a numb state of grief—the same kind of frozen despair she'd felt when her mother had died—Ana walked away from her office. She didn't think about where she was going until she found herself on the dirt road back to Villa Rosso, its mellow stone and terracotta tiles gleaming in the afternoon sun.

She was going home.

The villa was quiet when she entered, her footsteps falling softly on the tiled floor of the foyer. She headed for the stairs but heard her father's voice call out from his study.

'Hello? Is someone there?'

'It's me, Papà.' Ana paused on the stairs; her father came to the hall. He took one look at her face—Ana could only imagine how terrible she looked—and gasped aloud.

'Ana! What has happened?'

Ana gave a sad little smile. She felt as if her whole body were breaking, her soul rent into pieces. 'I discovered you were right, Papà. Love isn't very comfortable, after all.'

Enrico's face twisted in sorrow, but Ana knew she could not bear even his sympathy now. She just shook her head and walked with heavy steps upstairs, to the room she had not slept in since she'd got married.

Married. Vittorio was her husband, yet she hardly knew what that meant any more.

She spent the night alone, lying on her bed, watching the moon rise and then descend once more. She didn't sleep. She found herself reliving the joy of the last few weeks, now made all the sweeter by its brevity. Vittorio kissing her, taking her in his arms. Laughing as they played *stecca* again; he'd won that time. Talking about the vineyards, and grapes, and wine, gesturing with their hands, shared enthusiasm in their voices. The way he touched her casually, a hand on hers, when they were reading in bed, simply because he wanted to feel her next to him. And then later, the way he touched her so her body cried out in pleasure. So many memories, so many wonderful, sweet, *terrible* memories, because she was afraid they were all she'd ever have.

Was their marriage actually over? She could hardly believe he had rejected her so utterly; she thought of trying to see him again and then knew she couldn't. She couldn't face that hard, blank face again. She couldn't face the feeling of being so raw, so exposed and rejected again. Not by Vittorio, not by the man—the only man—she'd ever love.

She pressed her face into her pillow and willed the tears to come; crying would bring relief of a sort. They didn't. Some things, Ana knew, were too deep for tears.

Enrico knocked on her door in the morning, begging her to take a bit of breakfast. 'Ana, have some toast at least,' he called, his voice sounding thin and frail. 'I told the cook not to make kippers. I know they put you off.'

Ana couldn't even summon a smile. 'Don't trouble yourself, Papà. I'm not hungry. I just need to be alone for a little while.'

She needed to be alone to grieve the ending of her marriage, for surely that was what this was. Vittorio had not come to see her and Ana dreaded some horrible letter, a cold official ending to their marriage. Although, she reminded herself, he'd said divorce was not an option.

Yet the alternative—the cold convenient marriage she'd once agreed to—would be so much worse, for affection and respect had been obliterated. All that was left was duty.

Funny, Ana thought distantly as she lay on her bed, watching the sun rise in the sky, still in her clothes from the day before, how she had once convinced herself she could accept such a thing. A loveless marriage, a business arrangement. She'd deceived herself. Love wasn't comfortable but it was everything.

In the early evening, Enrico knocked again. *'Dolcezza—'*

'I'm still not hungry,' Ana called.

'You don't need to eat,' her father called back, 'but your husband is here, and he wants to see you.'

Ana stilled. Her hands clenched into fists on her bed covers. 'I can't see him, Papà,' she said, her voice no more than a choked whisper.

'Please, Ana. He is desperate for you.'

'Desperate?' She said the word disbelievingly, yet still laced with damning hope.

'Desperate, *rondinella.*' Vittorio's voice, no more than a husky whisper, made Ana freeze. Distantly, she heard her father's footsteps patter down the hall and, after a moment, her heart beating with hard, heavy thuds, she went to open the door. Vittorio stood there, ushaven, his hair rumpled, still wearing his clothes from yesterday. His eyes remained grave as he gave her a small uncertain smile.

'You look as awful as I do,' Ana said.

Vittorio touched her cheek. 'You have not been crying, at least.' His own eyes looked red.

'Some things are too deep for tears,' Ana told him and he stepped into the room. She leaned against the door, her arms crossed, unwilling to relax her guard. Afraid to hope.

'Oh, Ana.' Vittorio shook his head, his voice choking a little bit. 'I made you so unhappy.'

'Yes, you did,' Ana agreed, and was amazed at how level her voice sounded, as if she wasn't affected at all. As if she wasn't dying inside.

'I was so angry,' Vittorio said quietly. 'And it blinded me. All I could see—feel—was betrayal.'

'I know.'

His smile was touched with sorrow. 'It's not an excuse, is it?'

'No.'

'Just a reason.' He sighed again. 'I have a lot to learn, I suppose, if you will consent to be my teacher.'

Ana shook her head. 'I don't want to be your teacher, Vittorio. I want to be your wife. And that means you need to trust me.'

'I know,' Vittorio said in a low voice. 'I know I should have, but I couldn't *think*—'

'It doesn't even matter.' Ana cut him off, her voice tight. 'I realize the bargain we made doesn't work for me, Vittorio. I can't... I can't accept our marriage on your terms.'

'What?' He looked shocked. 'What are you talking about?'

She swallowed, her voice raw. 'I need more from you than your trust. I need your love.'

He stared at her, slack-jawed, and Ana braced herself for his refusal. His rejection. It never came.

'I do love you, Ana,' Vittorio said, his voice a throb of intensity. 'And it has terrified me. That's why I acted like I did yesterday. Not another excuse—just the truth. I am sorry. So sorry. Please forgive me.'

Ana could hardly believe what he'd said. 'You love me?' she repeated, and he offered her a tremulous smile.

'Utterly. Unbearably. I spent the most wretched night last night, and for love of you—I thought I'd just gone and thrown out the most wonderful thing that's ever happened to me, and for what? My own pride?'

She shook her head. Hope bubbled up inside her, an everlasting well of joy. 'I shouldn't have acted without you, but I thought... I thought to help heal the past—'

'And you have,' Vittorio said. 'Already, it has begun. When you walked out of that office I realized you might actually be walking away from me for ever, and I was letting you go. I was devastated, in agony, and I knew I could not let my pride keep you from me. I spoke to Bernardo, and to my mother.' He took a breath, offering her a wry smile. 'It was not easy or comfortable for any of us. We have all committed wrongs against each other and there is still much to do, to say and to forgive. Yet we have begun. You have helped us, Ana. You are the best thing to have come into my life.'

Ana's throat ached with unshed tears and suppressed emotion. 'And you are the best thing in mine.' Still, she felt the fear lurking in the dark corners of her heart. It seemed so hard to believe, too wonderful to be true. To last. 'Yesterday you were so cold, so hard to me—'

Vittorio reached for her fingers and pressed them against his lips. 'I do not want to be a hard man,' he confessed, his voice a ragged whisper, his eyes glinting with unshed tears of his own. 'God knows, I don't. Yet, when I am afraid, I find that is how I become, for it is what I learned as a boy.'

'I know it is,' Ana whispered, remembering what both Constantia and Bernardo had told her. They'd helped her understand Vittorio, and she was grateful to them for that.

'It is no excuse,' Vittorio replied resolutely. 'And yet you have changed me, Ana. I am so grateful for that. I realized just how much you've changed me when you left me yesterday. I do not want to be that man any more. With you, I am not him.'

He touched her cheek, resting his forehead against hers. 'Can you forgive me, *rondinella*, for those moments when I became him again? Can you forgive me, and believe in the man I am trying to become?'

Ana thought of the man who had comforted her as a grieving child so many years ago; she remembered his many kindnesses over the last few months. She recalled the wonder and joy she'd felt in his arms. 'You are that man, Vittorio. You always have been.'

He kissed her then sweetly, so very sweetly, a kiss that was healing and hope together. 'Only because of you, Ana. Only because of you.'

She laughed, a tremulous, muffled sound, for the knowledge that Vittorio loved her—that this was *real*—was too wonderful, too overwhelming. She trusted it now; she believed in it, and it was good.

It was amazing.

Vittorio touched her cheek; it came away damp. 'It's all right to cry, *rondinella*,' he whispered and Ana laughed again, entwining his fingers with her own as she kissed him once more.

'For joy,' she said. 'This time for joy.'

* * * * *

The Truth Behind His Touch

Cathy Williams

Cathy Williams is originally from Trinidad, but has lived in England for a number of years. She currently has a house in Warwickshire, which she shares with her husband Richard, her three daughters, Charlotte, Olivia and Emma, and their pet cat, Salem. She adores writing romantic fiction, and would love one of her girls to become a writer—although at the moment she is happy enough if they do their homework and agree not to bicker with one another!

Recent titles by the same author:

THE SECRET SINCLAIR
HER IMPOSSIBLE BOSS
IN WANT OF A WIFE?
THE SECRETARY'S SCANDALOUS SECRET

CHAPTER ONE

CAROLINE FANNED HERSELF wearily with the guide book which she had been clutching like a talisman ever since she had disembarked from the plane at Malpensa airport in Milan, and took the time to look around her. Somewhere, nestled amongst these ancient, historic buildings and wide, elegant *piazzas*, lay her quarry. She knew that she should be heading directly there, bypassing all temptations of a cold drink and something sweet, sticky, chocolatey and deliciously fattening, but she was hot, she was exhausted and she was ravenous.

'It will take you no time at all!' Alberto had said encouragingly. 'One short flight, Caroline. And a taxi... Maybe a little walking to find his offices, but what sights you'll see. The Duomo. You will never have laid eyes on anything so spectacular. *Palazzos.* More than you can shake a stick at. And the shops. Well, it is many, many years since I have been to Milan, but I can still recall the splendour of the Vittorio Gallery.'

Caroline had looked at him with raised, sceptical eyebrows and the old man had had the grace to flush sheepishly, because this trip to Milan was hardly a sightseeing tour. In fact, she was expected back within forty-eight hours and her heart clenched anxiously at the expectations sitting heavily on her shoulders.

She was to locate Giancarlo de Vito, run him to ground and somehow return to Lake Como with him.

'I would go myself, my dear,' Alberto had murmured, 'but my health does not permit it. The doctor said that I have to rest as much as possible—the strain on my heart... I am not a well man, you understand...'

Caroline wondered, not for the first time, how she had managed to let herself get talked into this mission but there seemed little point dwelling on that. She was here now, surrounded by a million people, perspiring in soaring July temperatures, and it was just too late in the day to have a sudden attack of nerves.

The truth was that the success or failure of this trip was really not her concern. She was the messenger. Alberto, yes, *he* would be affected, but she was really just his personal assistant who happened to be performing a slightly bizarre duty.

Someone bumped into her from behind and she hastily consulted her map and began walking towards the small street which she had highlighted in bold orange.

She had dressed inappropriately for the trip, but it had been cooler by the lake. Here, it was sweltering and her cream trousers stuck to her legs like glue. The plain yellow blouse with its three-quarter-length sleeves had looked suitably smart when she had commenced her journey but now she wished that she had worn something without sleeves, and she should have done something clever with her hair. Put it up into some kind of bun, perhaps. Yes; she had managed to twist it into a long braid of sorts but it kept unravelling and somehow getting itself plastered around her neck.

Caught up in her own physical discomfort and the awkwardness of what lay ahead, she barely noticed the old mellow beauty of the cathedral with its impressive buttresses, spires and statues as she hurried past it, dragging her suitcase which behaved like a recalcitrant child, stopping and swerving and doing its best to misbehave.

Anyone with a less cheerful and equable temperament might

have been tempted to curse the elderly employer who had sent them on this impossible mission, which was frankly way beyond the scope of their duties. But Caroline, tired, hot and hungry as she was, was optimistic that she could do what was expected of her. She had enormous faith in human nature. Alberto, on the other hand, was the world's most confirmed pessimist.

She very nearly missed the building. Not knowing what exactly to expect, she had imagined something along the lines of an office in London. Bland, uninspiring, with perhaps too much glass and too little imagination.

Retracing her steps, she looked down at the address which she had carefully printed on an index card, and then up at the ancient exterior of stone and soft, aged pinks, no more than three storeys tall, adorned with exquisite carvings and fronted by two stone columns.

How difficult could Giancarlo be if he worked in this wonderful place? Caroline mused, heart lightening.

'I cannot tell you anything of Giancarlo,' Alberto had said mournfully when she had tried to press him for details of what she would be letting herself in for. 'It is many, many years since I have seen him. I could show you some pictures, but they are so out of date. He would have changed in all these years... If I had a computer... But an old man like me... How could I ever learn now to work one of those things?'

'I could go and get my laptop from upstairs,' she had offered instantly, but he had waved her down.

'No, no. I don't care for those gadgets. Televisions and telephones are as far as I am prepared to go when it comes to technology.'

Privately, Caroline agreed with him. She used her computer to email but that was all, and it was nigh on impossible trying to access the Internet in the house anyway.

So she had few details on which to go. She suspected, however, that Giancarlo was rich, because Alberto had told her in passing that he had 'made something of himself'. Her suspicion crystallised when she stepped into the cool, uber-modern, marbled portico of Giancarlo's offices. If the façade of the building looked as though it had stepped out of an architectural guide to mediaeval buildings, inside the twenty-first century had made its mark.

Only the cool, pale marble underfoot and the scattering of old masterpieces on the walls hinted at the age of the building.

Of course, she wasn't expected. Surprise, apparently, was of the utmost importance, 'or else he will just refuse to see you, I am convinced of it!'.

It took her over thirty-five minutes to try to persuade the elegant receptionist positioned like a guard dog behind her wood-and-marble counter, who spoke far too quickly for Caroline to follow, that she shouldn't be chucked out.

'What is your business here?'

'Ah...'

'Are you expected?'

'Not *exactly*...'

'Are you aware that Signore de Vito is an extremely important man?'

'Er...' Then she had practised her haltering Italian and explained the connection to Giancarlo, produced several documents which had been pored over in silence and the wheels of machinery had finally begun to move.

But still she would have to wait.

Three floors up, Giancarlo, in the middle of a meeting with three corporate financiers, was interrupted by his secretary, who whispered something in his ear that made him still and brought the shutters down on his dark, cold eyes.

'Are you sure?' he asked in a clipped voice. Elena Carli seldom made mistakes; it was why she had worked for him so successfully for the past five-and-a-half years. She did her job with breathtaking efficiency, obeyed orders without question and *seldom* made mistakes. When she nodded firmly, he immediately got to his feet, made his excuses—though not profusely, because these financiers needed him far more than he needed them—and then, meeting dismissed, he walked across to the window to stare down at the paved, private courtyard onto which his offices backed.

So the past he thought to have left behind was returning. Good sense counselled him to turn his back on this unexpected intrusion in his life, but he was curious and what harm would there be in indulging his curiosity? In his life of unimaginable wealth and vast power, curiosity was a rare visitor, after all.

Giancarlo de Vito had been ferociously single-minded and ruthlessly ambitious to get where he was now. He had had no choice. His mother had needed to be kept and after a series of unfortunate lovers the only person left to keep her had been him. He had finished his university career with a first and had launched himself into the world of high finance with such dazzling expertise that it hadn't been long before doors began to open. Within three years of finishing university, he'd been able to pick and choose his employer. Within five years, he'd no longer needed an employer because he had become the powerhouse who did the employing. Now, at just over thirty, he had become a billionaire, diversifying with gratifying success, branching out and stealing the march on competitors with every successive merger and acquisition and in the process building himself a reputation that rendered him virtually untouchable.

His mother had seen only the tip of his enormous success, as she had died six years previously—perhaps, fittingly, in the passenger seat of her young lover's fast car—a victim, as he had seen it, of a life gone wrong. As her only offspring, Giancarlo knew he should have been more heartbroken than he actually was, but his mother had been a temperamental and difficult woman, fond of spending money and easily dissatisfied. He had found her flitting from lover to lover rather distasteful, but never had he once criticized her. At the end of the day, hadn't she been through enough?

Unaccustomed to taking these trips down memory lane,

Giancarlo shook himself out of his introspection with a certain amount of impatience. Presumably the woman who had come to see him and who was currently sitting in the grand marble foyer was to blame for his lapse in self-control. With his thoughts back in order and back where they belonged, he buzzed her up.

'You may go up now.' The receptionist beckoned to Caroline, who could have stayed sitting in the air-conditioned foyer quite happily for another few hours. Her feet were killing her and she had finally begun cooling down after the hours spent in the suffocating heat. 'Signora Carli will meet you up at the top of the elevator and show you to Signore De Vito's office. If you like, you may leave your…case here.'

Caroline thought that the last thing the receptionist seemed to want was her battered pull-along being left anywhere in the foyer. At any rate, she needed it with her.

And, now that she was finally here, she felt a little twist of nervousness at the prospect of what lay ahead. She wouldn't want to return to the lake house empty-handed. Alberto had suffered a heart attack several weeks previously. His health was not good and, his doctor had confided in her, the less stress the better.

With a determined lift of her head, Caroline followed the personal assistant in silence, passing offices which seemed abnormally silent, staffed with lots of hard-working executives who barely looked up as they walked past.

Everyone seemed very well-groomed. The women were all thin, good-looking and severe, with their hair scraped back and their suits shrieking of money well spent.

In comparison, Caroline felt overweight, short and dishevelled. She had never been skinny, even as a child. When she sucked her breath in and looked at herself sideways through narrowed eyes, she could almost convince herself that she was curvy and voluptuous, but the illusion was always destroyed the second she took a harder look at her reflection. Nor was her hair of the manageable variety. It rarely did as it was told;

it flowed in wild abandon down her back and was only ever remotely obedient when it was wet. Right now the heat had added more curl than normal and she knew that tendrils were flying wildly out of their impromptu braid. She had to keep blowing them off her face.

After trailing along behind Elena—who had introduced herself briefly and then seen fit to say absolutely nothing else on the way up—a door was opened into an office so exquisite that for a few seconds Caroline wasn't even aware that she had been deposited like an unwanted parcel, nor did she notice the man by the window turning slowly around to look at her.

All she could see was the expanse of splendid, antique Persian rug on the marble floor; the soft, silk wallpaper on the walls; the smooth, dark patina of a bookshelf that half-filled an entire wall; the warm, old paintings on the walls—not paintings of silly lines and shapes that no one could ever decipher, but paintings of beautiful landscapes, heavy with trees and rivers.

'Wow,' she breathed, deeply impressed as she continued to look around her with shameless awe.

At long last her eyes rested on the man staring at her and she was overcome with a suffocating, giddy sensation as she absorbed the wild, impossible beauty of his face. Black hair, combed back and ever so slightly too long, framed a face of stunning perfection. His features were classically perfect and invested with a raw sensuality that brought a heated flush to her cheeks. His eyes were dark and unreadable. Expensive, lovingly hand-tailored charcoal-grey trousers sheathed long legs and the crisp white shirt rolled to the elbows revealed strong, bronzed forearms with a sprinkling of dark hair. In the space of a few seconds, Caroline realised that she was staring at the most spectacular-looking man she had ever clapped eyes on in her life. She also belatedly realised that she was gaping, mouth inelegantly open, and she cleared her throat in an attempt to get a hold of herself.

The silence stretched to breaking point and then at last the man spoke and introduced himself, inviting her to take a seat, which she was only too happy to do because her legs felt like jelly. His voice matched his appearance. It was deep, dark, smooth and velvety. It was also icy cold, and a trickle of doubt began creeping in, because this was not a man who looked as though he could be persuaded into doing anything he didn't want to do.

'So…' Giancarlo sat down, pushing himself away from his desk so that he could cross his long legs, and stared at her. 'What makes you think that you can just barge into my offices, Miss…?'

'Rossi. Caroline.'

'I was in the middle of a meeting.'

'I'm so sorry.' She stumbled over the apology. 'I didn't mean to interrupt anything. I would have been happy to wait until you were finished…' Her naturally sunny personality rose to the surface and she offered him a small smile. 'In fact, it was so wonderfully cool in your foyer and I was just so grateful to rest my legs. I've been on the go for absolutely ages and it's as hot as a furnace out there…' In receipt of his continuing and unwelcoming silence, her voice faded away and she licked her lips nervously.

Giancarlo was quite happy to let her stew in her own discomfiture.

'This is a fantastic building, by the way.'

'Let's do away with the pleasantries, Miss Rossi. What are you doing here?'

'Your father sent me.'

'So I gather. Which is why you're sitting in my office. My question is *why*? I haven't had any contact with my father in over fifteen years, so I'm curious as to why he should suddenly decide to send a henchman to get in touch with me.'

Caroline felt an uncustomary warming anger flood through her as she tried to marry up this cold, dark stranger with the old man of whom she was so deeply fond, but getting angry wasn't going to get her anywhere.

'And who *are* you anyway? My father is hardly a spring chicken. Don't tell me that he's managed to find himself a young wife to nurse him faithfully through his old age?' He leaned back in his chair and steepled his fingers together. 'Nothing too beautiful, of course,' he murmured, casting insolent, assessing eyes over her. 'Devotion in the form of a young, beautiful, nubile wife is never a good idea for an old man, even a rich old man...'

'How dare you?'

Giancarlo laughed coldly. 'You show up here, unannounced, with a message from a father who was written out of my life a long time ago... Frankly, I have every right to dare.'

'I am *not* married to your father!'

'Well, now the alternative is even more distasteful, not to mention downright stupid. Why involve yourself with someone three times your age unless you're in it for the financial gain? Don't tell me the sex is breathtaking?'

'I can't believe you're saying these things!' She wondered how she could have been so bowled over by the way he looked when he was obviously a loathsome individual, just the sort of cold, unfeeling, sneering sort she hated. 'I'm not involved with your father in any way other than professionally, *signore*!'

'No? Then what is a young girl like you doing in a rambling old house by a lake with only an old man for company?'

Caroline glared at him. She was still smarting at the way his eyes had roamed over her and dismissed her as 'nothing too beautiful'. She knew she wasn't beautiful but to hear it casually emerge from the mouth of someone she didn't know was beyond rude. Especially from the mouth of someone as physically compelling as the man sitting in front of her. Why hadn't she done what most other people would have in similar circumstances and found herself an Internet café so that she could do some background research on the man she had been told to ferret out? At least then she might have been prepared!

She had to grit her teeth together and fight the irresistible urge to grab her suitcase and jump ship.

'Well? I'm all ears.'

'There's no need to be horrible to me, *signore*. I'm sorry if I've ruined your meeting, or…or whatever you were doing, but I didn't *volunteer* to come here.'

Giancarlo almost didn't believe his ears. People never accused him of being *horrible*. Granted, they might sometimes think that, but it was vaguely shocking to actually *hear* someone come right out and say it. Especially a woman. He was accustomed to women doing everything within their power to please him. He looked narrowly at his uninvited visitor. She was certainly not the sort of rake-thin beauty eulogised in the pages of magazines. She was trying hard to conceal her expression but it was transparently clear that the last place she wanted to be was in his office, being interrogated.

Too bad.

'I take it my father manipulated you into doing what he wanted. Are you his housekeeper? Why would he employ an English housekeeper?'

'I'm his personal assistant,' Caroline admitted reluctantly. 'He used to know my father once upon a time. Your father had a one-year posting in England lecturing at a university and my father was one of his students. He was my father's mentor and they kept in touch after your father returned to Italy. My father is Italian. I think he enjoyed having someone he could speak to in Italian.

'Anyway, I didn't go to university, but my parents thought it would be nice for me to learn Italian, seeing that it's my father's native tongue, and he asked Alberto if he could help me find a posting over here for a few months. So I'm helping your father with his memoirs and also pretty much taking care of all the admin—stuff like that. Don't you want to know…um…how he is? You haven't seen him in such a long time.'

'If I had wanted to see my father, don't you think I would have contacted him before now?'

'Yes, well, pride can sometimes get in the way of us doing what we want to do.'

'If your aim is to play amateur psychologist, then the door is right behind you. Avail yourself of it.'

'I'm not playing amateur psychologist,' Caroline persisted stubbornly. 'I just think, well, I know that it probably wasn't ideal when your parents got divorced. Alberto doesn't talk much about it, but I know that when your mother walked out and took you with her you were only twelve...'

'I don't believe I'm hearing this!' Intensely private, Giancarlo could scarcely credit that he was listening to someone drag his past out of the closet in which it had been very firmly shut.

'How else am I supposed to deal with this situation?' Caroline asked, bewildered and dismayed.

'I am not in the habit of discussing my past!'

'Yes, well, that's not *my* fault.' She felt herself soften. 'Don't you think that it's a good thing to talk about the things that bother us? Don't you *ever* think about your dad?'

His internal line buzzed and he spoke in rapid Italian, telling his secretary to hold all further calls until he advised her otherwise. Suddenly, filled with a restless energy he couldn't seem to contain, he pushed himself away from the desk and moved across to the window to look briefly outside before turning around and staring at the girl on the chair who had swivelled to face him.

She looked as though butter wouldn't melt in her mouth—very young, very innocent and with a face as transparent as a pane of glass. Right now, he seemed to be an object of pity, and he tightened his mouth with a sense of furious outrage.

'He's had a heart attack,' Caroline told him abruptly, her eyes beginning to well up because she was so very fond of him. Having him rushed into hospital, dealing with the horror of it all on her own had been almost more than she could take. 'A very serious one. In fact, for a while it was touch and go.' She opened her satchel, rummaged around for a tissue and found a pristine white handkerchief pressed into her hand.

'Sorry,' she whispered shakily. 'But I don't know how you can just stand there like a statue and not feel a thing.'

Big brown eyes looked accusingly at him and Giancarlo flushed, annoyed with himself because there was no reason why he should feel guilty on that score. He had no relationship with his father. Indeed, his memories of life in the big house by the lake were a nightmare of parental warfare. Alberto had married his very young and very pretty blonde wife when he had been in his late forties, nearly twenty-five years older than Adriana, and was already a cantankerous and confirmed bachelor.

It had been a marriage that had struggled on against all odds and had been, to all accounts, hellishly difficult for his demanding young wife.

His mother had not held back from telling him everything that had been so horrifically wrong with the relationship, as soon as he had been old enough to appreciate the gory detail. Alberto had been selfish, cold, mean, dismissive, contemptuous and probably, his mother had maintained viciously, would have had other women had he not lacked even basic social skills when it came to the opposite sex. He had, Adriana had wept on more than one occasion, thrown them out without a penny—so was it any wonder that she sometimes needed a little alcohol and a few substances to help her get by?

So many things for which Giancarlo had never forgiven his father…

He had stood on the sidelines and watched his delicate, spoilt mother—without any qualifications to speak of, always reliant on her beauty—demean herself by taking lover after lover, searching for the one who might want her enough to stick around. By the time she had died she had been a pathetic shadow of her former self.

'You have no idea of what my life was like, or what my mother's life was like,' Giancarlo framed icily. 'Perhaps my father has mellowed. Ill health has a habit of making servants of us all. However, I'm not interested in building bridges. Is that why he sent you here—because he's now an old man and he wants my forgiveness before he shuffles off this mortal coil?' He gave a bark of cynical, contemptuous laughter. 'I don't think so.'

She had continued playing with the handkerchief, twisting it between her fingers. Giancarlo thought that when it came to messengers, his father could not have been more calculating in his choice. The woman was a picture of teary-eyed incomprehension. Anyone would be forgiven for thinking that she worked for a saint, instead of for the man who had made his mother's life a living hell.

His sharp eyes narrowed and focused, taking in the details of her appearance. Her clothes were a fashion disaster—trousers and a blouse in a strange, sickly shade of yellow, both of which would have been better suited to someone twice her age. Her hair seemed to be escaping from a sort of makeshift braid, and it was long—really long. Not at all like the snappy bobs he was accustomed to seeing on women. And it was curly. She was free of make-up and he was suddenly conscious of the fact that her skin was very smooth, satin smooth, and she had an amazing mouth—full, well-defined lips, slightly parted now to reveal pearly-white teeth as she continued to stare at him with disappointment and incredulity.

'I'm sorry you're still so bitter about the past,' she murmured quietly. 'But he would really like to see you. Why is it too late to mend bridges? It would mean the world to him.'

'So have you managed to see anything of our beautiful city?'

'What? No. No, I've come directly here. Look, is there anything I can do or say to convince you to…to come back with me?'

'You have got to be kidding, haven't you? I mean, even if I were suddenly infused with a burning desire to become a prodigal son, do you really imagine that I would be able to drop everything, pack a bag and hop on the nearest train for Lake Como? Surprise, surprise—I have an empire to run.'

'Yes, but…'

'I'm a very busy man, Miss Rossi, and I have already allotted you a great deal of my very valuable time. Now, you could keep trying to convince me that I'm being a monster in not clapping my hands for joy that my father has suddenly decided to get in touch with me thanks to a bout of ill health…'

'You make it sound as though he's had a mild attack of flu! He's suffered a very serious *heart attack*.'

'For which I am truly sorry.' Giancarlo extended his arms wide in a gesture of such phoney sympathy that Caroline had to clench her fists to stop herself from smacking him. 'As I would be on learning of any stranger's brush with death. But, alas, you're going to have to go back empty-handed.'

Defeated, Caroline stood up and reached down for her suitcase.

'Where are you staying?' Giancarlo asked with scrupulous politeness as he watched the slump of her shoulders. God, had the old man really thought that there would be no consequences to pay for the destructive way he had treated his wife? He was as rich as they came and yet, according to Adriana, he had employed the best lawyers in the land to ensure that she received the barest of settlements, accessed through a trustee who had made sure the basics, the *absolute* basics, were paid for, and a meagre allowance handed over to her, like a child being given pocket money, scarcely enough to provide any standard of living. He had often wondered, over the years, whether his mother would have been as desperate to find love if she had been left sufficient money to meet her requirements.

Caroline wearily told him, although she knew full well that he didn't give a damn where she was staying. He just wanted her out of his office. She would be returning having failed. Of course, Alberto would be far too proud to do anything other than shrug his shoulders and say something about having tried, but she would know the truth. She would know that he would be gutted.

'Well, you make sure you try the food market at the Rinascente. You'll enjoy it. Tremendous views. And, of course, the shopping there is good as well.'

'I hate shopping.' Caroline came to a stop in front of the office door and turned around to find that he was virtually on top of her, towering a good eight or nine inches above her and even more intimidating this close up than he had been sitting safely behind his desk or lounging by the window.

The sun glinted from behind, picking out the striking angles of his face and rendering them more scarily beautiful. He had the most amazing eyelashes, long, lush and dark, the sort of eyelashes that most women could only ever have achieved with the help of tons of mascara.

She felt a sickening jolt somewhere in the region of her stomach and was suddenly and uncomfortably aware of her breasts, too big for her height, now sensitive, tingly and weighty as he stared down at her. Her hands wanted to flutter to the neckline of her blouse and draw the lapels tightly together. She flushed with embarrassment; how could she have forgotten that she was the ugly duckling?

'And I don't want to be having this polite conversation with you,' she breathed in a husky, defiant undertone.

'Come again?'

'I'm sorry your parents got divorced, and I'm really sorry that it left such a mark on you, but I think it's horrible that you won't give your father another chance. How do you know exactly what happened between your parents? You were only a child. Your father's ill and you'd rather carry on holding a grudge than try and make the most of the time you have left of him. He might die tomorrow, for all we know!'

That short speech took a lot out of her. She wasn't usually defiant, but this man set her teeth on edge. 'How can you say that, even if you were interested in meeting him, you couldn't possibly get away because you're too important?'

'I said that I have an empire to run.'

'It's the same thing!' She was shaking all over, like a leaf, but she looked up at him with unflinching determination, chin jutting out, her brown eyes, normally mild, flashing fire. 'Okay, I'm not going to see you again…' Caroline drew in a deep breath and impatiently swept her disobedient hair from away her face. 'So I can be really honest with you.'

Giancarlo moved to lounge against the door, arms folded, an expression of lively curiosity on his face. Her cheeks were flushed and her eyes glittered. She was a woman in a rage and he was getting the impression that this was a woman who didn't *do* rages. God, wasn't this turning into one hell of a day?

'I don't suppose *anyone* is really ever honest with you, are they?' She looked around the office, with its mega-expensive fittings, ancient rug, worn bookshelves, the painting on the wall—the only modern one she had glimpsed, which looked vaguely familiar. Who was really ever that honest with someone as wealthy as he appeared to be, as good-looking as he was? He had the arrogance of a man who always got exactly what he wanted.

'It's useful when my man who handles my stocks and shares tells me what he thinks. Although, in fairness, I usually know more than he does. I should get rid of him but—' he shrugged with typical Italian nonchalance '—we go back a long way.'

He shot her a smile that was so unconsciously charming that Caroline was nearly knocked backwards by the force of it. It was like being in a dark room only to be suddenly dazzled by a ray of blistering sunshine. Which didn't distract her from the fact that he refused to see his father, a sick and possibly dying old man. Refused to bury the hatchet, whatever the consequences. Charming smiles counted for nothing when it came to the bigger picture!

'I'm glad you think that this is a big joke,' she said tightly.

'I'm glad that you can laugh about it, but you know what? I feel *sorry* for you! You might think that the only thing that matters is all…all *this*…but none of this counts when it comes to relationships and family. I think you're…you're *arrogant* and *high-handed* and making a huge mistake!'

Outburst over, Caroline yanked open the office door to a surprised Elena, who glanced at her with consternation before looking behind to where her boss, the man who never lost his steely grip on his emotions, was staring at the small, departing brunette with the incredulous expression of someone who has been successfully tackled when least expecting it.

'Stop staring,' Giancarlo said. He shook his head, dazed, and then offered his secretary a wry grin. 'We all lose our cool sometimes.'

CHAPTER TWO

MILAN WAS A diverse and beautiful city. There were sufficient museums, galleries, basilicas and churches to keep any tourist busy. The Galleria Vittorio was a splendid and elegant arcade, stuffed with cafés and shops. Caroline knew all this because the following day—her last day before she returned to Alberto, when she would have to admit failure—she made sure to read all the literature on a city which she might not visit again. It was tarnished with the miserable experience of having met Giancarlo De Vito.

The more Caroline thought about him, the more arrogant and unbearable he seemed. She just couldn't find a single charitable thing to credit him with. Alberto would be waiting for her, expecting to see her arrive with his son and, failing that, he would be curious for details. Would she be honest and admit to him that she had found his sinfully beautiful son loathsome and overbearing? Would any parent, even an estranged parent, be grateful for information like that?

She looked down to where her ice-cold glass of lemonade was slowly turning warm in the searing heat. She had dutifully spent two hours walking around the Duomo, admiring the stained-glass windows, the impressive statues of saints and the extravagant carvings. But her heart hadn't been in it, and now here she was, in one of the little cafés, which outside on a hot summer day was packed to the rafters with tourists sitting and lazily people-watching.

Her thoughts were in turmoil. With an impatient sigh, she glanced down at her watch, wondering how she would fill the remainder of her day, and was unaware of the shadow looming over her until she heard Giancarlo's velvety, familiar voice which had become embedded in her head like an irritating burr.

'You lied to me.'

Caroline looked up, shading her eyes from the glare of the sun, at about the same time as a wad of papers landed on the small circular table in front of her.

She was so shocked to see him towering over her, blocking out the sun like a dark avenging angel, that she half-spilled her drink in her confusion.

'What are you doing here? And how did you find me?' Belatedly she noticed the papers on the table. 'And what's all that stuff?'

'We need to have a little chat and this place isn't doing it for me.'

Caroline felt her heart lift a little. Maybe he was reconsidering his original stance. Maybe, just maybe, he had seen the light and was now prepared to let bygones be bygones. She temporarily forgot his ominous opening words and the mysterious stack of papers in front of her.

'Of course!' She smiled brightly and then cleared her throat when there was no reciprocal smile. 'I... You haven't said how you managed to find me. Where are we going? Am I supposed to bring all this stuff with me?'

Presumably, yes, as he spun round on his heels and was scouring the *piazza* through narrowed eyes. Did he notice the interested stares he was garnering from the tourists, particularly the women? Or was he immune to that sort of attention?

Caroline grabbed the papers and scrambled to follow him as

he strode away from the café through a series of small roads, leaving the crush of tourists behind.

Today, she had worn the only other outfit she had brought with her, a summer dress with small buttons down the front. Because it left her shoulders bare, and because she was so acutely conscious of her generous breasts, she had a thin pink cardigan slung loosely over her—which wasn't exactly practical, given the weather, but without it she felt too exposed and self-conscious.

With the ease of someone who lived in the city, he weaved his way through the busier areas until they were finally at a small café tucked away from the tourist hotspots, although even here the ancient architecture, the charming square with its sixteenth-century well, the engravings on some of the façades, were all photo opportunities.

She dithered behind him, feeling a bit like a spare part as he spoke in rapid Italian to a short, plump man whom she took to be the owner of the café. Then he motioned her inside where it was blessedly cool and relatively empty.

'You can sit,' Giancarlo said irritably when she continued to hover by the table. What did his father see in the woman? He barely remembered Alberto, but one thing he *did* remember was that he had not been the most docile person in the world. If his mother had been a difficult woman, then she had found her match in her much older husband. What changes had the years wrought, if Alberto was happy to work with someone who had to be the most background woman he had ever met? And once again she was in an outfit that would have been more suitable on a woman twice her age. Truly the English hadn't got a clue when it came to fashion.

He found himself appraising her body and then, surprisingly, lingering on her full breasts pushing against the thin cotton dress, very much in evidence despite the washed-out cardigan she had draped over her shoulders.

'You never said how you managed to find me,' Caroline repeated a little breathlessly as she slid into the chair opposite him.

She shook away the giddy, drowning feeling she had when she looked too hard at him. Something about his animal sex-appeal was horribly unsettling, too hard to ignore and not quite what she was used to.

'You told me where you were staying. I went there first thing this morning and was told by the receptionist that you'd left for the Duomo. It was just a question of time before you followed the herd to one of the cafés outside.'

'So...have you had a rethink?' Caroline asked hopefully. She wondered how it was that he could look so cool and urbane in his cream trousers and white shirt while the rest of the population seemed to be slowly dissolving under the summer sun.

'Have a look at the papers in front of you.'

Caroline dutifully flicked through them. 'I'm sorry, I have no idea what these are—and I'm not very good with numbers.' She had wisely tied her hair back today but still some curling strands found their way to her cheeks and she absent-mindedly tucked them behind her ears while she continued to frown at the pages and pages of bewildering columns and numbers in front of her, finally giving up.

'After I saw you I decided to run a little check on Alberto's company accounts. You're looking at my findings.'

'I don't understand why you've shown me this. I don't know anything about Alberto's financial affairs. He doesn't talk about that at all.'

'Funny, but I never thought him particularly shy when it came to money. In fact, I would say that he's always had his finger on the button in that area.'

'How would you know, when you haven't seen him for over a decade?'

Giancarlo thought of the way Alberto had short changed his mother and his lips curled cynically. 'Let's move away from that contentious area, shall we? And let's focus on one or two interesting things I unearthed.' He sat back as cold drinks were placed in front of them, along with a plate of delicate little *tor-*

tas and pastries. 'By the way, help yourself…' He gestured to the dish of pastries and cakes and was momentarily sidetracked when she pulled her side plate in front of her and piled a polite mound, but a mound nevertheless, of the delicacies on it.

'You're actually going to eat all of those?' he heard himself ask, fascinated against his will.

'I know, I shouldn't really. But I'm starving.' Caroline sighed at the diet which she had been planning for ages and which had yet to get underway. 'You don't mind, do you? I mean…they're not just here for *show*, are they?'

'No, *di niente*.' He sat back and watched as she nibbled her way through the pastries, politely leaving one, licking the sweet crumbs off her fingers with enjoyment. A rare sight. The stick-thin women he dated pushed food round their plates and would have recoiled in horror at the thought of eating anything as fattening as a pastry.

Of course, he should be getting on with what he wanted to say, but he had been thrown off course and he still was when she shot him an apologetic smile. There was an errant crumb at the side of her mouth and just for an instant he had an overwhelming urge to brush it off. Instead, he gestured to her mouth with his hand.

'I always have big plans for going on a diet.' Caroline blushed. 'Once or twice I actually did, but diets are deadly. Have you ever been on one? No, I bet you haven't. Well, salads are all well and good, but just try making them interesting. I guess I just really love food.'

'That's…unusual. In a woman. Most of the women I meet do their best to avoid the whole eating experience.'

Of course he would be the type who only associated with model types, Caroline thought sourly. Thin, leggy women who weighed nothing. She wished she hadn't indulged her sweet tooth. Not that it mattered because, although he might be good-looking—well, staggering, really—he wasn't the sort of man she would ever go for. So what did it matter if he thought that she was overweight and greedy into the bargain?

'You were saying something about Alberto's financial affairs?' She glanced down at her watch, because why on earth should he have the monopoly on precious time? 'It's just that I leave tomorrow morning and I want to make sure that I get through as much as possible before I go.'

Giancarlo was, for once in his life, virtually lost for words. Was she *hurrying him along*?

'I think,' he asserted without inflection, 'that your plans will have to take a back seat until I'm finished.'

'You haven't told me whether you've decided to put the past behind you and accompany me back to Lake Como.' She didn't know why she was bothering to ask the question because it was obvious that he had no such intention.

'So you came here to see me for the sole purpose of masterminding a jolly reunion...'

'It wasn't *my* idea.'

'Immaterial. Getting back to the matter in hand, the fact is that Alberto's company accounts show a big, gaping black hole.'

Caroline frowned because she genuinely had no idea what he was talking about.

'*Si,*' Giancarlo imparted without a shade of regret as he continued to watch her so carefully that she could feel the colour mounting in her cheeks. 'He has been leaking money for the past ten years but recently it's become something more akin to a haemorrhage...'

Caroline gasped and stared at him in sudden consternation. 'Oh my goodness... Do you think that that's why he had the heart attack?'

'I beg your pardon?'

'I didn't think he took an active interest in what happened in the company. I mean, he's been pretty much a recluse since I came to live with him.'

'Which would be how long ago?'

'Several months. Originally, I only intended to come for a few weeks, but we got along so well and there were so many things he wanted me to do that I found myself staying on.' She fixed anxious brown eyes on Giancarlo, who seemed sublimely immune to an ounce of compassion at the news he had casually delivered.

'Are you…are you sure you've got your facts right?'

'I'm never wrong,' he said drily. 'It's possible that Alberto hasn't played an active part in running his company for some time now. It's more than possible that he's been merrily living off the dividends and foolishly imagining that his investments are paying off.'

'And what if he only recently found out?' Caroline cried, determined not to become too over-emotional in front of a man who, she knew, would see emotion in a woman as repellent. Besides, she had cried on him yesterday. She still had the handkerchief to prove it. Once had been bad enough but twice would be unforgivable.

'Do you think that that might have contributed to his heart attack? Do you think that he became so stressed that it affected his health?' Horribly rattled at that thought, she distractedly helped herself to the last pastry lying uneaten on her plate.

'No one can ever accuse me of being a gullible man, Signorina Rossi.' Giancarlo was determined to stick to the script. 'One lesson I've learnt in life is that, when it comes to money, there will always be people around who are more than happy to scheme their way into getting their hands on some of it.'

'Yes. Yes, I suppose so. Whatever. Poor Alberto. He never mentioned a word and yet he must have been so worried. Imagine having to deal with that on your own.'

'Yes. Poor Alberto. Still, whilst poring over these findings, it occurred to me that your mission here might very well have been twofold…'

'The doctor said that stress can cause all sorts of health problems.'

'Focus, signorina!'

Caroline fell silent and looked at him. The sun wafting through the pane of glass made his hair look all the more glossy. She vaguely noticed the way it curled at the collar of his shirt. Somehow, it made him look very exotic and very European.

'Now are you with me?'

'There's no need to talk down to me!'

'There's every need. You have the most wandering mind of anyone I've ever met.'

Caroline shot him a look of simmering resentment and added 'rude' to the increasingly long list of things she didn't like about him.

'And you are the *rudest* person I've ever met in my entire life!'

Giancarlo couldn't remember the last time anyone had ever dared to insult him to his face. He didn't think it had ever happened. Rather than be sidetracked, however, he chose to overlook her offensive remark.

'It occurred to me that my father's health, if your story about his heart attack is to be believed, might not be the primary reason for your visit to Milan.'

'If my story is to be believed?' She shook her head with a puzzled frown. 'Why would I lie about something like that?'

'I'll answer a question with a question—why would my father suddenly choose *now* to seek me out? He had more than one opportunity to get in touch. He never bothered. So why now? Shall I put forward a theory? He's wised up to the fact that his wealth has disappeared down the proverbial tubes and has sent you to check out the situation. Perhaps he told you that, if I seemed amenable to the idea of meeting up, you might mention the possibility of a loan?'

Shocked and disturbed by Giancarlo's freewheeling assumptions and cynical, half-baked misunderstandings, Caroline didn't know where to begin. She just stared at him as the colour drained away from her face. She wasn't normally given to anger, but right now she had to stop herself from picking her plate up and smashing it over his arrogant head.

'So maybe I wasn't entirely accurate when I accused you of lying to me. Maybe it would be more accurate to say that you were conveniently economical with the full truth...'

'I can't believe I'm hearing you say these things! How could you accuse your own father of trying to squeeze money out of you?'

Giancarlo flushed darkly under her steady, clear-eyed, incredulous gaze. 'Like I said, money has a nasty habit of bringing out the worst in people. Do you know that it's a given fact that the second someone wins a lottery, they suddenly discover that they have a hell of a lot more close friends and relatives than they ever imagined?'

'Alberto hasn't sent me here on a mission to get money out of you or...or to ask you for a loan!'

'Are you telling me that he had no idea that I was now a wealthy man?'

'That's not the point.' She remembered Alberto's statement that Giancarlo had made something of himself.

'No? You're telling me that there's no link between one semi-bankrupt father who hasn't been on the scene in nearly two decades and his sudden, inexplicable desire to meet the rich son he was happy to kick out of his house once upon a time?'

'Yes!'

'Well, if you really believe that, if you're not in cahoots with Alberto, then you must be incredibly naïve.'

'I feel very sorry for you, Signor De Vito.'

'Call me Giancarlo. I feel as though we almost know each other. Certainly no one can compete with you when it comes to delivering offensive remarks. You are in a league of your own.'

Caroline flushed because she was not given to being offensive. She was placid and easy-going by nature. However, she was certainly not going to apologise for speaking her mind to Giancarlo.

'You are pretty offensive as well,' she retaliated quietly. 'You've just accused me of being a liar. Maybe in *your* world you can never trust anyone...'

'I think it's fair to say that trust is a much over-rated virtue. I have a great deal of money. I've learnt to protect myself, simple as that.' He gave an elegant shrug, dismissing the topic. But Caroline wasn't quite ready to let the matter drop, to allow him to continue believing, unchallenged, that he had somehow been targeted by Alberto. She wouldn't let him walk away thinking the worst of either of them.

'I don't think that trust is an over-rated virtue. I told you that I feel sorry for you and I really do.' She had to steel herself to meet and hold the dark, forbidding depths of his icy eyes. 'I think it's sad to live in a world where you can never allow yourself to believe the best in other people. How can you ever be happy if you're always thinking that the people around you are out to take advantage of you? How can you ever be happy if you don't have faith in the people who are close to you?'

Giancarlo very nearly burst out laughing at that. What planet was this woman from? It was a cutthroat world out there and it became even more cutthroat when money and finances were involved. You had to keep your friends close and your enemies a whole lot closer in order to avoid the risk of being knifed in the back.

'Don't go getting evangelical on me,' he murmured drily and he noted the pink colour rise to her cheeks. 'You're blushing,' he surprised himself by saying.

'Because I'm angry!' But she put her hands to her face and glared at him. 'You're so...so *superior*! What sort of people do you mix with that you would suspect them of trying to use you for what you can give them? I didn't know anything about you when I agreed to come here. I didn't know that you had lots of money. I just knew that Alberto was ill and he wanted to make his peace with you.'

The oddest thing seemed to be happening. Giancarlo could

feel himself getting distracted. Was it because of the way those tendrils of curly hair were wisping against her face? Or was it because her anger made her almond-shaped eyes gleam like a furious spitting cat's? Or maybe it was the fact that, when she leant forward like that, the weight and abundance of her breasts brushing against the small table acted like a magnet to his wandering eyes.

It was a strange sensation to experience this slight loss of self-control because it never happened in his dealings with women. And he was a connoisseur when it came to the opposite sex. Without a trace of vanity, he knew that he possessed a combination of looks, power and influence that most women found an irresistible aphrodisiac. Right now, he had only recently broken off a six-month relationship with a model whose stunning looks had graced the covers of a number of magazines. She had begun to make noises about 'taking things further'; had started mentioning friends and relatives who were thinking of tying the knot; had begun to show an unhealthy interest in the engagement-ring section of expensive jewellery shops.

Giancarlo had no interest in going down the matrimonial path. There were two vital lessons he felt he had taken away from his parents: the first was that there was no such thing as a happy-ever-after. The second was that it was very easy for a woman to turn from angel to shrew. The loving woman who was happy to accommodate on every level quickly became the demanding, needy harridan who needed reassurance and attention round the clock.

He had watched his mother contrive to play the perfect partner on so many occasions that he had lost count. He had watched her perform her magic with whatever man happened to be the flavour of the day for a while, had watched her bat her eyelashes and flutter her eyes—but then, when things began winding down, he had seen how she had changed from eager to desperate, from hard-to-get to clingy and dependent. The older she had got, the more pitiful a sight she had made.

Of course, he was a red-blooded man with an extremely healthy libido, but as far as Giancarlo was concerned work was a far better bet when it came to reliability. Women, enjoyable as they might be, became instantly expendable the second they began thinking that they could change him.

He had never let any woman get under his skin and he was surprised now to find his thoughts drifting ever so slightly from the matter at hand.

He had confronted her, having done some background research, simply to have his suspicions confirmed. It had been a simple exercise in proving to her—and via her to Alberto—that he wasn't a mug who could be taken for a ride. At which point, his plan had been to walk away, warning guns sounding just in case they were tempted to try a second approach.

From the very second Caroline had shown up unannounced in his office, he had not allowed a shred of sentiment to colour his judgement. Bitter memories of the stories handed down to him from his mother still cast a long shadow. The truth he had seen with his very own eyes—the way her lack of any kind of robust financial settlement from a man who would have been very wealthy at the time had influenced her behaviour patterns—could not be overlooked.

'You must get bored out there,' Giancarlo heard himself remark when he should have really been thinking of concluding their conversation so that he could return to the various meetings waiting for him back at the office. Without taking his eyes off her, he flicked a finger and more cold drinks were brought to their table.

Caroline could no more follow this change in the conversation than she could have dealt with a snarling crocodile suddenly deciding to smile and offer her a cup of tea. She looked at him warily and wondered whether this was a roundabout lead-up to another scathing attack.

'Why are you interested?' she asked cautiously.

'Why not? It's not every day that a complete stranger waltzes into my office with a bombshell. Even if it turns out to be a bombshell that's easy to defuse. Also—and I'll be completely honest on this score—you don't strike me as the sort of person capable of dealing with the man I remember as being my father.'

Caroline was drawn into the conversation against her will. 'What do you remember?' she asked hesitantly. With another cold drink in front of her, the sight of those remaining pastries was awfully tempting. As though reading her mind, Giancarlo ordered a few more, different ones this time, smiling as they were placed in front of her.

He was amused to watch the struggle on her face as she looked down at them.

'What do I remember of my father? Now, let's think about this. Domineering. Frequently ill-tempered. Controlling. In short, not the easiest person in the world.'

'Like you, in other words.'

Giancarlo's mouth tightened because this was an angle that had never occurred to him and he wasn't about to give it house-room now.

'Sorry. I shouldn't have said that.'

'No, you shouldn't, but I'm already getting used to the idea that you speak before you think. Something else I imagine Alberto would have found unacceptable.'

'I really don't like you *at all*,' Caroline said through gritted teeth. 'And I take back what I said. You're *nothing* like Alberto.'

'I'm thrilled to hear that. So, enlighten me.' He felt a twinge of intense curiosity about this man who had been so thoroughly demonised by his ex-wife.

'Well.' Caroline smiled slowly and Giancarlo was amazed at how that slow, reluctant, suspicious smile altered the contours of her face, turning her into someone strangely beautiful in a lush, ripe way that was even more erotic, given the innocence of everything else about her. It put all sorts of crazy thoughts in his head, although the thoughts lasted only an instant, disappearing fast under the mental discipline that was so much part and parcel of his personality.

'He can be grumpy. He's very grumpy now because he hates being told what he can and can't eat and what time he has to go to bed. He hates me helping him physically, so he's employed a local woman, a nurse from the hospital, to help him instead, and I'm constantly having to tell him that he's got to be less bossy and critical of her.

'He was very polite when I first arrived. I think he knew that he was doing my dad a favour, but he figured that he would only have to be on good behaviour for a few weeks. I don't think he knew what to do with me, to start with. He's not been used to company. He wasn't comfortable making eye contact, but none of that lasted too long. We discovered that we shared so many interests—books, old movies, the garden. In fact, the garden has been invaluable now that Alberto is recovering. Every day we go down to the pond just beyond the walled rose-garden. We sit in the folly, read a bit, chat a bit. He likes me to read to him even though he's forever telling me that I need to put more expression in my voice... I guess all that's going to have to go...'

Giancarlo, who hadn't thought of what he had left behind for a very long time, had a vivid memory of that pond and of the folly, a weird gazebo-style creation with a very comfortable bench inside where he likewise had enjoyed whiling away his time during the long summer months when he had been on holiday. He shook away the memory as if clearing cobwebs from a cupboard that hadn't been opened for a long time.

'What do you mean that you guess that's all "going to have to go"?'

Caroline settled worried eyes on his face. For someone who was clearly so intelligent, she was surprised that he didn't seem to follow her. Then she realised that she couldn't very well explain without risking another attack on Alberto's scruples.

'Nothing,' she mumbled when his questioning silence threatened to become too uncomfortable.

'Tut tut. Are you going to get tongue-tied on me?'

The implication being that she talked far too much, Caroline concluded, hurt.

'What do you mean? And don't bother trying to be coy. It doesn't suit you.'

Caroline didn't think she could feel more loathing for another human being if she tried.

'Well, if Alberto has run into financial difficulties, then he's not going to be able to maintain the house, is he? I mean, it's enormous. Right now, a lot of it isn't used, but he would still have to sell it. And please don't tell me that this is a ploy to try and get money out of you. It isn't.' She sighed in weary resignation. 'I don't know why I'm telling you that. You won't believe me anyway.' Suddenly, she was anxious to leave, to get back to the house on the lake, although she had no idea what she was going to do once she got there. Confront Alberto with his problems? Risk jeopardising his fragile health by piling more stress on his shoulders?

'I'm not even sure your father knows the truth of the situation,' she said miserably. 'I'm certain he would have mentioned something to me.'

'Why would he? You've been around for five seconds. I suggest the first person on his list of confidants would probably have been his accountant.'

'Maybe he's told Father Rafferty. I could go and see him at the church and find out if he knows about any of this. That would be the best thing, because Father Rafferty would be able to put everything into perspective. He's very practical and upbeat.'

'Father Rafferty...?'

'Alberto attends mass at the local church every Sunday. Has done for a long time, I gather. He and Father Rafferty have become close friends. I think your father likes Father Rafferty's Irish sense of humour—and the odd glass of whisky. I should go. All of this...'

'Is probably very unsettling, and probably not what you contemplated when you first decided to come over to Italy.'

'I don't mind!' Caroline was quick to reply. She bit back the temptation to tell him that *someone* had to be there for Alberto.

Giancarlo was realising that his original assumption, which had made perfect sense at the time, had been perhaps a little too hasty. The woman was either an excellent, Oscar-winning actress or else she had been telling the truth all along: her visit had not been instigated for financial purposes.

Now his brain was engaged on a different path; he sat back and looked at her as he stroked his chin thoughtfully with one long, brown finger.

'I expect this nurse he's hired is a private nurse?'

Caroline hadn't given that a second's thought, but now she blanched. How much would that be costing? And didn't it prove that Alberto had no idea of the state of his finances? Why, if he did know, would he be spending money on hiring a private nurse who would be costing him an arm and a leg?

'And naturally he must be paying *you*,' Giancarlo continued remorselessly. 'How much?' He named a figure that was so ridiculously high that Caroline burst out laughing. She laughed until she felt tears come to her eyes. It was as though she had found a sudden outlet for her stressful, frantic thoughts and her body was reacting of its own volition, even though Giancarlo was now looking at her with the perplexed expression of someone dealing with a complete idiot.

'Sorry.' She hiccupped her way back to some level of seriousness, although she could still feel her mirth lurking close to the surface. 'You've got to be kidding. Take that figure and maybe divide it by four.'

'Don't be ridiculous. No one could survive on that.'

'But I never came here for the money,' Caroline explained patiently. 'I came here to improve my Italian. Alberto was doing me a favour by taking me in. I don't have to pay for food and I don't pay rent. When I return to England, the fact that I will be able to communicate in another language will be a great help to me when it comes to getting a job. Why are you staring at me like that?'

'So it doesn't bother you that you wouldn't be able to have much of a life given that you're paid next to nothing?' *Cheap labour,* Giancarlo thought. *Now, why am I not surprised?* A specialised nurse would hardly donate her services through the goodness of her heart, but a young, clearly inexperienced girl? Why not take advantage? Oh, the old man knew the state of his finances, all right, whatever she exclaimed to the contrary.

'I don't mind. I've never been fussed about money.'

'Guess what?' Giancarlo signalled to the waiter for the bill. When Caroline looked at her watch, it was to find that the time had galloped by. She hadn't even been aware of it passing, even though, disliking him as she did, she should have been counting every agonising minute.

'What?'

'Consider your little mission a success. I think it's time, after all, to return home…'

CHAPTER THREE

GIANCARLO'S LAST VIEW of his father's house, as he had twisted around in the back of the car, while in the front his mother had sat in stony silence without a backward glance, was of lush gardens and the vast stone edifice which comprised the back of the house. The front of the house sat grandly on the western shores of the lake, perfect positioning for a view of deep blue water, as still as a sheet of glass, that was breathtakingly beautiful.

It was unsettling to be returning now, exactly one week after Caroline had left, seemingly transported with excitement at the fact that she had managed to persuade him to accept the supposed olive-branch that had been extended.

If she was of the opinion that all was joyful in the land of reconciliation, then Giancarlo was equally and coldly reserved about sharing any such optimism. He was under no illusions when it came to human nature. The severity of Alberto's heart attack was open to debate and Giancarlo, for one, was coolly prepared for a man in fairly robust health who may or may not have persuaded a very gullible Caroline otherwise to suit his own purposes. His memories of his father were of a towering man, greatly into discipline and without an emotional bone in his body. He couldn't conceive of him being diminished by ill health, although rapidly disappearing funds might well have played a part in lowering his spirits.

The super-fast sports car had eaten up the miles of motorway and only now, as he slowed to drive through the picturesque towns and villages on the way to his father's house, were vague recollections beginning to surface.

He had forgotten how charming this area was. Lake Como, the third largest and the deepest of the Italian lakes, was picture-postcard perfect, a lush, wealthy area with elegant villas, manicured gardens, towns and villages with cobbled streets and *piazzas* dotted with Romanesque churches and very expensive hotels and restaurants which attracted the more discerning tourist.

He felt a pleasing sense of satisfaction.

This was a homecoming on *his* terms, just the way he liked it. A more in-depth perusal of Alberto's finances had shown a company torn apart by the ravaging effects of an unprecedented economic recession, mismanagement and an unwillingness to move with the times and invest in new markets.

Giancarlo smiled grimly to himself. He had never considered himself a vengeful person but the realisation that he could take over his father's company, rescue the old man and thereby level the scales of justice was a pleasing one. Really, what more bitter pill could his father ever swallow than know that he was indebted, literally, to the son he had turned his back on?

He hadn't mentioned a word of this to Caroline when they had parted company. For a few minutes, Giancarlo found himself distracted by thoughts of the diminutive brunette. She was flaky as hell; unbelievably emotional and prone to tears at the drop of a hat; jaw-droppingly forthright and, frankly, left him speechless. But, as he got closer and closer to the place he had once called his home, he realised that she had managed to get under his skin in a way that was uniquely irritating. In fact, he had never devoted this much time to thinking about any one woman, but that, he reasoned sensibly, was because this particular woman had entered his life in a singularly weird way.

Never again would he rule out the unexpected. Just when you thought you had everything in control, something came along to pull the rug from under your feet.

In this instance, it wasn't all bad. He fiddled with the radio, got to a station he liked and relaxed to enjoy the scenery and the pleasing prospect of what lay ahead.

He gave no house room to nerves. He was on a high, in fact, fuelled by the self-righteous notion of the wheel having turned full circle. Yes, he was curious to reacquaint himself with Alberto, but over the years he had heard so many things about him that he almost felt as though there was nothing left to know. The steady drip, drip, drip of information from a young age had eroded his natural inclination to question.

If anything, he liked to think that Alberto would be the one consumed by nerves. His business was failing and sooner or later, ill health or no ill health, Giancarlo was certain that his father would turn the conversation around to money. Maybe he would try and entice him into some kind of investment. Maybe he would just ditch his pride and ask outright for a loan of some sort. Either approach was possible. Giancarlo relished the prospect of being able to confirm that money would indeed be forthcoming. Wasn't he magnanimous even though, all things considered, he had no reason to be? But a price would have to be paid. He would make his father's company his own. He would take it over lock, stock and barrel. Yes, his father's financial security would rest on the generosity of his disowned son.

He intended to stay at the villa just long enough to convey that message. A couple of days at most. Thereafter it would be enough to know that he had done what he had to do.

He didn't anticipate having anything to say of interest to the old man. Why should he? They would be two strangers, relieved to part company once the nitty-gritty had been sorted out.

He was so wrapped up in his thoughts that he very nearly

missed the turning to the villa. This side of the lake was famous for its magnificent villas, most of them eighteenth-century extravaganzas, a few of which had been turned into hotels over the years.

His father's villa was by no means the largest but it was still an impressive old place, approached through forbidding iron gates and a long drive which was surrounded on both sides by magnificent gardens.

He remembered the layout of these glorious spreading lawns more than he had anticipated. To the right, there was the bank of trees in which he had used to play as a child. To the left, the stone wall was barely visible behind rows upon rows of rhododendrons and azaleas, a vibrant wash of colour as bright and as dramatic as a child's painting.

He slowed the car in the circular courtyard, killed the engine and popped the boot, which was just about big enough to fit his small leather overnight case—and, of course, his computer bag in which resided all the necessary documents he would need so that he could begin the takeover process he had in mind for his father's company.

He was an imposing sight. From her bedroom window, which overlooked the courtyard, Caroline felt a sudden sick flutter of nerves.

Over the past seven days, she had done her best to play down the impact he had made on her. He wasn't *that* tall, *that* good-looking or *that* arrogant, she convinced herself. She had been rattled when she had finally located him and her nerves had thrown everything out of perspective.

Unfortunately, staring down at Giancarlo as he emerged from his sports car, wearing dark sunglasses and walking round to swing two cases out of the miniscule boot of his car, she realised that he really *was* as unbelievably forbidding as she had remembered.

She literally flew down the corridor, took the staircase two steps at a time and reached the sitting-room at the back of the house, breathless.

'He's here!'

Alberto was sitting in a chair by the big bay window that had a charming view of the gardens stretching down to the lake, which was dotted with little boats.

'Anyone would think the Pope was paying a visit. Calm down, girl! Your colour's up.'

'You're going to be nice, aren't you, Alberto?'

'I'm always nice. You just fuss too much, get yourself worked up over small things—it's not good for you. Now, off you go and let the boy in before he climbs back into his car and drives away. And on your way you can tell that nurse of yours that I'm having a glass of whisky before dinner. Whether she likes it or not!'

'I'll do no such thing, Alberto De Vito. If you want to disobey doctor's orders, then you can tell Tessa yourself—and I would love to see how she takes that.' She grinned fondly at the old man, who was backlit by the evening sun glinting through the window. Having met Giancarlo, she found the similarities between them striking. Both had the same proud, aristocratic features and the long, lean lines of natural athletes. Of course, Alberto was elderly now, but it was easy to see that he must have been as striking as his son in his youth.

'Oh, stop that endless chattering, woman, and run along.' He waved her off and Caroline, steadying her nerves, got to the front door just as the doorbell chimed.

She smoothed nervous hands along her skirt, a black maxi in stretch cotton which she wore with a loose-fitting top and, of course, the ubiquitous cardigan, although at least here it was more appropriate thanks to the cooling breeze that blew off the lake.

She pulled open the door and her mouth went dry. In a snug-fitting cream polo-necked shirt and a pair of tan trousers with very expensive-looking loafers, he was every inch the impeccably dressed Italian. He looked as though he had come straight from a fashion shoot until he raised one sardonic eyebrow and said coolly, 'Were you waiting by the window?'

Remembering that she *had*, actually, been at her window when his car had pulled into the courtyard, Caroline straightened her spine and cleared her throat.

'Of course I wasn't! Although I *was* tempted, just in case you didn't show up.' She stood aside; Giancarlo took a step through the front door and confronted the house in which he had spent the first twelve years of his life. It had changed remarkably little. The hall was a vast expanse of marble, in the centre of which a double staircase spiralled in opposing directions to meet on the impressive galleried landing above. On either side of the hall, a network of rooms radiated like tentacles on an octopus.

Now that he was back, he could place every room in his head: the various reception rooms; the imposing study from which he had always been banned; the dining-room in which portraits of deceased family members glared down at the assembled diners; the gallery in which were hung paintings of great value, another room from which he had been banned.

'Why wouldn't I show up?' Giancarlo turned to face her. She looked more at home here, less ill at ease, which was hardly surprising, he supposed. Her hair which she had attempted to tie back in Milan was loose, and it flowed over her shoulders and down her back in a tangle of curls, dark brown streaked with caramel where the sun had lightened it.

'You might have had a change of heart,' Caroline admitted in a harried voice, because yet again those dark, cloaked eyes on her were doing weird things to her tummy. 'I mean, you were so adamant that you didn't want to see your father and then all of a sudden you announced that you'd changed your mind. It didn't make sense. So I thought that maybe you might have changed your mind again.'

'Where are the staff?'

'I told you, most of the house is shut off. We have Tessa, the nurse who looks after Alberto. She lives on the premises, and two young girls take care of cleaning the house, but they live in the village. I'm glad you decided to come after all. Shall we go and meet your father? I guess you'll want to be with him on your own.'

'So that we can catch up? Exchange fond memories of the good old days?'

Caroline looked at him in dismay. There was no attempt to disguise the bitterness in his voice. Alberto rarely mentioned the past, and his memoirs, which had taken a back seat over the past few weeks, had mostly got to the state of fond reminiscing about his university days and the places he had travelled as a young man. But she could imagine that Alberto had not been the easiest of fathers. When Giancarlo had agreed to visit, she had naïvely assumed that he had been willing, finally, to overlook whatever mishaps had drastically torn them apart. Now, looking at him, she was uneasily aware that her simple conclusions might have been a little off the mark.

'Or even just agree to put the past behind you and move on,' Caroline offered helpfully.

Giancarlo sighed. Should he let her in to what he had planned? he wondered.

'Why don't you give me a little tour of the house before I meet my father?' he suggested. 'I want to get a feel of the old place. And there are a couple of things I want to talk to you about.'

'Things? What things?'

'If you don't fancy the full tour, you can show me to my bedroom. What I have to say won't take long.'

'I'll show you to your room,' she said stiffly. 'But first I'll go and tell Alberto where we are, so he doesn't worry.'

'Why would he worry?'

'He's been looking forward to seeing you.'

'I'm thinking I will be in my old room,' Giancarlo murmured. 'Left wing. Overlooking the side gardens?'

'The left wing's not really used now.' Making her mind up, she eyed his lack of luggage and began heading up the stairs.

'I'll take you up to where you'll be staying. If we're quick, I'm sure your father won't get too anxious. And you can tell me whatever it is you have to tell me.'

She could feel her heart beating like a sledgehammer inside her as she preceded him up the grand staircase, turning left along the equally grand corridor, which was broad enough to house a *chaise longue* and various highly polished tables on which sat bowls of fresh flowers. Caroline had added that touch soon after she had come to live with Alberto and he had grumpily acquiesced, but not before informing her that flowers inside a house were a waste of time. Why bother when they would die within the week?

'Ah, the Green Room.' Giancarlo looked around him and saw the signs of disrepair. The room looked tired, the wallpaper still elegant but badly faded. The curtains he dimly remembered, although this was one of the many guest rooms into which he had seldom ventured. Nothing had been changed in over two decades. He dumped his overnight bag on the bed and walked across to the window to briefly look down at the exquisite walled garden, before turning to her.

'I feel I ought to tell you that my decision to come here wasn't entirely altruistic,' he told her bluntly. 'I wouldn't want you having any misplaced notions of emotional reunions, because if you have, then you're in for a crashing disappointment.'

'Not entirely altruistic?'

'Alberto's rocky financial situation has—how shall I put it?—delivered me the perfect opportunity to finally redress certain injustices.'

'What injustices?'

'Nothing you need concern yourself with. Suffice to say that Alberto will not have to fear that the banks are going to repossess this house and all its contents.'

'This house was going to be repossessed?'

'Sooner or later.' Giancarlo shrugged. 'It happens. Debts accumulate. Shareholders get the jitters. Redundancies have to be made. It's a short step until the liquidators start converging like vultures, and when that happens possessions get seized to pay off disgruntled creditors who are out of pocket.'

Caroline's eyes were like saucers as she imagined this worst-case scenario.

'That would devastate Alberto,' she whispered. She sidled towards the bed and sat down. 'Are you sure about all this? No. Forget I asked that. I forgot that you never make mistakes.'

Giancarlo looked at the forlorn figure on the bed and clicked his tongue impatiently. 'Isn't it a good thing that he'll be spared all of that? No bailiffs showing up at the door, demanding the paintings and the hangings? No bank clamouring for the house to be put on the market to the highest bidder, even if the price is way below its worth?'

'Yes.' She looked at him dubiously.

'So you can wipe that pitiful look from your face immediately!'

'You said that you were going to…what, exactly? Give him the money? Won't that be an awful lot of money? Are you *that* rich?'

'I have enough,' Giancarlo stated drily, amused by her question.

'How much is enough?'

'Enough to ensure that Alberto's house and company don't end up in the hands of the receivers. Of course, there's no such thing as a free lunch.'

'What do you mean?'

'I mean…' He pushed himself away from the window and strolled through the bedroom, taking in all those little signs of neglect that were almost impossible to spot unless you were looking for them. God only knew, the house was ancient. It was probably riddled with all manner of damp, dry rot, termites in the woodwork. Having grown up in a house that dated back centuries, Giancarlo had made sure that his own place was unashamedly modern. Dry rot, damp and termites would never be able to get a foothold.

'I *mean* that what is now my father's will inevitably become mine. I will take over his company and return it to its once-thriving state and naturally I will do the same with this villa. It's in dire need of repair anyway. I'll wager that those rooms that have been closed off will be in the process of falling to pieces.'

'And you won't be doing any of that because you care about Alberto,' Caroline spoke her thoughts aloud while Giancarlo looked at her through narrowed eyes, marvelling at the way every thought running through her head was reflected in the changing nuances of her expressions.

'In fact,' she carried on slowly, her thoughts rearranging themselves in her head to form a complete picture of what was really going on, 'you're not interested in reconciling with your father at all, are you?'

Giancarlo wasn't about to encourage any kind of conversation on what she considered the rights and wrongs of his reasons for coming to the lake, so he maintained a steady silence—although the resigned disappointment in her voice managed to pierce through his rigid self-control in a way that was infuriating. Her huge, accusing eyes were doing the same thing as well and he frowned impatiently.

'It's impossible to reconcile with someone you can barely recall,' he said in a flatly dismissive voice. 'I don't know Alberto.'

'You know him enough to want to hurt him for what you think he did to you.'

'That's a ridiculous assumption!'

'Is it? You said yourself that you were going to buy him out because it would give you the chance to redress injustices.'

Giancarlo was fiercely protective of his private life. He never discussed his past with anyone and many women had tried. They had seen it as a stepping stone to getting to know him better, had mistakenly thought that, with the right amount of encouragement, he would open up and pour his heart out. It was always a fatal flaw.

'Alberto divorced my mother and did everything legally possible to ensure that, whilst the essentials were paid, she was left with the minimum, just enough to get by. From *this*—' he gestured in a sweeping arc to encompass the villa and its fabulous surroundings '—she was reduced to living in a small modern box in the outskirts of Milan. You can see that I carry a certain amount of bitterness towards my father.

'However, it has to be said that, were I a truly vengeful person, I would not have returned here and I certainly would not be contemplating a lucrative buy-out. Lucrative from Alberto's point of view, that is. A lot less lucrative from where I'm standing, because his company will need a great deal of money pouring into it to get it off the starters' gate. Face it, I could have read those financial reports, turned my back, walked away. Waited until I read about the demise of his company in the financial section of the newspapers. Believe me, I seriously considered that option, but then... Let's just say that I opted for the personal touch. So much more satisfying.'

Caroline was finding it impossible to tally up Giancarlo's version of his father with her own experiences of Alberto. Yes, he was undoubtedly difficult and had probably been a thousand times more so when he had been younger, but he wasn't stingy. She just couldn't imagine him being vindictive towards his ex-wife, although how could she know for sure?

One thing she *did* know now was that Giancarlo might justify his actions as redressing a balance but it was revenge of a hands-on variety and no part of her could condone that. He would rescue his father in the certain knowledge that guilt would be Alberto's lifelong companion from then onwards. He would attack Alberto's most vulnerable part: his pride.

She stood up, hands on her hips, and looked at him with blazing eyes.

'I don't care how you put it, that's absolutely *rotten*!'

'*Rotten*, to step in and bail him out?' Giancarlo shook his head grimly and took a couple of steps towards her.

He had his hands in the pockets of his trousers and his movements were leisurely and unhurried, but there was an element of threat in every step he took that brought him closer and Caroline fought to stay her ground. She couldn't wrench her eyes away from him. He had the allure of a dangerous but spectacularly beautiful predator.

Looking down at her, Giancarlo's dark eyes skimmed the hectic flush in her cheeks, her rapid, angry breathing.

'You're a spitfire, aren't you...?' he murmured lazily, which thoroughly disconcerted Caroline. She wasn't used to dealing with men like this. Her experience of the opposite sex was strictly confined to the two men she had dated in the past, both of whom were gentle souls with whom she still shared a comfortable friendship, and work colleagues after she had left school.

'No, I'm not! I never argue. I don't like arguing.'

'You could have fooled me.'

'You do this to me,' she breathed, only belatedly realising that somehow that didn't sound quite right. 'I mean...'

'I get you worked up?'

'Yes! No...'

'Yes? No? Which is it?'

'Stop laughing at me. None of this is funny.' She drew her cardigan tightly around her in a defensive gesture that wasn't lost on him.

'For a young woman, your choice of clothes is very old-fashioned. Cardigans are for women over forty.'

'I don't see what my clothes have to do with anything.' But she stumbled over her words. Was he trying to throw her? He was succeeding. Now, along with anger was a creeping sense of embarrassment.

'Are you self-conscious about your body?' This was the sort of question Giancarlo never asked any woman. He had never been a big fan of soul-searching conversations. He had always preferred to keep it light, and yet he found that he was really curious about the hell cat who claimed not to be a hell cat. Except when in his presence.

Caroline broke the connection and walked towards the door but she was shaking like a leaf.

She stood in the doorway, half-in, half-out of the bedroom, which suddenly seemed as confining as a prison cell when he was towering above her.

'And when do you intend to tell Alberto everything?'

'I should imagine that he will probably be the one who brings up the subject,' Giancarlo said, still looking at her, almost regretful that the conversation was back on a level footing. 'You seem to have a lot of faith in human nature. Take it from me, it's misplaced.'

'I don't want you upsetting him. His doctor says that he's to be as stress-free as possible in order to make a full recovery.'

'Okay. Here's the deal. I won't open the conversation with a casual query about the state of his failing company.'

'You really don't care about anyone but yourself, do you?' Caroline asked in a voice tinged with genuine wonder.

'You have a special knack for saying all the wrong things to me,' Giancarlo muttered with a frown.

'What you mean is that I say things you don't want to hear.' She stepped quickly out into the corridor as he walked towards her. She was beginning to understand that being too close to him physically was like standing too close to an electric field. 'We should go downstairs. Alberto will be wondering where we've got to. He tires easily now, so we'll be having an early supper.'

'And tell me, who does the cooking? The same two girls who come in to clean?' He fell into step alongside her, but even though the conversation had moved on to a more neutral topic he was keenly aware of her still clutching the cardigan around her. His first impression had been of someone very background. Now, he was starting to review that initial impression. Underneath the straightforward personality there seemed to be someone very fiery and not easily intimidated. She had taken a deep breath and stood up to him in a way that not very many people did.

'Sometimes. Now that Alberto is on a restricted diet, Tessa tends to prepare his meals, and I cook for myself and Tessa. It's a daily fight to get Alberto to eat bland food. He's fond of saying that there's no life worth living without salt.'

Giancarlo heard the smile in her voice. For his sins, his father had found himself a very devoted companion.

For the first time he wondered what it would have been like to have had Alberto as a father. The man had clearly mellowed over time. Would they have had that connection? How much had he suffered because of his constant warfare with his wife?

Irritated with himself for being drawn back into a past he could not change, Giancarlo focused on sustaining the conversation with a number of innocuous questions as they walked back down the grand staircase, Caroline leading the way towards the smallest of the sitting-rooms at the back of the house.

Even with the majority of the rooms seemingly closed off, there was still a lot of ground to cover. Yet again he found himself wondering what the appeal was for a young woman. Terrific house, great grounds, pleasing views and interesting walks—but take those things out of the equation and boredom would gradually set in, surely?

How bored had his mother been, surrounded by all this ostentatious wealth, trapped like a bird in a gilded cage?

Alberto had met her on one of his many conferences. She had been a sparkling, pretty waitress at the only fancy restaurant in a small town on the Amalfi coast where he had gone to grab a couple of days of rest before the remainder of his business trip. She had been plucked from obscurity and catapulted into wealth, but nothing, she had repeatedly complained to her son over the years following her divorce, could compensate for the horror of living with a man who treated her no better than a servant. She had done her very best, but time and again her efforts had been met with a brick wall. Alberto, she had said with bitterness, had turned out to be little more than a difficult, unyielding and unforgiving man, years too old for her, who had thwarted all her attempts at having fun.

Giancarlo had been conditioned to loathe the man whom his mother had held responsible for all her misfortunes.

Except now he was prey to a disturbing sensation of doubt as he heard Caroline chatter on about his father. How disagreeable could the man be if she was so attached to him? Was it possible for a leopard to change its spots to that extreme extent?

Before they reached the sitting-room, she paused to rest one small hand lightly on his arm.

'Do you promise that you won't upset him?'

'I'm not big into making promises.'

'Why is it so hard to get through to you?'

'Believe it or not, most people don't have a problem. In our case, we might just as well be from different planets, occupying different time zones. I told you I won't greet him with an enquiry about the health of his finances, and I won't. Beyond that, I promise nothing.'

'Just try to get to know him,' Caroline pleaded, her huge brown eyes welded to his as she dithered with her hand still on his arm. 'I just can't believe you know the real Alberto.'

Giancarlo's mouth thinned and he stared down pointedly at her hand before looking down at her, his dark eyes as cold and frozen as the lake in winter.

'Don't presume to tell me what I know or don't know,' he said with ice in his voice, and Caroline removed her hand quickly as though she had been burnt suddenly. 'I've come here for a purpose and, whether you like it or not, I will ensure that things are wrapped up before I leave.'

'And how long are you intending to stay? I never asked, but you really haven't come with very much luggage, have you? I mean, one small bag...'

'Put it this way, there will be no need to go shopping for food on my account. I plan on being here no longer than two days. Three at the very most.'

Caroline's heart sank further. This was a business visit, however you dressed it up and tried to call it something else. Two days? Just long enough for Giancarlo to levy his charge for Alberto's past wrongdoings, whatever those might have been, with interest.

She didn't think that he was even prepared to get to know his father. The only thing that interested him, his only motivation for coming to the villa, was to dole out his version of revenge, whether he chose to call it that or not.

'Now, any more questions?' Giancarlo drawled and Caroline shook her head miserably, not trusting herself to speak. Once again, he felt a twinge of uninvited and unwelcome doubt. 'I'm surprised at your level of attachment to Alberto,' he commented brusquely, annoyed at himself, because would her answer change anything? No.

'Why?' Her eyes were wide and clear when she looked at him. 'I didn't have a load of prejudices when I came here. I came with an open mind. I found a lonely old man with a kind heart and a generous nature. Yes, he might be prickly, but it's what's inside that counts. At least, that's how it works for me.'

He really shouldn't have been diverted into encouraging her opinion. He should have known that whatever chirpy, homespun answer she came out with would get on his nerves. He was very tempted to inform her that he was the least prejudiced person on the face of the earth, that if on this single occasion he was prey to a very natural inclination towards one or two preconceived ideas about Alberto, then no one could lay the blame for that at his door. He cut short the infuriating desire to be sidetracked.

'Well, I'm very pleased that he has you around,' Giancarlo said neutrally. Caroline bristled because she could just *sense* that he was being patronising.

'No, you aren't. You're still so mad at him that you probably would much rather have preferred it if he was still on his own in this big, rambling house with no one to talk to. And, if there *was* someone around, then I'm sure you'd rather it wasn't me, because you don't like me at all!'

'What gives you that idea?'

Caroline ignored that question. The promise of what was to come felt like a hangman's noose around her neck. She was fit to explode. 'Well, I don't like you either,' she declared with vehemence. 'And I hope you choke on your plans to ruin Alberto's life.' She spun away from him so that he couldn't witness the tears stinging her eyes. 'He's waiting for you,' she muttered in a driven voice. 'Why don't you go in now and get it over with?'

CHAPTER FOUR

GIANCARLO ENTERED A room that was familiar to him. The smallest of the sitting-rooms at the back of the house had always been the least ornate and hence the cosiest. Out of nowhere came the memory of doing his homework in this very room, always resisting the urge to sneak outside, down to the lake. French doors led out to the sprawling garden that descended to the lake via a series of landscaped staircases. Alberto sat in a chair by one of the bay windows with a plaid rug over his legs even though it was warm in the room.

'So, my boy, you've come.'

Giancarlo looked at his father with a shuttered expression. He wondered if his memory was playing tricks on him, because Alberto looked diminished. In his head, he realised that he had held on to a memory that was nearly two decades old and clearly out of date.

'Father…'

'Caroline. You're gaping. Why don't you offer a drink to our guest? And I will have a whisky while you're about it.'

'You'll have no such thing.' Back on familiar ground, Caroline moved past Giancarlo to adopt a protective stance by her employer, who made feeble attempts to flap her away. Looking at their interaction, Giancarlo could see that it was a game with which they were both comfortable and familiar.

Just for a few seconds, he was the outsider looking in, then that peculiar feeling was gone as the tableau shifted. Caroline walked across to a cupboard which had been reconfigured to house a small fridge, various snacks and cartons of juice.

He was aware of her chattering nervously, something about it being time efficient to have stuff at hand for Alberto because this was his favourite room in the house and he just wasn't as yet strong enough to continually make long trips to the kitchen if he needed something to drink.

'Of course, it's all supervised,' she babbled away, while the tension stretched silent and invisible in the room. 'No whisky here. Tessa and I know that that's Alberto's Achilles' heel so we have wine. I put some in earlier, would that be okay?' She kept her eyes firmly averted from the uncomfortable sight of father and son, but in her head she was picturing them circling one another, making their individual, quiet assessments.

Given half a chance, she would have run for cover to another part of the house, but her instinct to protect Alberto kept her rooted to the spot.

When she finally turned around, with drinks and snacks on a little tray, it was to find that Giancarlo had taken up position on one of the chairs. If he was in any way uncomfortable, he wasn't showing it.

'Well, Father, I have been told that you've suffered a heart attack—'

'How was the drive here, Giancarlo? Still too many cars in the villages?'

They both broke into speech at the same time. Caroline drank too much far too quickly to calm her nerves and lapsed into an awkward silence as ultra-polite questions were fielded with ul-tra-polite answers. She wondered if they were aware that many of their mannerisms were identical—the way they both shifted and leaned forward when a remark was made; the way they idly held their glasses, slightly stroking the rim with their fingers. They should have bonded without question. Instead, Giancarlo's cool, courteous conversation was the equivalent of a door being shut.

He was here. He was talking. But he was not conversing.

At least he had kept his word and nothing, so far, had been mentioned about the state of Alberto's finances, although she knew that her employer must surely be curious to know why his son had bothered to make the trip out to Lake Como when he displayed so little enthusiasm for the end result.

Dinner was a light soup, followed by fish. One of the local girls had been brought in, along with the two regular house-keepers, to take care of the cooking and the clearing away. So, instead of eating in the kitchen, they dined in the formal dining-room, which proved to be a mistake.

The long table and the austere surroundings were not conducive to light-hearted conversation. Tessa had volunteered to have her meal in the small sitting-room adjoining her bedroom, in order to give them all some space to chat without her hovering over Alberto, checking to make sure he stuck to his diet. Caroline heartily wished she could have joined her, because the atmosphere was thick with tension.

By the time they had finished their starters and made adequately polite noises about it, several topics of conversation had been started and quickly abandoned. The changes in the weather patterns had been discussed, as had the number of tourists at the lakes, the lack of snow the previous winter and, of course, Alberto asked Giancarlo about his work, to which he received such brief replies that that too was a subject quickly shelved.

By the time the main course was brought to them—and Alberto had bemoaned the fact that they were to dine on fish rather than something altogether heartier like a slab of red meat— Caroline had frankly had enough of the painfully stilted conversation.

If they didn't want to have any kind of meaningful conversation together, then she would fill in the gaps. She talked about her childhood, growing up in Devon. Her parents were both teachers, very much into being 'green'. She laughed at memories of the chickens they had kept that laid so many eggs at times that her mother would bake cakes a family of three had no possibility of eating just to get rid of some of them. She would contribute them to the church every Sunday and one year was actually awarded a special prize for her efforts.

She talked about exchange students, some of whom had been most peculiar, and joked about her mother's experiments in the kitchen with home-grown produce from their small garden. In the end, she and her father had staged a low-level rebellion until normal food was reintroduced. Alberto chuckled but he was not relaxed. It was there in the nervous flickering of his eyes and his subdued, downturned mouth. The son he had desperately wanted to see didn't want to see him and he wasn't even bothering to try to hide the fact.

All the while she could feel Giancarlo's dark eyes restively looking at her and she found that she just couldn't look at him. What was it about him that brought her out in goose bumps and made her feel as though she just wasn't comfortable in her own skin? The timbre of his low, husky voice sent shivers down her spine, and when he turned to look at her she was aware of her body in such miniscule detail that she burned with discomfort.

By the time they adjourned for coffee back in the small sitting-room, Caroline was exhausted and she could see that Alberto was flagging. Giancarlo, on the other hand, was as coldly composed as he had been at the start of the evening.

'How long do you plan on staying, my boy? You should get yourself out on the lake. Beautiful weather. And you were always fond of your sailing. Of course, we no longer have the sailboat. What was the point? After, well, after...'

'After what, Father?'

'I think it's time you went to bed, Alberto,' Caroline interjected desperately as the conversation finally threatened to explode. 'You're flagging and you know the doctor said that you really need to take it easy. I'll get hold of Tessa and—'

'After you and your mother left.'

'Ah, so finally you've decided to acknowledge that you ever had a wife. One could be forgiven for thinking that you had erased her from your memory completely.' No mention had been made of Adriana. Not one single word. They had tiptoed around all mention of the past, as though it had never existed. Alberto had been on his best behaviour. Now Giancarlo expected to see his real father, the cold, unforgiving one, the one who, from memory, had never shied away from arguing.

'I've done no such thing, my son,' Alberto surprised Giancarlo by saying quietly.

'It's time you went to bed, Alberto.' Caroline stood up and looked pointedly at Giancarlo. 'I will not allow you to tire your father out any longer,' she said, and in truth Alberto was showing signs of strain around his eyes. 'He's been very ill and this conversation is *not* going to help anything at all.'

'Oh, do stop fussing, Caroline.' But his pocket handkerchief was in his hand and he was patting his forehead wearily.

'*You*—' she jabbed a finger at Giancarlo '—are going to wait *right here* for me while I go to fetch Tessa because I intend to have a little chat with you.'

'The boy wants to talk about his past, Caroline. It's why he's come.'

Caroline snorted without taking her eyes away from Giancarlo's beautiful face. If only Alberto knew!

She spun back around to look at her employer. 'I'm going to fetch Tessa and tomorrow you won't have your routine disrupted. Your son is going to be here for a few days. There will be time enough to take a trip down memory lane.'

'*A few days?*' They both said the same thing at the same time. Giancarlo was appalled and enraged while Alberto was hesitantly hopeful. Caroline decided to favour Giancarlo with a confirming nod.

'Maybe even as long as a week,' she threw at him, because wasn't it better to be hanged for a sheep than a lamb? 'I believe that's what you said to me?' She wondered where on earth this fierce determination was coming from. She always shied away from confrontation!

'So tomorrow,' she continued to both men, 'there will be no need for you to worry about entertaining your son, Alberto. He will be sailing on the lake.'

'I'll be *sailing on the lake*?'

'Correct. With me.' This in case he decided to argue the rules she was confidently laying down, with a silent prayer in her head that he wasn't going to launch into an outraged argument which would devastate Alberto, especially after the gruesome evening they had just spent together.

'I thought you couldn't sail, Caroline,' Alberto murmured and she drew herself up to her unimpressive height of a little over five-three.

'But I've been counting down the days I could start learning.'

'You told me that you had a morbid fear of open water.'

'It's something I've been told I can only overcome by facing it…on open water. It's a well-known fact that, er, that you have to confront your fears to overcome them…'

She backed out of the room before Alberto could pin her down and flew to Tessa's room. She could picture the awkward conversation taking place between Giancarlo and Alberto in her absence, and that was a best-case scenario. The worst-case scenario involved them both taking that trip down memory lane, the one she had temporarily managed to divert. It was a trip that could only lead to the sort of heated argument that would do no good to Alberto's fragile recovery. With that in mind, she ran back to the sitting-room like a bat out of hell and was breathless by the time she reappeared ten minutes later.

It was to discover that Giancarlo had disappeared.

'The boy has work to do,' Alberto told her.

'At this hour?'

'I remember when I was a young man, I used to work all the hours God made. Boy's built like me, which might not be such a good thing. Hard work is fine but the important thing is to know when to stop. He's a fine-looking lad, don't you think?'

'I suppose there might be some who like that sort of look,' Caroline said dismissively. With relief, she heard Tessa approaching. Alberto drew no limits when it came to asking whatever difficult questions he had in his head. It was, he had proclaimed, one of the benefits of being an old bore. The last thing she wanted was to have an in-depth question-and-answer session on what she thought of his son.

'Bright, too.'

Caroline wondered how he could be so clearly generous in his praise for someone who had made scant effort to meet him halfway. She made an inarticulate noise under her breath and tried not to scowl.

'Said he'd meet you by his car at nine tomorrow morning,' Alberto told her, while simultaneously trying to convince Tessa, who had entered the room at a brisk pace, that he didn't need to be treated like a child all the time. 'Think he'll enjoy a spot of sailing. It'll relax him. He seems tense. Of course, I totally understand that, given the circumstances. So don't you mind me, my dear. Think I'll rise and shine, but not with the larks, and the old bat here can take me for my constitutional walk.'

Tessa winked at Caroline and grinned behind Alberto's back as she helped him up.

'Anyone would think he wasn't a complete poppet when I settle him at night,' she said, unfazed.

Having issued her dictate to Giancarlo for 'a chat', Caroline realised that chatting was the last thing she wanted to do with him. All her bravado had seeped out of her. The prospect of a morning in his company now seemed like an uphill climb. Would he listen to her? He hadn't as yet revealed to Alberto the real reason for his visit but he would the following day; she knew it. Just as he would declare that his visit was not going to last beyond forty-eight hours, despite what she had optimistically announced to Alberto.

There was no way that she would be able to persuade Giancarlo into doing anything he didn't want to do and the past few hours had shown her that grasping the olive branch was definitely not on his agenda.

She had a restless night. The villa was beautiful but no modernisation had taken place for a very long time. Air-conditioning was unheard of and the air was still and sluggish.

She barely felt rested when she opened her eyes the following morning at eight-thirty. It took her a few seconds to remember that her normal routine was out of sync. She wouldn't be having a leisurely breakfast with Alberto before taking him for a walk, then after lunch settling into sifting through some of his first-edition books which, in addition to his memoirs, was one of her jobs for him: sorting them into order so that he could decide which ones might be left to the local museum and which would be kept. He had all manner of historical information about the district, a great deal of which was contained in the various letters and journals of his ancestors. It was a laborious but enjoyable task which she would be missing in favour of a sailing trip with Giancarlo.

She dressed quickly: a pair of trousers, a striped tee shirt and, of course, her cardigan, a blue one this time; covered shoes. She didn't know anything at all about being on a boat, but she knew enough to suspect that a skirt and sandals would not be the required get-up. Impatiently, she tied her hair back in a long braid for the purpose of practicality.

There was no time for breakfast and she walked from one wing of the villa to the other, emerging outside into a blissfully sunny day with cloudless skies, bright turquoise shot through with milk. Giancarlo was standing by his car, sunglasses on, talking into his mobile phone. For a few seconds she stared at him, her heart thudding. He might have severed all ties with his aristocratic background, but he couldn't erase it from the contours of his face. Even in tattered clothes and barefoot he would still look the ultimate sophisticate.

He glanced across, registered her presence and snapped shut his phone to lounge indolently against the car as she walked towards him.

'So,' he drawled, staring down at her when she was finally in front of him. 'I'm apparently here on a one-week vacation.' He removed the sunglasses to dangle them idly between his fingers while he continued to look at her until she felt herself blush to the roots of her hair.

'Yes, well…'

'Maybe you could tell me how I had this week planned out? Bearing in mind that you seemed to have arranged it.'

'You *could* make just a little polite conversation before you start laying into me.'

'Was I doing that?' He pushed himself off the car and swung round to open the door for her, slamming it shut as she clambered into the passenger seat. 'I distinctly recall having told you that the most I would be staying would be a matter of two days. Tell me how you saw fit to extend that into a week?' He had bent down, propping himself against the car with both hands so that he could question her through her open window. He felt so close up and personal that she found herself taking deep breaths and gasping for air.

'Yes, I realise that,' Caroline muttered mutinously when he showed no signs of backing off. 'But you made me mad.'

'I—made—you—mad?'

Caroline nodded mutely and stared straight ahead, keenly aware of his hawk-like eyes boring into her averted profile. She visibly sagged when he strode round to get into the car.

'And how,' he asked softly, 'do you think I felt when you backed me into a corner?'

'Yes, well, you deserved it!'

'Do you know, I can't believe you.' He exited the gravelled

courtyard with a screeching of angry tyres and she clenched her fists so tightly that she could feel her nails biting into the palms of her hands. 'I didn't come here for relaxation!'

'I know! Don't you think you made that pretty obvious last night?'

'I gave you my word that I wouldn't introduce the contentious issue of money on day one. I kept my word.'

'*Just about.* You didn't make the slightest effort with Alberto. You just sat there *sneering*, and okay, so maybe I was wrong to imply that you were staying a tiny bit longer than you had planned.'

'You are the master of understatement!'

'But when you mentioned your mother, well, I just wanted to avert an argument, so possibly I said the first thing that came into my head. Look, I'm sorry. I guess you could always tell Alberto that I made a mistake, that I got the dates wrong. I know you have lots of important things to do and probably can't spare a week off, whatever the reason, but just then I didn't think I had a choice. I had to take the sting out of the evening, give Alberto something to hang on to.'

'What a shame you couldn't use your brain and think things through before you jumped in feet first! I take it the little *chat* you had in mind last night has now been covered?'

'It was an awkward evening. Alberto really tried to make conversation. Do you know, after you disappeared to work he actually seemed to understand? It was almost as though he wasn't prepared to see anything wrong in his son coming to see him for the first time in years, barely making an effort and then vanishing to work!'

Giancarlo flushed darkly. The evening had not gone quite as he had envisaged, and now he wasn't entirely sure *what* he had envisaged. He just knew that the argumentative man—the one who had loomed larger than life in his head thanks to Adriana's continuing bitterness; the one who would have made it so easy for him to treat with the patronising contempt he had always assumed would be richly deserved—had not lived up to expectations.

For starters, it was clear that Alberto's ill health was every bit as grave as Caroline had stated, and even more surprising, instead of a conversation spiked with the sort of malice and bitterness to which he had become accustomed with his mother over the years, there had been no mention made of a regrettable past and a miserable marriage. Alberto had been so wildly different from the picture in his head that Giancarlo had spent the time when he should have been working trying to figure out the discrepancies.

Naturally, the question of money, the *raison d'être* for his presence at the villa, would rear its ugly head in due course. He might have been weirdly taken aback at the man he had found, but sooner or later the inevitable begging bowl would emerge. However, not even that certainty could still the uneasy doubt that had crept stealthily through him after he had vacated the sitting-room.

'Perhaps,' he said, glancing around at scenery that felt more familiar with every passing second, 'a few days away from Milan might not be such a terrible idea.' The very second he said it, Giancarlo knew that he had made the right decision.

'Sorry?'

'I wouldn't call it a holiday, but it is certainly more restful here than it is in Milan.' He looked sideways at Caroline. Through the open window, the breeze was wreaking havoc with her attempts at a neat, sensible hair-style, flinging it into disarray.

'I guess you don't really do holidays,' she said tentatively. Even if his intention was still to consume his father's house and company, a few days spent with Alberto might render him a little less black and white in his judgement, might invest him with sufficient tact so that Alberto wasn't humiliated.

'Time is money.'

'There's more to life than money.'

'Agreed. Unfortunately, it usually takes money to enjoy those things.'

'Why have you decided to stay on? Just a short while ago you were really angry that I had put you in a difficult position.'

'But put me in it you did, and I'm a man who thinks on his feet and adjusts to situations. So I might be here for a bit longer than I had anticipated. It could only work to my advantage when it comes to constructing the sort of business proposal my father will understand. I'll confess that Alberto isn't the man I had expected. I initially thought that talk of his ill health might have been exaggerated.'

His eyes slid across to her face. Predictably, her expression was one of tight-lipped anger. 'Now I see for myself that he is not a well man, which would no doubt explain his unnaturally docile manner. I am not a monster. I had intended to confront him with his financial predicament without bothering with the tedious process of beating around the bush. Now I accept that I might have to tiptoe towards the conclusion I want.'

The scenery rushing past him, the feeling of open space and translucent light, was breathtaking. He was behind the wheel of a car, he was driving through clear open spaces with a view of glittering blue water ahead, and for the first time in years he felt light-headed with a rushing sense of freedom.

'Besides,' he mused lazily, 'I haven't been to this part of the world for a long time.'

He was following signs to one of the many sailing jetties scattered around the lake and now he swerved off the main road, heading down towards the glittering water.

Caroline forgot all her misgivings about Giancarlo's mission. She forgot how angry and upset she was at the thought of Alberto being on the receiving end of a son who had only agreed to see him out of a misplaced desire for revenge.

'I don't think I can go through with this,' she muttered as the car slowed to a stop.

Giancarlo killed the engine and turned to face her. 'Wasn't this whole sailing trip *your* idea?'

'It was supposed to be *your* sailing trip.' There were tourists milling around and the sailing boats bobbed like colourful playthings on the calm water. Out on the lake many more of them skirted over the aquamarine surface. At any given moment, one might very well sink, and where would that leave those happy, smiling tourists on board? She blanched and licked her lips nervously.

'You're white as a sheet.'

'Yes, well...'

'You're seriously scared of water?'

'Of *open* water. Anything could happen. Especially on something as flimsy as a sailboat.'

'Anything could happen to anyone, anywhere. Driving here was probably more of a risk than that boat out there.' He opened his door and swung his long body out, moving round to open the passenger door for her. 'You were right when you said that you can't kill an irrational fear unless you confront it.' He held out one hand and, heart beating fast, Caroline took it. The feel of his fingers as they curled around hers was warm and comforting.

'How would you know?' she asked in a shaky voice as she eased herself out of the car and half-eyed the lake the way a minnow might eye a patch of shark-infested water. 'I bet you've never been scared of anything in your life.'

'I'll take that as a compliment.' He kept his fingers interlinked with hers as he led her down towards the jetty.

Hell, he never thought he'd live to see the day when there were no thoughts of work, deals to be done or lawyers to meet impinging on his mind. His mother's uncertain finances—the details of which he had never been spared, even when he had been too young to fully understand them—had bred a man to whom the acquisition of money was akin to a primal urge. The fact that he was very, very good at it had only served to strengthen his rampant ambition. Women had come and gone, and would continue to come and go, for his parents were a sad indictment of the institution of marriage, but the challenge of work would always be a constant.

Except, now, it appeared to have taken a back seat.

And he barely recognised the boyish feeling inside him as her fingers tightly squeezed his the closer they got to the jetty.

'Hey, trust me,' he told her. 'It'll be worth it. There's nothing like the freedom of being out on the lake and it's not like being on the sea. The edge of the lake is always visible. You'll always be able to orienteer yourself by the horizon.'

'How deep is it?'

'Don't think about that. Tell me why you're so scared.'

Caroline hesitated. She disapproved of everything about this man and yet his invitation to confide was irresistible. *And* her fingers were still entwined with his. Suddenly conscious of that, she wriggled them, which encouraged him to grasp them slightly harder.

'Well?'

'I fell in a river when I was a child.' She sighed and glanced up at him sheepishly. 'I must have been about seven, just learning how to swim. There were four of us and it was the summer holidays. Our parents had all arranged this picnic in the woods.'

'Sounds idyllic.'

'It was, until the four of us kids went off to do a bit of exploring. We were crossing a bridge, just messing around. Looking back now, the river must not have been more than a metre deep and the bridge was just a low, rickety thing. We were playing that game, the one where you send a twig from one side of the bridge and race to the other side to see it float out. Anyway, I fell, headlong into the river. It was terrifying. Although I could swim enough to get out, it was as though my mind had blanked that out. All I could taste was the water and I could feel floating weeds on my face. I thought I was going to drown. Everyone was screaming. The adults were with us within seconds and there was no harm done, but ever since then I've hated the thought of open water.'

'And when I was fourteen, I tried my hand at horse riding and came off at the first hurdle. Ever since then I've had an irrational fear of horses.'

'No, you haven't.' But she grinned up at him, shading her eyes from the glare of the sun with one hand.

'You're right. I haven't. But it's a possibility. I've never been near a horse in my life. I can ski down any black run but I suspect a horse would have me crying with terror.'

Caroline laughed. She was relaxing, barely noticing that the sailboat was being rented, because Giancarlo had continued to talk to her in the soothing voice of someone intent on calming a skittish animal, describing silly scenarios that made her smile. He was certain that he would have a fear of horses. Spiders brought him out in a sweat. Birds brought to mind certain horror movies. He knew that he would definitely have had a phobia of small aircraft had he not managed to successfully bypass that by owning his own helicopter.

Giancarlo hadn't put this much effort into a woman in a long time. It was baffling, because had someone told him a week ago that he would be held to account by a woman who didn't know the meaning of tact, he would have laughed out loud. And had that someone then said that he would find himself holed up at his father's villa for a week, courtesy of the same woman who didn't know the meaning of tact, he would have called out the little men with strait-jackets because the idea was beyond ridiculous.

Yet here he was: reaching out to help a woman with unruly brown hair streaked with caramel, who didn't seem to give a damn about all the other nonsense other women cared about, onto a sailboat. And enjoying the fact that he had managed to distract her from her fear of water by making her laugh.

Obeying an instinctive need to rationalise his actions, Giancarlo easily justified his uncharacteristic behaviour by assuming that this was simply his creative way of dealing with a situation. So what would have been the point in tearing her off a strip for having coerced him into staying at the villa longer than he had planned? He would still do what he had come to do, and anyway it made a relaxing change to interact with a woman in whom he had no sexual interest. He went for tall, thin blondes with a penchant for high-end designer clothes. So take away the sometimes-tedious game of chase and catch with a woman and it seemed that he was left with something really quite enjoyable.

Caroline was on the sailboat before she really realised what had happened. One minute she was laughing, enjoying his silly remarks with the sun on her face and the breeze running its balmy fingers through her hair and gradually undoing her loose plait—the next minute, terra firma was no longer beneath her feet and the swaying of the boat was forcibly reminding her of everything she feared about being out at sea, or in this case out on the lake.

Did he even know how to handle this thing? Wasn't he supposed to have had a little pep talk from the guys in charge of the rentals—a refresher course in how to make sure this insignificant piece of plywood with a bit of cloth didn't blow over when they were in the middle of the lake?

Giancarlo saw her stricken face, the panicked way she looked over her shoulder at the safety of a shoreline from which they were drifting.

He reacted on pure gut impulse.

He kissed her. He curled his long fingers into her tangle of dark hair and with one hand pulled her towards him. The taste of her full lips was like nectar. He felt her soft, lush body curve into him, felt her full breasts squash softly against his chest. He had taken her utterly by surprise and there was no resistance as the kiss grew deeper and more intimately exploring, tasting every part of her sweet mouth. God, he wanted to do more! His arousal was fast and hard and his fabled self-control disappeared so quickly that he was at the mercy of his senses for the first time in his life.

He wanted to strip off her shirt, tear off her bra, which wouldn't be one of those lacy slips of nothing the women he dated wore but something plainly, resolutely and impossibly sexy. He wanted to lose himself in her generous breasts until he stopped thinking altogether.

Caroline was in the grip of something so intensely powerful that she could barely breathe.

She had never felt like this in her life before. She could feel her body melting, could feel her nipples tightening and straining against her bra, knew that she was hot and wet between her legs...

Her body was behaving in a way it had never behaved before and it thrilled and terrified her at the same time.

When he eventually broke free, she literally felt lost.

'You kissed me,' she breathed, still clutching him by the shirt and looking up at him with huge, searching eyes. She wanted to know *why*. She knew why *she* had responded! Underneath her disapproval for everything he had done and said, there was a strong, irresistible current of pure physical attraction. She had been swept along by it and nothing she had ever experienced in her life before had prepared her for its ferocity. Lust was just something she had read about. Now she knew, firsthand, how powerful it could be. Was he feeling the same thing? Did he want to carry on kissing her as much as she wanted him to?

She gradually became aware of their surroundings and of the fact that, with one hand, he had expertly guided the small sailboat away from shore and out into the open lake. They had become one of the small bright toys she had glimpsed from land.

'You kissed me. Was that to distract me from the fact that we were heading away from land?'

Hell, how did *he* know? He just knew that he had been blown away, had lost all shreds of self-control. It was not something of which he was proud, nor could he understand it. Rallying quickly, he recovered his shattered equilibrium and took a couple of steps back, but then had to look away briefly because her flushed cheeks and parted mouth were continuing to play havoc with his libido.

'It worked, didn't it?' He nodded towards the shore, still not trusting himself to look at her properly. 'You're on the water now and, face it, you're no longer scared.'

CHAPTER FIVE

CAROLINE REMAINED POSITIONED in the centre of the small boat for the next hour. She made sure not to look out to the water, which made her instantly conjure up drowning scenarios in her head. Instead, she looked at Giancarlo. It was blissfully easy to devote all her attention to him. He might not have sailed for a long time but whatever he had learnt as a boy had returned to him with ease.

'It's like riding a bike,' he explained, doing something clever with the rudder. 'Once learnt, never forgotten.'

Caroline found herself staring at his muscular brown legs, sprinkled with dark hair. Having brought just enough clothes to cover a one-night stay, he had, he had admitted when asked, pulled strings and arranged for one of the local shops to open up early for him. At eight that morning, he had taken his car to the nearest small town and bought himself a collection of everyday wear. The khaki shorts and loose-fitting shirt, virtually unbuttoned all the way down, were part of that wardrobe and they offered her an incredible view of his highly toned body. Every time he moved, she could see the ripple of his muscles.

Now he was explaining to her how he had managed to acquire his expertise in a boat. He had always been drawn to the water. He had had his first sailing lesson at the age of five and by the age of ten had been adept enough to sail on his own, although he had not been allowed. By the time he had left the lake for good, he could have crewed his own sailboat, had he been of legal age.

Caroline nodded, murmured and thought about *that kiss*. She had been kissed before but never like that. Neither of the two boyfriends she'd had had ever made her feel as though the ground was spinning and freewheeling under her feet; neither had ever made her feel as if the rules of time and space had altered, throwing her into a wildly different dimension. With an eye for detail she never knew she possessed, she marvelled at how a face so coldly, exquisitely beautiful could inspire such craven weakness deep inside her when she had never previously been drawn to men because of how they looked. She wondered at the way she had fallen headlong into that kiss, never wanting it to stop when she barely liked the guy she had been kissing.

'Hello? Calling Planet Earth…'

'Huh?' Caroline blinked and realised that the sailboat was now practically at a standstill. The sound of the water lapping gently against the sides was mesmeric.

'If you stay in that position any longer, your joints will seize up,' Giancarlo informed her drily. 'Stand up. Walk about.'

'What if I topple the boat over and fall in?'

'Then I'll rescue you. But you'll be easier to rescue if you stripped off to your swimsuit. You *are* wearing a swimsuit underneath those clothes, aren't you?'

'Of course I am!'

'Then, off you go.' To show the way, he dispensed with his shirt, which was damp from his exertions, and laid it flat to dry.

Caroline felt her breath catch painfully in her throat as all her misbehaving senses went into immediate overdrive. Her lips felt swollen and her breasts were tender. She wanted to tell him to look away but knew that that would have been childish. She gave herself a stern little lecture—how many times had she worn this swimsuit? Hundreds! In summer, she would often go down to the beach with her friends. She never went in the water but she lazed and tanned and had never, not once, felt remotely self-conscious.

With a mental shrug, she quickly peeled off her clothes, folding them neatly and accepting the soft towel which Giancarlo had packed in a waterproof bag, then she stood up and took a few tentative steps towards the side of the boat. In truth, she felt much, much calmer than when she had first stepped on the small vessel. There were far too many other things on her mind to focus on her fears.

Watching her, Giancarlo felt a sudden, unexpected rush of pure sexual awareness. She was staring out to sea, her profile to him, offering him a view of the most voluptuous body he had ever laid eyes on, even though her one-piece black swimsuit was the last word in old-fashioned and strove to conceal as much as possible. She had the perfect hourglass figure that would drive most men mad. With the breeze making a nonsense of her plait, she had finally unravelled it and her hair fell in curls almost to her waist. He found that his breathing had become shallow, and his arousal was so prominent and painful that he inhaled sharply and began busying himself with the other towel which he had packed.

A youth spent on water had primed him for certain necessities: towels, drinks, something to snack on and, of course, sun-tan lotion.

He had taken up a safer position, sitting on his towel, when she turned to him with a little frown. He was tempted to tell her to cover herself up as he looked through half-closed eyes at her luscious breasts, which not even her sensible swimsuit could downplay.

'I never even asked,' Caroline said abruptly. 'Are you married?' Proud of herself for having ventured into the unknown and terrifying realms of standing at the side of the boat, she now made her way to where he was sitting and spread her towel alongside his to sit.

'Do I look like a married man?'

Caroline considered her father. 'No,' she admitted. 'And I know that you're not wearing a wedding ring, but lots of married men don't like jewellery of any kind. My dad doesn't.'

'Not married. No intention of ever getting married. You're staring at me as though I've just announced a ban on Christmas Day. Have I shocked you?'

'I just don't understand how you can be so certain of something.'

Giancarlo remained silent for such a long time that she wondered whether he was going to answer. He was now lying down on the towel, his hands folded behind his head, a brooding, dangerous Adonis in repose.

'I don't talk about my private life.'

'I'm not asking you to bare your soul. I was just curious.' She hitched her legs up and wrapped her arms around them. 'You're so... uptight.'

'Me—*uptight*?' Giancarlo looked at her with incredulity.

'It's as though you're scared of ever really letting go.'

'Scared? *Uptight*?'

'I don't mean to be offensive.'

'I never knew I had such a boundless capacity for patience,' Giancarlo confessed in a staggered voice. 'Do you ever think before you speak?'

'I wouldn't have said those things if you had just answered my question but it doesn't matter now.'

Giancarlo sighed heavily and raked his fingers through his hair in sheer frustration as Caroline stubbornly lay down, closed her eyes and enjoyed the sunshine.

'I've seen firsthand how unreliable the institution of marriage is,' he admitted gruffly. 'And I'm not just talking about the wonderful example set by my parents. The statistics prove conclusively that only an idiot would fall for that fairy-tale nonsense.'

Caroline opened her eyes, propped herself up on one elbow and looked at him with disbelief.

'I'm one of those so-called idiots.'

'Now, I wonder why I'm not entirely surprised?'

'What right do you have to say that?'

Giancarlo held both hands up in surrender. 'I don't want to get into an argument with you, Caroline. The weather's glorious, I haven't been out on a sailboat for the longest while. In fact, this is pretty much the first unscheduled vacation I've had in years. I don't want to spoil it.' He waited for a few seconds and then raised his eyebrows with amusement. 'You mean you aren't going to argue with me?' He shot her a crooked grin that made her go bright red.

'I hate arguing.'

'You could have fooled me.'

But he was still grinning lazily at her. She felt all hot and flustered just looking at him, although she couldn't drag her eyes away. It was impossibly still out here, with just the sound of gentle water and the far-away laughter of people on the nearest sailboat, which was still a good distance away. Suddenly, and for no reason, Caroline felt as though they were a million miles from civilisation, caged in their own intensely private moment. Right now, she wanted nothing more than to be kissed by him again, and that decadent yearning was so shocking that her mouth fell half-open and she found that she was holding her breath.

'Okay, but you have to admit that you give me lots to argue about.'

'I absolutely have to admit that, do I?'

The soft, teasing amusement in his voice made her blush even harder. Suddenly it seemed very important that she remind herself of all the various reasons she had for disliking Giancarlo. She loathed arguing and had never been very good at it, but right now arguing seemed the safest solution to the slow, burning, treacly feeling threatening to send her mind and body off on some weird, scary tangent.

'So, what about girlfriends?' she threw recklessly at him.

'What about *girlfriends*?' Giancarlo couldn't quite believe that she was continuing a conversation which he had deemed to be already closed. She had propped herself up on one elbow so that she was now lying on her side, like a figure from some kind of crazily erotic masterpiece. The most tantalizing thing about her was that he was absolutely convinced that she had no idea of her sensational pulling power.

'Well, I mean, is there someone special in your life at the moment?'

'Why do you ask?'

'I… I just don't want to talk about Alberto…' Caroline clutched at that explanation. In truth, the murky business between Giancarlo and his father seemed a very distant problem as they bobbed on the sailboat, surrounded by the azure blue of the placid lake.

'And nosing where you don't belong is the next best thing?' He should have been outraged at the cavalier way with which she was overstepping his boundaries, but he didn't appear to be. He shrugged. 'No. There's no one special in my life, as you call it, at the moment. The last special woman in my life was two months ago.'

'What was she like?'

'Compliant and undemanding for the first two months. Less so until I called it a day two months later. It happens.'

'I guess most women want more than just a casual fling. Most women like to imagine that things are going to go somewhere after a while.'

'I know. It's a critical mistake.' Giancarlo never made it a habit to enquire about women's pasts. The present was all that interested him. The past was another country, the future a place in which the less interest shown, the better.

Breaking all his own self-imposed restrictions, he asked, with idle curiosity, 'And what about you? Now that we've decided to shelve our arguments over Alberto for a while, you never told me how it is that someone of your age could be tempted to while away an indefinite amount of time in the middle of nowhere with only an old man for company. And forget all that nonsense about enjoying walks in the garden and burying yourself in old books. Did you come to Italy because you were running away from something?'

'Running away from what?' Caroline asked in genuine bewilderment.

'Who knows? Maybe the country idyll proved too much, maybe you got involved with someone who didn't quite fit the image, was that it? Was there some guy lurking in paradise who broke your heart? Was that why you escaped to Italy? Why you're content to hide away in a big, decaying villa? Makes sense. Only child…lots of expectations there…doting parents. Did you decide to rebel? Find yourself the wrong type of man?'

'That's crazy.' She flushed and looked away from those too-penetrating, fabulous bitter-chocolate eyes.

'Is it? Why am I getting a different impression here?'

'I didn't get involved with the wrong type of guy.' Caroline scoffed nervously. 'I'm not attracted to… This is a silly conversation.'

'Okay, maybe you weren't escaping an ill-judged, torrid affair with a married man, but what then? Were the chickens and the sheep and the village-hall dances every Friday night all a little too much?'

Caroline looked at him resentfully from under her lashes and then hurriedly looked away. How had he managed to turn this conversation on its head?

'Well?' Giancarlo asked softly, intrigued. 'You can't make the rules to only suit yourself. Two can play at this little game of going where you don't belong…'

'Oh, for goodness' sake! I *may* have become just a little bored, but so what?' She fidgeted with the edge of the towel and glared at him, because she felt like a traitor to her parents with that admission, and it was *his* fault. 'Italy seemed like a brilliant idea,' she admitted, sliding a sideways look at him, realising that he wasn't smirking as she might have expected. 'London was just too expensive. You need to have a well-paid job to go there and actually be able to afford somewhere to rent, and I didn't want to go to any of the other big cities. When Dad suggested that he get in touch with Alberto, that brushing up on my Italian would be a helpful addition to my CV, I guess I jumped at the chance. And, once I got here, Alberto and I just seemed to click.'

'So why the guilty look when I asked?'

'I think Mum and Dad always expected that I'd stay in the country, live the rural idyll just round the corner from them, maybe get married to one of the local lads...'

'They said so?'

'No, but...'

'They would have wanted you to fly the nest.'

'They wouldn't. We're very close.'

'If they wanted to keep you tied to them, they would never have suggested a move as dramatic as Italy,' Giancarlo told her drily. 'Trust me, they aren't fools. This would have been their gentle way of helping you to find your own space. Shame, though.'

'What do you mean?'

'I was really beginning to warm to the idea of the unsuitable lover.'

Caroline's breath caught sharply in her throat because she was registering how close they were to one another, and lying on her side, she felt even more vulnerable to his watchful dark eyes. Conscious of her every movement, she awkwardly sat up and half-wrapped the towel over her legs.

'I... I'm not attracted to unsuitable men,' she croaked, because he appeared to be waiting for a reply to his murmured statement, head slightly inclined.

'Define *unsuitable*...' He lazily reached over to the cooler bag which he had brought with him, and which she had barely noticed in her panic over the dreaded sailing trip, and pulled out two cold drinks, one of which he handed to her.

Held hostage to a conversation that was running wildly out

of control, Caroline could only stare at him in dazed confusion. She pressed the cold can to her heated cheeks.

'Well?' Giancarlo tipped his head back to drink and she found that she couldn't tear her eyes away from him, from the motion of his throat as he swallowed and the play of muscles in his raised arm.

'I like kind, thoughtful, sensitive men,' she breathed.

'Sounds boring.'

'It's not boring to like *good guys*, guys who won't let you down.'

'In which case, where are these guys who don't let you down?'

'I'm not in a relationship at the moment, if that's what you're asking,' Caroline told him primly, hoping that he wouldn't detect the flustered catch in her voice.

'No. Good guys can be a crashing disappointment, I should imagine.'

'I'm sure some of your past girlfriends wouldn't agree with that!' Bright patches of colour had appeared on her cheeks, and her eyes were locked to his in a way that was invasive and thrilling at the same time. Had he leant closer to her? Or had she somehow managed to shorten the distance between them?

'I've never had any complaints in that department,' Giancarlo murmured. 'Sure, some of them have mistakenly got it into their heads that they could persuade me to be in it for the long term. Sure, they were disappointed when I had to set them straight on that, but complaints? In the sex department? No. In fact—'

'I'm not interested,' Caroline interrupted shrilly.

Giancarlo dealt her a slashing smile tinged with a healthy dose of disbelief.

'I guess you haven't met a lot of Italian studs out here,' he said, shamelessly fishing and enjoying himself in a way that had become alien to him. His high-pressured, high-octane, high-stressed, driven everyday life had been left behind on the shores of Lake Como. He was playing truant now and loving every second of it. His dark eyes drifted down to her full, heaving breasts.

She might have modestly half-covered her bare legs with the towel but she couldn't hide what remained on display, nor could he seem to stop himself from appreciating it.

'I didn't come here to meet anyone! That wasn't the point.'

'No, but it might have been a pleasant bonus—unless, of course, you've left someone behind? Is there a local lad waiting for you in the wings? Someone your parents approve heartily of? Maybe a farmer?'

Caroline wondered why he would have picked a *farmer*, of all people. Was it because he considered her the outdoor kind of girl, robust and healthy with pink cheeks and a hearty appetite? The kind of girl he would never have kissed unless he had been obliged to, as a distraction from the embarrassment of having the girl in question make a fool of herself and of him by having a panic attack at the thought of getting into a boat? She sucked her stomach in, gave up the losing battle to look skinny and stood up to move to the side of the boat, where she held the railings and looked out to the lake.

The shore was a distant strip but she wasn't scared. Just like that, her irrational fear of water seemed to have subsided. There wasn't enough room for that silly phobia when Giancarlo was doing crazy things to her senses. And, much as he got under her skin, his presence was weirdly reassuring. How did *that* work?

She was aware that he had moved to stand behind her and in one swift movement she turned around, her back to the waist-high railing. 'It's so peaceful and beautiful here.' She looked at him steadily and tried hard to focus just on his face rather than on his brown, hard torso and its generous sprinkling of dark hair that seemed horribly, unashamedly masculine. 'Do you miss it? I know Milan is very busy and very commercial, but you grew up here. Don't you sometimes long for the tranquillity of the open spaces?'

'I think you're confusing me with one of those sensitive types you claim to like,' Giancarlo murmured. He clasped the railing on either side of her, bracing himself and locking her into a suffocating, non-physical embrace, his lean body only inches away from her. 'I don't do nostalgia. Not, I might add, that I have much to be nostalgic about.'

The smile he shot her sent a heat wave rushing through her body. She was barefoot and her toes curled against the smooth wooden planks of the sailboat. God, she could scarcely breathe! Their eyes tangled and Caroline felt giddy under the shimmering intensity of his midnight-dark eyes.

She could barely remember what they had been talking about. The quiet sounds of the water had receded and she thought she could hear the whoosh of blood rushing through her veins and the frantic pounding of her heart.

She wasn't aware of her eyes half closing, or of her mouth parting on a question that was never asked.

Giancarlo was more than aware of both those things. The powerful scent of lust made his nostrils flare. He realised that this was exactly what he wanted. Her lush, sexy body combined with her wide-eyed innocence had set up a chain reaction in him that he hadn't been able to control.

'And as for getting away from it all...' Some of her long hair blew across his face. She smelled of sun and warmth. 'I have a place on the coast.' From nowhere sprang such a strange notion that he barely registered it. He would like to take her there. He had never had any such inclination with any woman in the past. That was purely his domain, his private getaway from the hassle of everyday life, always maintained, waiting and ready for those very rare occasions when he felt the need to make use of it.

'You have the most amazing hair.' He captured some of it, sank his fingers into its untamed length. 'You should never have it cut.'

Caroline knew that he was going to kiss her and she strained up towards him with a sigh of abandon. She never knew that she could want something so much in her life. She lifted her hand and trembled as her fingers raked through his fine, dark, silky hair.

With a stifled groan, Giancarlo angled down and lost himself in a kiss that was hungry and exploring. His questing tongue melded with hers and, as the kiss deepened, he spanned her rib cage with urgent, impatient hands. They were out in the open but visible to no one. Other boats, dotted on the sparkling, still water, were too far away to witness his lack of control.

The push of her breasts as she curved her body up to him was explosive to his libido and he hooked his fingers under the straps of her swimsuit. He couldn't pull them down fast enough, and as her breasts spilled out in their glorious abundance he had to control the savage reaction of his throbbing arousal.

'God, you're beautiful,' he growled hoarsely.

'Beautiful' had never been one of those things Caroline had ever considered herself. Friendly, yes. Reasonably attractive, perhaps. But *beautiful*?

Right now, however, as she looked at him with a fevered, slumberous gaze, she believed him and she was infused with a heady, wanton feeling of total recklessness. She wanted to bask in his open admiration. It was a huge turn-on. He looked down and her nipples tightened and ached in immediate response. Her ability to think and to reason had been scattered to the four winds and she moaned and arched her back as his big hands covered her breasts, massaging them, pushing them up so that her swollen nipples were offered up to his scorching inspection. The sun on her half-naked body was beautifully warm. She closed her eyes, hands outstretched on the railing on either side of her.

It was a snapshot of an erotic, abundant goddess with her hair streaming back, and Giancarlo lowered his head to close his mouth over the pulsating pink disc of a surrendered nipple.

Reaching down, Caroline curled her fingers into his hair. She felt like a rag doll and had to stop herself from sinking to the floor of the boat as he plundered her breasts, first one then the other, suckling on her nipple, drawing it into his mouth so that he could tease the distended tip with his tongue. She felt powerful and submissive at the same time as he feasted on her, licking, nipping, sucking, driving her crazy with his mouth.

When his hand clasped her thigh, she nearly fainted. The swimsuit was pulled lower and he trailed kisses over each inch of flesh that was gradually exposed. The paleness of her stomach was a sharp contrast to the golden colour she had acquired over the summer months.

Giancarlo found that he liked that. It was a *real* body, the body of a living, breathing, fulsome woman, unlike the statue-perfect, all-over-bronzed bodies of the stick insects he was accustomed to. He rose to his feet and pushed his leg between her thighs, moving it slowly and insistently which made the boat rock ever so slightly. Caroline, with her phobia of water, barely noticed. She was on a different planet and experiencing sensations that were all new and wonderful.

She only surfaced, abruptly and rudely, when the sound of an outboard motor broke through her blurry, cotton-wool haze. She gasped, shocked at her state of undress and mortified at her rebellious body, which had disobeyed every law of self-preservation to flirt perilously with a situation that instinctively screamed danger.

Struggling to free herself, she felt the boat sway and rock under her and she stumbled to rebalance herself.

'What the hell are you doing? You're going to capsize this thing. Stay still!'

He tried to hold her arms as she frantically endeavoured to pull up her swimsuit and hide the shameful spectacle of her nudity.

'How *could* you?' Caroline was shaking like a leaf as she cautiously made her way back to the centre of the boat. Her huge brown eyes were wide with accusation, and Giancarlo, who had never in living memory experienced any form of rejection from a woman, raked his hand impatiently through his hair.

'How could I *what*?'

'You *know* what!'

He took a couple of steps towards her and was outraged when she shrank back. Did she find him *threatening*?

'What I *know*—' his voice was a whiplash, leaving her no leeway to nurse fanciful notions of being seduced against her will '—is that you *wanted* it, and it's no good huddling there like a virtuous maiden whose virginity has been sullied. Snap out of it, Caroline. You practically threw yourself at me.'

'I did no such *thing*,' Caroline whispered, distraught, because she had, she really *had*, and she couldn't for the life of her understand why.

Giancarlo shook his head with such rampant incredulity that she was forced to look away. When she next sneaked a glance at him, it was to see him preparing to sail back to shore. His face was dark with anger.

With agonising honesty, Caroline licked her lips and cleared her throat. It was no good letting this thing fester in simmering silence. She had had a terrible moment of horrifying misjudgement and she would just have to say something.

'I'm sorry,' she said bravely, addressing his profile, which offered nothing by way of encouragement. 'I know I was partly to blame...'

Giancarlo glanced over to her with a brooding scowl. 'How kind of you to rethink your accusation that I was intent on taking advantage of you.'

'I know you weren't! I never meant to imply that. Look...' With urgent consternation, Caroline leaned towards him. 'I don't know what happened. I don't even *like* you! I disapprove of everything about you.'

'*Everything*, Caroline? Let's not labour that statement too much. You might find that you need to retract it.' Not only was Giancarlo furious at her inexplicable withdrawal, when it had been plain to see that she had been as hot and ready for him as he had been for her, but he was more furious with himself for not being able to look at her for fear of his libido going haywire all over again.

'You took me by surprise.'

'Oh, we're back to that old chestnut, are we? I'm the arch-seducer and you're the shrinking violet!'

'It's the heat,' she countered with increasing desperation. 'And the situation. I've never been on the water like this before. Everything must have just been too much.' She continued to look at him earnestly. 'It's *impossible* for me to be attracted to you.' She sought to impose an explanation for her wildly out-of-character behaviour. 'We don't get along at *all* and I disapprove of why you decided to come here to see Alberto. I don't care about money and I've never been impressed by people who think that making money is the most important thing in the world. And, furthermore, I just don't get it with guys who are scared of commitment. I have no respect for them. So...so...'

'So, despite all of that, you still couldn't resist me. What do you think that says?'

'That's what I'm trying to tell you. It doesn't say *anything*!'

Giancarlo detected the horror in her voice and he didn't quite know how to deal with it. He would have made love to her right there, on the boat, and he certainly couldn't think of any other woman who wouldn't have relished the experience. The fact that this woman was intent on treating it as something she had to remove herself from as quickly as possible was frankly an insult of the highest order.

Caroline felt that she was finally in possession of her senses once again. 'I think you'll agree that that unfortunate episode is something we'd best put right behind us. Pretend it never happened.'

'You're attracted to me, Caroline.'

'I'm not. Haven't you listened to a word I've just been saying? I got carried away because I'm here, on a boat, out of my comfort zone. I don't go for men like you. I know you probably find that horribly insulting but it happens to be the truth.'

'You're attracted to me, and the faster you face that the better off you'll be.'

'And how do you figure that out, Giancarlo? How?'

'You've spent your life thinking that the local lad who enjoys the barn dance on a Saturday and whose greatest ambition is to have three kids and buy a semi-detached house on the street next to where your parents live is your ideal man. Just as you tried to kid yourself that never leaving the countryside was what you wanted out of life. Wrong on both counts. Your head's telling you what you should want, but here I am, a real man, and you just can't help yourself. Don't worry. Amazingly, it's mutual.'

Caroline went white at his brutal summary of everything she didn't want to face. Her behaviour made no sense to her. She didn't approve of him one bit, yet she had succumbed faster than she could ever have dreamt possible.

It was lust, pure and simple, and he wanted to drag that shameful admission out of her because he had an ego the size of a liner and he didn't care for the fact that she had rejected him. Had he thought that he was complimenting her when he told her that, *amazingly*, he found her attractive? Did he seriously think that it felt good to be somebody's novelty for five minutes before he returned to the sort of woman he usually liked?

Warning bells were ringing so loudly in her head that she would have been a complete idiot not to listen to them. She found that she was gripping the sides of the salty plank of wood sufficiently hard for her knuckles to whiten.

Glancing across at her, Giancarlo could see the slow, painful realisation of the truth sinking in. He had never thought himself the kind of loser who tolerated a woman who blew hot and then blew cold. Women like that were a little too much like hard work. But this woman…

'Okay.' Caroline's words tumbled over one another and she kept her eyes firmly fixed on the fast-approaching shoreline. 'So I find you attractive. You're right. Satisfied? But I'm glad you've dragged that out of me because it's only lust and lust doesn't mean anything. Not to me, anyway. So there. Now it's out in the open and we can both forget about it.'

CHAPTER SIX

IT WAS AFTER five by the time they were finally back at the villa. The outing on the lake had taken much longer than she had thought and then, despite its dramatic conclusion, Giancarlo had insisted on stopping somewhere for them to have a very late lunch.

To add insult to injury, he had proceeded to talk to her as naturally as though nothing had happened between them. He pointed out various interesting landmarks; he gave her an informative lecture on the Vezio Castle, asking her whether she had been there. She hadn't. He seemed to know the history of a lot of the grand mansions, monuments to the rich and famous, and was a fount of information on all the local gossip surrounding the illustrious families.

Caroline just wanted to go home. She was bewildered, confused and in a state of sickening inner turmoil. As he had talked, gesticulating in a way that was peculiarly Italian, she had watched those hands and felt giddy at the thought of where they had been—on her naked body, touching and caressing her in a way that made her breathing quicken and brought a flush of hectic colour to her cheeks. She looked at his sensual mouth as he spoke and remembered in graphic detail the feel of his lips on her breasts, suckling her nipples until she had wanted to scream with pleasure.

How was she supposed to laugh and chat as though none of that had happened?

And yet, wasn't that precisely what she wanted, what she had told him to do—pretend that nothing had happened? Sweep it all under the carpet and forget about it?

She hated the way he could still manage to penetrate her tight-lipped silence to make her smile at something he said. Obviously, *she* was the only one affected by what had happened out there on the lake.

'Thank you for today,' she told him politely as she opened the car door almost before he had had time to kill the engine.

'Which bit of it are you thanking me for?' Giancarlo rested glittering eyes on her and raised his eyebrows in a telling question that made her blush even more ferociously. She was the perfect portrait of a woman who couldn't wait to flee his company. In fact, she had withstood his polite onslaught over an unnecessarily prolonged lunch with the stoicism of someone obliged to endure a cruel and unusual punishment and, perversely, the fiercer her long-suffering expression, the more he had become intent on obliterating it. Now and again he had succeeded, making her laugh even though he could see that she was fighting the impulse.

Giancarlo didn't understand where his reaction to her was coming from.

She had made a great production of telling him just why she couldn't possibly be attracted to a man like him—all lies, of course, as he had proceeded to prove. But she had had a valid point. Where was the common ground between them? She was gauche, unsophisticated and completely lacking in feminine wiles. In short, nothing like the sort of women he went out with. But, hell, she turned him on. She had even managed to turn him on when she had been sitting there, at the little trattoria, paying attention to everyone around them and only reluctantly looking at him when she'd had no choice.

What was that about? Was his ego so inflated that he couldn't abide the thought of wanting a woman and not having instant and willing gratification? It was not in his nature to dwell on anything, to be remotely introspective, so he quickly shelved that thorny slice of self-examination.

Instead, he chose to focus on the reality of the situation. He was here, dragged back to his past by circumstances he could never have foreseen. Although he had a mission to complete, one that had been handed to him on a plate, it was, he would now concede, a mission that would have to be accomplished with a certain amount of subtlety.

In the meantime, reluctant prisoner though he might be, he found himself in the company of a woman who seemed to possess the knack of wreaking havoc with his self-control. What was he to do about it? Like an itch that had to be scratched, Giancarlo found himself in the awkward and novel position of wanting her beyond reason and knowing that he was prepared to go beyond the call of duty to get her. It was frustrating that he knew she wanted him too and was yet reluctant to dip her toes in the water. Heck, they were both adults, weren't they?

Now, faced with a direct question, she stared at him in mute, embarrassed silence.

'I haven't seen as much of the countryside around here as I would have liked,' Caroline returned politely, averting her eyes to stare just behind his shoulder. 'I have a driving licence, and of course Alberto said that I was more than welcome to use the car, but I haven't been brave enough to do much more than potter into the nearest town. Before he fell ill, we did take a couple of drives out for lunch, but there's still so much left to explore.'

Giancarlo smiled back at her through gritted teeth. He wanted to turn her face to him and *make* her look him in the eyes. It got on his nerves the way she hovered, as if waiting for permission to be dismissed.

He also hated the way he could feel himself stirring into unwelcome arousal, getting hard at the sight of her, her soft, ultra-feminine curves and her stubborn, pouting full mouth. He wanted to snatch her to him and kiss her into submission, kiss her until she was begging him to have his way with her. He almost laughed at his sudden caveman-like departure from his normal polished behaviour.

'Any time,' he said shortly and she reluctantly looked at him.

'Oh, thanks very much, but I doubt the occasion will arise again. After all, you're not here for much longer and I'll be returning to my usual routine with Alberto from tomorrow. Do you need a hand taking anything in? It's just that I'm really hot and sticky and dying to have a shower...'

'In that case, off you go. I think I can manage a couple of towels and a cool bag.'

Caroline fled. She intended on ducking into the safety of her room, which would give her time to gather herself. Instead, she opened the front door to be confronted with a freshly laundered Alberto emerging from the kitchens, with Tessa in tow.

He paused in the middle of a testy row, which Tessa was enduring with a broad smile, to look shrewdly at Caroline from under beetling brows.

'Been a long time out there, my girl. What have you been getting up to, eh? You look tousled.'

'Leave the poor woman alone, Alberto. It's none of your business *what* she's been getting up to!'

'I haven't been getting up to *anything*!' Caroline addressed both of them in a high voice. 'I mean, it's been a lovely day out...'

'Sailing? I take it my son managed to cure your fear of water?'

'I... I... Turns out I wasn't as scared of the water as I'd thought. You know how it is...childhood trauma...long story. Anyway, I'm awfully hot and sticky. Are you going to be in the sitting-room, Alberto? Shall I join you there as soon as I've had my shower?'

'Where's Giancarlo?'

'Oh, he's just taking some stuff out of the car.' The devil worked on idle hands, and a day spent lazing around had made Alberto frisky. Caroline could spot that devilish glint in his eyes a mile away and she eyed the staircase behind him with longing.

'So you two got along, then, did you? Wasn't sure if you would, as you seem very different characters, but you know what they say about opposites attracting...' Inquisitive eyes twinkled at her as a tide of colour rose into her face. Next to him, Tessa was rolling her eyes to the ceiling and shooting her a look that said, 'Just ignore him—he's in one of his playful moods.'

'I'm not in the *slightest* attracted to your son!' Caroline felt compelled to set the record straight. 'You're one-hundred percent right. We're completely different, *total* opposites. In fact, I'm *surprised* that I managed to put up with him for such a long time. I suppose I must have been so *engrossed* with the whole sailing business that *I barely noticed* him at all.' By the time she had finished that ringing declaration, her voice was shrill and slightly hoarse. She was unaware of Giancarlo behind her and when he spoke it sent shivers of awareness racing up and down her spine, giving her goose bumps.

'Now, now,' he drawled softly. 'It wasn't as bad as all that, was it, Caroline?'

The way he spoke her name was like a caress. Alberto was looking at them with unconcealed, lively interest. She had to put a stop to this nonsense straight away.

'I never said it was bad. I had a lovely day. Now, if you'll all excuse me...' As an afterthought, she said to Tessa, 'You'll be joining us tonight for dinner, won't you?' But, as luck would have it, Tessa was going to visit her sister and would be back later, in time to make sure that Alberto took his medication—which at least diverted the conversation away from her. She left them to it, with Alberto informing Tessa that he was feeling better and better every day, and he would be in touch with the consultant to see whether he could stop the tablets.

'And then, my dearest harridan, you'll be back to the daily grind at the hospital, tormenting some other poor, innocent soul. You'll miss me, of course, but don't think for a moment that I'll be missing you.' Caroline left him crowing as she hurried towards the staircase.

She took her time having a long, luxurious bath and then carefully choosing what she would wear. Everything, even the most boring and innocuous garments, seemed to be flagrantly revealing. Her tee shirts stretched tautly across her breasts; her jeans clung too tightly to her legs; her blouses were all too low-cut and her skirts made her think how easy it would be for his hand to reach under to the bare skin of her thighs.

In the end she settled for a pair of leggings and a casual black top that screamed 'matronly'.

She found them in the sitting-room where a tense silence greeted her arrival.

Alberto was in his usual position by the window and Giancarlo, on one of the upright chairs, was nursing what looked like a glass of whisky.

Caught off-guard by an atmosphere that was thick and uncomfortable, Caroline hovered by the door until Alberto waved her impatiently in.

'I can't face the dining-room tonight,' he declared, waving at a platter of snacks on the sideboard. 'I got the girl to bring something light for us to nibble on here. For God's sake, woman, stop standing there like a spectre at the feast and help yourself to something to drink. You know where it all is.'

Caroline slid her eyes across to Giancarlo. His long legs were stretched out, lightly crossed at the ankles. For all the world he looked like a man who was completely relaxed, but there was a threatening stillness about him that made her nervous.

She became even more nervous when Alberto said, with a barb to his voice, 'My son and I were just discussing the state of the world. And, more specifically, the state of *my* world, as evidenced in my business interests.'

Giancarlo watched for her reaction with brooding, lazy interest. So the elephant in the room had been brought out into the open. Why not? If the dancing had to begin, why not be the one to start the music instead of waiting? So much easier to be the one in control and, of course, control was a weapon he had always wielded with ruthless efficiency.

'Your colour's up, Alberto,' Caroline said worriedly. She glared at Giancarlo, who returned her stare evenly. 'Perhaps this isn't the right time to…'

'There is no right time or wrong time when it comes to talking about money, my girl. But maybe we should carry on our little *discussion* later, eh, my boy?' He impatiently gestured for Caroline to bring him the tray of snacks but his sharp eyes were on Giancarlo.

So he'd done it, Caroline thought in a daze, he'd *actually* gone and done it. She could feel it in her bones. Giancarlo had tired of dancing around the purpose for his visit to the villa. Maybe her rejection had hastened thoughts of departure and he had decided that this would be as good a time as any to finally achieve what he had intended to achieve from the very start. Perhaps Alberto's declarations of improving health had persuaded Giancarlo that there was no longer any need to beat around the bush. At any rate, Alberto's flushed face and Giancarlo's cool, guarded silence were saying it all.

Caroline felt crushed by the weight of bitter disappointment. She realised that there had been a part of her that had really hoped that Giancarlo would ditch his stupid desire for revenge and move on, underneath the posturing. She had glimpsed the three-dimensional, complex man behind the façade and had dared to expect more. God, she'd been a fool.

She sank into the deepest, most comfortable chair by the sprawling stone fireplace. From there, she was able to witness, in ever-increasing dismay, the awkwardness between father and son. The subject of money was avoided, but it lay unspoken in the air between them, like a Pandora's box waiting for the lid to be opened.

They talked about the sailing trip. Alberto politely asked what it felt like to be back on the water. Giancarlo replied that, of course, it was an unaccustomed pleasure bearing in mind that life in Milan as a boy had not included such luxuries as sailing trips, not when money had been carefully rationed. In a scrupulously polite voice, he asked Alberto about the villa and then gave a little lecture on the necessity for maintenance of an old property because old properties had a nasty habit of falling apart if left unattended for too long. But of course, he added blandly, old places *did* take money… Had he ever thought of leaving or was possession of one of the area's most picturesque properties just too big a feather in his cap?

After an hour and a half, during which time Ella had removed the snacks and replaced them with a pot of steaming coffee, Caroline was no longer able to bear the crushing discomfort of being caught between two people, one of whom had declared war. She stood up, said something polite about Tessa being back soon and yawned; she would be off to bed. With a forced smile, she parroted something to Alberto about making sure he didn't stay up much longer, that he was to call her on her mobile if Tessa was not back within the hour so that she could help him upstairs. She couldn't look at Giancarlo. His brooding silence frightened her.

'You should maybe come up with me.' She gave it her last best shot to avert the inevitable, but Alberto shook his head briskly.

'My son and I have matters to discuss. I can't pretend there aren't one or two things that need sorting out, and might as well sort them out now. I've never been one to run from the truth!' He was addressing Caroline but staring at Giancarlo. 'It's much better to get the truth out than let things fester.'

Caroline imagined the showdown—well, in Giancarlo's eyes, it was a showdown that had been brewing for the best part of his life and he had come prepared to win it at all costs. She was being dismissed but still she hesitated, searching valiantly for some miracle she could produce from nowhere, like a magician pulling a rabbit from a hat. But there was no miracle and she retreated upstairs. The villa was so extensive that there was no way she could possibly pick up the sound of raised voices, nor could she even hear whether Tessa had returned or not to rescue Alberto from his own son.

She fell into a fitful sleep and awoke with a start to the moon slanting silver light through the window. She had been reading and her book had dropped to the side of the bed. It took a few seconds for her eyes to adjust to the darkness and a few more seconds for her to remember what had been worrying her before she had nodded off: Alberto and Giancarlo. The unbearable tension, like a storm brewing in the distance, waiting to erupt with devastating consequences.

Groaning, she heaved herself out of the four-poster bed, slipped on her dressing gown and headed downstairs, although she wasn't quite sure what she expected to find.

Alberto's suite of rooms lay at the far end of the long corridor, beyond the staircase. Hesitating at the top of the winding staircase, Caroline was tempted to check on him, but first she would go downstairs, make sure that the two of them weren't still locked in a battle to the bitter end. Truth, as Alberto had declared, was something that could take hours to hammer out—and in this case the outcome would be certain defeat for Alberto. He would finally have to bow to Giancarlo and put his destiny in his hands. With financial collapse at his door, what other alternative would there be?

She arrived at the sitting-room to see a slither of light under the shut door. Although she couldn't hear any voices, what else could that light mean except that they were both still in the room? She pushed open the door before she could do what she really wanted to do, which was to run away.

The light came from one of the tall standard lamps that dotted the large room. Sprawled on the chair with his head flung back, eyes closed and a drink cradled loosely in one hand, Giancarlo looked heart-stoppingly handsome and, for once, did not appear to be a man at the top of his game. His hair was tousled, as though he had raked his fingers through it too many times, and he looked ashen and exhausted.

She barely made a sound, but he opened his eyes immediately, although it seemed to take him a few seconds before he could focus on her, and when he did he remained where he was, slumped in the chair.

'Where is Alberto?'

Giancarlo swirled the liquid in his glass without answering and then swallowed back the lot without taking his eyes from her face.

'How much have you *drunk*, Giancarlo?' Galvanised into sudden action, Caroline walked briskly towards him. 'You look terrible.'

'I love a woman who tells it like it is.'

'And you haven't told me where Alberto is.'

'I assure you, he isn't hiding anywhere in this room. You have just me for the pleasure of your company.'

Caroline managed to extract the glass from him. 'You need sobering up.'

'Why? Is there some kind of archaic house rule that prohibits the consumption of alcohol after a certain time?'

'Wait right here. I'm going to go and make a pot of coffee.'

'You have my word. I have no intention of going anywhere, any time soon.'

For once, Caroline failed to be awed by the size and grandeur of the villa. For once, she wished that the kitchens didn't involve a five-minute hike through winding corridors and stately reception rooms. She could barely contain her nerves as she anxiously waited for the kettle to boil, and by the time she made it back to the sitting-room, burdened with a tray on which was piled a mound of buttered toast and a very large pot of black, strong coffee, she half-expected to find that Giancarlo had disappeared.

He hadn't. He had managed to refill his glass and she gently but firmly removed it from him, brought the tray over to place it on the oval table by his chair and then pulled one of the upright, velvet-covered stools towards him.

'What are you doing here, anyway? Did you come down to make sure that the duel at dawn hadn't begun?'

'You should eat something, Giancarlo.' She urged a slice of toast on him and he twirled it thoughtfully between his fingers, examining it as though he had never seen anything like it before.

'You are a very caring person, Caroline Rossi, but I expect you've been told that before. I can't imagine too many women preparing me toast and coffee because they were worried that I'd drunk too much. Although...' He half-leaned towards her, steadying himself on the arm of his chair. 'I've never drunk too much—least of all when in the company of a woman.' He bit into the toast with apparent relish and settled his lustrous dark eyes on her.

'So, what happened? I don't mean to pry...'

'Of course you mean to pry.' He half-closed his eyes, shifted a little in the chair, indicated that he wanted more toast and drank some of the very strong coffee. 'You have my father's welfare at heart.'

'We can talk in the morning, when you're feeling a little less, um, worse for wear.'

'It would take more than half a bottle of whisky to make me feel worse for wear. I've the constitution of an ox. I made a mistake.'

'I know. Well. That's what people always say after they've drunk too much. They also say that they'll never do it again.'

'You're not following me. I made a *mistake*. I screwed up.'

'Giancarlo, I don't know what you're talking about.'

'Of course you don't. Why should you? To summarise—you were right and I was wrong.' He rubbed his eyes, sighed heavily, thought about standing up and discovered that he couldn't be bothered. 'I came here hell-bent on setting the record straight.

There were debts to be settled. I was going to be the debt collector. Well, here's one for the book—the invincible Giancarlo didn't get his facts straight.'

'What do you mean?'

'I was always led to believe that Alberto was a bitter ex-husband who had ensured that my mother got as little as possible in her divorce settlement. I was led to believe that he was a monster who had walked away from a difficult situation, having made sure that my mother suffered for the temerity of having a mind of her own. I was drip-fed a series of half-truths! I think another glass of whisky might help the situation.'

'It won't.'

'You told me that there might be another side to the story.'

'There always is.' Her heart constricted in sympathy. Unused to dealing with any kind of emotional doubt, Giancarlo had steadily tried to drink his way out of it. More than anything in the world, Caroline wanted to reach out and smooth away the lines of bitter self-recrimination from his beautiful face.

'My mother had been having affairs. By the time the marriage dissolved, she was involved with a man who turned out to be a con artist. There was a massive settlement. My mother failed to do anything with it. Instead, she handed it over to a certain Bertoldo Monti who persuaded her that he could treble what she'd had. He took the lot and disappeared. Alberto showed me all the documents, the letters my mother wrote begging for more money. Well, he carried on supporting her, and in return she refused to let him see me. She informed him that I was settled, that I didn't want contact. Letters he sent me were returned unopened. He kept them all.'

Giancarlo's voice was raw with emotion. Caroline could feel tears begin to gather at the back of her eyes and she blinked them away, for the last thing a man as proud as Giancarlo would want would be any show of sympathy. Not now, not when his eyes had been ripped open to truths he had never expected.

'I expect that the only reason I received the top education that

I did was because the money was paid directly to the school. It was one of those *basics* that Alberto made sure were covered because, certainly, there seems little question that my mother would have spent it or given it away to one of her many lovers, had she had it in her possession.'

'I'm sure, in her own way, she never thought that what she was doing was bad.'

'Ever the cheerful optimist, aren't you?' He laughed harshly, but when he looked at her, his eyes were wearily amused. 'So, it would seem, is my father. Do you know, I used to wonder what you had in common with Alberto. He was a bitter and twisted old man with no time for anyone but himself. You were young and innocent. Seems you two have more in common than I ever imagined. He, too, told me the same thing—my mother was unhappy. He worked too hard. She was bored. He blamed himself for not being around sufficiently to build up a relationship with me and she took advantage of that. She took advantage of his pride, threatened to air all their dirty linen in public if he tried to pursue custody, convinced him that he had failed as a father and that visits would be pointless and disruptive. I was her trump card and she used me to get back at him.

'God, do you know that when she died, Alberto requested to see me via a lawyer and I knocked him back? She behaved badly, she warped my attitudes, but the truth is she was a simple waitress who was plucked from obscurity and deposited into a lifestyle with which she was unfamiliar and ill at ease. The whole thing was a mess. *Is* still a mess. Alberto didn't know the extent of his financial losses. He's relied on his trusted accountant for the past ten years and he's been kept pretty much in the dark about the true nature of the company accounts. Of course, like a bull in a china shop, that was one of my choice opening observations.'

'Stop blaming yourself, Giancarlo. You were a child when you left here. You weren't to know that things weren't as they seemed. Was…was Alberto okay when he heard? I guess in a way it's quite a good thing that you came along to tell him, because if you hadn't none of these secrets would have ever emerged. He's old. How good is it for the two of you that all these truths have come out? How much better for you both to have reached a place where new beginnings can start, even though the price you've both paid has been so high?'

This time Giancarlo offered her a crooked smile. 'I suppose that's one upbeat way of looking at it.'

'And I know the situation between you hasn't been *ideal*, but when it comes to Alberto and the money, how much worse for him to have been called into an impersonal office somewhere, told that everything he'd spent your life working for had been washed down the tubes?'

'As things turn out.' He closed his eyes briefly, giving her some stolen moments to savour the harsh, stunning contours of his face. Seeing him like this, vulnerable and flawed but brutally, fiercely honest with himself, did something strange inside her. A part of her seemed to connect with him in a way that was scary and thrilling.

'As things turn out?' she prompted, while her mind drifted to things going on in her head that made her heart beat faster and her pulses race. Could she be *falling* for the guy? Surely not? She would be crazy to do something like that, and she wasn't crazy. But he made her feel *alive*, took her to a different level where all her emotions and senses were amplified in a way that was new and dangerous but also wonderful.

'As things turn out, reparation is long overdue. I don't blame my mother for the things she did. She was who she was, and I have to accept my own portion of responsibility for failing to question when I was old enough to do so.' He held his hand up as though to forestall an argument, although the last thing Caroline was about to do was argue with him. First and foremost, she wanted to get her thoughts in order. She looked at him with a slightly glazed expression.

'Right,' she said slowly, blinking and nodding her head

thoughtfully. She noticed that, even having been at the bottle, he was still in control of all his faculties, still able to rationalise his thoughts in a way that many sober people couldn't. He might be ruthless with others who didn't meet his high standards, but he was also ruthless with himself, and that was an indication of his tremendous honesty and fairness. Throw killer looks into the mix, and was it any wonder that her silly, inexperienced head had been well and truly turned? Surely that natural reaction could not be confused with love.

'The least I can do—' he murmured in such a low voice that she had to strain to hear him '—and I have told Alberto this— is to get people in to sort out the company. Old friends and stalwarts are all well and good, but it appears that they have allowed time to do its worst. Whatever it takes, it will be restored to its former glory and an injection of new blood will ensure that it remains there. And there will be no transfer of title. My father will continue to own his company, along with his villa, which I intend to similarly restore.'

Caroline smiled without reservation. 'I'm so glad to hear that, Giancarlo.'

'You mean, you aren't going say "I told you so", even though you did?'

'I would never say anything like that.'

'Do you know, I'm inclined to believe you.'

'I'm really glad I came downstairs,' she confessed honestly. 'It took me ages to fall asleep and then I woke up and wanted to know that everything was all right, but I wasn't sure what to do.'

'Would you believe me if I told you that I'm glad you came downstairs too?'

Caroline found that she was holding her breath. He was staring at her with brooding intensity and she couldn't drag her fascinated eyes away from his face. Without realising it, she was leaning forwards, every nerve in her body straining towards him, like a flower reaching towards a source of heat and light.

'Really?'

'Really,' Giancarlo said wryly. 'I'm not the sort of man who thinks there's anything to be gained by soul searching but you appear to have a talent for listening.'

'And, also, drink lowers inhibitions,' Caroline felt compelled to add, although she was flushed with pleasure.

'This is true.'

'So what happens next?' Caroline asked breathlessly. She envisaged him heading off to sort out companies and a bottomless void seemed to open up at her feet. 'I mean, are you going to be leaving soon?' she heard herself ask.

'For once, work is going to be put on hold.' Giancarlo looked at her lazily. 'I have a house on the coast.'

'So you said.'

'A change of scenery might well work wonders with Alberto and it would give us time to truly put an uncomfortable past behind us.'

'And would I stay here to look after the villa?'

'Would that be what you wanted?'

'No! I… I need to be with Alberto. It's part of my job, you know, to make sure that he's okay.' Silence descended. Into it, memories of that passing passion on the boat dropped until her head was filled with images of them together. Her pupils dilated and she couldn't say a word. She was dimly aware that she was shamelessly staring at him, way beyond the point of politeness.

She was having an out-of-body experience. At least, that was what it seemed like and so it felt perfectly natural to reach out, just extend her hand a little and trace the outline of his face.

'Don't touch, Caroline.' He continued to look at her with driving intensity. 'Unless you're prepared for the consequences. Are you?'

CHAPTER SEVEN

CAROLINE PROPPED HERSELF up on one elbow and stared at Giancarlo. He was dozing. Due to the throes of love-making, the sheets had become a wildly crumpled silken mass that was draped half-on, half-off the bed, and in the silvery moonlight, his long, muscular limbs in repose were like the silhouettes of a perfectly carved fallen statue. She itched to touch them. Indeed, she could feel the tell-tale throb between her legs and the steady build-up of dampness that longed for the touch of his mouth, his hands, his exploring fingers.

He had asked her, nearly a fortnight ago, whether she was prepared for the consequences. Yes! Caroline hadn't thought twice. Of course, that first time—and, heck, it seemed like a million years ago—they hadn't made love. Not properly. He was scrupulous when it came to contraception. No, they had touched each other and she had never known that touching could be so mind-blowing. He had licked every inch of her body, had teased her with his tongue, invaded every private inch of her until she had wanted to pass out.

For Caroline, there had been no turning back.

The few days originally planned by Giancarlo for his visit had extended into two weeks and counting, for he had taken it upon himself to personally oversee the ground changes that needed to be made to Alberto's company. With the authority of command, he had snapped his fingers and in had marched an army of his loyal workforce, who had been released into the company like ants, to work their magic. They stayed at one of the top hotels in the nearby town while Giancarlo remained at the villa, taking his time to try and rebuild a relationship that had been obliterated over time. He would vanish for much of the day, returning early evening, where a routine of sorts had settled into place.

Alberto would always be found in his usual favourite chair in the sitting-room, where Giancarlo would join him for a drink, while upstairs Caroline would ready herself with pounding heart for that first glimpse of Giancarlo of the day.

Alberto didn't suspect a thing. It was in Caroline's nature to be open and honest, and she was guiltily aware that what she was enjoying was anything but a straightforward relationship. The fact that she and Giancarlo had met under very strange circumstances and that, were it not for those strange circumstances, their paths would never have been destined to cross, was an uneasy truth always playing at the back of her mind. She preferred not to dwell on that, however. What was the point? From that very moment when she had closed her eyes and offered her lips to him, there had been no going back.

So late at night, with Alberto safely asleep, she would creep into Giancarlo's bedroom, or he would come to her, and they would talk softly, make love and then make love all over again like randy teenagers who couldn't get enough of one another.

'You're staring at me.' Giancarlo had always found it irritating when women stared at him, as though he was some kind of poster-boy pin-up, the equivalent of the brainless blonde bimbo. He had found, though, that he could quite happily bask in Caroline's openly appreciative gaze. When they were with Alberto and he felt her eyes slide surreptitiously over him, it was a positive turn-on. On more than one occasion he had had to fight the desire to drag her from the room and make love to her wherever happened to be convenient, even if it was a broom cupboard under the stairs. Not that such a place existed in the villa. 'Was I?'

'I like it. Shall I give you a bit more to stare at?' Lazily, he shrugged off the sheet so that his nakedness was fully exposed and Caroline sighed softly and shuddered.

With a groan of rampant appreciation, Giancarlo reached out for her and felt her willingly fall into his arms. He opened his eyes, pulled her on top of him and ground her against him so that she could feel the rock-hard urgency of his erection. As she propped herself up on his chest, her long hair tumbled in a curtain around her heart-shaped face. Roving eyes took in the full pout of her mouth, the sultry passion in her eyes, the soft swing of her generous breasts hanging down, big nipples almost touching his chest.

What was it about this woman's body that drove him to distraction?

They had made love only an hour before and he was ready to go again; incredible. He pulled her down to him so that he could kiss her, and now she no longer needed any prompting to move her body in just the right way so that he felt himself holding on by a slither.

'You're a witch,' he growled, tumbling her under him in one easy move, and Caroline smiled with satisfaction, like the cat that not only had got the cream but had managed to work out where there was an unlimited supply.

He pushed her hair back so that he could sweep kisses along her neck while she squirmed under him.

The thrill of anticipation was running through her like a shot of adrenaline. She couldn't seem to get enough of his mouth on her, and as he closed his lips around one nipple she moaned softly and fell back, arms outstretched, to receive the ministrations of his tongue playing against the erect bud of her nipple. She arched back and curled her fingers in his hair as he sucked and suckled, teasing and nipping until the dampness between her legs became pleasurably painful.

She wrapped her legs around him and as he began moving against her she gave a little cry of satisfaction.

They had arrived at his house on the coast only two days previously, and although it wasn't nearly as big as the villa it was still big enough to ensure perfect privacy when it came to being noisy. Alberto and Tessa were in one wing of the house, she and Giancarlo in the other. It was an arrangement that Caroline had been quick to explain, pointing out in too much detail that it was far more convenient for Tessa to be readily at hand, and the layout of the villa predicated those sleeping arrangements. She had been surprised when Alberto had failed to put up the expected argument, simply shrugging his shoulders and waving her lengthy explanation away.

'Not so fast, my sexy little witch.' Giancarlo paused in his ministrations to stare down at her bare breasts, which never failed to rouse a level of pure primal lust he had hitherto not experienced with any other woman. The circular discs of her nipples were large and dark and he could see the paleness of her skin where the sun hadn't reached. It was incredibly sexy. He leant down and licked the underside of her breasts, enjoying the feel of their weight against his face, then he traced a path down her flat stomach to circle her belly button with his tongue. She was salty with perspiration, as he was, even though it was a cool night and the background whirr of the fan was efficiently circulating the air.

Caroline breathed in sharply, anticipating and thrilling to what was to come, then releasing her breath in one long moan as his tongue flicked along the pulsating sensitised tip of her clitoris, endlessly repeating the motion until she wanted to scream.

In a mindless daze, she looked down at the dark head buried between her thighs and the eroticism of the image was so powerful that she shuddered.

She could barely endure the agony of waiting as, finally, he slipped on protection and entered her in a forceful thrust that sent waves of blissful sensation crashing through her. His hands were under her buttocks as he continued to drive into her, his motions deep and rhythmic. The wave of sensation peaked, and she stiffened and whimpered, her eyes fluttering shut as she was carried away to eventually sag, pleasurably sated, on the bed next to him.

Similarly spent, Giancarlo rolled off her and lay flat, one arm splayed wide, the other clasped around her.

Not for the first time, Caroline was tempted to ask him where they were going, what lay around the corner for the two of them. Surely something that was as good as this wasn't destined to end?

And just as quickly she bit back the temptation. She had long given up on the convenient delusion that what she felt for Giancarlo was nothing more than a spot of healthy lust. Yes, it was lust, but it was lust that was wrapped up in love—and instinctively she knew that love, insofar as it applied to Giancarlo, was a dangerous emotion, best not mentioned.

All she could do was hope that day by day she was becoming an indispensable part of his life.

Certainly, they enjoyed each other's company. He made her laugh and he had told her countless times that she was unique. Unique and beautiful. Surely that meant something?

She steered clear of perilous thoughts to say drowsily, 'I've got to get back to my room. It's late and I'm really, really tired...'

'Too tired for a bath?'

Caroline giggled and shifted in little movements so that she was curled against him. 'Your baths are not good for a girl who needs to get to sleep.'

'Now, what would make you say that?' But he grinned at her as she delicately hid a yawn.

'Not many women fall asleep on me,' he said sternly and she smiled up at him.

'Is that because you tell them that they're not allowed to?'

'It's because they never get the chance. I've never been a great fan of post-coital situations.'

'Why is that?' Thin ice stretched out in front of her because she knew that she could easily edge towards a conversation that might be off-limits with him. 'Is that because too much conversation equals too much involvement?'

'What's brought this on?'

Caroline shrugged and flopped back against the pillows. 'I just want to know if I'm another in a long line of women you sleep with but aren't really involved with.'

'I'm not about to get embroiled in a debate on this. Naturally, I've conversed with the women I've dated. Over dinner. After dinner. On social occasions. But my time after we've made love has been for me. I've never encouraged lazing around between the sheets chatting about nothing in particular.'

'Why not? And don't tell me that I ask too many questions. I'm just curious, that's all.'

'Remember what they say about curiosity and cats...'

'Oh, forget it!' Caroline suddenly exploded. 'It was just a simple question. You get so defensive if someone asks you something you don't want to hear.'

Giancarlo discovered that his gut instinct wasn't to ditch the conversation, even though he didn't like where it was going. What did she expect him to say?

'Maybe I've never found the woman I wanted to have chats with in bed...' he murmured softly, drawing her back to him and feeling her relent in his arms. 'Let's not argue,' he said persuasively. 'This riviera is waiting to be explored.'

'Are you sure you can take all that time off work?'

'Surprisingly, I'm beginning to realise the considerable benefits of the World Wide Web. My father may be a dinosaur when it comes to anything technological, but it's working wonders for me. Almost as good as being at an office but with the added advantage of having a sexy woman I can turn to whenever I want.'

He smoothed his big hands along her waist then up to gently caress the softness of one of her breasts.

'*And* you're teaching him.' Caroline was glad to put that moment of discomfort behind them. Questions might be jostling for room in her head but she didn't want to argue. She didn't want to explore the outcome of any arguments. 'He's really enjoying those lessons,' she confided, running her hand along his shoulder and liking the hard feel of muscle and sinew. 'I think he finds the whole experience of having a son rather wonderful. In fact, I know *you* feel maybe a bit guilty that you lived with a past that wasn't quite what you thought it was, but he feels guilty too.'

'He's told you that?'

'He called himself a proud old fool the other day when we were out in the garden, which is his way of regretting that he never got in touch with you over the years.' She glanced behind Giancarlo to where the clock on the ornate bedside table was informing her that it was nearly two in the morning. Her eyelids felt heavy. Should she just grab fifteen minutes of sleep before she trudged back to her bedroom? The warmth of Giancarlo's body next to her dulled her senses but she began edging her way out of the bed.

'Stay,' he urged, pulling her back to him.

'Don't be silly.' Caroline yawned.

'Alberto doesn't get up until at least eight in the morning and by the time he gets his act together it's more like ninethirty before he makes an appearance in the breakfast room. You can be up at seven and back in your room by five past.' He grinned wolfishly at her. 'And isn't the thought of early-morning sex tempting…?' The suggestion had come from nowhere. If he didn't encourage after-sex chat, he'd never encouraged any woman to stay the night. In fact, no one ever had.

He was playing truant from his real life. At least, that was what it felt like, and why shouldn't he enjoy the time out, at least for a little while? Having been driven all his adult life, having poured all his energies into the business of making money, which had been an ambition silently foisted onto him by his mother, why the hell shouldn't he now take time out under these extraordinary circumstances?

Neither he nor his father had been inclined to indulge in lengthy, analytical conversations about the past. In time and at leisure, they could begin to fill in the gaps, and Giancarlo was looking forward to that. For the moment, Alberto had explained what needed to be explained, and his scattered reminiscences had built a picture of sorts for Giancarlo, a more balanced picture than the one he had been given as a child growing up, but the blame game hadn't been played. After an initial surge of anger at his mother and at himself, Giancarlo was now more accepting of the truth that the past couldn't be changed and so why beat himself up over the unchangeable?

However, he could afford to withdraw from the race for a few weeks, and he wanted to. If Alberto had lost his only child for all those years, then Giancarlo had likewise been deprived of his father and it was a space he was keen to fill. Slowly, gradually, with them both treading the same path of discovery and heading in the same direction.

His thoughts turned to Caroline, so much a part of the complex tableau...

Acting out of character by asking her to spend the night with him was just part and parcel of his time out.

He could feel her sleepily deliberating his proposal. To help her along with her decision, he curved one big hand over her breast and softly massaged the generous swell. Tired she might very well be, and spent after their urgent, hungry love-making, but still her nipple began to swell and pulse as he gently rolled his thumb over the tip.

'Not fair,' Caroline murmured.

'Since when would you expect me to play fair?'

'You can't always get what you want.'

'Why not? Don't you want to wake up in the morning with

me touching you like this? Or like this?' He slid his hand down to the damp patch between her legs and slowly stroked her, on and on until she felt her breathing begin to quicken.

Giancarlo watched her face as he continued to pleasure her, enjoyed her heightened colour and then, a whole lot more, enjoyed her as she moved against his fingers, her body gently grinding until she came with a soft, startled gasp.

There seemed to be no end to his enjoyment of her body and he had ceased to question the strange pull she had over him. He just knew that he wanted her here with him in his bed because he wanted to wake up next to her.

'Okay. You win and I lose.' Caroline sighed. She shouldn't. She knew that. She was just adding to the house of cards she had fabricated around herself. She loved him and it was just so easy to overlook the fact that the word *love* had never crossed his lips. It shamed her to think how glad she was to have him, whatever the price she would have to pay later.

He kissed her eyelids shut; she was *so* tired...

The next time Caroline opened her eyes, it was to sunshine pouring through the open slats of the wooden shutters. She swam up to full consciousness and to the weight of Giancarlo's arm sprawled possessively over her breasts. Their tangled nakedness galvanised her into immediate action and she leapt out of the bed as he groggily came to and tried to tug her back down to him.

'Giancarlo!' she said with dismay. 'It's after seven! I have to go!'

Fully awake, Giancarlo slung his long legs over the side of the bed and killed the instinct to drag her back to him, to hell with the consequences. She was anxiously scouring the ground for her clothes and he sat for a while on the side of the bed to watch her.

'Are you looking for these, by any chance?' He held up her bra, a very unsexy cotton contraption which led him to think that he would quite like to buy her an entirely new set of lingerie, stuff that he would personally choose, sexy, lacy stuff that would look great on her fabulously lush body.

Caroline tried to swipe them and missed as he whipped them just out of reach.

'You'll have to pay a small penalty charge if you want your bra,' he chided. Sitting on the edge of the bed with her standing in front of him put her at just the perfect height for him to nuzzle her breast.

'We haven't got time!' She tried to slap him away and grab her bra, but put up next to no struggle when he yanked her on top of him and rolled her back on the bed.

'I'll shock you at how fast I can be.'

Fast and just as blissfully, sinfully satisfying. It was past seven-thirty as Caroline quietly opened the bedroom door.

She knew that she was unnecessarily cautious because Giancarlo was right when he had pointed out that his father was a late riser. Very early on in her stay, Alberto had told her that he saw no point in rushing in the morning.

'Lying in bed for as long as you want in the morning,' he had chuckled, 'is the happy prerogative of the teenager and the old man like myself. It's just about the only time I feel like a boy again!'

So the very last thing she expected as she opened the door and let herself very quietly out of Giancarlo's bedroom was to hear Alberto say from behind her, 'And what do we have *here*, my dear?'

Caroline froze and then turned around. She could feel the hot sting of guilt redden her cheeks. Alberto, walking stick in hand, was looking at her with intense curiosity.

'Correct me if I'm wrong, but isn't that my *son's* bedroom?'

He invested the word *bedroom* with such heavy significance that Caroline was lost for words.

'I thought you would still be asleep,' was all she could manage to dredge from her befuddled mind. He raised his bushy eyebrows inquisitively.

'Do you mean that you *hoped* I would still be asleep?'

'Alberto, I can explain...'

As she racked her brains to try and come up with an explanation, she was not aware of Giancarlo quietly opening the bedroom door she had previously shut behind her.

'No point. My father wasn't born yesterday. I'm sure he can jump to all the right conclusions.'

As if to underline his words, Caroline spun round to find that Giancarlo hadn't even bothered to get dressed. He had stuck on his dressing gown, a black silk affair which was only loosely belted at the waist. Was he wearing anything *at all* underneath? she wondered, subduing a frantic temptation to laugh like a maniac. Or would some slight shift expose him in all his wonderful naked glory? Surely not.

The temptation to laugh gave way to the temptation to groan out loud and bash her head against the wall.

Alberto was looking between them. 'I'm not sure how to deal with this shock,' he said weakly, glancing around him for support and finally settling on the dado rail. 'This is not what I expected from either of you!'

'I'm so sorry.' Caroline's voice was thin and pleading. She was suddenly very ashamed of herself. She was in her twenties and yet she felt like a teenager being reprimanded.

'Son, I'll be honest with you—I'm very disappointed.' He shook his head sadly on a heavy sigh and Giancarlo and Caroline remained where they were, stunned. Giancarlo, however, was the first to snap out of it. He took two long strides down the corridor, where a balmy early-morning breeze rustled against the louvres and made the pale voile covering them billow provocatively.

'Papa...'

Alberto, who had turned away, stopped in his unsteady progress back to his wing of the house and tilted his head to one side.

Giancarlo too temporarily paused. It was the first time he

had used that word, the first time he had called him 'Papa' as opposed to Alberto.

'Look, I know what you're probably thinking.' Giancarlo raked his fingers through his bed-tousled hair and shook his head in frustration.

'I very much doubt you do, son,' Alberto said mournfully. 'I know I'm a little old-fashioned when it comes to these things, and I do realise that this is your house and you are a grown man fully capable of making his own rules under his own roof, but just tell me this—how long? How long has this been going on? Were you two misbehaving while you were in the villa?'

'*Misbehaving* is not exactly what I would term it,' Giancarlo said roughly, his face darkly flushed, but Alberto was looking past him to where Caroline was dithering on legs that felt like jelly by the louvred window.

'When your parents sent you over to Italy, I very much think that this is not the sort of thing they would have expected,' he told her heavily, which brought on another tidal wave of excruciating guilt in her. 'They entrusted your well-being to me, and by that I'm sure they were not simply referring to your nutritional well-being.'

'Papa, enough.' Giancarlo plunged his hands into the deep pockets of his dressing gown. 'Caroline's well-being is perfectly safe with me. We are both consenting adults and...'

'Pah!' Alberto waved his hand impatiently.

'We're not idiots who haven't stopped to consider the consequences.' Giancarlo's voice was firm and steady and Alberto narrowed his eyes on his son.

'Carry on.'

Caroline was mesmerised. She had inched her way forwards, although Giancarlo's back was still to her, a barrier against the full force of Alberto's disappointment.

'I may have been guilty in the past of fairly random relationships...' Just one confidence shared with his father after several drinks. 'But Caroline and I…er…have something different.' He glanced over his shoulder towards her. 'Don't we?'

'Um?'

'In fact, only yesterday we were discussing where we were going with what we have here…'

'Ah. You mean that you're serious? Well, that's a completely different thing. Caroline, I feel I know you well enough to suspect that you're the marrying kind of girl. I'm taking it that marriage no less is what we're talking about here?' He beamed at them, while a few feet away Caroline's jaw dropped open and she literally goggled like a goldfish.

'Marriage changes everything. I might be old but I'm not unaware of the fact that young people are, shall we say, a little more experimental before marriage than they were in my day. I can't believe you two never breathed a word of this to me.'

He chose to give them no scope for interruption. 'But I have eyes in my head, my boy! Could tell from the way you're relaxed here, a changed man, not to put too fine a point on it. And, as for Caroline, well, she's so skittish when she's around you. All the signs were there. I can't tell you what this means to me, after my brush with the grim reaper!'

'Er, Alberto…'

'You get to my age and you need to have something to hold on to, especially after my heart attack. In fact, I think I might need to rest just now after all this excitement. I wish you'd told me instead of letting me find out for myself, not that the end result isn't the same!'

'We didn't say anything because we didn't want to unduly excite you.' Giancarlo strolled back to her and proceeded to sling his arm over her shoulder, dislodging the robe under which he was thankfully decently clad in some silk boxers. 'It's been a peculiar time, why muddy the waters unnecessarily?'

'Yes, I see that!' Alberto proclaimed with an air of satisfaction. 'I'm thrilled. You must know by now, Giancarlo, that

I think the world of your fiancée. Can I call you that now, my dear?'

Fiancée? Engaged? Getting married? Had she been transported into some kind of freaky parallel universe?

'We were going to break it to you over dinner tonight,' Giancarlo announced with such confidence that Caroline could only marvel at his capacity for acting. How much deeper was he going to dig this hole? she wondered.

'Of course, you two will want to have some time off to do the traditional thing—buy a ring. I could come with you,' Alberto tacked on hopefully. 'I know it's a private and personal thing, but I can't think of a single thing that would fill me with more of a sense of hope and optimism, a reason for *going on*.'

'A reason for going on where?' Tessa demanded, striding up towards them. 'You're worse than a puppy off a leash, Alberto! I told you to wait for me and I would help you down to the breakfast room.'

'Do I look as though I need help, woman?' He waggled his cane at her. 'Another week and I won't even need this damnable piece of tomfoolery to get around! And, not that it's part of your job description to be nosing around, but these two love birds are going to be married!'

'When?' Tessa asked excitedly, while she did something with Alberto's shirt, tried to rearrange the collar; predictably he attempted to shoo her away.

'Good question, my shrewish nurse. Have you two set a date yet?'

Finally, Caroline's tongue unglued itself from the roof of her mouth. She stepped out of Giancarlo's embrace and folded her arms. 'No, we certainly haven't, Alberto. And I think we should stop talking about this. It's…um…still in the planning stage.'

'You're right. We'll talk later, perhaps over a dinner, something special.' Alberto glowered at Tessa, who smiled serenely back at him. 'Get in a couple of bottles of the finest champagne, woman, and don't even think of giving me your "demon drink" lecture. Tonight we celebrate and I fully intend to have a glass with something drinkable in it when we make a toast!'

'Okay,' Giancarlo said, once his father and Tessa had safely disappeared down the stairs and out towards the stunning patio that overlooked the crystal-clear blue of the sea from its advantageous perch on the side of the hill. 'So what else was I supposed to do? I feel like I'm meeting my father for the first time. How could I jeopardise his health, ruin his excitement? You heard him, this gives him something to cling to.'

Caroline felt as though she had done several stomach-churning loops on a roller-coaster which had slackened speed, but only temporarily, with the threat of more to come over the horizon.

'What else were you *supposed to do*?' she parroted incredulously. Engagement? Marriage? All the stuff that was so important to her, stuff that she took really seriously, was for Giancarlo no more than a handy way of getting himself out of an awkward situation.

'My mother slept around,' Giancarlo told her abruptly, flushing darkly. 'I knew she wasn't the most virtuous person on the face of the earth. She was never afraid of introducing her lovers to me but she was single, destroyed after a bad marriage, desperate for love and affection. Little did I know at the time that her capacity for sleeping around had started long before her divorce. She was very beautiful and very flighty. My father refrained from using the word *amoral*, but I'm guessing that that's what he thought.

'Here I am now. The estranged son back on the scene. I'm trying to build something out of nothing because I want a relationship with my father. Finding out that we're sleeping together, him thinking that it's nothing but a fly-by-night romance, well, how high do you think his opinion is going to be of me? How soon before he begins drawing parallels between me and my mother?'

'That's silly,' Caroline said gently. 'Alberto's not like that.' But how far had Giancarlo come? It wasn't that long ago that he had agreed to see Alberto purely for the purpose of revenge. He felt himself on fragile ground now. His plans had unravelled on all sides, truths had been exposed and a past rewritten. She could begin to see why he would do anything within his power not to jeopardise the delicate balance.

But at what price?

She had idiotically flung herself into something that had no future and when she should be doing all she could to redress the situation—when, in short, she should be pulling back—here she now was, even more deeply embedded and through no fault of her own.

The smell of him still clinging to her was a forceful reminder of how dangerous he could prove to be emotionally.

'If I dragged you into something you didn't court, then I apologise, but I acted on the spur of the moment.'

'That's all well and good, Giancarlo,' Caroline traded with spirit. 'But it's a *crazy* situation. Alberto believes we're *engaged*! What on earth is he going to do when he finds out that it was all a sham? Did you hear what he said about this giving him something to *carry on for*?'

'I heard,' Giancarlo admitted heavily. 'So the situation is not ideal. I realise it's a big favour, but I'm asking you to play along with it for a while.'

'Yes, but for how long?' A pretend engagement was a mocking, cruel reminder of what she truly wanted—which, shamefully, was a real engagement, excited plans for the future with the man she loved, *real* plans for a *real* future.

'How long is a piece of string? I'm not asking you to put your life on hold, but to just go with the flow for this window in time—after all, many engagements end in nothing.' Giancarlo propped himself up against the wall and glanced distractedly out towards breathtaking scenery, just snatches of it he could glimpse through the open shutters. 'In the meantime, anything could happen.' Why, he marvelled to himself, was this sitting so comfortably with him?

'You mean Alberto will come to accept that you're nothing like your mother, even though it's in your nature to have flings with women and then chuck them when you get bored?'

'Yet again your special talent for getting right to the heart of the matter,' Giancarlo gritted.

'But it's true, isn't it? Oh, I guess you could soft-soap him with something about us drifting apart, not really being suited to one another.'

'Breaking news—people *do* drift apart, people *do* end up in relationships only to find that they weren't suited to each other in the first place.'

'But you're different.' Caroline stubbornly stood her ground. 'You don't give people a chance. Relationships with you never get to the point where you drift apart because they're rigged to explode long before then!'

'Is this your way of telling me that you have no intention of going along with this? That, although we've been sleeping together, you don't approve of me?'

'That's not what I'm saying!'

'Then explain. Because if you want me to tell Alberto the truth, that we're just having a bit of fun, then I will do that right now and we will both live with the consequences.'

And the consequences would be twofold: the fledgling relationship Giancarlo was building with his father would be damaged—not terminally, although Giancarlo could very well predetermine an outcome he might gloomily predict. And, of course, Alberto would be disappointed in her as well.

'I feel boxed in,' Caroline confessed. 'But I guess it won't be for long.' Would she have been able to sail through the pretence if her heart hadn't been at stake? She would have thought so, but if she felt vulnerable then it was something she would have to put up with, and who else was to blame if not herself? Had she ever thought that what she had with Giancarlo qualified for a happy-ever-after ending? 'I feel awful about deceiving your father, though.'

'Everyone deserves the truth, but sometimes a little white lie is a lot less harmful.'

'But it's not really *little*, is it?'

Giancarlo maintained a steady silence. It was beginning to dawn on him that he didn't know her as well as he had imagined. Or maybe he had arrogantly assumed that their very satisfying physical relationship would have guaranteed her willingness to fall in with what he wanted.

'Nor is it really a lie,' he pointed out softly. 'What we have *is* more than just a bit of fun.'

With all her heart, Caroline wanted to believe him, but caution allied with a keen sense of self-preservation prevented her from exploring that tantalising observation. How much *more* than just a bit of fun? she wanted to ask. How much did he *really* feel for her? Enough to one day love her?

She felt hopelessly vulnerable just thinking like that; she felt as though he might be able to see straight into her head and pluck out her most shameful, private thoughts and desires. She wondered whether he had not dangled that provocative statement to win her over. Giancarlo would not be averse to a little healthy manipulation if he thought it might suit his own ends. But he needn't have bothered trying to butter her up, she thought gloomily. There was no way that she could ever conceive of jeopardising what had been a truly remarkable turnaround between father and son. She would have had to be downright heartless to have done so.

'Okay,' she agreed reluctantly. 'But not for long, Giancarlo.'

Lush lashes lowered over his eyes, shielding his expression. 'No,' he murmured. 'We'll take it one day at a time.'

CHAPTER EIGHT

CAROLINE WISHED DESPERATELY that this new and artificial dimension to their relationship would somehow wake her up to the fact that they weren't an item. A week ago, when they had launched themselves into this charade, she had tried to get her brain to overrule her rebellious heart and pull back from Giancarlo, but within hours of Alberto's crazy misconceptions all her plans had nosedived in the face of one unavoidable truth.

They were supposedly a couple, madly in love, with the clamour of wedding bells chiming madly in the distance, so gestures of open physical affection were suddenly *de rigeur*. Giancarlo seemed to fling himself into the role of besotted lover with an enthusiasm that struck her as beyond the call of duty.

'How on earth are we ever going to find the right time to break it to your father that we're *drifting apart*, when you keep touching me every time we're together? We're not giving the impression of two people who have made a terrible mistake!' she had cried, three days previously after a lazy day spent by his infinity pool. Those slight brushes against her, the way he had held her in the water under Alberto's watchful gaze, were just brilliant at breaking down all her miserable defences. In fact, she was fast realising that she had no defences left. Now and again, she reminded herself to mutter something pointed to Giancarlo under her breath, but she was slowly succumbing to the myth they had fabricated around themselves.

'One day at a time,' he had reminded her gently.

He was beautifully, staggeringly, wonderfully irresistible and, although she *knew* that it was all a fiction which would of course backfire and injure her, she was lulled with each passing hour deeper and deeper into a feeling of treacherous happiness.

Alberto made no mention of their sleeping arrangements. Ideally, Caroline knew that she and Giancarlo should no longer be sleeping together. Ideally, she should be putting him at a distance, and sleeping with him was just the opposite of that. But every time that little voice of reason popped up, another more strident voice would take charge of the proceedings and tell her that she no longer had anything left to lose. She was with Giancarlo on borrowed time so why not just enjoy herself?

Besides, whether he was aware of it or not, he was burying all her noble intentions with his humour, his intelligence, his charm. Instead of feeling angry with him for putting her in an unenviable position with Alberto, she felt increasingly more vulnerable. With Alberto and Tessa, they explored the coastline, stopping to have lunch at any one of the little towns that clung valiantly to the hilltop from which they could overlook the limpid blue sea. Giancarlo was relaxed and lazily, heart-stoppingly attentive. Just walking hand in hand with him made her toes curl and her heart beat faster.

And now they were going to Milan for three days. The last time she had gone to Milan, her purpose for the visit had been entirely different. Today she was going because Giancarlo had stuff to do that needed his physical presence.

'I think I should stay behind,' she had suggested weakly, watching while he had unbuttoned her top and vaguely thinking that her protestations were getting weaker with every button undone.

'You're my beloved fiancée.' Giancarlo had given her a slashing smile that brooked no argument. 'You should *want* to see where I work and where I live.'

'Your *pretend* fiancée.'

'Let's not get embroiled in semantics.'

By which time he had completely undone her blouse, rendering her instantly defenceless as he stared with brazen hunger at her abundant, bra-less breasts. As he closed his eyes, spread his hands over her shoulders and took one pouting nipple into his mouth, she completely forgot what she had been saying.

By the time they made it to Milan, Caroline had had ample opportunity to see Giancarlo in work mode. They had taken the train, because Giancarlo found it more relaxing, and also because he wanted the undisturbed time to focus and prepare for the series of meetings awaiting him in Milan. An entire first-class carriage had been reserved for them and they were waited on with the reverential subservience reserved for the very wealthy and the very powerful.

This was no longer the Giancarlo who wore low-slung shorts and loafers without socks and laughed when she tried to keep up with him in the swimming pool. This was a completely different Giancarlo, as evidenced in his smart suit, a charcoal-grey, pin-striped, hand-tailored affair, the jacket of which he had tossed on one of the seats. In front of his laptop computer—frowning as he scrolled down pages and pages of reports; engaging in conference calls which he conducted in a mixture of French, English and Italian, moving fluently between the languages as he spoke with one person then another—he was a different person.

Caroline attempted to appreciate the passing scenery but time and again her eyes were drawn back to him, fascinated at this aspect to the man she loved.

'I'm just going to get in your way,' she said at one point, and he looked up at her with a slow smile.

'I hope so. Especially at night. In my bed. I definitely want you in my way then.'

It was late by the time they made it to Milan. Meetings would start in the morning, which was fine, because there was so much she wanted to see in the city that she had not found the time for on her previous visit. While Giancarlo worked, she would explore the city, and she had brought a number of guide books with her for that purpose.

Right now, as they were ushered into the chauffeur-driven car waiting for them at the station, she was just keen to see where he actually lived.

After the splendid seclusion of his villa on the coast and the peaceful tranquility of the view over the sea, the hectic frenzy of Milan, tourists and workers peopling the streets and pavements like ants on a mission, was an assault on all the senses. But it was temporary, for his apartment was in one of the small winding streets with its stunning eighteenth-century paving with a view of elegant gardens. Caroline didn't need an estate agent to tell her that she was in one of the most prestigious postcodes in the city.

The building in front of which the air-conditioned car finally stopped was the last word in elegance. A historic palace, it had clearly been converted into apartments for the ultra-wealthy and was accessed via wrought-iron gates, as intricate as lace, which led into a beautiful courtyard.

She openly goggled as Giancarlo led the way through the courtyard into the ancient building and up to his penthouse which straddled the top two floors.

He barely seemed to notice the unparalleled, secluded luxury of his surroundings. In a vibrant city, the financial beating heart of Italy, this was an oasis.

His apartment was not at all what she had expected. Where his villa on the coast was cool and airy, with louvred windows and voile curtains that let the breeze in but kept the ferocity of the sun out, this was all dark, gleaming wooden floors, rich drapes, exquisite furniture and deep, vibrant Persian rugs.

'This is amazing,' she breathed, standing still in one spot and slowly turning round in a circle so that she could take in the full entirety of the vast room into which she had been ushered.

Much more dramatically than ever before, she was struck by the huge, gaping chasm between them. Yes, they were lovers, and yes, he enjoyed her, lusted after her, desired her, couldn't keep his hands off her, but really and truly they inhabited two completely different worlds. Her parents' house was a tiny box compared to this apartment. In fact, the entire ground floor could probably have slotted neatly into the entrance hall in which she was now standing.

'I'm glad you approve.' He moved to stand behind her and wrapped his arms around her, burying his face in her long hair, breathing in the clean smell of her shampoo. She was wearing a flimsy cotton dress, with thin spaghetti straps and he slowly pulled these down, and from behind began unfastening the tiny pearl poppers. She wasn't wearing a bra and he liked that. He had long disbanded any notion of her in fine lingerie. If he had his way, she would never wear any at all.

'Show me the rest of the apartment.' She began doing up the poppers he had undone but it was a wasted mission because as fast as she buttoned them up he proceeded to unbutton them all over again.

'I'm hungry for you. I've had a long train trip with far too many people hovering in the background, making it impossible for me to touch you.'

Caroline laughed with the familiar pleasure of hearing him say things like that, things that made her feel womanly, desirable, heady and powerful all at the same time.

'Why is sex so important to you?' she murmured with a catch in her voice as he began playing with her breasts, his big body behind her so that she could lean against him, as weak as a kitten as his fingers teased the tips of her nipples into tight little buds.

'Why do you always initiate deep and meaningful conversations when you know that talking is the last thing on my mind?' But he chuckled softly. 'I should be making inroads into my reports but I can't stop wanting you for long enough,' he murmured roughly.

'I'm not sure that's a good thing.' She had arched back and was breathing quickly and unsteadily, eyes fluttering closed as he rolled the sensitised tips of her nipples between gentle fingers.

'I think it's a *very* good thing. Would you like to see my bedroom?'

'I'd like to see the *whole* apartment, Giancarlo.'

He gave an elaborate sigh and released her with grudging reluctance. He had long abandoned the urge to get to the bottom of her appeal. He just knew that, the second he was in her presence, he couldn't seem to keep his hands off her. Hell, even when she wasn't around she somehow still managed to infiltrate his brain so that images of her were never very far away. It was one reason he hadn't hesitated to ask her to accompany him to Milan. He just couldn't quite conceive not having her there when he wanted her. He also couldn't believe how much time he had taken off work. He wondered whether his body had finally caught up with him after years of being chained to the work place.

'Okay.' He stepped back, watched with his hands in his pockets as she primly and regrettably did up all those annoying little pearl buttons that ran the length of her dress. 'Guided tour of the apartment.'

While he was inclined to hurry over the details, Caroline took her time, stopping to admire every small fixture; gasping at the open fireplace in the sitting-room; stroking the soft velvet of the deep burgundy drapes; marvelling at the cunning way the modern appliances in the kitchen sat so comfortably alongside the old hand-painted Italian tiles on the wall and the exquisite kitchen table with its mosaic border and age-worn surface.

His office, likewise, was of the highest specification, geared for a man who was connected to the rest of the working world twenty-four-seven. Yet the desk that dominated the room looked to be centuries old and on the built-in mahogany shelves spanning two of the walls, first-edition books on the history of Italy nestled against law manuals and hardbacks on corporate tax.

Up a small series of squat stairs, four enormous bedrooms shared the upstairs space with a sitting-room in which resided the only television in the apartment.

'Not that I use it much,' Giancarlo commented when he saw her looking at the plasma screen. 'Business news. That's about it.'

'Oh, you're so boring, Giancarlo. *Business news!* Don't you get enough business in your daily life without having to spend your leisure time watching more of it on the telly?'

Giancarlo threw back his head and laughed, looking at her with rich appreciation. 'I don't think anyone's ever called me *boring* before. You're good for me, do you know that?'

'Like a tonic, you mean?' She smiled. 'Well, I don't think anyone has ever told me that before.'

'Come into my bedroom,' he urged her along, restlessly waiting as she poked her head into all of the bedrooms and emitted little cries of delight at something or other, details which he barely noticed from one day to the next. Yes, the tapestry on that wall behind that bed was certainly vibrant in colour; of course that tiffany lamp was beautiful and, sure, those narrow strips of stained glass on either side of the window were amazing. He couldn't wait to get her to his bedroom. He was tormented at the prospect of touching her and feeling her smooth, soft, rounded body under his hands. His loss of self-control whenever she was around still managed to astound him.

'Your mother must have been really proud of you, Giancarlo, to have seen you scale these heights.'

'Mercenary as I now discover she really was?' He shot her a crooked smile and Caroline frowned. 'How long have you been storing up that question?'

'You're so contained and I didn't want to bring up an uncomfortable subject. Not when things have been going so well between you and Alberto, yet I can't help but think that you must be upset at finding out that things weren't as you thought.'

'Less than I might have imagined,' Giancarlo confessed, linking his fingers with hers and leading her away from where she was heading towards one of the windows through which she would certainly exclaim at the view outside. It was one which still managed to impress him, and he was accustomed to it. 'Hell, I should be livid at the fact that my mother rewrote the past and determined my future to suit the rules of her own game, but...'

But he wasn't, because Caroline seemed to cushion him, seemed to be the soothing hand that was making acceptance easier. She was the softly spoken voice that blurred the edges of a bitterness that failed to surface. It made his head spin when he thought about it.

'I'm old enough to be able to put things in perspective. When I was younger, I wasn't. My youth helped determine my hardline attitude to my father but now that I'm older I see that my mother never really grew up. In a funny way, I think she would have been happier if Alberto really had been the guy she portrayed him as being. She would have found toughness easier to handle than understanding. He actually kept supporting her even when she had shown him that she was irresponsible with money, and would have taken everything and thrown it all away had Alberto not had the good sense to lock most of it up. He had bank statements going back for well over a decade.'

He hesitated. 'Three years after we left, she made an attempt to get back with my father. He turned her down. I think that was when she decided that she could punish him by making sure he never saw me.'

'How awful.' Caroline's eyes stung with sympathy but Giancarlo gave an expressive, philosophical shrug.

'It's in the past, and don't feel sorry for me. Adriana might have had dubious motivations for her behaviour—she certainly did her best to screw up whatever relationship I might have had with my father—but she could also be great fun and something of an adventurer. It wasn't all bad. She just spoke without thinking, acted without foreseeing consequences and was a little too gullible when it came to the opposite sex. In the end she was as much a victim of her own bitterness as I was.'

They had reached his bedroom and he pushed open the door, gazing with boyish satisfaction at her look of pleasure as she tentatively stepped into the vast space.

One wall was entirely dominated by a massive arched window that offered a bird's-eye view of Milan. She walked towards it, looked out and then turned round to find him watching her with a smile.

'I know you think I'm gauche.' She blushed.

'Don't worry about it. I happen to like that.'

'Everything's so *grand* in this apartment.'

'I know. I never thought it would be my style. Maybe I find it restful, considering the remainder of my life is so hectic.' He walked slowly towards her and Caroline felt that small frisson of anticipated pleasure as he held her gaze. 'It's easy to forget that the rest of the world exists outside this apartment.' He curved one hand around her waist. With the other, he unhooked the heavy taupe drape from a cord, instantly shrouding the room in semi-darkness.

He gathered her into his arms and they made love slowly. He lingered on her body, drawing every last breath of pleasure out of her, and in turn she lingered over his so that the chocolate-brown sheets and covers on the bed became twisted under their bodies as they repositioned themselves to enjoy one another.

It was dark by the time they eventually surfaced. A single phone call ensured that food was brought to them so that they could eat in the apartment, although Caroline was laughingly appalled at the fact that his fridge was bare of all but the essentials.

Despite the opulence of the decor, this was strictly a bachelor's apartment. Lazing around barefoot in one of his tee shirts, she teased him about his craziness in stocking the finest cheeses in his fridge but lacking eggs; having the best wines and yet no milk; and she pointed to all the shiny, gleaming gadgets and made him list which he was capable of using and which were never touched.

She let herself enjoy the seductive domesticity of being in his space. After a delicious dinner, they washed the dishes together—because he frankly hadn't a clue how to operate the dishwasher—and then she curled into him on the huge sofa in the sitting-room, reading while he flicked through papers with his arm lazily around her.

It all felt so right that it was easy to push away the notion that her love was making a nonsense of her pride and her common sense.

'Wake me up before you leave in the morning,' she made him promise, turning to him in bed and sliding her body against his. She had always covered herself from head to toe whenever she had gone to bed but he had changed all that. Now she slept naked and she loved the feel of his hard body against hers. When she covered his thigh with hers, the pleasure was almost unbearable.

Giancarlo grinned and kissed the corner of her mouth as she tried to disguise a delicate yawn.

'Have I worn you out?'

'You're insatiable, Giancarlo.'

'Only for you, *mi amore*, only for you.'

Caroline fell asleep clutching those words to herself, safeguarding them so that she could pull them out later and examine them for content and meaning.

When she next opened her eyes, it was to bright sunshine trying to force its way through the thick drapes. Next to her the bed was empty and a sleepy examination of the apartment revealed that Giancarlo had left. She wondered what time he had gone, and tried to squash the niggling fear that he might be going off her. Was he? Or was she reading too much in the fact that he had left without saying goodbye? It was hardly nine yet. In the kitchen, prominently displayed on the granite counter, were six eggs, a loaf of bread, some milk and a note informing her that he could be as twenty-first-century as any other man when it came to stocking his larder.

Caroline smiled. It was hardly an outpouring of emotion, but there was something weirdly pleasing about that admission, an admission of change whether he saw it as such or not. She made herself some toast and scrambled eggs, finally headed out with her guide books at a little after ten and, pleasantly exhausted after several hours doing all those touristy things she had missed out on first time around, returned with the warming expectation of seeing him later that evening.

'I might be late,' he had warned her the night before. 'But no later than eight-thirty.'

It gave her oodles of time to have a long, luxurious bath and then to inspect herself in the mirror in the new outfit she had bought that morning. It was a short flared skirt that felt lovely and silky against her bare skin and a matching vest with three tiny buttons down the front. When she left the buttons undone, as she now did, her cleavage was exposed and she knew that without a bra he would be able to see the swing of her heavy breasts and the outline of her nipples against the thin fabric.

Of course she would never go bra-less in public, not in something as thin and flimsy as this top was, but she imagined the flare in his dark eyes when he saw her and felt a lovely shiver of anticipation.

With at least another couple of hours to go, she was thrilled to hear the doorbell ring.

She was smiling as she pulled open the door. Very quickly, her smile disappeared and confusion took over.

'Who are you?'

The towering, leggy blonde with hair falling in a straight sheet to her waist spoke before Caroline had time to marshal her scattered thoughts.

'What are you doing here? Does Giancarlo know that you're here? Are you the maid? Because, if you are, then your dress code is inappropriate. Let me in. Immediately.'

She pushed back the door and Caroline stepped aside in complete bewilderment. She hadn't had time to get a single word in, and now the impossibly beautiful blonde in the elegant short silk shift with the designer bag and the high, high heels that elevated her to over six feet, was in the apartment and staring around her through narrowed, suspicious eyes which finally came to rest once more on Caroline's red, flustered face.

'So.' The blonde folded her arms and looked at Caroline imperiously. 'Explain!'

'Who *are* you?' She had to crane her neck upwards to meet the other woman's eyes. 'Giancarlo didn't tell me that he was expecting anyone.'

'*Giancarlo?* Since when is the maid on first-name terms with her employer? Wait until he hears about this.'

'I'm *not* the maid. I'm… I'm…' There was no way that he would want her to say anything along the lines of 'fiancée', not when it was a relationship fabricated for Alberto's benefit, not when it meant nothing. 'We're…involved.'

The blonde's mouth curled into a smile that got wider and wider until she was laughing with genuine incredulity, while Caroline stood frozen to the spot. Her brain seemed to have shifted down several gears and was in danger of stalling completely. Next to such stupendous beauty, she felt like a complete fool.

'You have *got* to be joking!'

'I'm not, actually.' Caroline pulled herself up to her unimpressive height of a little over five-three. 'We've been seeing each other for a few weeks now.'

'He'd never go out with someone like you,' the blonde said in an exaggeratedly patient voice, the voice of someone trying to convey the obvious to a deluded lunatic.

'Sorry?' Caroline uttered huskily.

'I'm Lucia. Giancarlo and I were an item before I broke it off a few months ago. Pressure of work. I'm a model, by the way. I hate to tell you this, but *I'm* the sort of woman Giancarlo dates.'

There was an appreciable pause during which Caroline deduced that she was to duly pay heed, take note and join the dots: Giancarlo dated models. He liked them long, leggy and blonde; short, round and brunette was not to his liking. She wished, uncharitably, that she was wearing an engagement ring, a large diamond cluster which she could thrust into the blonde's smirking face, but the trip to the jeweller's had not yet materialised despite Alberto's gentle prodding.

'Look, tell him I called, would you?'

Caroline watched as Lucia—elegant name for an elegant blonde—strutted towards the door.

'Tell him…' Lucia paused. Her cool blue eyes swept over Caroline in a dismissive once-over. 'That he was right. Crazy hours flying all over the world. Tell him that I've decided to take a rest for a while, so he can reach me whenever he wants.'

'Reach you to do *what*?' She forced the question out, although her mouth felt like cotton wool.

'What do you think?' Lucia raised her eyebrows knowingly. Despite her very blonde hair, her eyebrows were dark; a stunning contrast. 'Look, you must think I'm a bitch for saying this, but I'll say it anyway because it's for your own good. Giancarlo might be having a little fun with you because he's broken up about me, but that's all you are and it's not going to last. Do yourself a favour and get out while you can. *Ciao*, darling!'

Caroline remained where she was for a few minutes after Lucia had disappeared. Her brain felt sluggish. It was making connections and the process hurt.

This was Giancarlo's real life—beautiful women who suited his glamorous life. He had taken time out and had somehow ended up in bed with her and now she knew why. In extraordinary circumstances, he had behaved out of character, had fallen into bed with the sort of woman who under normal circumstances he would have overlooked, because she was the sort of woman he might employ as his maid.

Even more terrifying was the suspicion that she had just

been *there*, a convenient link between himself and his father. She had bridged a gap that could have been torturously difficult to bridge, and by the way had leapt into bed with him as an added bonus. He had found himself in a win-win situation and, Giancarlo being Giancarlo, he had taken full advantage of the situation. The note she had found, which she had optimistically seen as the sign of someone learning to really share, now seemed casual and dismissive, a few scribbled lines paying lip service to someone who had made his life easier; a willing bed companion who gave him the privileges of a real relationship while conveniently having expectations of none.

Caroline hurt all over. She felt ridiculous in her stupid outfit and was angry and ashamed of having dressed for him. She was mortified at the ease with which she had allowed herself to be taken over body and soul until all her waking moments revolved around him. She had dared to think the impossible— that he would love her back.

She hurried to change. Off came the silly skirt and the even sillier top. She found that her hands were shaking as she rifled through her belongings, picking out a pair of jeans and a tee shirt. It was like stepping back into her old life and back into reality. She stuffed the new outfit—which only hours before had given her such pleasure as she had looked at her reflection in the changing room of the overpriced Italian boutique—into the front pocket of her suitcase which she usually kept for her shoes and dirty clothes.

She very much wanted to run away, but she made herself turn the telly on, and there she was when an hour and a half later she heard Giancarlo slot his key into the door.

She had a horrid image of herself in her silly outfit, scampering to the front door like a perfectly trained puppy greeting its master, and she forced herself to remain exactly where she was in front of the television until he walked into the sitting-room. As he strolled towards her, with that killer smile curving his mouth, he began loosening his tie and unbuttoning his shirt.

Bitter and disillusioned as she was, Caroline still couldn't contain her body's instinctive reaction, and she strove to quell the feverish race of her pulse and the familiar drag on her senses. She pulled up the image of the blonde and focused on that.

'You have no idea how much I've been looking forward to coming back…' Tie undone, he tossed it onto one of the sofas and walked towards her, leaning down over the chair into which she was huddled, his arms braced on either side, caging her in.

Caroline had trouble breathing.

'Really?'

'Really. You're very bad for me. Somehow trying to work out the logistics of due diligence is a lot less fun than thinking about you waiting for me back here.'

Like a faithful, mindless puppy.

'I left my chief in command at the meeting. The option of seeing you here, well, it wasn't a difficult choice.'

Seeing me here…in your bed…

'Food first? My man at the Capello can deliver within the hour.'

Because why would you take me out and cut into the time you can spend in bed with me? Before you get bored, because I'm nothing like the girls you want to date, girls who look good hanging on your arm… Long, leggy girls with waist-length blonde hair and exotic, sexy names like Lucia…

'You're not talking.' Giancarlo vaulted upright and strolled towards the closest chair, where he sat and then leaned forwards, his arms on his thighs. 'I'm sorry I couldn't go sightseeing with you today. Believe me, I would have loved to have shown you my city. Were you bored?'

Caroline unfroze and rediscovered the power of speech. 'I had a very nice time. I visited the Duomo, the museum and I had a very nice lunch in one of the *piazzas*.'

'I'm guessing that there's a 'but' tacked on to that description of your *very nice* day with the *very nice* lunch?' Something was going on here. Giancarlo could feel it, although he was at a loss to explain it.

He had woken next to her at a ridiculously early hour and had paused to look at her perfectly contented face as she slept on her side, one arm flung up, her hands balled into fists, the way a baby would sleep. She had looked incredibly young, and incredibly tempting. He had had to resist the urge to wake her at the ungodly hour of five-thirty to make love. Instead he had taken a cold shower and had spent most of the day counting down to when he would walk through the front door. Never before could he remember having such a craving to return to his apartment. 'Wherever he laid his hat' had never been his definition of home.

He frowned as a sudden thought occurred to him.

'Did something happen today?' he asked slowly. 'I take no responsibility for my fellow Italians, but it's not unheard of for some of them to be forward with tourists. Did you get into some bother while you were sightseeing? Someone follow you? Made a nuisance of himself?' He could feel himself getting hot under the collar, and he clenched and unclenched his fists at the distasteful thought of someone pestering her, making her day out a misery.

'Something *did* happen,' Caroline said quietly, her eyes sliding away from him because even the sight of him was enough to scramble her brains. 'But nothing like what you're saying. I didn't get into any bother when I was out. And, by the way, even if someone *had* made a nuisance of himself I'm not a complete idiot. I would have been able to handle the situation.'

'What, then?'

'I had a visit.' This time she rested her eyes steadily on his beautiful face. A person could drown in those dark, fathomless eyes, she thought. Hadn't *she*?

'A visit *here*?'

Caroline nodded. 'Tall. Leggy. Blonde. You might know who I mean. Her name was Lucia.'

CHAPTER NINE

GIANCARLO STILLED.

'Lucia was *here*?' he asked tightly. The hard lines of his face reflected his displeasure. Lucia Fontana was history, one of his exes who had taken their break-up with a lot less grace than most. She was a supermodel at the height of her career, accustomed to men lusting after her, paying homage to her beauty, contriving to be in her presence. She was also, in varying degrees, annoying, superficial, vain, self-centred and lacking in anything that could be loosely termed *intelligence*. She had met him at a business function, an art exhibition which had been attended by the glitterati, and she had pursued him. His mistake had been lazily to go along for the ride. 'What the hell was she doing here?'

'Not expecting to find *me*,' Caroline imparted tonelessly. She toyed with the idea of telling him that the blonde had, at first, assumed that she was the maid, the hired help dressed inappropriately for the job of scrubbing floors and cleaning the toilets. She decided to keep that mortifying titbit to herself.

'I apologise for that. Don't worry. It won't happen again.'

Caroline shrugged. Did he expect her to be grateful for that heartening promise, just because she happened to be the flavour of the month, locked in a situation which neither of them

could ever have foreseen? She felt an uncharacteristic temptation to snort with disgust.

'I expect there's probably a whole barrel-load of them lurking
in the woodwork, waiting to crawl out at any minute.'

'What the hell are you talking about?'

'Women. Exes. Glamorous supermodels you threw over or,
in the case of this one, a glamorous supermodel who threw
you over.'

'Lucia? Did she tell you that she left me?' Giancarlo felt a
surge of white-hot rage rip through him. He knew that he had
badly dented her ego when he had dumped her, but the thought
of her coming to his apartment and lying through her pearly-
white teeth made him see red.

'Well, I guess it must have been difficult for her to conduct a
relationship with someone when she was travelling all over the
place, but she said that she's back now and you can contact her
whenever you want. Pick up where you left off.'

No; he was not going to start explaining himself. No way.
That was a road he had never been down and he wasn't about
to go down it now. It just wasn't in his nature to justify his behaviour, not that he had anything *to* justify!

'And this is what you'll be expecting me to do, is it?' he
asked coolly.

Caroline felt her heart breaking in two. She hadn't realised
how much she had longed to hear him deny everything the other
woman had said. His silence on the subject was telling. Okay,
so maybe he wasn't going to race over to Lucia's apartment and
fling himself at her feet, but surely if the other woman had been
lying he would have denied her story?

'You've gone into a mood because, despite everything, you
don't trust me.'

'I'm not in a mood!'

'That's not what my eyes are telling me. Lucia and I were
finished months ago.'

'But did you end it or did *she*?'

'What difference does it make? You either trust me or you don't.'

'Why should I trust you, Giancarlo?' She had been determined not to lose her rag, but looking at his proud, aristocratic face she wanted to slap him. Her own crazy love for him, her stupidity in thinking that what they had meant something, rose up like bile to her throat.

'You wouldn't have looked twice at someone like me if we'd met under more normal circumstances, would you?'

'I refuse to get embroiled in a hypothetical discussion of what might or might not have happened. We met and you've had more than ample proof of how attracted I am to you.'

'But I'm not *your type*. I guess I knew that all along—deep down. But your girlfriend made it very clear that—'

'Lucia is *not* my girlfriend. Okay, if it means that much to you to know what happened between us, I'll tell you! I went out with the woman and it turned out to be a mistake. There's only room for one person in Lucia's life and that's Lucia. She's an airhead who can only talk about herself. No mirror is safe when she's around, and aside from that she's got a vicious tongue.'

'But she's beautiful.' Caroline found that she no longer cared about who had done the breaking up. What did it matter? Dig deep and the simple fact was that Lucia was more his type than *she* was. He liked them transient; playthings that wouldn't take up too much of his valuable time and wouldn't make demands of him.

'I dumped her and she took it badly.' He hadn't meant to explain himself but in the end he had been unable *not* to.

'Well, it doesn't matter.'

'It clearly does or you wouldn't be making such a big deal of this.'

Caroline thought that what was nothing to him was a very big deal for her, except there was no way that he would understand that because he hadn't dug himself into the same hole that she had. Every sign of hurt would be just another indication to him of how deeply embedded she had become in their so-called relationship.

What would he do if he discovered that she was in love with him? Laugh out loud? Run a mile? Both? She was determined that he wouldn't find out. At least then she would be able to extract herself with some measure of dignity instead of proving Lucia right, proving that she had made the fatal error of thinking that she meant more to Giancarlo than she did.

Unable to contain her agitation, she stood up and paced restlessly towards the window, peering outside in search of inspiration, then she perched on the broad ledge so that she was sitting on her hands. That way, they kept still.

'I was embarrassed,' Caroline told him. She swallowed back the tears of self-pity that were vying for prevalence over her self-control. 'I hadn't expected to open the door to one of your ex-girlfriends, although it's not your fault that she showed up here. I realise that. She said some pretty hurtful things and that's not your fault either.'

Considering that he was being exonerated of all blame from the sound of it, Giancarlo was disturbed to find that he didn't feel any better. And he didn't like the remote expression on her face. He preferred it when she had been angry, shouting at him, backing him into a corner.

'It *did* make me think, though, that what we're doing is... Well, we need to stop it.'

'Work that one through for me. One stupid woman turns up uninvited on my doorstep and suddenly you've decided that what we have is a bad idea? We're adults, Caroline. We're attracted to one another.'

'We're deceiving an old man into thinking that this is something that it isn't, and I should have listened to my conscience from the start. It's not just about having fun, never mind the consequences.'

Giancarlo flushed darkly, for once lost for words. If Lucia had been in the room, he would have throttled her. It was unbelievable just how wrong the evening had gone. The worst of it was that he could feel Caroline slipping away from him and there was nothing he could do about it.

'The fact is, that woman was right. I'm not your type.' She couldn't help herself. She left a pause, a heartbeat of silence, something he could fill with a denial. 'You're not my type. We've been having fun, and in the process leading Alberto into thinking that there's more to what we have than there actually is.'

'It's crazy to come back to the hoary subject of *type*.' Even to his own ears he sounded like a man on the back foot, but any talk about the value of 'having fun', which seemed to have become dirty words, would land him even further in the quagmire. He raked frustrated fingers through his hair and glowered at her.

'Maybe if Alberto wasn't involved things might have been a bit different.'

'Isn't it a bit late in the day to start taking the moral high ground?'

'It's never too late in the day to do the right thing.'

'And a woman who meant nothing to me, who was an albatross around my neck after the first week of seeing her, has brought you to this conclusion?'

'I've woken up.' She felt as though she was swallowing glass and her nerves went into frantic overdrive as he stood up to walk towards her.

Everything about him was achingly familiar, from the smell of him to the supple economy of his movements. Her imagination only had to travel a short distance to picture the feel of his muscular arms under his shirt.

She half-turned but her breathing was fast. More than anything else in the world, she didn't want him to touch her.

'I know it's late, but I really think I'd like to get back to the villa.'

'This is crazy!'

'I need to be—'

'Away from me? Because if you stay too close you're scared that your body might take over?' He muttered a low oath in the face of her continuing silence.

'I don't mind heading back tonight.'

'Forget it! You can leave in the morning, and I'll make sure that I'm not under your feet tonight. I'll instruct my driver to be here for you at nine. My private helicopter will take you back to the villa.' He turned away and began striding towards the bedroom. After a second's hesitation, Caroline followed him, galvanised into action and now terrified of the void opening up at her feet, even though she knew that there was no working her way around it.

'I know you're concerned about Alberto getting the wrong impression of you.'

She hovered by the door, desperate to maintain contact, although she knew that she had lost him. He was turning away, stripping off his shirt to hurl it on the antique chair that sat squarely under the window.

'I'll tell him that your meetings were so intensive that we thought it better for me to head back to the coast, to get out of the stifling heat in Milan.'

Giancarlo didn't answer. She found her feet taking her forwards until she was standing in front of him.

'Giancarlo, please. Don't be like this.'

He paused and looked at her with a shuttered expression. 'What do you want me to say, Caroline?'

She shrugged and stared mutely down at her feet.

'Where are you going to go? I mean, tonight? You said that you'll make sure that you aren't under my feet.' She placed one small hand on his arm and he looked down at it pointedly.

'If you want to touch, then you have to be prepared for the consequences.'

Caroline whipped her hand away and took a couple of unsteady steps back. He had said that before. Once. And back then, light-years ago, she had reached out and touched because she had wanted to fall into bed with him. Now she wanted to run as fast as she could away from him. How had she managed to breach the space between them? It was as if her body, in his presence, had a mind of its own and was drawn to him like a moth to a flame.

'This is your apartment. It's—it's silly for you to go somewhere else for the night,' she stammered.

'What are you suggesting? That I climb into bed next to you and we both go to sleep like chaste babes in the wood?'

'I could use one of the spare bedrooms.'

'I wouldn't trust me if I were you,' Giancarlo murmured, keen eyes watching her as she went a delicate shade of pink. 'You might just wake up to find me a little too close for comfort. Now, I'm going to have a shower. Do you want to continue this conversation in the bathroom?'

Her heart was still beating fast twenty minutes later when Giancarlo reappeared in his sitting-room, showered, changed and with a small overnight bag. He looked refreshed, calm and controlled. She, on the other hand, was perched on the edge of the sofa, her back erect, her hands primly resting on her knees. She looked at him warily.

'You do know,' he said, dropping his bag on one of the sprawling sofas and strolling towards the kitchen, where he proceeded to pour himself a drink, 'that I'll be heading back to the coast once this series of meetings is finished? So I need to know exactly what I'm going to be walking into.'

'Walking into?' She was riveted by the sight of him in a pair of faded jeans and a polo shirt in a similar colour, so different from the businessman who had walked through the door, and all over again she agonised as to whether she had made the right decision. Distressed and disconcerted by Lucia's appearance, had she overreacted? She loved Giancarlo! Had she blown whatever chance she had of somehow getting him to feel the way she felt? If they had continued seeing one another, would love eventually have replaced lust?

As soon as she started thinking like that, another scenario rushed up in her head. It was a scenario in which he became bored and disinterested, in which she became more and more needy and clingy. It was a scenario in which another Lucia clone came along, leggy, blonde and dim-witted, to lure him away from the challenge of someone who spoke too freely. He might find her frankness a novelty now, but it was not a trait he was used to—and did a leopard ever change its spots?

But the way he looked…

She swallowed and told herself just to *focus*.

'Now that you've seen the light, are you even planning on being there at the end of the week?'

'Of course I am! I told you that I'm prepared to go along with this for a short while longer, but we're going to have to show your father that we're drifting apart so that he won't be upset when we announce that it's over between us.'

'And any clues on how we should do that? Maybe we could stage a few arguments? Or you could play with the truth and tell him that you met one of my past girlfriends and you didn't like what you saw.'

Caroline thought of Lucia and she glanced hesitantly at Giancarlo. 'Were all your girlfriends like that?'

'Come again?'

'All your girlfriends, were they like Lucia?'

Giancarlo frowned, taken aback by the directness of the question and the gentle criticism he could detect underlying it.

'I know that Lucia might have annoyed you,' she continued. 'But were they all like her? Have you ever been out with someone who wasn't a model? Or an actress? I mean, do you just go out with women because of the way they look?'

'I don't see the relevance of the question.' Nor could he explain how it was that a beautiful, intellectually unchallenging woman could be less of a distraction than the other way around. But that was indeed the case as far as he was concerned. He had not been programmed for distraction. Somewhere along the line, that hard-wiring had just failed.

'No. It's not relevant.' She looked away from him and he was savagely tempted to force himself into her line of vision and bring her back to his presence.

Instead, he slung his holdall over his shoulder and began heading towards the front door.

Caroline forced herself to stay put, but it was hard because her disobedient feet wanted to fly behind him and cling, keep him there with a few more questions. She wanted to ask him what he ever saw in her. She wasn't beautiful, so was there something else that attracted him? She wanted to prise anything favourable out of him but she bit back the words before they could tumble out of her mouth.

She thought of this so-called distancing that would have to take place and immediately missed the physical contact and the easy camaraderie. And the laughter. And everything else that had hooked her in.

She heard the quiet click of the front door shutting and the apartment suddenly felt very big and very, very empty.

With her mind in complete turmoil, she had no idea how she was ever going to get to sleep, but in actual fact she fell asleep easily and woke to thin grey light filtering through the crack in the heavy curtains. It took her a few seconds for the links in her mind to join up. Giancarlo wasn't there. The bed was empty. It hadn't been slept in. He was gone. For a few seconds more, she replayed events of the evening before. She was a spectator at a film, condemned to watch it even though she knew the ending and hated it.

The chauffeur was there promptly at nine, and Caroline was waiting for him, her bags packed. Right up until the last minute, she half-hoped to see Giancarlo appear. She guiltily allowed herself the fantasy of him appearing with a huge bouquet of flowers, red roses, full of apologies and possibly with a ring in a small box.

In the absence of any of that, she spent both the drive and the brief helicopter ride sickeningly scared at the very real possibility that he had left the apartment to seek solace in someone else's arms.

Would he do that? She didn't know. But then, how well did she know him, after all?

She had sworn that she had seen the complete man, but she had been living in a bubble. The Giancarlo she had known was not the same Giancarlo who dated supermodels because they were undemanding and because they looked good on his arm.

She felt a pang of agonising emptiness as finally, with both the drive and the helicopter ride behind her, the villa at last approached, cresting the top of the cliff like an imperious master ruling the waves beneath it.

What they had shared was over. She had been so busy dwelling on that that she had given scant thought as to what she would actually say to Alberto when she saw him.

Now, as she stepped out of the taxi which had taken her from the helipad close by to the house, her thoughts shifted into another gear.

They had as left the happy couple. How easy was it going to be to convince Alberto that in the space of only a few hours that had all begun unravelling?

As she frantically grappled with the prospect of yet more half-truths, and before she could slot the spare key which she had been given when they first arrived at the villa into the lock, the front door was pulled open and she was confronted with the sight of a fairly flabbergasted Alberto.

Caroline smiled weakly as he peered around her in search of Giancarlo.

'What's going on? Shouldn't you be in Milan on the roof terraces of the Duomo with the rest of the tourists, making a nuisance of yourself with your camera and your guide book and getting in the way of the locals?' He frowned keenly at her. 'Something you want to tell me?' He stood aside. 'I was just on

my way out for a little stroll in the gardens, to take a breather
from the harridan, but from the looks of it we need to talk...'

Giancarlo looked at his watch for the third time. He was battle-
hardened when it came to meetings, but this particular one
seemed to be dragging its feet. It was now nearly four in the
afternoon and they had been at it since six-thirty that morning, a
breakfast meeting where strong coffee had made sure all partici-
pants were raring to go. There was a hell of a lot to get through.

Unfortunately, his mind was almost entirely preoccupied with
the woman he had left the previous evening.

He scowled at the memory and distractedly began tapping his
pen on the conference table until all eyes were focused on him
in anticipation of something very important being said. This
was just the sort of awestruck respect to which he had become
accustomed over time and which he now found a little irritating. Didn't any of these people have minds of their own? Was
there a single one present who would dare risk contradicting
anything he had to say? Or did he just have to tap a pen inadvertently to have them gape at him and fall silent?

He pushed his papers aside and stood up. Several half-rose
and then resumed their seats.

Having spent the day in the grip of indecision, with his
mind caught up in the last conversation he'd had with Caroline, Giancarlo had now reached a decision, and was already
beginning to regain some of his usual self-assured buoyancy.

Step one was to announce to the assembled crew that he
would be leaving, which was met with varying degrees of
shock and surprise. Giancarlo walking out of a meeting was
unheard of.

'Roberto.' He looked at the youngest member of the team, a
promising lad who had no fear of long hours. 'This is your big
chance for centre stage. You're well filled-in on the details of
this deal. I will be contactable on my mobile, but I'm trusting

you can handle the technicalities. Naturally, nothing will proceed without my final say-so.'

Which made at least one person extremely happy.

Step two involved a call to his secretary. Within minutes he was ready for the trip back to the coast. The helicopter was available but Giancarlo chose instead the longer option of the train. He needed to think.

Once on the train he checked his mobile for messages, stashed his computer bag away, because the last thing he needed was the distraction of work, and then gazed out of the window as the scenery flashed past him in an ever-changing riot of colour.

He was feeling better and better about his decision to leave Milan. Halfway through his trip, he reached the decision that he would start being more proactive in training up people who could stand in for him. Yes, he had a solid, dependable and capable network of employees, but he was still far too much the figurehead of the company, the one they all turned to for direction. Hell, he hadn't had time out for years!

It was dark by the time he arrived at the villa, and as he stood in front of it he paused to look at its perfect positioning and exquisite architectural detail. As getaways went, it was one that had seldom been used. He had just never seemed to find the down time. Getaways had been things for other people.

He let himself in and headed straight for the breezy patio at the front of the house. He knew the routine. His father would be outside, enjoying the fresh air, which he claimed to find more invigorating than the stuffiness of the lakes.

'Must be the salt!' he had declared authoritatively on day one, and Giancarlo had laughed and asked for medical proof to back up that sweeping statement.

It was a minute or two before Alberto was alerted to Giancarlo's shadowy figure approaching, and a few more seconds for Caroline to realise that they were no longer alone.

They had not switched on the bank of outside lights, preferring instead the soothing calm of the evening sky as the colours of the day faded into greys, reds and purples before being extinguished by black.

'Giancarlo!' Caroline was the first to break the silence. She stood up, shocked to see him silhouetted in front of her, tall and even more dramatically commanding because he was backlit, making it impossible for her to clearly see his face.

'We weren't expecting you.' Alberto looked shrewdly between them and waved Caroline back down. 'No need to stand, my girl. You're not in the presence of royalty.'

'What are you doing here?'

'Since when do I need a reason to come to my own house?'

'I just thought that in the light of what's happened you would remain in Milan.'

'In the light of what's happened?'

'I've told your father everything, Giancarlo. There's no need to pretend any longer.'

A thick silence greeted this flat statement and it stretched on and on until Caroline could feel herself begin to perspire with nervous tension. She wished he would move out to the patio. Anything but stand there like a sentinel, watching them both with a stillness that sent a shiver through her.

Caroline glanced over to Alberto for some assistance and was relieved when he rose to the occasion.

'Of course, I was deeply upset by this turn of events,' Alberto said sadly. 'I'm an old man with health problems, and perhaps I placed undue pressure on the both of you to feign something just for the purpose of keeping me happy. If that was the case, son, then it was inexcusable.'

'Aren't you being a little over-dramatic, Alberto?' Giancarlo stepped out to the patio and shoved his hands in his pockets.

'There is nothing over-dramatic about admitting to being a misguided old fool, Giancarlo. I can only hope that my age and frailty excuse me.' He stood up and gripped the arm of the chair, steadying himself and flapping Caroline away when she rose to help him.

'I'm old, but I'm not dead yet,' he said with a return of his feisty spirit. 'Now I suppose you two should do some talking. Sort out arrangements. I believe you mentioned to me that you would be thinking of heading back to foreign shores, my girl?'

Caroline frantically tried to remember whether she had said any such thing. Had she? Perhaps she had voiced that thought out loud. It certainly hadn't been one playing on her mind. In fact, she hadn't really considered her next move at all, although now that the suggestion was out in the open didn't it make horrible sense? Why would she want to stick around when the guy who had broken her heart would always be there on the sidelines, popping in to see his father?

Besides, surely she had a life to lead?

'Er...'

'In fact, it might be appropriate for us to leave the coast, come to think of it. Head back to the lakes. We wouldn't want to take advantage of your hospitality, given the circumstances.'

'Papa, please. Sit down.'

'And I could have sworn that you two had chemistry. Just goes to show what a hopeful fool I was.'

'We got along fine.' Caroline waded in before Alberto could really put his foot in it. She had confessed everything to her employer, including how she felt about his son. Those were details with which he had been sworn to secrecy. 'We...we... We're just... I'm sure we'll remain friends.'

Giancarlo threw her a ferocious scowl and she wilted. So, not even friendship. It had been an impractical suggestion, anyway. There was no way she could remain friends with him. It would always hurt far too much.

'I'll toddle off now. Tessa will probably be fretting. Damn woman thinks I'm going off the rails if I'm not in bed by ten.'

Mesmerised by Giancarlo's unforgiving figure, Caroline was only dimly aware of Alberto making his way towards the sitting-room by the kitchen, where Tessa was watching her favourite soap on the television. Alberto would join her. Caroline was convinced that he was becoming hooked on it even though he had always been the first to decry anything as lightweight as a soap opera.

'So,' Giancarlo drawled, slowly covering the space between them until he was standing right in front of her.

'I know I said I wouldn't say anything to Alberto, but I got here and it all just poured out. I'm sorry. He was okay with it. We underestimated him. I don't understand why you came back, Giancarlo.'

'Disappointed, are you?' he asked fiercely. He stepped away from her and walked towards the wooden railing to lean heavily against it and stare out at the glittering silver ocean below.

He turned round to face her.

'Just surprised. I thought you had so much to do in Milan.'

'And if I hadn't shown up here tonight, would you have disappeared back to England without saying a word?'

'I don't know,' Caroline confessed truthfully. She bowed her head and stared down at her feet.

'Well, at least that's more honest than the last lot of assurances you gave me—when you said that you'd say nothing to my father. I can't talk to you here. I keep expecting Alberto to pop out at any minute and join in the conversation.'

'What's there to talk about?'

'Walk with me on the beach. Please.'

'I'd rather not. Now that your father has no expectations of us getting married or anything of the sort, we need to put what we had behind us and move on.'

'Is that what you want?' Giancarlo asked roughly. 'If I recall, you said that, were it not for Alberto, you would consider us... Well, Alberto is now out of the picture.'

'There's more to it than that,' Caroline mumbled. The breeze lifted her hair, cooled her hot face. Beneath her, the sound of the waves crashing against rocks was as soothing as an orchestral beat, although she didn't feel in the least soothed.

'I need more than just a physical relationship, Giancarlo, and

I suppose that was what I finally faced up to when your ex-girl-friend paid a visit to your apartment. She's reality. She's the life you lead. I was just a step out of time. When you decided, for whatever reason, to return to Lake Como to see your father, you were doing something totally out of the ordinary. I was just part and parcel of your time out. It was fun but I want more than to just be someone's temporary time-out girl.'

'Don't tell me we're not suited to one another. I can't accept that.'

'Because you just can't imagine someone turning you down? I believe you when you say that you dumped Lucia—and yet there she was, a woman who could snap her fingers and have anyone she wanted, ready to do whatever it took to get you back.'

'And now the boot's on the other foot,' Giancarlo said in a husky undertone. 'Now I've found out what it's like to be that person who is willing to do whatever it takes to get someone back.'

CHAPTER TEN

'YOU'RE JUST SAYING THAT,' Caroline whispered tautly. 'You just can't bear the thought of someone walking away from you.'

'I don't care who walks away from me. I just can't bear the thought that that person would be *you*.'

Caroline didn't want to give house room to any hope. One false move and it would begin taking over, like a pernicious weed, suffocating all her common sense and noble intentions. And then where would she be?

'Look, let's go down to the beach. It's private there.'

Caroline thought that that was exactly what she was scared of. Too much privacy with Giancarlo had always proved to be a disaster. On the other hand, what had he meant when he'd said that he would do whatever it took to get her back? Had she misheard?

'Okay,' she agreed, dragging that one word out with a pointed show of reluctance, just in case he got it into his head that he might have the upper hand. 'But I want to get to bed early. In the morning I think it would be best all round for us to leave, return to the lakes, and then I can start thinking about heading back to the U.K.' Her mind instantly went blank and she felt a sense of vague panic.

'I've already been in Italy far too long!' she babbled on

brightly. 'Mum's started asking when I plan to return. It's been a brilliant experience over here. I may not be incredibly fluent but I can hold my own now in Italian. I think it's going to be so much easier to get a really good job.'

'I'm not all that interested in your prospective CV.'

'I'm just saying that I have lots of stuff planned for when I return home and, now that Alberto is back on his feet and this silliness between us is over, there's no reason for me to stay on.'

'Do you really think that what we had could be termed *silly*?'

Caroline fell silent. When on a frustrated sigh Giancarlo began heading towards the lawns, to the side gate that opened onto a series of steps that had been carved into the hillside so that the cove beneath could be accessed, she followed him. It was dark, but the walk down was lit and the steps, in a graceful arch, were broad, shallow and easily manoeuvred thanks to iron railings on either side. She had no idea what the cove was like. The walk was a bit too challenging for Alberto and she had hesitated to go on her own. In Giancarlo's presence, her fear of open water was miraculously nonexistent. Without him around, she had been dubious at the prospect of the small beach on her own. What if the tide rushed up and took her away?

'The water is very shallow here,' Giancarlo said, reading her mind. 'And very calm.'

'I wasn't scared.'

He paused to turn around and look at her. 'No. Why would you be? I'm here.'

Her heart skipped a beat and she licked her lips nervously. Although it was after nine, it was still warm. In the distance, the sea beyond the protected cove glinted silver and black, constantly changing as the waves rose, fell, crashed against rocks and ebbed away. It was an atmosphere that was intimate and romantic but all she felt was trepidation and an incredible sadness that her last memories of Giancarlo would probably be of him right here, on his own private beach. Whatever he said about doing whatever it took, she would know what he meant: he didn't want to lose.

The cove was small and private. Giancarlo slipped off his shoes and he felt the sand under his feet with remembered delight. Then he walked to the water's edge and looked out to the black, barely visible horizon.

Behind him, Caroline was as still as the night. In fact, he could hardly hear her breathing. What was she talking about, leaving the country, returning to the U.K.? Uncertainty made him unusually hesitant. She had confessed everything to Alberto. For him, that said it all. He turned round to see her perched on a flat slab of rock, her knees drawn up, her arms wrapped around herself. She was staring out to sea but as he walked towards her she looked up at him warily.

'I don't want you to leave,' he said roughly, staring down at her. 'I came back here because I had to see you. I couldn't concentrate. Hell, that's never happened to me before.'

'I'm sorry.'

He sat next to her on the sand. 'Is that all you have to say? That you're sorry? What about the bit where I told you that I don't want you to leave?'

'Why don't you? Want me to leave, that is?'

'Isn't it obvious?'

'No. It's not.' Caroline shifted her gaze back to the inky sea. 'This is all about you being attracted to me,' she said in a low, even voice. 'I don't suppose you expected that to happen when you first came to see your father. In fact, I don't suppose you expected lots of things to happen.'

'If by that you mean that I didn't expect to reconcile with Alberto, then you're right.'

'I'm just part of an unexpected chain of events.'

'I have no idea what you're talking about.'

'That's the problem.' Caroline sighed. 'You don't know what I'm talking about.'

'Then why don't you enlighten me?'

Caroline wondered how she could phrase her deeply held fear that she had been no more than a novelty. How many times, as they had laughed and made love and laughed again, had he marvelled at the feeling of having taken time out of his ordinary life? Like someone going on holiday for the first time, he had picked her up and enjoyed a holiday romance with her, but had he ever mentioned anything permanent? Had he ever made plans for a future? Now that she had found the strength to walk away from him, he had come dashing back because she hadn't quite outstayed her welcome. But she would.

'I feel that my life's been on hold and now it's time for me to move on,' she said in a low voice. 'I never really meant to stay for this length of time in Italy in the first place, but Alberto and I got along so well together, and then when he fell ill I didn't want to leave him to on his own.'

'What does that have to do with us?' A cold chill was settling in the pit of his stomach. This had all the signs of a Dear John letter and he didn't like it. He refused to accept it.

'I don't want to just hang around here, living with Alberto, waiting for the occasional weekend when you decide to come down to visit until you get sick of me and go back to the sort of life you've always led.'

'What if I don't want to go back to the life I've always led?'

'What are you saying?'

'Maybe I've realised that the life I've always led isn't all that it's cracked up to be.'

Caroline gave him a smile of genuine amusement. 'So you've decided that you'll take to the lakes and become a sailing instructor?'

'You're so perfect for me. You never take me seriously.'

On the contrary, Caroline thought that she took him *far* too seriously.

'You swore to me that you weren't going to say a word to my father.'

How did they get back to this place? Caroline frowned her

puzzlement but then she gave an imperceptible shrug. 'I hadn't planned to,' she confessed truthfully. 'But Alberto was at the front door when I got back. I think if I'd had time to get my thoughts in order—I don't know… But he opened the door to me and I took one look at him and I just knew that I couldn't carry on with the deception. He deserved the truth. It doesn't matter now, anyway.'

'It matters to me. I came here to try and persuade you that I didn't want us to break up. We're good for one another.'

For that, Caroline read 'we're good in bed together'. She looked at him sceptically.

'You don't believe me.'

'I believe that you've had a good time with me, and maybe you'd like the good time to continue a little bit longer, but it's crazy to confuse that with something else.'

'Something else like what?' he asked swiftly and Caroline was suddenly hot and flustered.

'Like a reason for not breaking up,' she muttered. 'Like a reason for trying to persuade me to stay on in Italy when I'm long overdue for my return trip. Like a reason for persuading me to think that it's okay to put my life on hold because we're good in bed together.'

'And let's just say that I want you in my life for longer than a few weeks? Or a few months? Or a few years? Let's just say that I want you in my life for ever?'

Caroline was so shocked that she held her breath and stared at him wide-eyed and unblinking.

'You're not the marrying sort. You don't even like women getting their feet through your front door.'

'You have an annoying habit of quoting me back to myself.' But he shot her a rueful grin and raked his fingers through his hair. 'You also have an annoying habit of making me feel nervous.'

'*I* make *you* feel nervous?' But her mind was still wrapped up with what he had said about wanting her in his life for ever.

She desperately wanted to rewind so that she could dwell on that a bit longer. Well, a lot longer. What had he meant? Had she misheard or was that his way of proposing to her in a round-about manner? Really proposing? Not just asking her to marry him as a pretence...?

Logically, there was no need for him to continue the farce of trying to pull the wool over Alberto's eyes. And Giancarlo was all about logic. Which meant...

Her brain failed to compute.

'I'm nervous now,' Giancarlo said roughly.

'Why?'

'Because there are things I want to say to you. No, things I *need* to say to you. Hell, have I mentioned that that's another annoying trait you have? You make me say things I never thought I would.'

'It's good to be open.'

'I love your homespun pearls of wisdom.' He held up one hand as though to prevent her from interrupting, although in truth she couldn't have interrupted if she had wanted to, not when that little word *love* had been uttered by him, albeit not exactly in the context she would have liked.

'I never knew how much I had been affected by my past until you came along,' he said in such a low voice that she had to lean forward in the darkness to follow him.

'Sure, I remembered my childhood, but it had been coloured by my mother and after a while her bitterness just became my reality. I accepted it. The financial insecurity was all my father's fault and my job was to know exactly where the blame lay and to make sure that I began rectifying the situation as soon as I was capable of doing that. I never questioned the rights or wrongs of being driven to climb to the top. It felt like my destiny, and anyway I enjoyed it. I was good at it. Making money came naturally to me and if I recognised my mother's inability to control her expenditures then I ignored it. The fact is, in the process, I forgot what it meant to just take each day at a time and learn to enjoy the little things that had nothing to do with making money.

'Am I boring you?' He smiled crookedly at her and Caroline's heart constricted.

'You could never do that,' she breathed huskily, not wanting to disturb the strange, thrilling atmosphere between them.

Giancarlo, who had never suffered a moment's hesitation in his life before, took comfort from that assertion.

'Ditto.' He badly wanted to reach out and touch her. It was an all-consuming craving that he had to fight to keep at bay.

'But you never got involved with anyone. Never had the urge to settle down?' It was a question she desperately needed answering. Yes, he might have been driven to make money—it might have been an ambition that had been planted in him from a young age, when he had been too young to question it and then too old to debate its value—but that didn't mean that he couldn't have formed a lasting relationship somewhere along the way.

'My mother,' Giancarlo said wryly. 'Volatile, embittered, seduced by men who made empty promises and then vanished without a backward glance. I don't suppose she was the ideal role-model. Don't get me wrong, I accepted her and I loved her, but it never occurred to me that I would want someone like that in my life as a partner. I worked all the hours God made, and in a highly stressed environment the last thing I needed was a woman who was high maintenance and I was quietly certain that all women were. Until I met you.'

'I'm not sure that I should take that as a compliment.' But she was beaming. She could barely think straight and her heart was beating like a sledgehammer inside her. Take it as a compliment? She was on a high! She felt as though she had received the greatest compliment of her life! She had felt so inadequate thinking about the exciting, glamorous women he had dated. How could she ever hope to measure up? And yet here he was, reaching deep to find the true essence of her, and filling her with a heady sense of self-confidence that was frankly amazing.

'You're fishing.'

'Okay, you're right. I am. But can you blame me? I've spent weeks trying not to tell you how crazy I am about you.'

Giancarlo grinned and at last reached out and linked his fingers through hers. Warmth spread through him like treacle, heating every part of his body. He rubbed his thumb over hers.

'You're crazy about me,' he murmured with lazy satisfaction and Caroline blushed madly. Liberated from having to hold back what she would otherwise have confessed because she was so open by nature, she felt as though she was walking on cloud nine.

'Madly,' she admitted on a sigh, and when he pulled her towards him she relaxed against his hard body with a sensation of bliss and utter completion. 'I thought you were the most arrogant person on the face of the earth, to start with, but then I don't know what happened. You made me laugh and I began to see a side to you that was so wonderfully complex and fascinating.'

'Complex and fascinating. I like it. Carry on.'

She twisted to look up at him and smiled when he kissed her, his lips tracing hers gently at first, then with hungry urgency. Her breathing quickened and she moaned as he pushed up her top, quickly followed by her bra. He bent his legs slightly, supporting her so that she could lean back in a graceful arch as he began suckling on her nipples, pulling one then the other into his mouth, greedy to taste her.

She understood sufficient Italian now to know that his hoarse utterances were mind-blowingly erotic, although nothing was as erotic as when, temporarily sated, he looked down seriously at her flushed face to say with such fierce tenderness that her heart flipped over, 'I love you. I don't know when it started. I just knew when I was in Milan that I couldn't stand not being close to you. I missed everything about you.

'Meetings and conferences and lawyers and stockpiling wealth faded into insignificance. I was broken up by the way things had ended between us, and I had to get here as quickly as I could because I was so damned scared that I was on the verge of losing you. Damn it, I wondered whether I'd ever had you in the first place!'

It was unbearably touching to know that this big, strong man, so self-assured and controlled, had been uncertain.

'I love you so much,' she whispered.

'Enough to marry me? Nothing short of that will ever be enough.'

EPILOGUE

CAROLINE LOOKED AT the assembled guests with a smile. It wasn't a big wedding. Neither of them had wanted that, although they had had to restrain Alberto from his vigorous efforts to have a full-blown wedding of the century.

'Let's wake up these old bores in their big houses,' he had argued with devilish amusement. 'Give them something to talk about for the next ten years!'

They had chosen to be married in the small church close to where Alberto lived and where Giancarlo had grown up. It felt like home to Caroline, especially over the past two months, when the giddy swirl of having her parents over and planning the wedding had swept her off her feet.

She had never been happier. Giancarlo had proven himself to be a convert to the art of working from home and, along with all the marvellous renovations to the villa, had installed an office in one of the rooms from which he could work at his own chosen pace. Which included a great deal of down time with his bride to be.

Her gaze shifted to the man who was now her husband. Amongst the hundred or so guests—friends, family and neighbours who had delightedly enjoyed reconnecting with Alberto, who had become something of a recluse over the years—he stood head and shoulders above them all.

Right now, he was smiling, chatting to her parents, doubtless charming them even more than they had already been charmed, she thought.

Unconsciously, she placed a hand on her stomach, and just at that instant their eyes connected. And this time his smile was all for her, locking her into that secret, loving world she shared with him and him alone.

As everyone began moving towards the formal dining-room, onto which a magnificent marquee had been cleverly attached so that the guests could all be seated comfortably for the five-course meal, he strode across to her, pulling her into the small sitting-room, now empty of guests.

'Have I told you how much I love you?' He curved his hand behind the nape of her neck and tilted her face to his.

'You have. But you need to remind me how much of this is down to Alberto.'

'The wily old fox.' Giancarlo grinned. 'To think that he knew exactly what he was doing when he decided that we were going to be married. Anyone would be forgiven for thinking, listening to his little speech in the drawing-room, that he had masterminded the whole thing.'

Caroline laughed and thought back affectionately to Alberto's smug declaration that anyone in need of match-making should seek him out.

'I know. Still, how can you do anything but smile when you see how thrilled he is that everything worked out according to his plans, if he's to be believed? I heard him telling Tessa the day before yesterday that there was no way he was going to allow us to go our separate ways because we were pig-headed. He would sooner have summoned the ambulance and threatened to jump in unless we came to our senses.'

'He now has a son and a daughter-in-law and you can bet that I'll be raising my glass to him during my after-dinner speech.

He deserves it. You look spectacular tonight. Have I already mentioned that?'

'Yes, but I've always loved it when you repeat yourself.' Her eyes danced with amusement for he never tired of reminding her of his love.

'Have I also told you that I'm hard for you right now?' As if any proof were needed, he guided her hand to where his erection was pressing painfully against his zip. 'It's awkward having to constantly think of trivia to distract myself from the fact that I've spent the past four hours wanting to rip that dress off you.'

Caroline giggled and glanced down at her ivory dress, which was simple but elegant and had cost a small fortune. She was horrified at the thought of Giancarlo ripping it off her, and amazingly turned on by the image at the same time.

'But I guess I'll have to wait for a few more hours until I have you all to myself.' He curved his hand over her breast, gently massaged it just enough for her to feel that tell-tale moisture dampening between her legs, just enough for her eyelids to flutter drowsily and her pulses to begin their steady race.

He kissed the side of her mouth and then dipped his tongue inside to explore further until she was gasping, so tempted to pull him towards her, even though she knew that there was no way they could abandon their own reception even for the shortest of time.

But she wanted him to herself just for a few moments longer. Just long enough to tell him her news.

'I can't wait for us to be alone,' he murmured fervently, before she could speak. He relinquished his hold with evident regret and then primly smoothed the ruffled neckline of her dress. 'Talking and laughing, and making love and making babies, because in case you didn't know that cunning father of mine has already started making noises about wanting grandchildren while he still has the energy to play with them. And he's not above pulling any stunt he wants if it means he can get his way.'

'That seems to be a family trait but, now that you mention

it...' Caroline couldn't contain her happiness a second longer. She smiled radiantly up at him and reached to stroke his cheek, allowing her hand to be captured by his. 'You might find that there's not much need to try on the making babies front.'

'What are you telling me?'

'I'm telling you that I'm a week late with my period, and I just couldn't hold off any longer so I did a pregnancy test this morning—and we're going to have a baby. Are you happy?'

Silly question. She knew that he would be. From the man who had made a habit of walking away from involvement, he had become a devoted partner; he would be a devoted husband and she couldn't think of anyone who would be a more devoted father.

The answer in his eyes confirmed everything she already knew.

'My darling,' he said brokenly. 'I am the happiest man on the face of the earth.' He took both her hands in his and kissed them tenderly. 'And my mission is to make sure that you never forget that.'

* * * * *

Keep reading for an excerpt of
The Bride Who Said No
by Susan Mallery.
Find it in the
Desert Rogues anthology,
out now!

Chapter One

"I know marrying the crown prince and eventually being queen *sounds* terrific," Daphne Snowden said in what she hoped was a calm I'm-your-aunt-who-loves-you-and-I-know-better voice instead of a shrill, panicked tone. "But the truth of the matter is very different. You've never met Prince Murat. He's a difficult and stubborn man."

Daphne knew this from personal experience. "He's also nearly twice your age."

Brittany looked up from the fashion magazine she'd been scanning. "You worry too much," she said. "Relax, Aunt Daphne. I'll be fine."

Fine? Fine? Daphne sank back into the comfortable leather seat of the luxury private jet and tried not to scream. This could not be happening. It was a dream. It had to be. She refused to believe that her favorite—and only—niece had agreed to marry a man she'd never met. Prince or no prince, this could be a disaster. Despite the fact that she and Brittany had been having the same series of conversations for nearly three weeks now, she felt compelled to make all her points again.

"I want you to be happy," Daphne said. "I love you."

Brittany, a tall willowy blonde with delicately pretty features in the tradition of the Snowden women, smiled. "I love you, too, and you're worrying about nothing. I know Murat is, like, really old."

Daphne pressed her lips together and tried not to wince. She knew that to an eighteen-year-old, thirty-five was practically geriatric, but it was only five years beyond her own thirty years.

"But he's pretty cute," her niece added. "And rich. I'll get to travel and live in a palace." She put down the magazine and stuck out her feet. "Do you think I should have gone with the other sandals instead of these?"

Daphne held in a shriek. "I don't care about your shoes. I'm talking about your *life* here. Being married to the crown prince means you won't get to spend your day shopping. You'll have responsibilities for the welfare of the people of Bahania. You'll have to entertain visiting dignitaries and support charities. You'll be expected to produce children."

Brittany nodded. "I figured that part out. The parties will be great. I can invite all my friends, and we'll talk about, like, what the guy who runs France is wearing."

"And the baby part?"

Brittany shrugged. "If he's old, he probably knows what he's doing. My friend Deanna had sex with her college boyfriend and she said it was totally better than with her boyfriend in high school. Experience counts."

Daphne wanted to shake Brittany. She knew from dozens of after-midnight conversations, when her niece had spent the night, that Brittany had never been intimate with any of her boyfriends. Brittany had been very careful not to let things go too far. So what had changed? Daphne couldn't believe that the child she'd loved from birth and had practically raised, could have turned into this shallow, unfeeling young woman.

She glanced at her watch and knew that time was running short. Once they landed and reached the palace, there would be no turning back. One Snowden bride-to-be had already left

Murat practically at the altar. She had a feeling that Brittany wouldn't be given the opportunity to bolt.

"What was your mother thinking?" she asked, more to herself than Brittany. "Why did she agree?"

"Mom thought it would be completely cool," Brittany said easily. "I think she's hoping there will be some amazing jewelry for the mother of the bride. Plus me marrying a prince beats out Aunt Grace's piggy Justin getting into Harvard any day, right?"

Daphne nodded without speaking. Some families were competitive about sports while others kept score using social status and money. In her family it was all about power—political or otherwise. One of her sisters had married a senator who planned to run for president, the other married a captain of industry. She had been the only sibling to pick another path.

She scooted to the edge of her seat and took Brittany's perfectly manicured hands into her own.

"You have to listen," she said earnestly. "I love you more than I've ever loved another human being in my life. You're practically my daughter."

Brittany's expression softened. "I love you, too. You know you've been there for me way more than my own mother."

"Then, please, please, think this through. You're young and smart and you can have anything you want in the world. Why would you be willing to tie yourself to a man you've never met in a country you've never visited? What if you hate Bahania?"

Daphne didn't think that was possible—personally she loved the desert country—but at this point she was done playing fair.

"Travel isn't going to be what you think," Daphne continued before Brittany could interrupt. "Any visits will be state events. They'll be planned and photographed. Once you agree to marry the prince you'll never be able to just run over and see a girlfriend or head to the mall or the movies."

Brittany stared at her. "What do you mean I can't go to the mall?"

Daphne blinked. Was this progress at last? "You'll be the future queen. You won't be able to rush off and buy a last-minute cashmere sweater just because it's on sale."

"Why not?"

Daphne sighed. "I've been trying to explain this to you. You won't get to be your own person anymore. You'll be living a life in a foreign country with unfamiliar rules and expectations. You will have to adhere to them."

None of which sounded all that tough to her, but she wasn't the one signing up for a lifetime of queenhood.

"I never thought about having to stay in the palace a lot," Brittany said slowly. "I just sort of figured I could fly back home whenever I wanted and hang with my friends."

"Bahania will be your home now."

Brittany's eyes darkened. "I wouldn't miss Mom and Dad so much, but Deanna and you." She bit her lower lip. "I guess if I love the prince…"

"Do you?" Daphne asked. "You've never met him. You're risking a whole lot on the off chance you two will get along." She squeezed her niece's fingers. "You've only had a couple of boyfriends, none of them serious. Do you really want to give all that up? Dating? College?"

Brittany frowned. "I can't go to college?"

"Do you think any professor is going to want the future queen in his class? How could he or she give you a real grade? Even if you did get that worked out, you'd just be attending classes part-time. You couldn't live on campus."

"That's right. Because I'd be in the palace."

"Possibly pregnant," Daphne added for good measure.

"No way. I'm not ready to have a baby *now*."

"And if Prince Murat is?"

Her niece glared at her. "You're trying to scare me."

"You bet. I'm willing to do just about anything to keep you from throwing away your life. If you'd met someone and had fallen in love, then I wouldn't care if he was a prince or an alien from planet Xeon. But you didn't. I would have gotten involved with this sooner, but your mother did her best to keep the truth from me."

Brittany sighed. "She's pretty determined to have her way."

"I'm not going to let that happen. Tell me honestly. Tell me you're completely committed to this and I'll back off. But if you have even one hint of a doubt, you need to give yourself time to think."

Brittany swallowed. "I'm not sure," she admitted in a tiny voice. "I want things to go great with the prince, but what if they don't?" Tears filled her eyes. "I've been trying to do what my parents want me to do and I'm scared." She glanced around the luxury plane. "The pilot said we were landing in twenty minutes. That's about up. I can't meet the prince and tell him I'm not sure."

Daphne vowed that when she returned to the States she was going to kill her oldest sister, Laurel. How dare she try to guilt her only daughter into something like this? Outrage mingled with relief. She held open her arms, and Brittany fell into her embrace.

"Is it too late?" the teenager asked.

"Of course not. You're going to be fine." She hugged her tight. "You had me worried for a while. I thought you were really going through with this."

Brittany sniffed. "Some parts of it sounded pretty fun. Having all that money and crowns and stuff, but I tried not to think about actually being married to someone that old."

"I don't blame you." The age difference was impossible, Daphne thought. What on earth could Murat be thinking, considering an engagement to a teenager?

"I'll take care of everything," she promised. "You'll stay on the plane and go directly home while I handle things at the palace."

Brittany straightened. "Really? I don't even have to meet him?"

"Nope. You go back and pretend this never happened."

"What about Mom?"

Daphne's eyes narrowed. "You can leave her to me, as well."

Just over an hour later Daphne found herself in the back of a limo, heading to the fabled Pink Palace of Bahania. Because of the long plane trip, she expected to find the city in darkness, but with the time difference, it was late afternoon. She sat right by the window so she could take in everything—the ancient buildings that butted up against the new financial district. The amazing blue of the Arabian Sea just south of the city. The views were breathtaking and familiar. She'd grown to love this country when she'd visited ten years ago.

"Don't go there," she told herself. There was no time for a trip down memory lane. Instead she needed to focus and figure out what she was going to say to Murat.

She glanced at her watch. With every second that ticked by, finding the perfect words became less and less important. Once Brittany landed back in the States, she would be safe from Murat's clutches. Still, she couldn't help feeling a little nervous as the long, black car turned left and drove past elegant wrought-iron gates.

The car pulled to a stop in front of the main entrance. Daphne drew in a deep breath to calm herself as she waited for one of the guards to open the door. She stepped out into the warm afternoon and glanced around.

The gardens were as beautiful as she remembered. Sweet, lush scents competed for her attention. To the left was the gate that led to the private English-style garden she'd always loved. To the right was a path that led to the most perfect view of the sea. And in front of her...well, that was the way into the lion's den.

She tried to tell herself she had no reason to be afraid, that she'd done nothing wrong. Murat was the one interested in marrying a teenager nearly half his age. If anyone should be feeling foolish and ashamed, it was him.

But despite being in the right, and determined to stand strong against any and all who might try to get in her way, she couldn't help a tiny shiver of apprehension. After all, ten years ago she'd been a guest in this very palace. She'd been young and in love and engaged to be married.

To Murat.

Then three weeks before the wedding, she'd bolted, leaving him without even a whisper of an explanation.

Subscribe and fall in love with a Mills & Boon series today!

You'll be among the first to read stories delivered to your door monthly and enjoy great savings.